Arcane Gateway

C.L. Carhart

ARCANE GATEWAY

Book 1 of His Name Was Augustin series

ISBN: 978-1-954807-00-6 (paperback)

ISBN: 978-1-954807-01-3 (eBook)

https://www.clcarhart.com

Cover Design © J. L. Wilson Designs | https://jlwilsondesigns.com

For Carter
my eternal inspiration
who brings light to my darkness

Brief Pronunciation Guide

Bayerisch – BEYE-rish (eye is pronounced like eyeball)
Dane – DAH-nuh
Eihalbe – EYE-hahl-buh (eye is pronounced like eyeball)
Isar – EE-zahr
Leutascher Ache – LOY-tah-sher AH-khuh
Lise – LEEZ-uh
Swanhilde – Swan-HIL-duh
Thaden – TODD-n
Torstein – TOR-stein (stein is pronounced like a beer stein)
Traudl – TROW-dool (trow is pronounced like cow)
Vreni – FRAY-nee

Table of Contents

Prologue

I lounged on the banks of the pool in our inner gardens, without a care in the world, on the day when Augustin first insisted that I should write out the story of my life. His suggestion took me completely off guard, for of the two of us, he is the writer and I the musician. I tilted my head toward where he rested beneath our silver oak tree with a sketchbook in his lap, his cobalt eyes focused on the page before him, his right hand directing the pen with an artistry that forever enchanted me. "Are you being serious?" I questioned, thinking of all of the volumes he had recorded for history's sake. "Pretty sure my life story wouldn't interest scholars."

Augustin chuckled at my assertion. "As true as that may be, you have told me many times that in your century especially, people enjoy reading the stories of . . . how would you say it . . . tragic heroines? Flawed saints, perhaps?" He looked toward me with a wry expression.

I scoffed quietly and turned my head around to face the pool, lightly tracing its waters with my fingertips. "Sure, I could call it 'Annals of the Teuton Witch.' From purity to degeneracy. Definitely a bestseller."

"Ach, Swanhilde, you ought not to assume the worst. You need to write out your story because your life has been very momentous." I looked back toward him, and he clarified, "I doubt too many other young women have bent the threads of time in an eternal quest for the truth." His fiery blue eyes seemed to carry a silent rebuke, and his pen no longer beautified his page.

I could not argue that point, but I gave the traditional response. "Everything worked out in the end."

He smiled darkly and appended my declaration with another inarguable point. "To an extent."

I sighed, knowing that I was beginning to give in. "Why don't you write it instead?" I hedged. "I mean, you're the experienced chronicler, anyway. It would read a lot better if you wrote it."

"I have written enough over the years for history's sake," he replied. "I have chronicled our recent history and my own discoveries in more than one language, but it is all from my perspective. I am sure that many Teutons in your century would be curious to read our recent history from a female perspective."

I chuckled, though he might have been right. "I don't know. Some Teutons in the modern era are still really old fashioned, especially the ones who care at all about the past. A lot of people still haven't gotten over the gender gap." I frowned.

Augustin smiled in a cynical fashion. "We know that they never will. In spite of this, I am certain that in the future there will be at least one Teuton who would be very interested in reading *your* history." He nodded significantly at me.

With those words, I abruptly understood his purpose. I shook my head a bit in shock, then stared over at him. "You're thinking of my son."

Augustin nodded again. "Well, someone needs to think of him. You never told him the entirety of your story, did you?" I acknowledged the truth of this, and Augustin finished, "I think he is one person who deserves to know all of it. I am sure that he would view both himself and you in

2

a more positive light, should he discover the motives behind your decisions. And who knows? With his position, he may be able to share your story with others, even with outsiders."

"Outsiders?" I repeated the word with a touch of skepticism. "They'd think my story was just a fantasy novel. No one in my era believes in magic."

"I pity their narrow-mindedness." Augustin had returned to his drawing, his right hand adding sweeping strokes to the page in his lap.

"What language should I use when I write it?" I asked, turning my attention back to the cirrus clouds flecking the sky above. "Teutonica?"

"If you want your son to share your story, I would suggest using whichever language is the most widely understood."

"American English it is," I said in the same tongue, snickering at memories of the days I had spent in southern New Jersey.

"I was thinking of Latin, actually." I burst out laughing, and when I looked at Augustin he rolled his eyes at me, his expression clearly revealing his thoughts on the modern era. He belonged in another one entirely.

Now here I sit at Augustin's writing desk, surrounded by his pens, inkwells, and sheets of parchment, contemplating the task of putting my life story into words. How long will it take me to fully explain my life? How long will I compose words on these sheets before I deem my story complete? So many events swirl in my head, and I do not know where or when to begin . . . .

Max. Though you may not refer to yourself that way anymore, when you find this record someday I want you to know that I have never cared much for tradition. I have cared only that the truth be discovered, and that the Teutons finally appreciate how special a people they are. If my record is to be read only by you and others of your ilk, my writing is not in vain. In my heart, you will always be Max, my son . . . just as Augustin will always be Augustin. In your hands, my son, you hold the keys to our people's future along with the means to break a piteous cycle. They must understand the past to face today.

This record is for you.

Chapter One:
The Autumn Party

That night was to be the most wondrous night the Thaden house had known since my father first purchased it six months prior. After years of pushing against the malicious cloud of sickness and loss that seemed to hover around our family, he had taken a step forward, furnishing our new home with an elegance that few could criticize. Anticipation had gnawed at my heart that entire week. I had spent most of my after school hours watching the hired help bustling here and there to prepare our home to receive over a hundred guests—the first party my father had held since my mother had passed away in 1985. Memories of earlier parties had brightened my imagination with colors—rich ladies in fabulous attire floating through the gardens like fairies, chatting and laughing, dancing and drinking, nibbling on cheeses and chocolates, patting my head and complimenting my girlish dress.

When I had first learned of the upcoming party, I had fully expected to be included. I had always attended our family's parties when I was a little girl, when my radiant mother had danced in my father's arms. But for some reason, my father had decreed that I must spend the entire evening and night upstairs in my room, away from the cavorting adults, away from the music and colors, away from the savory dishes made only for this day.

I did not understand, and the greater part of me longed to pitch a fit, for all of my attempts to persuade him otherwise had fallen flat. I could not comprehend what had prompted my amiable father to transform into a tyrant who would lock his only daughter away in a tower. We usually got along well, the two Thadens who had risen above to conquer, to succeed. But he hardly looked at me as I confronted him one final time in the front parlor, having dressed myself in a dusky autumn-colored dress printed with oversized flowers and trimmed with gold. It was one of my best dresses; its lifted bust made me look older than thirteen.

"But Pappi, I spent over an hour getting ready when I got home today! I even had Lise do my nails—" I waved their golden sparkles toward his face "—and she did my braids, too—"

"Lise was just humoring you," my father interrupted, his expression looking as though it had been chiseled from stone, his gray eyes turned away from me, toward the picture window. "She knows quite well that the matter is settled. Tonight's party is for business contacts, for adults."

"But Leon and Lothar are coming. They're not *that* much older than me!" I retorted. "I saw their names on the guest list with Onkel Derek!"

My father sighed and shook his head, his gaze drifting to the left but passing over me, settling on something in the entrance hall behind where I stood with my fists pressed against my hips. "A gathering of my clients is no place for you."

"But there's going to be *dancing!*" I pointed out, gesturing at the five musicians my father had hired to provide music for the gala. They were in the process of tuning their violins, cello, and guitars in the far corner of the room, studiously ignoring the row between father and daughter. "They wouldn't be here if there wasn't going to be dancing. Ava and Morgen went to the Wagner party last month, and they've been going on and on about dancing and flirting—"

"As if I'd want my daughter to gain the reputation of a flighty vamp!" my father responded with a vehemence that derailed my train of thought. He glared down at me and took a step forward, reaching out to brush away the single tear that had escaped my left eye. I felt moisture welling behind both eyes and glowered at my father from behind my glasses. I hated how quickly the tears would come whenever I tried to argue. I knew that made me look weak.

"It's time for you to go back upstairs with Lise," my father told me gently, doubtless sensing my wavering emotions. "She can bring you first dibs on the food before it's set out in the dining room and parlors. Something from every dish if you want." His lips curled into a conciliatory smile. He pitied me.

"Come on, Swanie." Lise beckoned me from the foot of the front staircase, but I was still too provoked to go quietly. I blinked against my tears, and I felt my cheeks starting to burn at the direction of my thoughts. But I had to get it out.

"I'm n-not going to . . . do it with one of your guests." I stepped backward when I said it, suddenly horrified at myself. My heart thudded beneath my dress.

My father laughed once and waved for me to go. "No, you certainly are not, but that wouldn't necessarily stop some of them from trying." My father's chief servant stepped to his side to murmur something in his right ear before sliding away to vanish through the doorway to the other parlors. "That's what I thought. Swanie, get upstairs. People are starting to arrive." He strode toward the vestibule, shoving me in front of him as he went, directing me to where Lise stood at the base of the steps.

I sniffed and heaved a sigh, thinking that maybe I should plot some sort of revenge against my father. How could he possibly lump me in with the ditzy girls in my class at school? Sure, maybe they were the only ones who gushed about going to parties with adults, but still. "Mutti would have let me dance with her," I threw toward my father's back as I paused on the first step; I heard Lise gasp. "And Dane would have wanted me to go so I could tell him all about it. *I* was the one who told him stories, never you."

"*Enough!*" my father roared, and Lise fairly dragged me up the stairs. But I thought I saw his proud shoulders falter a bit, where he stood waiting to greet his guests. *Good, he needs to hurt as much as I do,* I thought.

I heard Lise shut my bedroom door behind us soon afterward, but by then I could not see straight thanks to my tears. "Really, Swanie, you shouldn't have said those things to your Pappi," Lise chided me, though her voice sounded comforting. "Tonight is a happy night for him, for your family."

"I don't care. I want to d-dance with everybody else," I insisted. My words began to break when images of the hospital bed in the room across from mine assaulted me, the sounds of machinery and wheezing, of the grim voices of doctors. "I w-want to . . . t-tell . . . Dane . . . ab-about dancing. I . . . want to tell . . . I want D . . . Dane . . . ." Sobs overtook me, and I collapsed into my nanny's arms.

My mother had been gone for over eight years now, and my memories of her had grown hazy with time, though I often missed her when I went to bed at night, recalling her sweet voice singing lullabies to me until I fell asleep. But my younger brother had not yet been gone a year, and dark memories of his suffering arose at times when I least expected them—like the last time I went to the doctor's office to get a booster shot. I had panicked, and I was told later that several nurses had to carry me from the waiting room to the exam room. Apparently I had sobbed while the doctor tried to listen to my heartbeat and breathing. I had been sent to a psychiatrist at his request, and I had been given pills that I had stubbornly thrown away. They had muddled my thoughts, which exacerbated my pain.

Lise held me until I cried myself out, leaving the room with a pledge to bring back a little of everything from the kitchen in a few minutes' time. The unspoken warning was clear: do not bother trying to sneak out.

In her absence, I plodded toward the bathroom and removed my glasses, disgusted at the sight of my streaked mascara and blush. "You really have to get over this," I said after I had washed off my makeup, blinking sternly at the gray eyes in the mirror—they matched my father's exactly. "Pappi will never let you go to any of his parties if you can't get it together. And Dane's not coming back. He's with God now. With Mutti. And people don't come back from there."

By the time Lise came back with a tray in tow, I sat primly upon my bright blue couch, ready to put forth the appearance of contentment. Lise tried to cheer me up while I ate, telling tales about silliness in the kitchen. I blocked out most of her words, concentrating instead on the food, for my father had given it his all for this party. Even when unhappy, I still relished filet mignon, fresh curried herring, white truffles, and pasta Bolognese. My father had ordered a case of Almdudler from Austria for guests who preferred non-alcoholic drinks, and the taste of that beverage brought a smile to my face at last. "You need to swipe more cans of this to put in my fridge before they're all gone," I told Lise, glancing toward where my mini fridge sat with a microwave on top, two paces away from my stereo.

We danced together for a short time once I had determined myself stuffed, her servant's Dirndl whirling with my more stylish dress. I put on the music that my classmates deemed cool at the time—Snap! and U96—and we playfully switched styles as the songs changed, covering the entirety of my room and balcony. Finally Lise begged for a break, saying that she was getting winded, her graying blond curls having escaped their pins long before. So I collapsed on my bed while she rested on the couch before loading up her tray with our used dishes and silverware. "I'm not going to lock the door," she mentioned on her way out, "because I trust you not to get caught if you decide to prowl around."

I jerked into an upright position on my bed, my mouth dropping open as my eyes darted toward my bedroom door just in time to catch her wink. One final song from U96's CD chugged away on my stereo before I decided how to react. When the song ended, I jumped up and switched the music off, then darted for my closet, intending to discard my brilliant dress for my most obscure set of pajamas.

Some time later, I positioned myself in a shadowy alcove behind where the railing to the front staircase curved toward the second floor hallway, trusting my navy blue patterned pajamas and black hair to keep me concealed from the revelers below. My spot afforded me a decent view of the entryway and the edge of the front parlor, from which drifted the smooth sounds of a nocturne. I took mental notes on the fashion and agility of the dancers that passed through my line of vision, soon convincing myself that my skills far outweighed most of theirs. But of course many of the adults were already drunk. I wondered whether my skills at ballroom dancing and ballet would slip away from me if I was drunk.

So absorbed was I in the dancers that I did not notice him standing behind me in the dark hallway until he spoke. "Watching the festivities, are you?"

My heart leapt into my throat, and I spun around, my fingers fastened to the iron bars of the railing. I quickly recognized Hans standing there in his serving attire—perfectly pressed black suit, snow white button-up shirt, black bow tie, shiny black shoes, white gloves—regarding me with a rather shrewd expression. Though I had rarely spoken to Hans, I knew that he was my father's chief servant, a middle-aged man usually in the background of things who said little. As long as he decided not to tell on me, he was safe; and he probably would not, since his first words to me had had nothing to do with my presence in the hallway. So I relaxed my tense stance and answered his question. "Yes, I am."

"And what do you think?" He looked past me now, over the railing at the guests thronging the wide vestibule. They had paused in their dancing as the song transitioned into a waltz by Schumann; soon all began again.

I turned back to look, feeling a touch of envy. "I think it's amazing," I replied with feeling. "I can't wait until I can be down there, too."

There was a pause, and then Hans made a rather dismissive sound. I turned back to him and found him leaning against the wall within arm's reach of me, looking down at the dancers with a critical expression. "That's not *real* dancing, that down there," he commented.

I frowned, taken aback, and stepped away from him. "What do you mean?"

He crossed his arms and shook his head once. "Down there they dance with their bodies and with the private lusts of fantasy." I blushed at this and almost fled from him right there, thinking back to what I had said to my father earlier. I wondered if Hans had overheard that. But he was still eyeing the dancers and went on, oblivious to my reaction. "If you really want to dance . . . you have to dance with your *soul* . . . with your heart . . . ." His voice trailed off, and he cocked his head to look down at me with a strange triumph in his dark blue eyes.

There was something mystical glittering in his eyes, igniting my curiosity. "What do you mean, dance with the heart?" I asked, beating down my discomfiture at his earlier remark. "They're dancing just like I'm learning in school, and I'm sure they're doing it with sincerity." Except for the drunks, of course.

Half of Hans' mouth curled upward in a mocking smile. "That may be, but they don't know how the Teutons dance." He looked back at the guests again.

With that statement he had me hooked. At that point in my life, I knew little about Teutons besides what I had learned in history class in school. I knew that my family had Teutonic blood, for I had overheard a few adult conversations on the subject. I had no idea what that meant, but now I was determined to learn. If my father did not want me to take part in the rowdiness of drunken dancing, I might as well learn some sort of historical tradition instead. If nothing else, it would help distract me from thinking of Dane. "How exactly *do* the Teutons dance?" I asked when Hans looked down at me again.

He looked at me for a long moment, straightening from his casual stance against the wall. He uncrossed his arms, and his expression grew thoughtful for a moment, his eyes narrowed. At last, he seemed to make a choice, and he smiled suddenly, showing his teeth. It was one of the first times I ever saw him really smile. He gestured at the dark hallway behind him and said, "Come. I'll show you."

My eyes widened. "*Now?*" He nodded. "But I'm too young!"

Hans' smile turned wry as he said, "Not for *that*." He turned swiftly away, headed down the halls toward the back staircase. I stared after him for a moment, thousands of emotions seizing me—fear, anticipation, horror, excitement. Then I raced after him.

At first I had no idea where we were going. Hans reached the bottom of the back staircase, me six steps behind, and threaded his way through the kitchen, nodding once at the extra cooks and servers my father had hired for the party. A few of them glanced at him absently and returned to their work, while most ignored him entirely. I slipped past them unnoticed and followed Hans into the pantry and the laundry room, and finally through the back door to the garage. I was starting to get confused now, for he had not looked back at me after taking off down the upstairs hall—had he been joking, or was he crazy? I entered the garage just in time to see Hans flinging open the side door to the backyard. He halted just outside and turned back to me, the same wry smile curling on his lips. "Are you coming?"

"Out there?" I shivered once from the autumn wind blowing into the garage. Hans nodded, and I protested, "But it's cold, and I don't have a coat with me!"

"You won't need it." He stood waiting, holding the door for me.

I had a feeling that I would truly be treading unfamiliar ground tonight if I followed him. But anticipation overtook me, and I had never really feared any of my father's servants. After all, if he did something to hurt me, I could get him fired. I had heard adults say that Hans was a Teuton priest, and if there was something to know about traditional Teutonic dancing, a priest would know all. So I threw hesitation aside and walked through the door into the crisp night air.

Hans closed the door behind me and swept his gaze over the entire yard at once. "We'll have to do this some distance from the house," he noted, "for we would not want to disturb the guests." He scoured the hedges and shadows with a fierce expression. The waxing gibbous moon cast the landscape in a silvery hue.

I agreed with him wholeheartedly. If my father found us out here, he would kill me, since I was supposed to be upstairs in my room. After a moment's consideration, I suggested, "Maybe we'd be safe out by the stream and the gazebo."

"Hmm." Hans frowned thoughtfully, then nodded. "You may be right." In the same second, he turned his stride toward the trees some thirty meters out, keeping to the sides of the yard near the curved wall coated with ivy.

The Thaden house stood on the outskirts of München on about two hectares of land. My father had bought the house just that April after two very profitable years for his company, Süddeutsche Getriebe. Before that, we had always lived in his father's house, which was somewhat smaller and on the other side of the city. He never told me how much it had cost, but it had to be a staggering amount. Since his business continued to prosper in subsequent years, he never regretted his purchase. The backyard was magnificent, covered in gardens and woods with a tiny stream running through the back. The house and the gazebo by the stream were about a hectare apart, which would not have been a terribly long walk had I not been trying to keep up with Hans. He moved through the yard swiftly and silently like a cat, finding and melding with every shadow. By the time I reached the clearing in the trees where the gazebo stood, I was out of breath and no longer felt the cold air. He was right; I did not need a jacket.

Hans stood at the doorway to the small white gazebo, his face turned toward the water and the waxing moon above. He shifted his gaze to me when I emerged from the trees. I paused at the edge of the clearing to recover my breath, and the tranquility of the night in this tiny forest took hold of me. The chattering stream and the whispering breeze reminded me of how it felt to relax in the Englischer Garten—in a bustling city but set apart from the fray. *I need to spend more time out here,* I realized, for apart from school and dance classes I had cloistered myself in the house while I mourned my brother, channeling my grief into music and books. Maybe some sort of primal dance was what I really needed.

Hans had removed his white gloves and stepped onto the grass while I stood lost in thought at the edge of the clearing. I looked back at him at last, and he stretched one hand out toward me. "Come dance with me, child," he intoned.

I stepped toward him slowly, shivering slightly with the autumn breeze. I paused several steps away and looked down at his hand, ghostly pale in the moonlight, then up at his face. His eyes shone with some internal glory now, almost like a flame of fire somehow. I trembled again and wondered for a fleeting moment what I had gotten myself into. Then I reached for his hand.

I pulled away immediately as a searing pain shot through my skin. I gasped and took a step back, staring down at my hand. There were no outward signs, but I felt as though I had been burnt. The pain disappeared as quickly as it had come; I shook my hand in confusion and heard Hans sigh. When I met his eyes again, they evinced a deep disappointment. "Ach, Teuton child, it is not truly that difficult," he murmured. I frowned, and he went on. "I don't know what element you are, since your father chose to stifle your ancestral spirit all these years, but you certainly are *some*thing. You must relax, let go of your cares, bring out your soul, and embrace this night." He swept his arm in a wide arc, indicating the trees, the brook, the sky. "To dance as a Teuton, you must be free," he finished, then held out his right hand again. "Dance with me, Teuton princess." His voice was low; his gaze burned deep.

I had listened to his every word, and I tried to concentrate on the night air, on this little bucolic glade in the middle of the suburbs, alone with nature. I took a deep breath, and now the chattering of the stream overshadowed all other sounds. I closed my eyes and stepped forward with more surety to take Hans' hand.

I heard a new sound when our hands touched, as he clasped my hand in his. I felt no pain this time, but it seemed as though I heard something sizzling quietly. When I opened my eyes I saw what looked like a bit of steam rising from our entwined hands. I stared and breathed out, noticing that I could see my breath now. Hans looked down at our hands, then at my face, and his eyes burned with amazement. "*Ice* princess," he said, correcting his earlier label of me. *Ice?* I breathed out again, staring in wonder at my frigid breath. For some reason my vision had grown fuzzy. My eyebrows came together, and I reached up to touch my glasses with my left hand. Yes, they were still there, though slightly fogged. Hans' face shone with amusement, and he brought his left hand forward to remove my glasses, fold them up, and place them in his pocket.

I blinked in amazement at the clarity of the glade in the moonlight. It was as though I could somehow *see* the life emanating from the trees and stream, all in a frosty shade of blue. "The awakening of a Teuton's element improves the senses," Hans explained with a snicker. I blinked a few times and put my left hand to my head, not knowing what to say. Had I stumbled into a fairytale? Suddenly, Hans flexed his grip on my right hand and swung it into the air, pulling my body against his with his other hand. I gawked at him in shock, and he warned me teasingly, "Don't let me melt you, Swan of Ice." In the next instant, we were dancing.

This Teutonic dancing was not like the dancing I had learned in class. On some occasions our feet found the traditional steps of the waltz or the polka, but in general we danced a far more primitive dance, whirling astride the wind. We leapt from tree to tree, into the gazebo and out again, sometimes breaking apart and bounding through the dell in an olden form of tag. I found myself chortling almost the entire time, feeling no cold, just the thrill of exhilaration in the night. I was the stream, an icy river breaking over rocks, crashing over waterfalls. My partner took the form of a black fire, leaping high into the air, consuming everything in his path. At the start I feared that he might consume *me*, that his skill and ferocity might overwhelm my inexperience, but as the dance progressed I found my own element, the ice, to be as strong as his. His fire could not burn me, and I could not freeze him. We were equals, even though he danced with far more expertise.

I could have danced this way, this instinctive, heart-felt dance, until the dawn and not grown tired. Ultimately it ended, though, about the same as it had begun. Hans brought us to a graceful stop just outside the gazebo, easing my hand down to my side much more gently than he had lifted it into the air at the start. He let go of me but did not back away, and for a long moment we stared into each other's faces. My eyes were wide with shock and likely a little blue from the ice I had just discovered within me. His were black as the night sky, glowing with an inner fire and perhaps with something more. Slowly he raised his right hand again and brought it to my face, tracing the side of it with a tenderness that shocked me all over again. A beautiful smile spread across his face again, as I stood frozen, and he whispered an accolade: "*Sconi* . . . ."

I did not know what that word meant, but I began to tremble with a tumble of teenage emotions. Then Hans dropped his hand to his side and looked back toward the house. "We should go before someone starts looking for you," he said in a normal voice, as though my entire world had not transformed completely in a single hour. He

16

handed my glasses back to me and left the glade, but I remained for a while longer, my breaths still dotting the air with frost.

"What . . . *was* that . . . ?" Dread had begun to supersede my wonder.

Chapter Two:
Elemental Uncertainties

I did not make it back to my room unseen. As the adrenaline from my dance with Hans gradually wore off, I began to feel as though the forest watched me, the breeze eerily rustling the leaves to discuss the birth of a Teuton. *This sort of thing doesn't just happen,* I told myself, the chill of the air beginning to seep through my icy protection. *The Teutons are just one of the ancient German tribes, not this . . . this mysterious witchy thing . . . .*

At length I huffed and put my glasses back on, shutting my eyes and taking a moment to breathe deeply in an attempt to calm down enough to take the bluish sheen off of my vision. I wondered whether my irises looked as blue as my vision did when I awakened my ice. *My ice.* This was madness. How could Hans just walk away from me after deftly demonstrating that the supernatural was real?

And what had he meant by that word? *Sconi.* I needed to look it up, but I did not know what dialect it was, or what language in general. I also needed to see what the encyclopedia said about Teutons. I barked out a laugh at that thought. Maybe what I really needed to do was find one of my grandfather's books of olden fairytales. Maybe there was one I had missed in childhood that said that sometimes people had elemental powers that came out at night. Or was I some modern version of the Snow Queen, or the White Witch?

But with the elements, it's usually just earth, air, water, and fire, I thought while sprinting back to the house, still feeling as though something was watching me. *Hans was fire, black fire, like hell fire I guess. But why is my water frozen? Is it supposed to be that way, or am I a freak?*

I entered the house through the side door to the garage, which Hans had left unlocked, thankfully. I crept as unobtrusively as possible toward the back staircase, where I encountered a rotund man wobbling about halfway up, garbling nonsense about having a tryst with a girl in a red dress. He did not seem to notice me, though he loosed a belch when I slipped past, rolling my eyes at the collective stupidity of partying adults. *Maybe that's why Pappi wanted me to stay out of sight,* I realized. I should have thought of that earlier, but I had been too enchanted by the concept of ballroom dancing. The dance I had experienced was far afield from that.

In the library I encountered a couple half-dressed on the couch, the man's mouth at work on the woman's right breast while she giggled and tugged at his hair. "There are bedrooms for that, you know," I muttered in disgust, heading straight for the shelf that held my father's encyclopedias. I pulled out the one for the letter T and settled onto the floor, paging through until I found the entry on "Teutons." I skimmed the entry quickly, seeing that it repeated the same tale I had heard in school. The Teutons were a generalized term for the German tribes as a whole, though there had been several tribes from millennia ago that actually called themselves by that name. They had settled in Alpine areas. The other Germanic tribes like the Saxons, Alemanni, and Goths had populated other sections from the Italian border to the North Sea. The Teutons had helped keep the Romans on the far side of the Rhine and the Alps.

But the encyclopedia gave no hint that they had elemental powers or any sort of magical gifts at all. I should not have expected otherwise. Real people did not just manifest random elemental powers. Only characters in fantasy novels and fairytales did things like that.

"Adi . . . there's a kid in here." The lazy female voice broke my concentration, and I looked up from the encyclopedia to see the woman's flushed face pointed in my direction over the back of the couch, her ruby red lipstick slightly mangled.

"No there's not," I heard the man mumble in response, his head hidden from view. I heard a smacking noise. I figured I had better not test my luck. Though the pair seemed fully engaged, they could conceivably reveal my presence to my father. So I left the encyclopedia on the floor and sped to the door, slipping quickly into the shadowed hallway, bound for my bedroom.

I spent several hours pacing here and there in my room, sometimes sitting on the couch, sometimes stepping outside to the balcony, sometimes curling into a ball on the edge of my canopied bed. I knew that I needed to sleep, but I could not turn off my brain, which seemed insistent upon contemplating every possible problem with having an elemental gift of ice. Was this the type of thing that could erupt without notice, now that I had discovered its existence? How was I supposed to keep this hidden? *Was* I supposed to keep this hidden? Were there other Teutons in München aside from Hans and me? Was my father a Teuton? Could he summon ice, too? Was this the sort of thing that meant I had to quit regular schooling and attend some secret magical boarding school, like in the *Discworld* novels or *The Worst Witch* series? I would be behind everybody else if I had to do that; I had only just learned about my ice that very night.

I wish I could tell Dane about this . . . .

Eventually I ended up in my bathroom again, squinting my gray eyes at the mirror as I tried to grasp exactly what I had to do to awaken my ice again. I tried to quiet my mind, to recall how I had felt in the glade with Hans, abruptly wondering whether I needed to be outside for it to work. Or maybe I needed a Teuton partner to guide me into the sphere of the unknown. Maybe I needed a middle-aged man who was not particularly unattractive, his black hair transforming into a dark flame of fire while we danced . . . .

"You're an idiot, Swanie," I whispered to myself, leaning forward to touch my forehead to the mirror while I squeezed my eyes shut. "It was just a dance. You can't just start feeling something for a guy who works for your Pappi."

I had never really felt attracted to anyone before, at that point in my life. I had played along with various girlfriends as a kid, pretending to have a crush on this boy or that boy. My American cousin Beth and I had once "liked" a boy her age who went to her church, but we had decided to stop liking him after watching him bite into the bottom of his sneaker. It had all been fun and games until now. Now I was spending too much time remembering the feel of Hans' fingers linked with mine, the sensation of his fire brushing perfectly against my ice. Too much time remembering that I was only thirteen with underdeveloped breasts and a child's figure. My father would kill me if he caught wind of my thoughts. I hoped that Teutons did not have psychic powers too.

Eventually I fell into a shallow slumber on my bed, having resolved to hunt Hans down later that morning. It was Saturday, and even if he did not come to the main house at all this weekend, I could find him at his cottage out back. Our property had three small cottages, two of which were occupied, one by Hans and the other by Lise and her husband, who took care of the gardens and did simple repairs. If I headed that way first thing in the morning, my father should remain unaware of my activities. Alcohol was a vice of his, especially at parties, though I knew that he drank to forget his wife and son more than for any other reason. He probably would not crawl out of bed before noon at the earliest.

I woke shortly after eight a.m., having gotten maybe six hours of sleep tops. My first instinct was to go back to sleep since it was Saturday, but memories of the previous night returned in a flash. I jumped to my feet and headed for the bathroom to prepare for the day; my braids had not fared well in bed, so I undid them and put my hair up in a blue scrunchie. Then I entered my closet and sifted through my casual clothes for a while, finally settling on violet corduroy pants and a sweatshirt with ducks printed on it. I had gotten that one in the U.S. two years ago and would not be able to fit into it for much longer. Beth's grand-mother had given it to me for Christmas, back before my world had shattered into tiny pieces all over again.

Does this ice that I apparently have mean that something good is going to happen to me finally? I wondered while heading downstairs. *Not that I haven't had any good things before. But this better not be one of those things that will put my family in danger. There'd better not be some elemental war going on in the shadows.* I shuddered a little and entered the kitchen, where some of the extra staff from last night were finishing up their cleaning. I asked the one who appeared to be in charge whether he had seen Hans that morning or not. He replied negatively and asked whether he could get me anything for breakfast. "No, I'll just get some Pop-Tarts, thanks," I answered, snagging the box from a cabinet as I spoke. Then I turned for the dining room with its glass doors that opened onto the back porch.

I did not feel as though the forest watched me make my way to Hans' cottage, so maybe what I had sensed before had been the work of my imagination. I finished the second Pop-Tart just as I reached his doorstep, which was of aged cement. I halted there and shook the crumbs from my fingers before stuffing the trash into my pants pocket, glancing toward the windows on each side of his front door. Their shutters were already open, and mums bloomed in oranges and yellows in his flower boxes. He was doubtless already awake, so all I needed to do was knock. *But how am I going to break the subject? So what was that thing you showed me last night when we danced? How widespread is this elemental thing? Why can't I get the thought of you out of my head?* I grimaced, embarrassment heating my cheeks. I could not bring that part up, not at all. Hans was in his forties, and I was thirteen. There was nothing for it. I just needed to find out more about this magical madness that had intruded upon my life.

I had planned to knock, but I found myself twisting the knob instead. The door slid open silently, revealing a cozy living space: brown, three-cushioned sofa against the far wall, dark mahogany coffee table, small TV on a wheeled stand, five-shelved bookcase, two tall lamps, one on, one off. The window beside the front door let in enough sunlight to render the lamps superfluous, truthfully. A soft chair that matched the sofa stood before the window, and that was where Hans sat clad in a green flannel shirt and tan trousers, the morning paper in his lap, his right hand cradling a mug of coffee. "Guten Morgen, Swanie," he greeted after I had stood awkwardly in the doorway for a few seconds, silently cursing my impropriety. His tone did not sound surprised in the slightest, and that wry smile had curled upon his lips again.

I shook myself and turned away to shut the door, returning his greeting in a voice laden with uncertainty. I stood facing the door with my hand on the knob for a count of five, gathering my courage. Then I heard Hans get to his feet. "Have a seat, if you would, and I'll make us some more coffee."

"No thanks. I don't like coffee," I murmured as he went through a doorway that I assumed led to the kitchen.

"How about tea, then? Or milk or orange juice. Have you had anything to eat this morning?" He had paused in the doorway, his eyes scrutinizing me from head to toe, like they had done in the hallway last night.

I fairly flew to the couch before he could notice my blush rising once more. "I had Pop-Tarts, but I'll take some milk, thanks." He muttered his assent and left the room, so I sat stiffly on the cushion closest to the door with my arms wrapped around my body, feeling as uncomfortable as I felt whenever I had to give a speech in class. I still had not worked out how to broach the subject of Teutons. Something caught my eye against the glass panes of the window—a jarred candle sat on the sill, having burned halfway through its wax already. The flame atop the wick was a solid black. It cast no light.

I kept staring at it until Hans returned and handed me a glass of milk. "You don't look like you slept very well," he remarked while heading for his chair, a fresh mug of coffee in his hand.

A hysterical giggle escaped my lips with a shocking suddenness. "How could you expect me to *sleep* after that?!" I demanded, abruptly irritated.

Hans chuckled in response and took a sip of coffee. "How indeed."

He sounded so casual, as though the candle at his windowsill had a regular old flame burning upon it. I frowned at him and drank some milk, firmly ordering myself to keep my cool. I needed his help to understand what had happened to me. "So it . . . doesn't just happen at night, I guess?" I nodded toward the black flame.

Hans chuckled again, seeming entertained by my ignorance. "The time of day has no effect on a Teuton's gifts. Our elements are a product of our blood, yes, but they stem from our spirits, from inside of us." He leaned back in his chair and shifted a lidded gaze to his candle. The flame reformed itself into a perfect sphere.

I stared, feeling as though my eyes were as round as an owl's. "How do you just . . . *put* it there like that?" My questions hardly made sense.

"It takes practice to create and manipulate one's element with precision," Hans replied, taking another sip from his mug before looking back toward me. The flame regained its natural shape, and I just gaped, my hands starting to tremble around my glass of milk. I set it down onto the coffee table. "This all came as a shock to you, I suppose, and I don't know if I can really grasp how confused you must be. Most Teutons are taught about the elements from childhood. And most discover their own at a young age, sometimes as early as four."

I felt my eyebrows come together, and I blinked rapidly at Hans from behind my glasses. "You . . . you said . . . last night . . . that my Pappi had . . . stifled me? What does that mean? Is he a Teuton, too? Why didn't he tell me anything about this?" Betrayal scratched at my heart again. First the party, now this. I had thought that my father had always been open with me.

Hans sighed heavily, and his dark blue eyes took on a hue of sadness. "It's a hard subject, Swanie, but his silence is one of his ways of dealing with your family's losses. Childbirth can be hard for a Teuton woman." I stiffened. "And when your brother's element began coming out during his sickness—"

"*What are you saying?!*" I shouted, clenching my fists, panic contracting my chest. "My Mutti died because she was a *Teuton?* And Dane . . . Dane was . . . what element did he *have?!*" The last phrase came out in a screech, and my eyes welled up with tears. I choked, gasping for breath, my heart pounding in a ribcage that felt far too tight. I pressed my fists into the cushion beneath me.

"Swanie, please." Hans' voice trickled into my consciousness from the far end of a tunnel, a tunnel that was a hospital wing, that smelled of pungent medicine and hopelessness. I think he said something else, but now my brain was drowning in memories, truths I had never grasped haltingly clicking into place. My mother had died because childbirth was difficult for Teuton women. My father had watched it happen and decided not to tell me. My brother had somehow found his element during his sickness, likely during that final bout early this year, when his lungs had slowly smothered themselves. The doctors had said that cystic fibrosis patients usually last much longer than he had. Being a Teuton was a death sentence. I had been right. This was not the beginning of good things for me.

I had curled into a ball on the sofa when I heard Hans' voice speaking much closer to me. "Did you take your pills this morning?"

"They . . . they don't . . . not happy . . . they can't . . . I can't . . . think . . ." My speech slurred from German to Bayerisch to English. What I wanted to say was that the pills did not make me happy; they only made it hard to think. I had thrown each one out as soon as Lise had stopped watching me take them with breakfast.

"Swanhilde, look at me," Hans commanded, prying my left arm away from my body and enclosing my wrist in an iron grip. I gave out a strangled gasp, and then I felt him take hold of my chin. "Look at me," he repeated, his thumb pressing hard upon the center of my left wrist. I was still struggling to breathe. I realized that if I could not get my panic under control, Hans may very well call some doctor to stick pills down my throat, or worse. *Look at me,* he had said, so I clutched onto that command like a lifeline and pried my eyes open.

All I could see before me was a blur, and the tears felt crusty upon my eyelids. A large form sat before me on the floor, and I blinked, trying to focus on his face. I could not. "Breathe slowly with me. In, out. In, out." Hans softly repeated himself until I had nearly managed to match my breaths to his; then he told me to recite the Lord's Prayer in German. Something basic and unrelated to drag my mind out of the muck. I whispered the words bit by bit, and when I had finished he asked me to say the prayer again in Bayerisch, and then in English. By the time I had recited the last phrase of the English prayer, I could see clearly again, though I sensed the traces of ice upon my face. Apparently tears could come out as a person's element.

I had certainly been learning a lot today.

Hans had let go of my chin after I had finished the first prayer, and his grip on my wrist moved to rest upon my pulse while I spoke. "That might be the last language I know it in," I said in English.

Hans snickered and released my wrist, rising to his feet. He had moved the coffee table toward the center of the room to give him space to kneel before me. "That may be, but if you can't recite it in Latin, you're no scholar." He shifted the table back toward the sofa, and I noticed that my milk had not spilled.

"Really?" I muttered in response to his jibe, launching immediately into the Latin version of the Lord's Prayer. He chuckled again and returned to his chair, sitting down and lifting his mug from the floor, watching me minutely while I said the Latin words, this time trying to take their meaning to heart. Mutti and Dane were with God now. It was no use to cry about it. And I did not have cystic fibrosis. It was just my stupid panic that told me I could not breathe.

"So I guess elements come out when you're upset," I observed when I had finished the prayer, switching back to dialect without a hitch. "I've been upset a lot this year. I wonder why my ice never came out before."

"Normally Teuton children are informed of their elemental potential and are taught how to control or suppress it, depending on the circumstances." Hans favored me with a thoughtful expression, and I picked up my glass of milk again. "Whether informed or not, though, a Teuton's element may manifest itself when a person is in mortal danger, which may explain what happened with your brother."

"Did his lungs . . . freeze inside of him?" I bit my lip after I put the question into words, not sure whether I really wanted the answer.

Hans shook his head once, and I relaxed a little. "He was not ice. He seemed to manifest either water or mist; I am unsure which one. But the excess of liquid damaged him in a tragic way." I took a large gulp of milk to hide my face from Hans, unsure whether that sounded worse or better than having frozen lungs. "Now that you have discovered your ice, it would behoove you to actually take your medicine," he added in a barbed tone. "You don't want to be having panic attacks like that one while out in public."

He had a point, but that raised another question in my mind. "Do I have to go to some elemental magic boarding school now?"

Hans laughed outright, and I saw the black flame of his candle increase in size in response to his amusement. "No, Teutons have no such place. But there's an elderly Lady in our city that would like to meet you, one who has taught Teuton girls about their gifts for many years. I'll have to arrange for you to meet with her and with your peers of the same age the next time your Pappi is away."

I found myself smiling at the thought, for it was clear by the look on Hans' face that he respected this Lady very much. Maybe being an icy Teuton would turn out to be a good thing after all.

Chapter Three:
My Teuton Peers

In the weeks before I went to visit Lady Muniche for the first time, I learned more about the Teuton people thanks to a book Hans leant me before I left his cottage that Saturday. He answered a few more of my basic questions, but claimed that I would find out most of what I needed to know from that book. Titled *Der Weg Teutonisch,* he called it the official history of our people, first compiled long ago in the 1000s by a Catholic priest named Paulus von Bayern. "The most recent update was published in 1904, after the final changes agreed upon by the General Conference of Teuton Priests," Hans told me, pointing to the date printed at the bottom of the title page beneath the name of a press I did not recognize.

"What did they change in 1904?" I asked, filing the concept of a conference of Teuton priests away for later consideration. The idea of such an authoritative conclave kind of freaked me out.

"It was only then that Teuton males with blood beneath the level of ninety percent were allowed to study for the priesthood," Hans answered. "Blood mixing between Teutons and outsiders has become more and more common in modern times, so the practice of exclusion of those with elemental control was deemed outdated."

I shut the book while Hans spoke, tracing my fingers over the title engraved upon it in golden lettering. "Exclusion?" I repeated.

Hans gave a slight clearing of his throat, and I looked up at his face. "Anyone with Teuton blood at the level of eighty-five percent or higher can learn the mastery of their element and everything that comes with that," he explained. "Despite the tolerance of the modern era, some Teutons still degrade those who marry outsiders and produce children who will never experience elemental control."

"Oh," I said, scrunching my eyebrows at the thought. "Guess that means my list of future husbands is pretty slim." Hans looked like he wished to comment on that, but before he could, I asked, "Has my blood ever been tested . . . for its percentage? How do you *do* that, anyway?"

"The test itself is nothing for you to worry about. Priests take care of that," Hans said with a chuckle. "Your blood is ninety-five percent Teutonic."

"Is that good?"

"It's certainly a high percentage in this day and age. Your blood matched your mother's exactly." I gave a soft cry at that, a sense of belonging warming me deep inside as I headed back to the house, ready to study my people's history.

I ate lunch with my father shortly after noon, having gotten through the first section of *Der Weg* that outlined the alliances of Teutonic tribes in the BCE years. I had yet to come across any information about blood magic or elemental powers, but my thoughts were effectively several millennia away when I sat down across from my father at our elegant dining room table. The extra staff that had organized the party had pretty much cleared out, and Gregor, our usual cook, had prepared a standard meal of Leberkäse with Spätzle and buttered cauliflower. "It's a lot more peaceful in here today," my father commented after I had seated myself.

I took a few seconds to look at him. He wore jeans and a light orange polo shirt—casual dress for him. His dark hair looked like he had slept on it wrong, he had not yet shaved, and his eyes appeared much less lively than they had looked last night. "Do you have a headache?" I asked, watching him rub his forehead.

He winced a little. "It'll pass, Swanie. But I think I know now why I haven't held any parties like this in a decade."

It hasn't been that long. "Have to keep your clients impressed," I rehearsed, having heard him say that more times than I could count over the years. I turned my attention to my plate and started cutting the meat, a sensation of estrangement creeping gradually up my spine. *I can't tell him anything about my ice, or he may get angry, or break down in front of me. I can't bring any of it up at all.*

"Are you still mad at me for shutting you away last night?"

I chewed a bite of Leberkäse before responding, briefly weighing whether it would be wiser to tell him part of the truth or act like I had slept soundly all night. He eyed me with an expression that implied that he knew of my wanderings, so I swallowed and admitted, "I saw a few things last night that helped me understand."

"Mitzi said she saw you in the library." My father chuckled.

"Maybe I should learn karate instead of dance. Then I could fight off all your crazy drunken guests."

"Just kick them in the nuts. Gives you time to get away."

I cocked my head at my father. "You want me to practice doing that?"

"There's a dummy in the exercise room for a reason." My father smirked, and then we both burst out laughing simultaneously. Once I had gotten control of myself, I smiled and tackled my cauliflower. Maybe I could still be cool with my father without bringing up the Teuton subject. I wondered what element he had, though. And how he had figured out how to wholly stifle it for years on end.

Hans drove me to Lady Muniche's apartment on the first Sunday in November, while my father was away presenting products at a conference in Stockholm. We headed there right after church, not having changed clothes first, so I wore a maroon velvet dress with a black bowed sash, nude stockings, and black heels. "I hope everybody else isn't in regular clothes," I remarked after climbing into the passenger seat of his gray Mercedes. I pulled the visor down to check my makeup.

"From what the Lady said, she'll have a total of six girls visiting her for lunch and lessons today. And a lot of Teutons are still religious, so I'm sure some of them will have come straight from church."

I looked over at Hans, who wore a gray suit with a blue shirt and tie, having played the organ at church that morning. His black hair was slicked back perfectly from his forehead, his blue eyes serious as he watched the street, waiting for a break in traffic. "Maybe we should go home first so I can change," I suggested, trying to keep my focus on that topic rather than on my temptation to gawk at Hans.

Hans snorted a little. "If your peers are too blind to notice the wealth your outfit implies, any criticisms they may have ought not to touch you."

He had a valid point, though I often felt like a stranger even among my rich peers at school. I had been the shortest girl in class for pretty much my entire life; that and my glasses had often made me the butt of jokes. I had felt more accepted among Beth's American classmates during the two years I had spent with her family, for while those kids could speak only one language, they were not wealthy snobs, and a German exchange student was an anomaly to them. I wondered how long it would be before my father would let me go back there for a year or two. *But would I really fit in there anymore, now that I have ice powers?*

"I finished *Der Weg*," I mentioned, breaking the sustained silence. Hans did not seem the type to expect constant conversation. That would not have bothered me had I not been anxious about meeting Teutons my own age.

Hans raised his right eyebrow at me. "Information overload, right?"

I watched a group of obvious tourists cross the street while we waited for a red light, not really sure where to begin on the subject of the Teuton history tome. It had raised more questions than it had answered, in some ways. "The stuff about Teuton cities was really interesting," I said, figuring that I ought to be able to find some type of belonging in that aspect at least, since I had been born in the largest one of all. "Like that mystical part about the collective souls of those who've served München in the past, and all of that being kept by Lady Muniche, who I'm going to meet today." I shivered in nervous excitement at the privilege of being trained by such an important person.

"Lady Muniche is truly the heart of our Teuton community here," Hans said in a tone that sounded both proud and respectful. "She has led our city well for many years and has created new opportunities for Teuton women."

"A lot of the ideas in *Der Weg* seemed old fashioned," I noted, something that had bothered me deep inside. "Like how they want all Teuton women to have kids when it's dangerous to do that."

"The modern age has given us more options in regards to that," Hans said, a smile that looked like it held a touch of mockery gracing his face. "Some Teuton women of high blood choose to use a C-section every time, and I've heard of some who have paid outsiders to bear children as surrogates."

I shrank back in the seat, the mere thought of medical procedures scratching at the edges of my brain. "Maybe we'd better not talk about that." I clutched my purse more tightly, taking deep, measured breaths. I had not taken any pills that day because I wanted to be able to fully ponder anything I learned. In recent weeks I had taken them more regularly, though.

We stopped at another traffic light, and Hans turned his head toward me, a toothy grin stretching across his face. "Some Teuton women ask witches for help with childbirth, though their advice should be taken with a grain of salt."

"*Der Weg* didn't have anything good to say about witches," I recalled.

"Teuton women who choose to delve into the deeper spirituality often find themselves in over their heads, so to speak," Hans stated with a laugh. "There's a reason only men become Teuton priests. Much of the deeper sorcery is rooted in a darkness beyond that of earth. And most male demons aren't homosexual."

My jaw dropped at that tidbit. "What?"

Hans parked the car at the curb in front of the Lady's apartment without offering further explanation. After engaging the parking break, he met my gaze with an encouraging smile. "Lady Muniche's door is right before you. I'll be back to pick you up at three."

I blinked at him. "*Demons?*" *Der Weg* had mentioned a few of those in passing, mainly one that went by the name of Wuotan, but such things had been put forth as though they were naught but remnants of old tradition. Several curses and spells had involved demons in times past, but I had a hard time believing that such things were still applicable today.

Hans just smiled and gestured for me to go. "She's waiting for you, Swanie."

I walked the path to the Lady's door in a haze, wondering now if one of my first fears may hold water after all. If actual demons were somehow involved with Teuton powers, was I about to get inducted into a platoon of teenaged girls? *I can't do that, if that's what this is about,* I resolved. *Not even if Hans does it on the side. My Pappi needs me alive; he's lost everybody else.*

I squared my shoulders and opened the door—the only purple door in the long, beige row of apartments—and found myself greeted by the boisterous yapping of a tiny dog. I shut the door just as a well-groomed Yorkie jumped at my ankles, slightly pricking my stockings. "Down, girl," I said automatically, seeing that she wore a pink collar, trying to divert my attention to the contents of the room. It appeared to be a small parlor similar to Hans' in size; my eyes ran quickly over an upright piano and a sewing loom loaded with a partially-finished weaving of greens and blues. An empty but well-loved recliner stood between the loom and a doorway that likely led to a dining room and kitchen, and several rods of incense burned at the windowsill, suffusing the chamber with a pleasant woodsy scent. The little dog had not yet left my ankles alone, so I sighed and knelt down to stroke her head, at last looking toward the blue-and-white-checkered sofa that stood before the window.

Three teenaged girls sat perched upon the sofa, and all three of them were staring at me with equally surprised expressions. Out of the three, only one wore a dress; the other two were in jeans and sweatshirts. I instantly felt overdressed. I looked back down at the Yorkie, anxiety rising within me again, and then one of the three girls declared in a loud voice, "Lady Muniche, I thought you said she was our age! She looks like a kid!"

My cheeks began to burn, and I stood up and faced the sofa, anger churning inside of me. Even in heels, I still looked like a kid. I searched for words to defend myself, but before I could, a quieter voice spoke from the doorway. "Oh Ina, she's the same age as Marga and the two sisters. I won't stand for any of you teasing or deriding poor Swanie. It's not her fault that she only just found out about our people. Now why don't you start setting up the TV trays, please."

I looked toward the elderly woman in the doorway, gratitude swelling within me. She was plump with beautiful silver curls and twinkling blue eyes, her smile clearly welcoming me into her mystical enclave. She also wore what looked like church attire: a navy blue skirt and soft lavender sweater, amethyst earrings hanging beneath her curls. A portion of my anxiety evaporated at the sight of her, and I nodded in greeting. "Thanks, Lady Muniche, but lots of people think I'm younger than I am. I'm used to it."

The elderly Lady chuckled and gave me a knowing look. "Well, if you're anything like your mother, your size won't hinder you in the slightest. You don't have to be tall to be influential." She gestured toward her parlor and added, "Feel free to sit wherever you like, in my chair if you wish it. Lunch will be ready soon."

I looked back toward the other girls in the room. Ina was in the process of unfolding a TV tray in front of what looked like a chair taken from a dining room table. She was tall and slim with a figure that belonged to someone in her twenties. She had apparently been teed off by the Lady's rebuke, for she kept her face turned away from me, her highlighted black hair flopping around in her ponytail. The girl in the dress, her red hair bobbed in a style similar to Beth's, looked me up and down with curiosity glinting in her hazel eyes. "Well, that's a first. She offered you her chair, so that must mean you're as important as you look." She grinned a saucy grin and approached me, offering her hand. "I'm Erika."

"Swanie." I smiled back and shook her hand, eyeing the pair of beanbag chairs sitting on either side of the sofa. "I think I'll just use the blue beanbag." That one was beside where Erika had sat on the sofa. I did not want to sit on the yellow beanbag. It was too close to where Ina had sat.

"Or you can squeeze onto the cushion with me. I don't bite."

"Much," the third girl put in, who I guessed was Marga. She was stocky with curly brown hair and painted fingernails that looked obviously chewed.

"Now that you bring it up, I could use a few more points of Teuton blood," Erika mused, shooting Marga a toothy grin and crouching like a lion.

"That's not how you raise your Teuton blood," I blurted, for *Der Weg* had been quite clear on that. Its various revelations swirled constantly inside my brain.

"Oh? I thought you were oblivious about everything except your element." Marga tilted her head at me, looking inquisitive. Erika scooped up the Yorkie and headed for the sofa, plopping back down next to Marga with the dog cradled in her lap. "And if you *could* raise Teuton blood that way, I'd be the last person you'd try it with," Marga said to Erika, looking slightly put out.

"I read *Der Weg*," I said by way of explanation, sitting down onto the blue beanbag chair and arranging my skirt around my legs. I set my purse down between myself and the sofa.

"But which version?" Erika queried, grinning down at me from around the dog, who was hopping up to lick her face.

"I'm going to see if Lady Muniche needs any help with the food," Ina stated, having set up a total of four TV trays. I suspected those of us on the beanbags would simply hold our plates in our laps. I watched Ina sweep from the room and felt just a twinge of envy at the grace with which she moved. I hoped that in a few years my body would fill itself out properly like hers.

"Did you read the 1904 version?" Erika prodded, having wrestled the dog into a ball on her lap.

"Um, yes? Hans said that one had the most recent edits."

"Yeah, that's the one where they took out all the spells and put, 'To be found among the priestly works.'" Marga looked scornful and reached over to stroke the Yorkie's head.

I felt my forehead wrinkle at this information. "So . . . you're saying that in the older versions of *Der Weg*, all of the spells were written out? Like how to do the test for Teuton blood?"

"Not just that one," Erika clarified, "almost all of them. Even the invocation for the blood-transfer was still in the one from the 1800s."

I cringed, remembering what little I had read about that particular ritual. "Why did they take all of that out?

Hans said they just updated it to say that men with elemental control could study for the priesthood."

"Too many women were getting literate," Erika answered with a smirk, but before I could question her on that, the Yorkie leapt off of her lap, yapping on her way to the door, which had opened to admit the final two guests.

I barely had a chance to look toward the door before an extremely familiar voice broke into my consciousness. "Back, Sonnig, back."

"You can't go out front—Swanie?"

"Swanie? Swanie!!!"

The two new arrivals charged at me like a freight train as my mouth slowly dropped open in recognition. Before I could react, they had smothered me in their embrace, talking over each other in their enthusiasm.

"FINALLY! I never thought—"

"—thought your Pappi would never—"

"—let us tell you anything—"

"—until you're an adult—"

"—and get away from him!"

"Can you two give me some space?" I squeaked, trying to worm my way out from beneath my two cousins Trudi and Traudl, twins just three months older than me. They were both dressed for church, their black hair in matching buns.

"Sorry, sorry—"

"—just a little overwhelmed."

They both pushed away from me but remained on the floor, their matching smiles lighting up the room, giving me a sense of having found my place at last. "So you're both Teutons, too?"

"Swanie, your entire *family* are Teutons, at least on the Thaden side," Trudi clarified, rolling her eyes. Traudl made a stink face.

I thought about what that meant for a moment, frowning as I realized that my mother's only sibling—a brother—had married an American and moved away permanently. *If Mutti's blood matched mine at ninety-five percent, then Onkel Jens must have high Teuton blood, too. But he married an outsider. Is that why he's brought his family to visit us only once? Did my grandparents disown him?*

My cousins continued to bubble over about my identity, and both Marga and Erika seemed surprised that my father was Max von Thaden. Apparently he was known among the Teuton community despite his decision to forsake it. "Her Pappi's a millionaire in his own right, so she's on a higher plane than us peons," I heard Trudi say, but my thoughts were oceans away now, in the U.S., wondering whether Beth knew anything about her German father's blood.

Chapter Four:
Lady Muniche's Gathering

Eventually Lady Muniche and Ina brought out bowls of hearty goulash with seeded rye breadsticks for dipping. I loaded up on napkins when they got passed around, and I accepted a bottle of Coke from Marga, who had taken it upon herself to pass out drinks. One corner of my mouth cringed momentarily when I realized that the Coke had not yet been refrigerated, but I opened it and took a swig anyway. That was one unfortunate habit I had picked up from my years in the U.S.: a preference for cold drinks, especially in the summer. But it was autumn now, and I was a guest in someone's home, so I would have to remain silently wistful of my fridge.

My cousins had plopped themselves on either side of me, having dragged the yellow beanbag over and mashed it up against its companion. I sat between the two, more on the floor than not, and they kept up a running commentary between bites of goulash, chattering about the elements that ran in their family and later the Thaden family as a whole. Apparently our Opa Hobart was fire— just straight fire, according to Traudl—while Oma Toni was dark energy. "What's dark energy?" I managed to ask around a mouthful of breadstick. I had read about the three types of energy in *Der Weg*—lightning, energy, and dark energy—but I had never wholly grasped how something that was naturally bright or invisible could present itself as dark.

"It's the combo of darkness and energy," Trudi said.

"And energy is the combo of fire and air," added Traudl.

"I think it'd be awesome to have dark energy, don't you?" Trudi asked.

"You could dart around in the shadows and nobody would know."

"And nobody could catch you!"

"Except for lightning," Traudl clarified.

"Because light is faster than darkness."

Both of them paused in their gushing to beam at me, their blue-gray eyes glimmering in excitement. I glanced from one to the other and chewed on my food, trying to figure out now what combination ice was supposed to be. Water plus cold? Was that even a thing? *Der Weg* had mentioned wintry wind and Föhn, though, so maybe it was a thing.

"Now girls, let's not start raising one element above another," Lady Muniche instructed when my cousins paused for breath. "Someone remind me what we've learned about the elements during our gatherings here." Her eyes twinkled around the rim of her mug of tea as they moved from one girl to another.

"All Teuton elements are equal in power," Erika rehearsed, giving her head a brief twist to slide a stray lock of red hair away from her face.

"All of them have different uses, all of which are equally important," Ina put in, offering Sonnig a small bite of bread. Apparently she was not as stuck up as she had appeared, at least where animals were concerned.

"But whether or not you can beat one in battle depends on how well you've learned to manipulate and enhance your power," Traudl informed me, giving my left shoulder a suggestive nudge. Then she stuffed a huge forkful of goulash into her mouth.

I blinked at my cousin, my earlier fears coming to the forefront of my brain. "In battle?" I repeated in a shaky voice. *This had better not be an induction into an army. If it is, I'm getting out of here. I don't care that my cousins are in on it.*

"Ach, Traudl, no need to scare your cousin," Lady Muniche reproved. "The Teuton community has been peaceful during much of its existence, particularly in this day and age. We're all better off if we keep our abilities in check rather than shout them from the rooftops." Her blue eyes held an unspoken warning.

I met her gaze and remembered, "From what I read in *Der Weg*, it sounded like Teutons don't really use their elements against invaders, even when they were at war in the Middle Ages."

"Elements have not been openly permitted in battle since before the time of Christ, when the German peoples were scattered," Lady Muniche confirmed. "With the advent of Christianity came the distrust of the unknown, and our people have never been able to multiply as others have, for many reasons."

I'll bet the childbirth thing is a big reason for that, I thought to myself. My eyebrows came together as I looked toward the three girls seated on the checkered sofa. *Did any of them lose their mother? I know my Tante Lena decided to quit having children after Trudi and Traudl. I've heard people say that she was in the hospital for a week afterward, and that she's never fully recovered . . . .*

The conversation drifted in another direction while I finished my goulash. I heard a few squeals from the sofa when one of the girls flicked droplets of water at another; Lady Muniche's voice quickly dispelled the impending elemental spat. I should have been watching the girls to see who had been involved and how, but I could not get thoughts of childbirth out of my head now. I sensed panic scratching at the edges of my chest, and I took a long drink of Coke, knowing that I needed to think about something else. But I needed answers.

"Lady Muniche," I said, prompting her friendly face to turn toward me again, "how many kids is a safe number for a Teuton woman to have?"

Utter silence overtook the parlor, aside from the quiet pants of the Yorkie, who had positioned herself beside Ina's place at the far end of the sofa. None of the girls looked toward me; in fact, they all seemed to be studiously looking away, even my cousins. The elderly lady heaved a sigh and glanced toward the colors spilling from her loom before meeting my gaze. "It depends on the strength of the Teuton blood, Swanie. Those of high blood take a higher risk in childbearing."

"That's one thing I shouldn't have to worry about," Marga declared from the middle of the couch, sounding rather proud of that fact. I looked toward her, and she smacked her palm against her chest and said, "Only eighty-five percent here." She wiggled her brown eyebrows at me and grinned.

"What a thing to be proud of." Ina rolled her eyes at her companion.

"We're both eighty-nine percent, so we should be okay, too," Trudi said, her eyes still averted from mine as she poked a final breadstick into her bowl.

"It's once you're over ninety that things get dicey," Traudl explained.

Ina made a dismissive noise, and Lady Muniche said, "Now girls, there's no need to portray childbearing as some dark process overseen by the Grim Reaper. While it's true that women of high Teuton blood take a greater risk, there are steps that can be taken beforehand to ensure the best outcome." She favored me with an empathetic smile and murmured, "With God's help, I was able to bear two daughters even though my blood is ninety-two percent Teutonic."

Seems like you're really asking for it if you try for more than two, I thought, wondering what that meant for my Tante Gerda, who had three children. How high was her Teuton blood? Was my Onkel Derek's really low like Marga's? Did that balance things out? Truth to be told, I had never seriously thought about whether I wanted children or not. I had always preferred to play with stuffed animals over dolls, anyway, so maybe I should just set the concept of childbirth on the back burner. I did not really agree with *Der Weg's* portrayal of women, anyway. We did not exist for the sole purpose of breeding.

Ina and Marga were in the middle of a conversation about the blood status of the Teuton boys they happened to like. Apparently, Teutonic festivals were a thing, and both seemed to agree that a good selection of Teuton boys could be found at such events. "If I end up with somebody like Fonsi, I'll have to give him kids right away, before my blood gets much higher," Ina remarked, and Marga nodded.

I cleared my throat and directed my next question toward Lady Muniche again. "So . . . what if someone's Teuton blood was kind of high, so she decided to marry an outsider. Would that make it safe for her to have kids?"

"Ha! That's a good way to get shunned," Traudl interpolated.

"Not worth it to just have 'Teutonic children.'" Trudi used air quotes.

"Ex*cuse* me?" Erika narrowed her hazel eyes at my cousins, looking seriously affronted. Meanwhile, I rearranged my butt between the two beanbag chairs, my eyes riveted upon the empty bowl in my lap. *I was right. My family must have disowned Onkel Jens.*

"Ach, girls, at the rate you are going on, Swanie's going to wish she'd never heard anything about Teutons and Teuton blood." Lady Muniche frowned toward my cousins. "The next one of you that blathers on about the trials of our people will find herself gasping for air. You've been warned."

All of the girls fell silent again, but Erika had been staring at me pointedly ever since she had voiced her complaint at my cousins. I shuddered all over, trying to keep myself in the present, to stop imagining what my future would hold as a Teuton woman of ninety-five percent. No one else in the room seemed to have blood at that sort of level. And *Der Weg* had not mentioned any way to lower one's Teuton blood. I shook my head and took another sip of Coke, then looked toward Erika at last. She eyed me earnestly, her mouth pressed into a thin line.

"Swanie, if you fall for an outsider, and it's serious, come talk to me, okay? Being a Teuton doesn't mean you have to do what's expected." The resolution in her eyes prompted me to nod at her in silent determination. No old book could tell us what to do. We could forge our own path.

The door opened again soon afterward, and a sturdy man dressed in casual clothes, who looked to be around forty, walked in with a toolbox in hand. "Oh no, I've stumbled into a coven of witches," he commented by way of greeting, his grin belying his words. He closed the door before Sonnig could get out and bent down to give the Yorkie a cordial pat.

"Ah, Rudi, so good to see you," Lady Muniche welcomed him with a smile, reaching a wrinkled right hand out to him.

He clasped her hand and bent down to kiss her cheek. "How are you today, *Leitalra*?" he murmured in a respectful tone, using an old term that applied only to the Ladies of a Teuton city. I straightened out of habit at his formality.

"Quite well, trying to keep my young witches from scaring our new friend out of her wits." She chuckled and gestured at me. "Swanie von Thaden."

Rudi looked toward me and adjusted his glasses, his square jaw shifting in what looked like incredulity. "Max's kid?" I nodded. "Well, it's about time. It's not healthy to stifle the truth. So what do you have for me today? Just the sink?"

"If you could load all our dishes into the dishwasher and collect our trash before you get started on the sink, that would be wonderful." Lady Muniche smiled and handed him her bowl, which he took into the kitchen along with his toolbox, returning in a short time to collect all of our bowls and utensils.

I saw Erika looking at me again, so I mouthed, *Who's he?*

"That's her boyfriend," Erika told me in a stage whisper. Both of my cousins started giggling.

"Rudi is one of the priests on the Teuton Council of München," our elderly hostess explained, a playful smirk curling upon her face. "All six of them help me with a variety of things, but he's been one of my closer confidants over the years. Now, why don't we all tell Swanie a bit about our personal elements, and give her a brief description of what we can do with them."

By the time Hans came to retrieve me at three, I had learned more than I had ever thought possible about how a Teuton could use her element subtly around the house and at school. Trudi, who was yellow fire, admitted to using her fire to heat up her food at school whenever the cafeteria served a dish that had not been fully cooked. And Marga used her earth to cultivate an herb garden year round in her family's front parlor. I had yet to completely grasp how to invoke my ice, but I would get there with time—and winter would be here soon.

"I want to read the older version of *Der Weg* from the 1800s," I told Hans once we were seated in his car, heading back toward the Thaden house. Out of all of the things that I had learned that afternoon, the idea of actually reading and practicing the ancient spells had settled like a seed in my heart, longing to be nurtured and grow. If it was too dangerous for me to have children, then I would learn all there was to know about my people, even the secrets held by the priests.

Hans gave a dark chuckle at my assertion. "You'd have to learn Teutonica first," he informed me, "and I can help you there."

Chapter Five:
Mind Over Matter Festival

Over the next few years, I devoured all of the information I could find on the Teuton people, on their history, on their traditions, on their gifts. Discovering my Teuton blood became the catalyst that spurred my recovery from the depression that had hampered me since I had lost Dane. I began taking solitary walks on the grounds, imagining that I could speak to him in the realm of nature, that he may somehow hear even though he had left the mortal world behind. I told him everything that I had learned, and when I went to the stream to practice with my ice, I celebrated my victories and laughed at my failures with him. After Hans taught me how to give my ice full control in order to set my spirit free, I pretended that Dane and I could dance together as Teuton spirits, both of us clad in watery sapphire, weaving amid the trees like two playmates that fate had not separated.

My Teutonic nature was a secret that I did not mind keeping, though I did tell Lise after a few months of trying to hide my icy exploits in my bathroom sink. She just chuckled and said that she had known all along that one day I would turn into an ice princess like my mother. "Then

Mutti was ice, too?" I asked, thrilled that I apparently had two things in common with my mother.

"That she was, and she wasn't shy about sprinkling its diamonds around the mobile above your crib," Lise reminisced. Her wistful smile prompted me to think back to those hazy days of my childhood and wonder how many times my mother had shown me her ice before I was old enough to understand.

When I went to school in the U.S. for tenth grade, I spilled my secret to Beth, who knew positively nothing about Teutons even though her dad was one. She did not take it well at first. I witnessed a horrific argument between her and my Onkel Jens once she had fully grasped the truth. She demanded to know why he had married her mother instead of a Teuton woman when he knew what that would mean for his potential offspring. After Beth had cried for a bit at the unfairness of it all, her father told her softly, "I married your Mom because I love her, and love crosses the bounds of blood and of nation. That's something you'll both understand one of these days—" he cast a glance toward where I stood watching in the hallway "—and you'll have to make what sacrifices your love requires."

The issue of love had nipped at me like an ever-present caterpillar ever since my Teutonic life had bloomed in 1992. The often-cited dangers of childbirth had curtailed my hopes for a boyfriend. As the years passed, I discovered that while girls like Ina and Marga had no trouble flirting with every eligible Teuton bachelor at the festivals, I felt no similar tug. Usually I would hang out with Erika instead, for she seemed uninterested in coy gyrations, preferring to discuss college plans. She wanted to study studio art in Vienna, and I would nod along while my eyes followed Hans' path, silently wishing that he would ask me to dance around the Maypole or in a festive jig. Clad in black priestly robes from chin to the ground, he carried himself with a poise that attracted me far more than the foolish Teutons my own age. The fact that he never showed preference to any one woman did not escape my notice. The only one with whom he shared regular conversations was my elderly friend and mentor, Lady Muniche, who sailed around every Teutonic gathering like a fairy queen, often cradling her dog Sonnig, her sage eyes claiming all of us as her personal entourage.

By the time I had reached my final year of high school, I had resolved to go to college at a liberal arts university in the U.S. with Beth. For many years, my father had hoped that I would either marry a gifted manager who could take his place at the head of Süddeutsche Getriebe—similar to my Onkel Derek, his brother-in-law, who worked as his CFO—or that I would ultimately prove myself capable of taking on the responsibility. My interest in management was limited, though; I much preferred the fields of art and music. I had taken organ lessons for years thanks to some things I had read in *Der Weg*, and if it had been up to me, I would have gone to a local conservatory to study organ performance. But my father wanted me to study business just in case my single status never changed, so Beth had helped me pinpoint a university in the U.S. that offered a wide variety of programs. We would embark on our next adventure in August of 1998, with business management and organ performance on my roster and creative writing on hers.

Though I looked forward to spending more time with my cousin—who was honestly my best non-Teuton friend—the idea of being away from München and everything Teutonic for such an extended period of time filled me with uncertainty. I had gotten used to living at home again over the past three years, getting to know my Teuton friends better, becoming wholly invested in their lives and future plans. Ina was mid-college with her eyes on a handsome Teuton man of high blood. Marga was in trade school with a boyfriend whose Teutonic blood was in the low eighties. She expected that he would stay with her long enough to gain elemental control. Erika had thrown herself into the Viennese art school with a verve that sometimes seemed inappropriate for one with the element of water, choosing to wear dresses more often than not, always eager to show off her most recent drawings. Trudi and Traudl were both in trade school themselves, studying massage therapy and auto mechanics respectively.

But Swanhilde von Thaden had decided to buck the trend and study far away in the U.S., a place where finding a man of high Teuton blood would likely remain improbable. All five of my friends tried to talk me out of it one last time a month before I planned to depart. We all sprawled together in a tent at the Mind Over Matter music festival, the acrid scent of cigarette smoke prompting me to burrow my nose under the fabric of my sleeping bag. I was not a fan of that particular vice.

"I just can't see *why* you'd want to study all the way in the U.S.," Traudl said at length, flopped halfway on top of her sister on their air mattress. Both of them had drunk heavily during the shows that day; Trudi had passed out the second she had hit the mattress. "What happens if one of us gets married?" Traudl yawned dramatically.

"You'll have to fly in for any weddings whether you like it or not," Marga asserted, sounding a lot more lucid than my cousin. Out of the six of us, she and I were the only ones still sober. I had had one beer at lunch, and she had had a shot of Schnapps with dinner.

"That won't be a problem," I assured the group, still burrowed beneath my sleeping bag. I was exhausted after being jostled by the crowd all day. I had refined my taste in music thanks to this festival, but the rock and metal crowd seemed to be a wild bunch. My T-shirt still smelled like beer after a bearded man in a kilt had swung his drink-filled horn a bit too freely. "I can let my Pappi know I might need to get home at a moment's notice."

"You ever going to tell your Pappi about what we really are?" Erika sounded half asleep. When I looked toward her, she took a drag on her cigarette, and I saw its embers reflecting in her eyes, an eerie orange glimmer.

"I don't know. Someday maybe I will. But every time I drop a vague hint, he acts like I handed him a cobra or something." I grimaced at the memory of our most recent conversation about potential boyfriends. He had offered names of some of his younger business contacts, and I had stated blandly that I needed to know their blood status before I would consider any of them. He had given me an arch look, grumbled something about rituals costing too many lives, then changed the subject completely.

"I like your Pappi," Ina mused, her words more slurred than usual. Her hair was half natural and half in dreadlocks, their ends spilling over her shoulder while she sat propped up on an elbow on her sleeping bag. "Wish he'd take someone my age. I'd be set up for life." She guffawed and slumped down onto her pillow.

I rolled my eyes at my oldest Teuton friend's crazy fantasies. "No thanks. I'd rather not have a stepmother just two years older than me. Erika, can you put out that cigarette? I need to get to sleep."

"I guess so," Erika sighed, squishing the smoldering end between her fingers, her water dousing its cinders. "You'd better be glad I like you," she added while in the process of worming her way into her sleeping bag. "But I *don't* like that you're leaving us for four whole years."

"Goodnight," I said in a tone of warning. We had more shows to attend the following day, and if I got no sleep, I would be a walking zombie.

On Sunday I followed my friends' wake from one stage to another, from the bars to the merch stands, picking up a few new CDs for myself as well as my father and his new hire, a single young man tasked with all house projects that involved heavy lifting. Therion's metal opera performance impressed me the most, followed by Oomph!, whose style reminded me of Rammstein. I limited myself to water that day, for I did not want to have a hangover the next morning. I would have to drive, carting Erika to our next stop on this final pre-college vacation of mine. Everyone else had to return home for work, and apparently Ina was to be designated driver. She drank only Fanta and Sprite.

"You *are* coming back home every summer, right?" Erika questioned that night, half-leaning on me while we made our way back to our tent. The camping field had taken on a more distasteful quality after three days' use.

Mud and garbage littered the ground along with the occasional stoned metalhead.

"Of course I am," I answered, keeping my focus on my Doc Martens, trying to steer us both away from the grimiest areas. Thankfully Trudi was still lucid enough to hold a patch of yellow fire in her palm to light our way. The previous night I had stepped in what had to be human dung, and I had kicked someone in the stomach, which had nearly resulted in the rise of a croaking swamp monster. "I might even come back for Christmas a couple times. My Pappi is planning on holding his grandest parties during the winter holidays."

"Inviting us?" Erika asked before leaning over to vomit.

I held her upright while she splattered the ground with beer and potatoes. "You can't drink like this for the rest of our trip," I reminded her. "The plan is to hike, and to be honest, my classmates hold their alcohol better than you do."

"They'll think I'm a gutter rat anyway. What does it matter?"

I sighed and pulled her toward our tent, which loomed in the darkness before us. Trudi had gotten there first and yanked open the zipper, holding her yellow fires over her head as a beacon for the rest of us. "Come on, everybody. Light's about to go out," she called, holding the tent flap open.

"If I could find that flashlight . . ." Marga mumbled on her way in, kicking her sneakers off without untying them.

I stripped down to my underwear and slid into my sleeping bag, grateful to embark on a different sort of escapade tomorrow morning. As much as I loved both rock music and my group of Teuton friends, I preferred camping in the forest to camping in a place thronged with drunken humanity. I had enjoyed many of the bands and the vibe during the concerts, but I decided that if I ever attended another music festival in the future, I would get a hotel room. Though I did not like to think of myself as a spoiled rich brat, there was some truth in that label, honestly. My years with Beth's family had not completely cured that part of me.

"So what was everyone's favorite band? Bands?" Ina asked once we had all settled in. Several voices muttered in response to her question, but she pressed on, undeterred by her friends' lethargy. "Blind Guardian gave the best show, I think. It's like they could really transport everyone to Middle Earth."

"Yeah, Blind Guardian," Marga mumbled before turning her body pointedly away from the rest of us.

"I liked Crematory," Erika stated blandly, and an instant later I heard the distinctive click of her lighter.

"Can you *not* start smoking right now?" I blurted in a voice that sounded more wounded than intended. "Your driver needs to sleep. And we can discuss our favorite bands while we break camp in the morning, right?"

"Fine then," Erika shot back before cursing me in Bayerisch and shifting around in her sleeping bag. "But I'm smoking in your Maserati. I don't care."

I rolled my eyes up to the creased ceiling of the tent and conceded, "Just put the window down first." Then I shut my eyes and my mind to my friends' words and drifted off to sleep, memories of opera metal weaving through fancies of myself in the U.S. in just over a month, branching out on my own for the first time.

Chapter Six:
The Lure of the Lake

The next morning, Erika and I loaded all of our stuff into my red Ghibli and helped our friends pack up Ina's squat Volkswagen in preparation for their journey home. "So jealous of you two," Trudi complained while I shoved the tent deep into my trunk—it belonged to Erika and thus would make the trip in my car. "Not only are you going to the lake country, you get to ride there in style."

"Artists get to have all the fun while the rest of us slave away," Traudl said in response, sounding more wistful than upset.

I finished with the tent and extracted myself from the trunk, closing it and pushing my glasses back into place before turning to face my cousins. "You two *could* ride with us as far as Stainach if you want. That's where we turn north."

My cousins looked at each other, their black hair braided in similar fashion. Though the two were identical, I found it easier to tell them apart now thanks to my years of Teutonic training. Traudl naturally exuded an air of sturdiness common for those with an earth-related element. Trudi, on the other hand, seemed flightier even at a glance—typical for a Teuton of fire.

"Don't steal all of my passengers, Swanie," Ina warned, sliding into her car and cranking the ignition. "You know my car can't keep up with yours."

"Doesn't sound like it's on its last legs yet," Traudl noted, her head tilted to study the sounds of Ina's engine. Marga made a coughing noise as she claimed the passenger seat, doing a pantomime of the Volkswagen dying a slow death.

I rolled my eyes at all of them. "We're not at home. Can't speed in Austria."

"130 is so freaking *slow*," I heard Erika complain while I situated myself in the driver's seat of my car. I turned the key and the engine purred to life. My father had given me the Maserati as my seventeenth birthday present, and I prided myself in the fact that I had not yet damaged the car in any way. Many of my wealthy peers had gone through multiple cars already in their attempts to prove themselves young and fearless.

"In the U.S. it's worse," I told Erika, who had pulled the passenger seat forward to let my cousins climb into the back. "Literally the fastest speed limit I've ever seen is about 113, I think."

"That's like turtle speed," Trudi laughed.

"How do they get anywhere before dying of old age?" Erika plopped down at my side and pushed the button to roll down her window.

"Well, if I come back this Christmas with gray hairs, you'll know why," I said with a grin, following Ina's car toward the street.

We paused at a McDonald's near Stainach for lunch, and there our group parted ways, Marga pledging to call Lady Muniche to schedule one final gathering before I headed to college in August. Erika and I did not speak much during the rest of the drive, for she preferred to enjoy a pair of CDs that she had picked up at the festival, often shouting out the lyrics in the midst of her cloud of smoke. "You think Vreni's really going to be able to invoke her fire someday?" she asked just as I turned my car off of the main road toward the mountains.

I glanced at Erika, her red hair now cropped into a pixie cut, her lidded eyes studying the landscape with an expression of muted interest. She planned on taking loads of pictures during this part of our vacation, wanting to add to her stockpile of backgrounds for landscape drawings. She referenced the only girl out of my three classmates that she had met before, Verena Scheele. Vreni and I had attended the same expensive private school during our years of secondary education, and out of all of my wealthy peers, she was the only one that I knew had a trace of Teutonic blood. Unfortunately her blood was at seventy-five percent, ten points away from the threshold of elemental control. In spite of this, her family occasionally attended the May festivals and the New Year celebrations, and I had once seen her mother at one of the Teuton-run tents during the Oktoberfest.

"Well, she *did* find a boyfriend with an element that could nudge her in the right direction," I replied at length, not particularly wanting to speculate on that subject. According to *Der Weg*, sexual intercourse was one of two ways to raise one's Teuton blood. Such ventures were more complicated when one of the partners did not have elemental control, though. It would not be safe for an outsider to properly mate with a Teuton of fire.

"What's Stefan's element again?"

"He's Föhn."

"Right." Erika heaved a sigh and then mentioned, "You know I heard that if you do anal, you get an extra percentage point right away."

My eyes widened, and I had to catch myself before my ice erupted in my veins. I could not allow my emotions to influence my element while driving. "What the *heck*, Erika?!" I had no wish to discuss weird sex with my friend.

"That's what I heard. It's because it's unnatural. Since our elements are tied in with Wuotan's sorcery, unnatural sex will raise—"

"But if that was true, then rape should be included," I interrupted, fighting to stifle a new image that had popped into my brain: myself with Hans on top of me. His Teuton blood was at ninety-seven percent, the highest status of any of the Teutons I personally knew.

"I doubt Wuotan cares about consent," Erika scoffed.

Probably not. "Why are we talking about this?" I slowed down for a curve.

"Maybe I should tell Vreni she should try sucking Stefan's dick."

I gagged. "You barely know her. You can't just blurt out something like that. Anyway, that might dry her mouth out." Erika guffawed, and I fought a smile.

We met up with Vreni, Morgen, and Ava at a four-star hotel on the banks of the Fuschlsee, one of several lakes clustered together in the Austrian Alps. They had come in Morgen's light blue Aston Martin, her second car; she had wrecked the first early that year while in the company of a rowdy businessman she had picked up at a party. My classmates greeted Erika and me with enthusiasm, and after we had unpacked, Ava and Morgen spent most of the evening questioning Erika about the Mind Over Matter festival. They seemed to find metal music amusing, though Ava interjected a few snide comments that implied that that type of musician would never make it to the Grammys. Erika shot me a few appalled looks every now and then. Apparently she was as bemused by my rich peers as they were by her.

Vreni and I reclined in lounge chairs while watching the sunset over the lake, discussing college plans. Neither Ava nor Morgen planned to attend college right away since their families were putting up the money for them to travel for a few years. I suspected that they were being set free while their families sought out proper matches for the two of them. Their fathers were financiers, so they would be expected to marry well. Hopefully both of them would settle down after their years of exploration. At this point they had an ongoing contest on who had screwed the most men, the richest men, the craziest men. They likely would not hesitate to talk about unusual sex with Erika.

Vreni produced a map of the surrounding area as the sky darkened, and we spent a good bit of time plotting out our itinerary for the following day. Our first stop would be the summit of the Schafberg, which sported an incomparable view of the many lakes and peaks nearby. I remarked that we ought to dress nicely since Erika would doubtless try to pose us for various photos, and Vreni grinned. "Well, if I wear my Prada skirt up there, I'll have to change before we go to the cave," she said, her dyed blue hair appearing argentine in the twilight.

"We can go there in the morning and come back here for lunch before hiking anywhere," I declared, anticipation inspiring my ice to lightly cool my body. I could hardly wait for tomorrow's escapades.

Tuesday passed in wondrous fashion. We admired the view from the peak, tasted local dishes at lunch, and explored a nearby cave and waterfall. My wealthy friends were all exhausted by the time we returned to our hotel for dinner, and Morgen insisted that we stay at the hotel on Wednesday to take advantage of its boats. Erika muttered in my ear that the rich had no endurance, but I did not mind the prospect of boating. Once we were far enough out on the lake, I would swim whether my friends did or not. In the water I could conjure my ice on the sly.

Morgen and Ava turned in early that night, and Vreni eventually left Erika and me alone on the banks of the lake, stating with a yawn that she would see us in the room. We had rented adjoining rooms with balconies, and Vreni had deigned to share our room while the other two had insisted upon taking the one with beds for only two guests.

"About time she left," Erika said once we heard the glass doorway to the hotel's enclosed porch shut behind my friend.

"Do they really bother you that much?" I asked, abruptly doubting the value of my plan to vacation with friends of disparate backgrounds. Erika's father was an engineer for BMW, and her mother worked as a secretary.

Though her family was hardly broke, they were not on my classmates' level either.

"It's not that," Erika replied in an unexpectedly sultry tone. I looked toward where she lay on the lounge chair to my left, snuffing her cigarette into an adjacent ashtray. She winked at me and confessed, "I was having Teutonic thoughts." Her gaze shifted toward the lake.

My eyebrows came together, and I glanced around the lawn. "Just because nobody's out here right now doesn't mean *some*body wouldn't see us. I think I can hear people talking on that balcony." I nodded to the right.

Erika smirked. "Sure they'd see us if we did it openly. I was thinking more along the lines of a spiritual frolic."

I felt my forehead wrinkle at her choice of words. The idea of skipping across the lake as a Teuton spirit sent an icy thrill through me, but . . . . "I thought you'd never successfully made the crossing." I cocked my head at my friend, sensing the freshness of her element gradually overtaking her aura. Her irises altered from hazel to a perfect blue while she met my gaze, a triumphant smile spreading across her face.

"I just recently figured it out while in the shower at my dorm," Erika told me with a snicker. "I think it's easier for me to grasp my element when I'm physically *in* the water. But I know you don't need snow to properly change, thanks to your creepy mentor." She wagged her tongue at me.

"Hans isn't creepy."

"He's a Teuton priest, and that makes him creepy, because you know all he wants to do is lock you into some submissive relationship for the rest of your life." Erika stood up and stretched, wriggling her fingers in the direction of the lake.

Embarrassment heated my cheeks, and I looked down at my hands in my lap. "He's older than my Pappi, Erika. If he'd wanted a submissive Teuton wife, he'd have found one years ago." I looked toward the lake myself, deciding that if Erika wanted to test her newfound abilities out there, I might as well join in. I had never danced as a

Teuton spirit with any of my female friends. Lady Muniche actually advised against such things, often repeating that many good Teutons had become criminals after diving into the spiritual realm. That was one of the major tasks of the Teuton Council of München, to ensure that no Teutons in their jurisdiction used their gifts indiscreetly. Hans had once told me that there was an ancient dungeon of sorts somewhere north of our city that housed Teutons who had used their elements for thievery or violence. *They are bound there until they prove themselves willing to properly contribute to society,* he had said, and then appended, *because any Teuton worth his salt would be able to break free from any modern prison.*

"If we hide ourselves in these reeds here, nobody ought to notice our watery bodies," Erika remarked from a short distance away. She stood with her bare feet in the water, her hands on her hips, her expression approving as she eyed a clump of leafy growth. "Come on, Swanie! What are you waiting for?"

I had finally pulled myself out of the lounge chair and stretched, wondering why thoughts of dark stone corridors and anguished moans had tainted my hopes for a romp on the water. "I don't know," I muttered, stepping into the water beside Erika. "Guess I just keep hoping we don't get caught. Women usually don't do this sort of thing. If some priest sees us, we might end up in big trouble."

"He'd have to beat us both in battle first."

I raised an eyebrow at my confident friend. "You think we could win against a priest? I'm not *that* good at fighting." Every time my friends and I had friendly elemental spats on the Thaden property, my cousins always wore me out. I could beat water, earth, and air, but yellow fire and metal generally proved too potent for my ice to withstand.

"He'd have to catch us first," Erika whispered in my ear. Then she crouched down among the reeds, sinking her hands into the water, its dampness creeping up her bare arms and legs, gradually soaking her hair. Her cerulean eyes met mine as she said, "Meet you at the middle of the lake." She took a deep breath, and then her body transformed into what appeared to be solid water, a naiad lurking in the reeds.

I pursed my lips and shook my head. "That looks so weird," I said to myself, trying to rein in my yearning to touch her watery arm, to see whether my fingers would pass through her form or not. I had studied my own body shortly after I had learned how to use my ice to enter the realm of the spirit; mine simply looked like an icy sculpture of a human woman. The water that encompassed Erika's mortal body did not appear wholly solid, though, the closer I studied her. I saw currents swirling on her skin and in her mermaid hair.

I shook my head again and crouched down beside her, gathering as many of the reeds to conceal myself as possible. Then I closed my eyes and centered myself on my element, on my ice, drawing it forth from where it lurked in my blood, in my heart, in my spirit. I felt it crusting my skin from my toes up, its chill reassuring me, welcoming me into its mystical realm. I shut my eyes and bolstered my ice until it seeped into my chest and coated my face—the moment when fear prompted many young Teutons, myself included, to lose focus right at the edge of the crossing. The first few times I had tried, I had panicked at the sensation of ice freezing my lungs, of my nostrils sealing over. But the breathlessness lasted only a few seconds, as my priestly tutor had patiently explained, and the victory of the spirit's liberation overshadowed any momentary discomfort.

My spirit burst into the sky an instant later, the warmth of the summer night prompting my robes to manifest as a brilliant blue that matched the waters of the Fuschlsee exactly. I grinned down at my spiritual robes, sensing their ever-present chill despite the season; then I threw my arms out and spun around in midair, my eyes scouring the stars above, amazed all over again at how clear they appeared. I had gotten contacts several years ago but still wore glasses more often than not, for ever since I had learned that my elemental vision perfected my eyesight in a way that corrective lenses never could, I had gotten into the habit of invoking my ice into my eyes whenever I needed to really look at something. And my ice had ruined quite a few pairs of contacts.

Hey Swanie, come on! Erika's spiritual voice sang along inside my head, and I looked toward the center of the lake, where I saw her drifting about a meter above the water, waving her left hand toward me.

Coming! I called back, darting down to the surface of the water, using its power to propel me swiftly toward my Teuton friend. I raised a low wave in my path, its crest peppered with ice.

Erika took the Lord's name in vain when I halted below her and lifted my face to grin up at her spirit. *Swanie, seriously, you are* gorgeous! *Now I wish I was ice, too, I mean, look at your hair!* She drifted down to my level and reached out to touch the icy locks that comprised my spiritual hair. Her ghostly fingers passed through them, and her lips contorted into a pout. *I forgot about that.*

I laughed, admiring my friend's hair in turn. It was much longer in her spiritual form than in her mortal form, and it undulated around her like the currents of a river, hued in mesmerizing shades of blue. *Well, your hair looks like countless forms of my favorite color, so no need to worship mine. Gosh, it's really a rush to be a spirit in a place like this,* I observed, the expansive water beneath me singing to my soul. *This is way better than doing it by my stream.*

Better than the shower, too! Erika swatted me with more force than appropriate. I felt her water pass through my shoulder like an unexpected eel.

Hey! I clawed at her with my fingers, their nails sharpening into icy points at my silent command. In the next instant we were chasing each other across the surface of the lake, hooting with laughter and raising unnatural waves. We romped until the moon had climbed a handbreadth in the sky above, sometimes diving into the waters and emerging with strange plants pulled from the depths. We tried to keep away from the pair of party boats floating along on opposite sides of the lake, although I suspected that if the partygoers noticed any of our activities, they would chalk them up to drunken hallucinations.

Eventually, though, I dropped a hint that we should return to our bodies and get some sleep. *Have to be awake for all the lounging planned for tomorrow,* Erika said with a mocking simper. Then she closed her eyes, and her spirit hovered for a moment before vanishing into thin air.

The lungs of my soul sighed in relief that she had agreed to halt our dance. The real reason I had suggested that we stop was because I had abruptly sensed another Teuton spirit somewhere close by, likely in human form. The Teuton that I sensed could have been someone sleeping in one of the lakeside hotels, but thoughts of being sent to some medieval dungeon for frolicking too freely brought caution to the forefront of my mind. Anytime Hans had taught me how to perfect some Teutonic gift that most Teutons did not use—like how to explore the world as a spirit—he always emphasized discretion and control. Never let others know the extent of your knowledge. Never let your emotions result in elemental chaos.

I did not tell Erika that I had sensed another Teuton nearby, and on our way back inside, she pulled me close in a side hug. "We should do this again tomorrow night," she whispered in my ear.

"Definitely, but next time let's check out some of the other lakes, too."

Chapter Seven:
The Leutasch Gorge

During the following week, we shifted our base from the Fuschlsee to the banks of a small stream in northern Tyrol, the Leutascher Ache. We would use our new site—a high-class bed-and-breakfast—as a springboard from which to explore the nearby towns of Mittenwald and Garmisch-Partenkirchen and all of the surrounding landscapes. Ava and Morgen had grown weary of the Fuschlsee after spending four nights with different male guests. None had been particularly entertaining, they claimed, and Ava remained thoroughly affronted that one of the men had tried to whip her with his tie. "I'm just not into the BDSM scene. It's so vulgar," she declared during breakfast on our last morning there.

"I've heard that BDSM is actually really popular among rich men," Erika put in with a look of faux innocence. "Apparently they feel like having money doesn't satisfy their cravings for power."

This prompted both Ava and Morgen to refuse to speak to Erika for the rest of the day, while I simply blushed at my food and shared a private glance with Vreni, who I could tell was trying hard to hold back laughter. When we arrived at our new destination, the two offended girls shut themselves into their suite to grumble together while Erika, Vreni, and I got settled in a slightly larger suite. Erika agreed to take the daybed this time around, so I would be sharing the main bed with Vreni. Hopefully I would not have any dreams that inspired my ice to manifest itself while I slept. That generally happened only with nightmares, though I had also awoken with traces of ice coating my flesh whenever I had raunchy dreams. Usually those sorts of dreams involved either Hans himself or an unknown Teuton priest of sizzling fire, his element complementing mine perfectly in my subconscious.

That was one thing that I hoped four straight years in the U.S. would purge from my system entirely. Though I hated to admit the truth to myself, I was in love with someone over thirty years my senior, someone who treated me as just another curious Teuton student, someone who had never reciprocated my feelings at all. I needed time away from Hans, and maybe immersing myself in a completely foreign culture would help quell my foolish yearnings. Even if I did end up with a Teuton man of high blood someday, I may not be willing to risk giving him children. And from what I had observed, all of the young Teuton men in München seemed hung up on the concept of preserving their family trees.

On our third night at the bed-and-breakfast, Erika joined Morgen and Ava in their drinking games, the two having forgiven her after she had introduced them to a pair of Austrian businessmen who had rented the apartment above ours. The three girls spent most of the evening at the hut's beer garden, their rowdy laughter occasionally drifting out to where I sat beside Vreni before the hut's fire pit. The two of us were in casual clothes—shorts, tank tops, and sandals—since we had all spent the day hiking around the lakes near Mittenwald. "So is it getting serious between you and Stefan yet?" I inquired at length, leaning back on my elbows and watching the flames dance in the pit. I wished that I could manipulate fire as well as ice.

Vreni sighed quietly, lying back on the lawn with her hands behind her head, her eyes on the stars above. "I like him a lot, but I don't know how long he's going to stay with me, you know? With the whole Teuton thing and all."

"Yeah," I answered, sympathy building within me at my friend's problem. "But just think, if he *does* decide to stay with you, then someday you'll be able to stick your hand into the heart of those flames."

Vreni chuckled, brushing a strand of blue back from her face; her hair had begun to escape its bun after our exertions that day. "Not sure if I'd really *want* to be able to manipulate my element," she murmured, sounding thoughtful, shifting position a bit on the ground. "I mean, think about it, Swanie. If the government ever got wind of Teutonic powers, all of you would either get stuck in science labs or be hunted to extinction."

"Yeah, I know." I looked up at the heavens myself, wishing for another world, one in which my people would not have to hide. "That's why we have to keep it contained and only tell people we trust. The secrecy really sucks sometimes." Vreni sighed again, and I closed my eyes to concentrate on my other senses—the sounds and heat of the crackling fire, the summer breeze caressing my cheeks, the scents of flowers and trees and grass . . . and the chattering waters of the shallow river that flowed not far from our bed-and-breakfast. I felt a familiar stirring in my soul and thought back to my recent romps with Erika. "This night is calling me to break free and dance . . . ." I said in an undertone. My Teuton friend would be too drunk to attempt anything tonight, I figured. I felt a niggling urge to set more than just my spirit free this time around.

"How can *that* be, when it's not even winter?" I looked toward Vreni and caught her skeptical eye.

I gave her a half-smile and jerked my head toward the trees beyond the fire pit, beyond the property of the bed-and-breakfast. "The Leutascher Ache is down there, in case you didn't notice." Vreni's incredulity showed no signs of departing, so I shrugged and added, "But there's still too many people around for that."

Vreni pursed her lips, but before she could comment, Ava appeared abruptly at our sides. "Hey you two, the beer garden's closing for the night, but Greg and Fritz have invited us to use their hot tub." I looked up at my lecherous friend, who swayed her hips and wiggled her blond eyebrows at me. "Figured I'd invite you two to take part if you wish. Your beggarly friend might need help making it back to your room, though, Swanie."

"Good grief, Ava, her dad's an engineer. And she lives in a *house*." I shook my head at my classmate's snobbery, and out of the corner of my eye I saw Erika bent over the railing surrounding the beer garden, vomiting onto the grass. All I could see of Morgen was her wave of auburn hair. She was locked in an embrace with one of the businessmen, having ditched my Teuton friend in her time of need.

"Whatever," Ava said, rolling her eyes and running the fingers of her right hand through her long ponytail. "You two can help her if you're not coming. We'll see you in the morning, or maybe the afternoon!" She blew Vreni and me a kiss and then flitted back to the beer garden, where the waitresses were cleaning tables.

"Bitches as always," Vreni noted with a disgusted scowl. "I'll go take care of Erika if you'd rather get icy with the stream." She pushed herself onto her feet and gave a big yawn as she stretched, her well-developed breasts bouncing noticeably beneath her sequined tank top.

"Those two guys would probably enjoy your company," I remarked before getting up myself, stretching and patting the pocket of my jean shorts to make sure I still had my room key. "I can help Erika back to our room." She was leaning upon the railing now, looking seasick.

"Unless they can improve my blood status, I'm not interested. Go have your fun, Swanie. I'll take care of Erika." She left the fireside before I could object, and I watched her hoist Erika's right arm and drape it across her shoulders, her left arm gripping her waist as she led her toward the back door into the bed-and-breakfast. They looked like an odd pair, both tall and willowy, one blue-haired in name brand clothing, the other in a flared Gothic skirt and Crematory T-shirt, their positions in life hardly equal. But they appeared to be kindred spirits anyway, somehow.

I stood lost in thought beside the fire pit until one of the waitresses came out to extinguish its remaining flames and remind me that the doors would soon lock for the night. "That's fine; I've got my key to come in the front," I assured her, glancing toward the third floor balcony, wondering whether I would eventually see my two crazy friends standing there naked, having splashed around madly in a hot tub. The patrons had all departed from the beer garden, and the balconies on both floors were empty of people. For now.

I pulled the case for my contacts from my pocket and poked them out of my eyes, deciding that it was time to take Vreni's advice. *Go have your fun, Swanie,* she had said. She was right. I should not have to fear the possibility of running into any witnesses around the Leutascher Ache. It was a shallow river girded by trees, mostly undeveloped. I allowed my element to rise within me, answering the call of its primary . . . *water* . . . . My sight altered with a haze of blue, sharpening my focus on the night around me, its darkness no longer a mystery to me. And I turned away from the bed-and-breakfast to head for the river, just a short walk through the trees.

It did not take me long to reach the water's edge, and when I did, I paused for a moment, reveling in the beauty of the night, the sounds of chirping insects and hooting owls melding with the chattering of the stream before me. Its waters were colored a pure light blue, though at such a late hour it appeared more of a midnight blue, the rays from the crescent moon above hardly touching its ripples. My friends and I had visited the waterfall that its currents created some distance downstream two days ago, but here beside our bed-and-breakfast it appeared calm and welcoming, its waters whispering to my soul. My eyes studied the stream from left to right, tracing its course among the trees, along the road that led from our calm hideaway in the Austrian Tyrol to our home state of Bavaria.

A smile spread slowly across my face at the mad idea that gradually came over me while I stood admiring nature's path. Erika and I had enjoyed spiritual dances upon the lakes on three different occasions while we vacationed beside the Fuschlsee, but we had never attempted a physical elemental dance upon it. There were always too many people around, even at night, but here? It should be possible here, and I had some experience with manipulating the flowing currents of the tiny stream on Thaden property. But did I dare to try such a thing with a *river,* with one that eventually entered an untamed gorge in its swift quest for the waterfall?

I kicked off my sandals anyway and knelt down to trace my fingers through the water, my mind toying with the idea despite its risks. The currents seemed to caress my skin, their chill speaking more deeply to my blood, to my ice. It began to overtake my veins more thoroughly, and I watched as my fingers took on a translucent sheen, creating tiny ice floes in the water they touched. One breath of cold air escaped my lips, and I swung my head around to look behind me at the line of trees, at the lights of the bed-and-breakfast further away, atop a slight incline. No people. There were still no people around.

In order to physically dance in Teutonic glory, one must put aside inhibitions and fully embrace one's element, allowing it to meld with the landscape in a per-fection of life . . . . I had read that phrase some time ago in *Der Weg,* and I had already put the concept to the test at home, in the safety of my own backyard. I had even danced once on the shallows of the River Isar, which traversed my hometown. If I could succeed there, I could manage it here as well. There was no one around to witness it, or to tell me to refrain from indulging myself.

So I threw caution aside and skipped into the waters of the Leutascher Ache, their cool temperature infusing my limbs with strength, awakening my ice to the fullest. I giggled at the foolishness of my actions, then lifted my arms as though to join them with a Teuton partner, imagining a moment of elemental unity. And my voice began to softly sing an ancient folk song of my people, my body beginning to sway gracefully, a thin coating of ice spreading itself down the skin of my arms, of my legs, of the shoulder-length locks of my black hair. At last, my confidence came to the fore with a triumphant burst of vigor, and I leaped from my stance in the center of the narrow river to the crest of a swell several meters downstream, my icy toes merging neatly with the water, freezing it solid.

My enthusiasm increased exponentially, and I chortled in the midst of my song, springing further downstream to create another ice floe, and then another. From time to time I neared the banks of the stream, my frozen fingers reaching up to brush overhanging branches with the frigid kiss of my ice. The currents of the Leutascher Ache seemed eager to carry me along with them, reinforcing my stamina with the melody of my strong and living primary: *water*. My element began to sense other creatures dancing with me amid the tree branches, some of which I noticed were of silver oak, one of several plants with special properties to the Teuton people. *Are the Eihalbae actually dancing with me?* I wondered, a delight I had not yet experienced quivering in my heart. I began to brush my ice against more and more branches as I progressed, hoping that the whimsical fairies may show themselves.

The idea of sharing a dance with the elusive fairies propelled me to abandon all restraints, to engross myself in my powers while I had the chance, before I found myself in the prison of a foreign country, a college campus filled to the brim with students and professors, with witnesses. I sprang from choppy waters to a boulder that jutted into the river, creating a rushing waterfall. I paused just long enough for my ice to begin crusting the stone beneath my toes, and then I jumped to the base of the waterfall, letting its spray coat the strands of my hair, where it promptly froze into jagged icicles. Laughter rang forth from my lips, echoing through the trees around me, reflected by the waters beneath me, their chill, swells, and speed ever increasing.

I finished singing another song, one about the Isar—changing the name *Isar* to *Leutasch,* since it seemed close enough—before thinking that it might be prudent to end my elemental gambol and return to the bed-and-breakfast before the night grew much later. I slowed to a halt on a small iceberg that seemed to arise from my feet themselves, then offered a brilliant smile to the river before me, to the waters around me. "Leutascher Ache and distinguished *Eihalbae,* it has been a pleasure." I spoke my compliment in Teutonica, suddenly wondering whether the stream itself had a spirit, that it could somehow appreciate my gratitude.

Then I turned to face what was behind me, and a horrified gasp escaped my lips.

The calm and peaceful mountain stream that I had eagerly danced upon had transformed into a swollen river with raging and rippling currents, my elemental potency having filled it to the brim of its banks. The waters shoved me forward with unyielding tenacity, as though they wished to mock my confidence, having danced down-stream toward more dangerous environs rather than upstream, which should have been my first choice, despite the difficulties it would have entailed. *Teutons with water-related elements, when dancing upon a river, should chose the downstream path in order to maximize their liveliness with that of the currents . . . .*

But *Der Weg Teutonisch,* as erudite as it was, did not stop to consider the consequences of dancing downstream when there happened to be a rock-walled gorge . . . and a large waterfall . . . downstream . . . .

I had not realized that I had gone *this* far . . . .

My eyes darted around to analyze my surroundings beyond the stream itself, and I saw that the trees had indeed given way to steep walls of earth and rock, grass poking out in clumps here and there, scraggly trees stretching to the sky high above my head. The river had narrowed, beginning to ram itself around stone ledges and fallen logs in a race for its grand plunge over a kilometer away.

And the hand of fear grasped my heart at the realization that I had reached the Leutasch Gorge, a lengthy ravine ignored by intrepid rock climbers, not yet developed into any type of attraction. I would not come upon anyone to help me get out of this dreaded place, not even once I reached the path to the waterfall, which was closed for the night. I had to rescue myself.

My first thought was to point my feet to the west, upstream, and fortify my ice with what little remained of my sanity, to allow it to conquer the raging waters at my back—my own creation. If I had caused this overflow, I should be able to tame it. But my fear had already prompted my grasp on my element to slacken, and suddenly a wave smashed me against a rock to my right, my feet sinking into the waters as they attempted to pull me under, a mere human overcome by her folly. I cried out in pain at the impact, reaching up to grasp hold of a tuft of grass sticking out above the rock. *If I can't ride the river back, maybe I can climb out of here and head for the road. It can't be too long of a walk . . . .*

I considered that option for a moment, my right hand clinging to the grass, my left scrabbling upon the rock, at last snatching its rough tip, my feet and lower legs still pounded by the angry waters of the Leutascher Ache. Though I had never used my ice to *climb* anything before, it would probably be safer than attempting to control the maddened river. So with a shout of determination, I channeled my ice into my fingers, transforming them into translucent claws, with which I began to scale the wall of the gorge, thrusting them into patches of earth, avoiding the stone.

Soon enough, I managed to pull my entire body out of the river, my toes also sharpened by my ice, stabbing themselves into the sides of the chasm. I pressed onward, away from the uncontrolled stream toward a sizeable elm tree that arched out from the rock, reaching for the sky and its life-giving heat. If I could pull myself atop the curve of its trunk, I could rest for a while, recover from this watery insanity that had conquered my confidence. So I clawed my way onto the trunk, some fifteen meters above the stream, panting with the effort, at last collapsing onto the bark and wrapping my arms around its girth. Shaky laughter pealed from my lips as belated shock flooded my veins, displacing my ice entirely.

What is this lunacy that drove me to this? I asked myself, closing my eyes and pressing my right cheek against the elm. *How could I have let my fantasies master my discretion? True, no one saw me . . . except for the fairies . . . but now I have to face the consequences of my elemental jaunt . . . and find a way back to the bed-and-breakfast . . . back to my friends who will wonder where I've been . . . and why I'll come back looking so bedraggled and drenched . . . .*

My thoughts turned to Hans, and a blush burned my face. *What will he think of me when he finds out about this?* I struggled to push aside my shock and fears and properly focus on a solution to my predicament. Here I sat, on a curved tree some distance from a stream rushing through a gorge, even further away from the top. I was no rock climber, and the awareness that I had already ascended this far without the aid of climbing ropes sent another rush of anxiety through me. I looked down at the dark currents below me, then squinted at the rim high above, trying to decide which path to take. My ice had contracted into my soul, so I focused upon it anew, pulling its blue veil over my eyesight, letting its chill freeze the nervous sweat that coated my skin. I looked up again, then down, the ice within me sensing the call of the Leutascher Ache once more, yearning to merge with something far suppler than the earth and stone above.

But I would have to go upstream . . . and I don't know if I can do it . . . even if the currents have calmed from my elemental storm, my uncertainty may lead to my destruction . . . .

Torn, I scowled, raising my eyes to the cliff above me. It was high, at least another thirty meters to the top, crags of rock protruding here and there amid bits of earth, grass, weeds, trees. *I can't do this. I really* can't *do this. I've trapped myself here where no one will find me, and my ice cannot save me from the wild.* Despair dug its nails into my heart, and my shoulders began to shake with sobs.

Chapter Eight:
An Unexpected Discovery

I do not know how long I wallowed in my gloom, weeping at my own foolishness and wishing that I could completely redo the past half hour. If I had danced in spirit form, I could have simply returned to my body once the stream grew too aroused. But no, I had to imagine myself as skilled as a Teuton priest, the master of all the elements around me as well as my own. *Hans is going to chew me out over this,* I knew, for there was no way I could keep it from him. He was the bearer of all of my Teuton secrets. *And now he'll think I'm still a ridiculous child, or worse, a naïve woman, just like* Der Weg *implies. One who needs a priestly husband to control her, but not him, no, never him . . . .*

"Zoubaraera . . . Teutona . . . ." The two words entered my mind like a wispy swath of silk, prompting my body to jerk upright; I had embraced the elm's trunk while indulging my misery. I endeavored to blink the tears—all of simple water—out of my eyes, invoking my ice to enhance my vision, to reveal who had encroached upon my failure. I wondered whether I had imagined the voice and its words, for its tenor had sounded like how Hans had described the voices of the *Eihalbae*. And there was no way such an entity would stoop to acknowledge me now.

Der Weg revealed little about the *Eihalbae* save that they embodied the spirits of the silver oaks, the most sacred tree to the Teuton people. They were said to possess ancient knowledge and sagacity, and they deigned only rarely to speak to human beings. Visible only to those who could enhance their eyesight with their elements, they generally inhabited the world unseen and unheard, considered mere myth by many of my people. But Hans had formally introduced me to the one who occupied the single silver oak on the Thaden grounds, a meeting that I would never forget. The *Eihalbe* had hidden itself amid a thick batch of silvery leaves and stared at me in silence, its almond-shaped eyes aglow with a prism of colors.

Now, to my astonishment, I found myself blinking at an *Eihalbe* hovering within arm's reach, its silvery body nearly blending in with the weathered wall of the gorge. A chill crept up my spine as I looked over the one who had intruded upon my anguish—the fairy was about the size of a squirrel, humanoid in form but with swiftly beating wings and a casually swaying tail. Its wavy hair shimmered around its body like mercury, making it appear female, though I knew that *Eihalbae* were genderless creatures. They did not reproduce like humans or animals; they came into being whenever a silver oak first produced acorns. They usually did not travel far from their own tree, but this one was *here*, hovering above an elm tree growing from the bluff of an Austrian gorge. And it had called me a Teuton witch.

I shuddered a little, gripping the bark beneath me more tightly as I pulled out all of the Teutonica I knew to properly greet my unexpected company. "Noble... *Eihalbe* ...." I began haltingly, meeting its mesmerizing gaze, "Please, I ... I'm not ... worthy to call myself a witch ... not after ... after ...." My voice broke, and I gestured wordlessly toward the river below, which still flowed more roughly than it should.

"Sorcery always exacts a price." Its kaleidoscope eyes bored seriously into mine, its lips curving strangely around the words. I noticed that its teeth were that of an herbivore; it had flat canines.

"True. Good advice," I murmured, nodding, my curiosity beginning to grow about my companion. I remembered all that Hans had told me. Be respectful. Never ask any questions. Offer gratitude for any counsel. "Thank you," I added belatedly, my eyes shifting downward again. The waters appeared to be calming at long last, so maybe I could safely ride the Leutascher Ache back to the glade where I had started my dance. What I really wanted to do was find out whether my companion had a name, what tree it inhabited, whether it had followed me in my dance, why it had decided to speak with me *now*, of all times. But when I raised my face to the fairy once more, it simply looked back at me in silence, its fingers slowly weaving a blade of grass that I had not seen before. Maybe it had pulled it from somewhere on the gorge wall. There were enough tufts of grass sticking out here and there.

"Looks like the river is calming," I mentioned, the fairy's silence rendering me uneasy. "I guess I should try to convince its waters to carry me back."

"The Teuton witch should climb." The *Eihalbe* looked over its right shoulder toward the top of the cliff, some thirty meters overhead.

I followed its gaze, the earthen wall seeming to tower over me. *Really? Is that what I should do?* I suddenly began to doubt the *Eihalbe's* wisdom. My element was ice, not earth, and the fairy certainly knew that. It would be easier to just let the river take me back—but then again, with an upstream course, I may run out of energy to direct its waters properly before I got there. My dance and subsequent scramble had exhausted me already. "It was hard to climb this far, noble *Eihalbe*," I pointed out as respectfully as possible.

"The Teuton witch seeks the abstruse. The Leutascher Ache she knows." My companion looked upward toward the edge of the cliff again, but this time I realized that its radiant eyes focused on something else, something below the edge. In the starlight I could see a crevice in a shadowy boulder about halfway between where I sat upon the elm and the top of the gorge. I squinted toward the cleft and sensed a strange tingle in my blood, an aura that made my Teuton spirit take notice.

"There's something up there. And I won't get it if I just commit my fate to the Leutascher Ache." I looked back at my companion, whose expression appeared pleased, as far as I could tell. It threaded the woven blade of grass into its hair and flitted away from the weathered wall, as if to give me space to start my climb. So I rose to my feet and placed my hands against the cliff before me, lifting my gaze to the crevice and the surrounding area one final time. There appeared to be enough clumps of grass and rocky indents to use as foot- and handholds on my way there. I bit my lip and summoned a courage I did not feel, awakening my ice more fully yet again, letting it protrude from my fingers and toes, solidifying it with all of my power. I felt my hair freeze into spikes as I twisted my face to the right to regard the *Eihalbe* one final time. "Thank you for your counsel, worthy *Eihalbe.*"

"Respect the price, *Zoubaraera Teutona.*" The fairy whizzed away before I could press the subject, quickly vanishing over the upper edge of the gorge. Apparently its tree was somewhere in the forest. No point in dawdling any longer. It had grown late, and Vreni had likely begun to wonder what had become of me. I shoved my hesitation aside and thrust my ice-coated fingers into the wall in a course for the mystery above.

I reached my goal after some struggle. The higher I ascended, the sparser the patches of earth and grass became, forcing me to push my ice back so that I could properly grip the multiplying crags of rock. At last, I balanced my toes on a thin ledge of stone, pulling my body into a standing position, my left hand precariously clutching a scrawny tree branch, rendering my face level with the dark crevice. There, deep in the shadows of the stone, I saw a small glimmer of crimson.

For a protracted moment, I stared at the reddish glow in silent confusion, wondering whether I dared to reach my right hand into the crevice to take hold of it, whether it might be enchanted somehow, whether it might burn me. *What in the world has that Eihalbe gotten me into? Some hidden ember?* I tried to think back to everything I had read in *Der Weg,* to recall if there existed some glowing amulet that harbored Teutonic magic. I did not think so, but then something else snared my concentration, something powerful, something atrocious, something very, *very* dark . . . .

And everything happened at once. My heart began to race, knives of horror prickling upon my flesh, and I plunged my right hand into the crevice, snatching that crimson curiosity and bringing it out into the night air before shoving it deep into the pocket of my jean shorts. My rash motions cost me my grip on the ledge beneath my feet, and I cried out in terror, my left hand tightening its grasp on the branch while my right hand scrabbled to clutch something, *anything* on the rock before me. My icy toes scraped desperately upon the cliff below, unable to find purchase on a more solid element, and I screamed, swinging my right hand over to the branch in desperation. I just barely managed to wrap my fingers around it, my arms taking the entirety of my weight, prompting their muscles to tremble with strain. *Did that fairy know that this would happen? Did it want me to die?*

The tree branch was truly bending now, and I caught a glimpse of the water far, far below, so shallow, not enough to cushion a fall from this height. I lifted my head to the top of the chasm, an impossible distance away . . . and there I saw the dark presence that had seized hold of my thoughts mere seconds before. Someone stood at the very edge of the gorge, wrapped in a blackness my eyesight could not pierce, its shadowed face turned downward, to me. In spite of the terror that enveloped me at the sight— so unexpected to see a human in an undeveloped ravine— I choked out a cry to whoever it was: "Help me!"

The branch bent further, accompanied by a creaking sound, and I knew that I had only seconds before I would die, tumbling to the rocky river below. The figure above me showed no signs of interest in my plight; in fact, it began to drift away. In hopelessness I shouted, "*Wait!*" My fingers had begun to slip from the branch.

The cloaked figure paused, and suddenly a sardonic male voice broke upon my ears, speaking a harsh indictment in Bayerisch. "Time and tide wait for none but the dead."

And a power tore me from my grip with a tenacity that I could neither match nor fight, sweeping me into an elemental storm that seemed a mix of deadly energy, a roaring gale, and an intense hurricane. It cast me down, down toward the rocks and water below, then swept me upstream, carrying me through the air centimeters above the river. I could not move my body as it hurtled out of the gorge and along the path of the Leutascher Ache, though my ice had erupted with an intensity that I had rarely experienced in my mortal form, possibly in defense, crystallizing my eyes, freezing my hair into a sheet upon my shoulders. My mouth was open in a soundless scream, and even my teeth had sharpened into razor icicles.

With an abruptness that could very well have caused my heart to leap out of my chest, the whirlwind ride had ceased, depositing me onto the very bank from which my adventure had begun. I found myself crouched upon the grass, panting, my heart still racing, my ice yet holding prominence over my body. I blinked my eyes several times, shook my head back and forth, and calmed my element, noticing my discarded sandals lying near a bush about a meter to my left. Lifting my head to the trees before me and the incline beyond, I saw the glimmering lights of the bed-and-breakfast piercing the darkness, inviting me to return to reality.

What . . . just . . . happened . . . ?

Now was not the time to consider it. I pushed myself to my feet and yanked my sandals from the grass, then sprinted away from that stream, from that specter, from that gorge, from those mad Teutonic whims. I yanked on the back door first before remembering that I had to use my key to get in from the front. I harrumphed in frustration and paused just long enough to stuff my sandals back onto my feet before running more slowly around the side of the building farthest from the gorge that had plunged my life into insanity. I dug around in my left hand pocket while crossing the parking lot, finding my contact case first, then the key. I pulled it out and held it to my chest like a lifeline, my sole connection to reality.

After gaining access to the lobby, I fairly fled up the stairs to the suite I had rented with my friends, locking its door firmly behind me, as though that could keep out the demons that now stalked my memories. Erika lay passed out on the daybed, not having changed her clothes. Vreni was curled up beneath the blanket on her side of our shared bed, soft snores exiting her open mouth. Both seemed to be sleeping soundly, not having noticed my prolonged absence.

And here I was, having danced like a naiad far down a stream, scaled a gorge without the aid of ropes or a harness, taken the unsolicited advice of a cryptic fairy, discovered something that had been hidden in the rock face for who knew how long, met a wraith with a power so strong, so noxious that it seemed impossible to exist . . . .

So what was this thing I had found, this thing that had called to both my ice and my blood? Now that I had made it safely back to this room, to the company of my Teutonic friends, it was high time to find out the truth. I moved to sit down upon my side of the bed, switching on the small light that shone above my pillow. I dug my contact case from my pocket first, seeing that it had cracked somehow in the fray, likely damaging the lenses inside. I sighed a little but laid the case down onto the bedside table in front of my glasses; I could simply wear those for the rest of our vacation, as usual. Then I stretched myself out upon the bed, relaxing my muscles, closing my eyes for a moment before reaching into the right pocket of my shorts to bring my new possession into the light.

It appeared to be a small, misshapen stone, about two centimeters in diameter and a deep dark red in color. It did not seem to give off any light, so how I had noticed its glow inside the crevice remained an enigma. Its color made me think of dark blood, perhaps from an artery, mingled with earth. What was more, the stone felt rather *unlike* a regular old stone, as I held it. It felt too smooth and somehow malleable, arcane. It felt like it could possibly be *used* for something.

A story arose in my mind, one I had read several times before in *Der Weg*, one of many tales in that historical text that most people believed to be legend. *In the eleventh century, at the height of the Teuton era, many Teutons still practiced the ancient traditions and studied the ancient arts, within the bounds of mysticism permitted by the Catholic Church. Some Teuton priests showed great interest in history, desiring not only to read what the chroniclers had written down, but to experience the events for themselves. One of them, at his death, created the Teutonic Torstein with his own blood . . . the gateway stone . . . the stone that could take a person back in time to observe, to become a part of history . . . .*

The Torstein, according to *Der Weg*, was supposedly a dark red in color and about the size of the rock I now held in my hand. It had disappeared sometime in the fifteenth century, and no one, not any of the Teuton scholars, knew where it had gone. It was thought to be lost forever.

It was not lost forever. The certainty had begun to grow in my mind. I had found the Torstein at the direction of an *Eihalbe*, deep in a crevice in the Leutasch Gorge. I was almost positive. But how could I know for sure . . . ?

I felt a shiver run up my spine as I answered my own question. *Hans would know. Of course he would know. But we're not going home for another three days.*

My eyes drifted to my right to where Vreni lay asleep, then toward the opposite end of the room where Erika sprawled stoned upon the daybed. I certainly could not tell either of them, not until I knew for sure whether this stone was the real deal or not. Maybe I could convince them to go to breakfast together in the morning, act like I needed to sleep longer. Somehow I had to evict them from the room so I could call my father's house in peace.

I shook my head at myself and placed the rock back into my pocket before getting to my feet and heading for the bathroom. I knew that I would get zero sleep that night, even though my adventure had exhausted my body. My brain swirled with ideas on how to use a power over time travel and all of the potential dangers involved, the stone lying heavily against my thigh. *Respect the price.*

Chapter Nine:
Confessions

I spent most of the night lying in bed replaying every aspect of my adventure and debating whether or not my discovery truly *was* the Torstein. I suspected that the *Eihalbe* would not have alerted me to its presence if it had no mystical significance. Even if the stone could not send me into history, perhaps it had some other magical properties. Eventually I nodded off, and when I awoke, daylight brightened the room, the sounds of the shower drifting outward from the attached bathroom. My alertness returned to me in a flash at the memory of what lay in my pocket, and I threw the covers off of my bed.

Vreni stood before the full-length mirror applying her makeup, which meant that Erika occupied the shower. I wondered whether my Teuton friend had a hangover; if so, she would need to get some coffee at the breakfast buffet downstairs. I looked toward the clock on the table to my left. 8:37.

"Did you have a wild dream or something?" Vreni had turned toward me, her eyes shifting from the blanket on the floor to my face. She wore a blue crop top that matched her hair, which she had pulled back from her face, the white leather shorts hugging her hips leaving little room for imagination.

I could not remember any of my dreams, but I sensed the rock pressing up against my leg in my pocket. "Not really, but it was a wild night," I admitted, getting up to stretch and comb my fingers through my hair. I could tell that I had a pretty obvious case of bed head.

The shower turned off, and Vreni raised her eyebrows at me. "The stream?" she inquired, looking curious. She drifted toward the dresser, setting her makeup kit atop it.

"Yeah, and I think I need a shower when Erika's done." I had not changed clothes from the night before, and I needed to clean up my appearance, since today we planned to ride the cable car to the top of the Zugspitze.

"Well, we're going down to breakfast as soon as she's finished. I'm starved, and she needs coffee and water." Vreni snickered and started rooting around in her purse. "You want us to bring you anything?"

"Don't worry about it. I'll get down there eventually. You may want to bring up some muffins for the two vixens upstairs."

Vreni laughed. "Haven't heard one sound from up there yet."

I spent the next few minutes rearranging the blanket on my bed and sorting through my suitcase for an appropriate outfit. I decided on a collared blue-and-green-striped blouse that emphasized my breasts and a pair of flared jean capris, knowing that it would doubtless be colder at the top of the Zugspitze than it was down here. Not that the cold would bother my ice. I would have to wear pants with pockets for the remainder of our vacation, anyway. I did not want to leave my new possession in the suite, nor did I trust it not to lose itself inside my purse.

Erika emerged from the bathroom wearing a flowing purple skirt and black top sprinkled with sparkles, her red hair pushed back with a violet band. She met my eyes almost immediately, her own appearing lifeless. "You got any ibuprofen, Swanie? Thought I had more, but I already used it up."

"Yeah, hold on," I said, heading for my suitcase to do some more digging. "You know if you just drink water, too, you wouldn't have this problem." I found the pill bottle beneath my Doc Martens and pulled it out.

"So says the teetotaler." Erika scrunched her nose at me and accepted the pills, unspoken gratitude in her hazel eyes.

"Hey, you know I've had beer on this trip more than once. And I'm prepping for my years in the U.S. You can't drink there until you're twenty-one." Both girls made a gagging noise, and I shooed them toward the door. "Go get some breakfast. I'll see you down there once I'm done in the shower."

After they had gone, I waited for a count of thirty, then dove for the phone on the bedside table. The clock beside the phone read 9:08 now, so if I called my house, Hans should be the one to answer since it was a weekday. I dialed the country code and then the number for my house, sitting down on the bed with my foot tapping the floor while I waited for the call to connect. I felt like the mysterious rock had begun to burn a hole in my pocket.

"Thaden household. This is Hans Meissner." The familiar voice broke upon my ears after the second ring, speaking a traditional business greeting.

"Hey Hans, it's Swanie," I responded in a low voice, my free ear monitoring the door to the hallway, checking for any listeners.

There was a pause, and then Hans sighed. "Swanie, you know that the purpose of this line is business, not frivolity," he rebuked me, sounding irritated.

"I know, I know, and I'm sorry," I answered, racing through my apology. "I guess I could have just left you a message, but last night I found something in the Leutasch Gorge. Something very . . . strange." I broke off, suddenly out of words. My right hand slipped into my pocket to finger my new possession.

"What?" Hans prompted, still sounding irritated.

"It's a rock, but it's not like a normal rock. It's . . . a dark red in color, about two centimeters in diameter, a little misshapen . . . ." I stumbled over the words as I tried to figure out how to describe my discovery. At last I came out with it in a low voice. "I think it might be the Torstein."

Dead silence for at least three seconds. Then a menacing voice, "Sebastian, get off the phone!" Another pause. My heart pounded, and my ice began to trickle into my veins. "I don't know if someone else in the house is listening. Why do you think it may be the Torstein?" Hans had switched over to Teutonica. He and I were the only two in our house who understood that language.

"It certainly looks like it," I began slowly, still having to translate words in my head whenever I spoke the ancient Teutonic dialect. I needed to work on that. "And when I first realized where it was, I . . . I *felt* like it was something more than just a rock. I felt something strange—"

"In your blood?" He cut me off.

How did he know? I gripped the phone more tightly and whispered, "*Yes.*"

"The Torstein disappeared centuries ago," Hans noted. "I don't see how it could have ended up in an Austrian gorge."

"I know, I know." I was probably crazy. "I just wish there was a way I could know for sure. It's burning in my soul, not knowing."

Another pause, and then Hans chuckled. "There's really only one way to know."

My eyes bugged, and I shivered once, all over. "I'd have to test it . . . ."

"Yes." Hans' voice sounded distracted now, and I pushed my ice back with effort, shifting my eyes toward the door. *Test it . . . but where? When . . . ?* "Don't try anything with it until you return home," he ordered. "Three more days, correct?"

"Yes." My voice shook.

"I'll find out all there is to find out about the Torstein before you return. Then we can decide for ourselves."

I choked in horror. "You . . . you're not going to . . . *tell* anyone about it, are you?" I gasped.

"Of course not." His voice was harsh. "That would make things complicated, and dangerous. I'll do the research on my own. Just make sure you bring the stone back unscathed, and don't tell any of your friends about it."

I thought of Erika, of whom Hans also likely thought, and exhaled, knowing that this discovery may truly be a secret to keep to myself. "I won't," I promised, "and I kind of need to get in the shower. We're going to the Zugspitze today."

"Noted. And Swanie?"

"Yes?"

Another pause, and Hans spoke one final phrase, this time in Bayerisch, our native dialect. "Be careful." The receiver clicked abruptly.

I brought the phone down from my ear, my arm moving slowly, like in a dream. I stared at the receiver for a few moments as my mind replayed his last words to me. Then I hung up the phone and bounced sprightly off of the bed, a shriek of bliss bursting from my lips. *He wants me to be careful, and if he didn't care about me, he wouldn't have said that!*

The door opened while I bounced beside the bed with a huge grin, warmth certainly noticeable on my cheeks. "Where's that key—what the heck, Swanie?"

I froze in place, blinking toward the doorway, where Erika stood reaching for a room key that lay upon the dresser. "Oh . . . yeah . . . I probably ought to lock the door while I'm in the shower," I blathered, spinning around to grab my clothes and underwear.

"Was that you that just squealed?"

My blush deepened as I ducked into the bathroom. "Um," I said vaguely, seriously considering locking myself in the bathroom.

I tossed my clothing onto the toilet seat and grabbed a towel, then turned for the doorway, where I found Erika giving me a suspicious look. "Vreni said you played around with the Leutascher Ache last night." A watery blue had begun to overtake her irises.

I scoffed at her choice of words. "'Played around.' You make it sound like I screwed the river or something."

"Ach, Swanie, we all know you're a virgin. I'm just a little annoyed that you didn't invite me." She scowled.

"You were wasted. You couldn't have made the crossing."

"You waited to do it the one night I decided to get drunk."

I sighed and started pulling my T-shirt over my head, rolling my eyes where Erika could not see. "You don't have to take it personally. We can play around out there tonight if you want." I tossed my shirt to the floor and added, "I think there's fairies in that forest, though, so if you—"

"*What?*" Erika's eyes had grown as wide as a cat's, their irises a deep blue.

"*Eihalbae.* You know, the fairies of silver oak trees?" I took off my bra and threw it on top of my T-shirt, then stood still, not wanting to remove my shorts and their numinous secret until my friend had gone.

Erika's eyes slid down my chest before returning to my face. "Are you hinting that one of them *spoke* to you? I didn't think they actually exist!"

"Of course they exist. There's one in my yard. And I didn't start the conversation." I turned toward the shower and started the water, trying to make it clear that I had had enough of this discussion. I felt my stomach growl, and images of the breakfast buffet arose in my mind.

"Well, what did it *say* to you?"

I sighed heavily and twisted my head back toward Erika. "It said to respect the price of magic. Can you get going? My stomach is starting to eat itself."

Erika backed out of the room while cursing me in Bayerisch and demanding that I tell her the whole story at breakfast. I waited until I knew that she had left the suite before shutting the bathroom door and turning the lock, then retrieving the stone from my pocket to stare at it again. It really did seem to shine with some otherworldly glow when I looked at it with my icy eyes. But I would have to wait another three days before finding out the truth.

Chapter Ten:
Seeking Answers

I pulled my Ghibli up to the front door of the Thaden house three days later, after having deposited Erika at her own home. I had listened to a CD by Haggard on my way home that gave a metal flair to medieval music—something that seemed far too appropriate now that I had a potential method of time travel in my pocket. Out of all of the shows I had seen at the Mind Over Matter festival, I had enjoyed the bands with female singers the most: Haggard, Tristania, and Therion. Metal music was still a new discovery for me at that point. I had only just become aware of its potential one year prior when my Teuton girlfriends and I saw The Gathering perform in Salzburg. The contrast of a female voice with heavy guitars and drums had implanted itself ever deeper into my psyche since then.

I exited the car with my purse in one hand and several CDs in the other, my eyes lifted to the front porch, where I saw Sebastian descending the steps. My father had hired him just over a year ago to help with what seemed to be an ever increasing number of projects involving our house and grounds. "Hey Swanie!" he greeted as he reached the passenger side of my car. "Is all your stuff in the trunk?"

"Yeah, and it's waiting for you. I got you a CD at the festival."

He paused after hefting my suitcase to the ground. "*Really?* You didn't have to, Swanie."

"Well, I know you're into NDH, so I saw this and thought of you." I handed him the latest album by Oomph!

"Wow, this is great! I've been meaning to get this one. Thanks!" He smiled down at me fondly, his cheeks dimpling, his hazel eyes warm with gratitude.

I smirked at him and pretended to fan my face with the other CDs I held. "I hope you've been keeping everyone in line without me," I teased, knowing full well that was not his responsibility. Hans was in charge of the Thaden house business; Sebastian just did the busy work.

"Oh yesss," Sebastian snickered, spreading his lips into an attractive smile, reaching to shut the trunk of my car before smoothing his wavy black hair in a silly gesture. If I had not been concerned about marrying someone with Teuton blood, I likely would have fantasized about Sebastian in spite of his position as my father's servant. But Sebastian was an outsider, and despite the risks of childbirth, I had no wish to partner myself with someone who could never grasp the intricacies of being a Teuton. I leered at him and followed him toward the front door, which he opened with finesse before observing, "Out of all of us, I think your Pappi missed you the most, actually."

"Not my fault he didn't take a business trip during my vacation." I stepped into the vestibule and stood still for a moment, pondering whether or not I would have any luck hunting for Hans on a weekend afternoon. Considering the gravity of what we needed to discuss, I would probably be better off waiting until after dark. I touched one hand to the right pocket of my khaki shorts, assuring myself that the mysterious stone still rested there. Then I heard someone quickly descending the front steps, and my father trapped me in his embrace before I could react.

"Welcome home!" he exclaimed, spinning me around like a child, prompting me to giggle in delight. He pulled back to look down at my face, his dark brown hair slicked back perfectly, his gray eyes aglow with affection. "Did you have a good time? You look tanner." He reached out to brush a stray hair away from my face.

I smiled brilliantly at him and answered, "It was *amazing*. The scenery in Austria is beautiful, and I got some really good pictures." I glanced toward the path Sebastian had taken with my bags; he would likely deposit them in my room. "I'll have to show them to you as soon as I get unpacked. Would have been a better trip if you'd been able to come, too." I cocked my head at my father.

He grinned at my comment, letting go of me and inquiring, "And how many handsome young men did Ava and Morgen manage to capture?"

I shook my head at my two friends' reputations and admitted, "A few."

"Then it's a darn good thing I *didn't* go, or they may have set their sights on me." My father winked and ran a hand through his hair, his muscular physique quite apparent beneath his pale green polo shirt.

I made a face, remembering Ina's muses in the tent. "I certainly hope not. Parents are off limits." I swatted at him playfully and then headed up the stairs myself, intending to unpack and sift through my vacation photos, wiling away the time until dinner, and then the evening.

I spent the afternoon unpacking and listening to all of my new CDs, sitting down at my desk to scroll through all of the new posts on the Teuton message board that Hans and I had started late last year. We had set it up to connect with younger internet users as a resource for all things Teutonic, and anyone who requested to join had to provide us with documented proof of their blood status. I had come to enjoy discussing various topics and bantering with the other users on the forum, although I was starting to get exasperated with a guy who went by the screenname *Idealismus*. He was a nineteen-year-old from Regensburg studying graphic design, and he had a crush on me. Thankfully he had not become lewd about it, but in the role-play forum he always trailed along in my wake.

He had sent me two private messages asking about my trip, and I replied to the more recent one before checking the moderation history. Hans had banned four spam bots and one fool from Berlin whose blood status was seventy percent. Our lower limit for acceptance was seventy, but this person had spent his entire month on the message board starting flame wars in the history forums. I sent Hans a quick message that said, "About time you nixed *Teuton Brother*," though he was not online and might not see the message before I sought him out later tonight.

It took me a while to sift through all of my vacation pictures, for aside from the ones from the festival, nearly all of them had come out very well, having been taken outside in the realm of nature. I laughed at quite a few pictures of my friends and me together in ridiculous poses. In my favorite one, the four of them had lifted me from the ground in preparation to toss me off a boat into the Fuschlsee. My face betrayed feigned trepidation, while my companions looked as though they found me much heavier to lift than they had expected. As the shortest one of the crowd, I was always relegated to stances such as that one in contrived group photos. I ended up setting that one as my desktop background.

I managed to enjoy dinner with my father soon afterward, although by that time my mind was thoroughly occupied by the crimson rock in my pocket, which had to remain a secret from him. Gregor the cook had prepared a very Bavarian dinner as a welcome home gift to me, Jägerschnitzel with bread dumplings and wine kraut. After dinner I played two fugues and three hymns on the small pipe organ in our music room, showered, and then played strings with my gray cat Thunar until the sky darkened into dusk. He seemed to grow weary of the game, so I picked him up and put him onto the bed at the top of his cat tree, stroking his fur for a while and musing about the mystery in my pocket. "Do you think this stone is the real thing, Thu?" I asked him, gazing into his sleepy yellow-green eyes as though he had the ability to answer. "Do you think your Mutti's going to become the Teuton world's first time traveler since the fifteenth century? Where do you think I should go?"

I had thought about that over the past three days, silently considering my options whenever my friends' chatter had subsided. From what I could remember, *Der Weg* stated that the Torstein had the power to take a person backward in time, not forward, so the future was not an option. There were quite a few moments in my own past that I would like to revisit—oh for the privilege of meeting Dane again, and before his final sickness, when we could play together in my grandfather's garden! I imagined telling him that I had a secret, that I had traveled time just to tell him about my Teutonic fantasies, my ice, my spiritual dances, my trusted friends. Or maybe I could go further into the past to see my mother again, maybe when she was a teenager like me. I could see whether we could pass for sisters, since those who had known her often said that I looked just like her. We could dance together in a snowy forest, our ice combining into a wintry wonder.

At ten p.m. I slipped out the back door into the yard, wearing black jeans, black shoes, and a black hoodie with the hood raised. With my hands stuffed into the pocket of the hoodie and curled around the stone, I paused on the deck to look up at my father's bedroom window. The shades were closed, and a dim light trickled through. He was probably in bed reading the Bible. No other lights were on in the house aside from the one in my bedroom window. I sprinted for the trees. I reached Hans' door quite out of breath and knocked quietly, then placed a hand against the doorframe and panted, adrenaline coursing through my veins.

Footsteps sounded on the hardwood floor inside, and the door swung open. Yellow light from a stand-up lamp lit the doorway, and Hans stood viewing me a bit disdainfully. "You ran?" He wore leather sandals, white socks, khakis, and a T-shirt bearing a picture of the Matterhorn.

I had almost regained my breath and held up a hand apologetically. "I had to." He made a face, acknowledging this, and gestured me inside, shutting the door quickly behind me.

I entered Hans' parlor and marched straight to the coffee table, setting the stone upon it and plopping down stiffly onto the brown sofa without a word. I noticed that a book by Rilke lay open upon the arm of Hans' chair, and while part of me longed to question him on his opinion of Rilke's works, tonight distraction held me fast. I glanced briefly around the room at the six framed pictures upon the walls. Three were portraits of different sections of München, one was a painting of the Rhine River, another a gorgeous photo of the Alps, and the last showed the inside of a cathedral in the Schwäbisch Gmund with its magnificent pipe organ. I looked away from the organ pipes quickly, thinking back to my reasons for learning how to play that instrument, a nervous chill agitating my body.

Hans, meanwhile, had knelt onto the floor beside the coffee table to peer closely at the stone. Presently, he lifted it from the table and held it up so that the weak light of his lamp hit it. It seemed to sparkle with different shades of crimson while Hans studied every angle, his eyes growing wider. At last, as the dull glow of the rock matched the fiery gleam in his eyes, he murmured, "Ach . . . you have truly discovered a wonder . . . Swanie . . . ."

I leaned forward on the cushion, my eyes as wide as his. "Do you think it really *is* . . . the Torstein?" I whispered.

He set the stone back onto the table carefully and took a step back, gazing at it with a thoughtful look. "If the descriptions that I've read in the past three days are correct, then there is a distinct probability. Yes." He ogled it for another moment, then walked over to the chair and sat down, crossing his legs and folding his hands pensively.

Excitement welled in my soul, and I may have given a little squeal of delight. "So what did you find out, in everything that you read?" I asked, my heart beginning to pound in anticipation.

Hans leaned back in his chair and looked at me darkly. "To this day there is little to be found on the Torstein," he began, "aside from its history and what it is supposedly capable of. Regarding the scant actual description of the stone itself, I'd say this one here matches the writings exactly." He nodded toward the stone, and I squealed again quietly, covering my mouth with my hands. Hans turned his eyes toward me once more. "You remember the history of the Torstein, of course, for I know that you've read it before."

That was true, but Hans was so good at telling Teuton stories—looking so horribly like a priest now even though he wore casual clothes—that I could not bear to rely on my own memory. "Tell me again," I begged him, stuffing my hands under my legs and leaning forward.

A tiny smile graced his serious face. "Very well. The Teutonic Torstein came to be in the summer of 1074, eight years after the fall of Muniche. You will recall that those years were very difficult for the Teutons of Bavaria, for their kingdom had been invaded by the Saxons of the north in the 1060s. By the early 1070s the Saxons had prevailed, scattering the remaining Teutons across Germanic and Slavic lands." I nodded vigorously, remembering, and Hans went on. "You will also remember that the previous decades had been the most prosperous in Teuton history up to that point due to the success of trade and agriculture.

"The Prince of the Teutons during this era was Otto Eduard Hildebrand von Bayern, a young man but an excellent ruler, the keyholder of Muniche. During the time of peace, Otto conducted much research and experiments involving Teutonic abilities, wanting to discover our greatest strengths. Prince Otto was also a musician like you and me." Hans eyed me significantly, and I nodded again. "He wrote many gorgeous songs, some said to have almost reached musical perfection. Most of these were lost long ago, but one song stood high above the rest, for Otto von Bayern discovered the song that could pierce the bounds of this earth, that could open the gates of time.

"It is said that Otto and his brother Paulus took many journeys using this song, and that both gained great wisdom from viewing history firsthand. Today, as you know, the beginning of Otto's song is still recorded, but the final lines—the part necessary to open the gates to the past—have been lost." I nodded again, for the song he spoke of was written for the organ, and both of us could play most of it. It was, as he described, incredibly beautiful but incomplete. "At the end of Otto's life, following the destruction of the Teutons in Bavaria, he was desperate enough to break the rules of time travel—to go back and change what had been done. He wanted to fix things so that the Saxon conquest would have failed. But he could remember the end of his song no longer, though for days he tried. He spent a full day mourning what had been lost, bleeding himself in agony and guilt.

"Thus it was that the Torstein came into existence, made from Otto's blood, his tears, and some dark earth from the Rhine River. Fate had smiled upon him after all, for he had regained the power he had lost, and he could have chosen then to fix all his mistakes. But by then, Otto knew that what he wished would have done no good, so he chose instead to commit ritual suicide and leave the Torstein to others. What exactly happened with it after its formation is not entirely known, as the Teutons were scattered and few concrete writings were made for some time. But it is known that it has the same power as Otto's forgotten song, and that in the fifteenth century, it fell out of Teuton hands and has been lost ever since."

Hans stopped here and looked at the stone again. I mulled over everything that he had said, and though I had heard the story before it awed me afresh, for now the Torstein was found, *here*, in our possession. So we thought. "But Hans," I said in a low voice, "If that really is the Torstein, we'll have to test it." I shivered with excitement and a touch of fear at the idea of testing it.

"If it is the Torstein," Hans began, still staring at it as if it could speak, "then it holds the greatest power that has fallen into Teuton hands in many years. But there are rules governing its use, and though most people would want to use it to change history, that is not advisable. Time is such a forceful current; it cannot be turned backward without cost. Changing one tiny event could alter history entirely, could kill people, could introduce new problems. Those who go back must pledge first that they go to observe, not to interfere."

I was on the edge of my seat. "And how does it work?" I cried out.

Hans frowned at my outburst but answered anyway. "If you were going to use it yourself, you must first decide *when* and where you want to go, the exact time, the exact place. It is said that if you're uncertain, you could wind up anywhere. You would hold the rock and picture in your mind the exact time and the exact place. You would speak this solemn spell in Teutonica: 'I go to observe, not to interfere. To become a part of the past, not to change what is past. I go to see with my own eyes, to hear with my own ears, that which cannot be fully understood another way. I seek the past to learn, to return forever changed. May the gates of time take me, and restore me as I was, but new.' Once you have said those words and meant them, the gates of time will open before your eyes, and you simply step through, into the past."

"Amazing," I whispered, many ideas whirling through my head. "It doesn't sound too hard . . . but I have to decide where to go, and when to go."

Hans smiled at me and nodded, looking pleased with my resolution. "Then you plan to test it, to step into the past."

"I have to," I replied, suddenly certain. "I found it, after all, and it seemed to call to me. I'm probably fated to use it, to see something I've never seen. I need to memorize the spell first," I added.

Hans was out of his chair and had vanished into his bedroom in an instant, and seconds later he returned, handing me a thin book with a worn cover. "This is a priest's book, so do not lose it. The correct lines are marked."

I nodded, taking the book carefully from him. Then I thought of something else. "How do you get back once you've gone?"

Hans raised an eyebrow. "The same way you went. There are different words to say upon your return. I marked those, as well."

"Fair enough." I rose from the sofa, book in hand, and scooped up the stone with my other hand, placing it back into the pocket of my hoodie. "I should get back to the house. But I'll let you know when I decide."

Hans followed me to his door and opened it, looking as though he wished to open other subjects before I left. But he simply nodded and said, "I look forward to it. And I got your message about *Teuton Brother,* by the way."

I paused on his threshold. "Oh good! That guy was really stirring things up with all his comments about how Teutons acted or didn't act in the past."

Hans leaned against his doorjamb and favored me with a loaded look. "A message board dedicated to Teutonic culture may attract a fair number of fools in time. Our people have not always been on the right side of history, unfortunately. But the one thing you ought to keep in mind is that it would never be wise to write about the Torstein or the Song of Time on the forum, or on the internet in general." His fiery eyes flared a warning at me.

I nodded and stuffed both of my hands into the pocket of my hoodie again, reminding myself that the stone was safe with me, at least for the time being. I did not know if any outsiders knew about the Torstein or believed in its existence, but it certainly retained a potential for misuse. It was a secret to keep to ourselves, for now. "Don't worry," I said to Hans, "I'm not going to wave it around for the world to see."

Chapter Eleven:
Dark Secrets

It took me an entire week to read the book Hans leant to me. Titled *Niofirgeban*, or *The Unforgiven,* the entire book had been written in Teutonica. It described the final years of the Saxon conquest and Prince Otto von Bayern's breakdown in 1074. Mainly focusing on history, I found it an intriguing though difficult read. At the very end, several pages were devoted to the creation and powers of the Torstein, and once I found the phrases marked by Hans, I copied them down into a Microsoft Word document and spent most of my free hours practicing them. I concentrated on the words necessary to return, for I figured that it would be worse to go back in time and end up stuck there than to not be able to go back in the first place.

I learned a bit more about the Torstein through Hans' book, more than he had told me Sunday night. Apparently the words spoken to open the gates of time were truly considered a solemn vow. Trying to alter the past in any way promised to bring terrible penalties. Forgetting what had happened during a trip or refusing to learn from it also presaged serious repercussions. Another disturbing warning I found advised those who traveled time to not participate in any Teutonic rituals that might be life-threatening. Death, according to the book, was an alternative way of returning to one's own era, but Teutonic ritual suicide meant certain and final death even for time travelers.

I knew the basics of Teutonic ritual suicide. Prince Otto had been the first to use it in 1074, and other Teutons had chosen that path from time to time, often to prove a point or to escape a tormented life. To commit ritual suicide, a Teuton would have to slit their wrists and throat with a stone knife and then jump into the Rhine River on the night of the new moon. I doubted I would ever have to worry about that, since I had no wish to kill myself despite my difficult past. I took a small bit of comfort in the thought that if I ever used the Torstein and ended up stuck in the past, I could return through death, as long as it was not some ritual death.

On Friday night, I informed Hans over ICQ that I had finished reading the book, and he summarily requested that I bring it back to him at his cottage. He had some issues that he wished to discuss with me regarding my new possession, and since we had not spoken more than a few words in passing that week, it was high time to reopen our dialogue about time travel. I agreed without complaint, for my time left at home grew ever shorter; I was scheduled to leave for the U.S. in just three weeks. I needed to sort out the mysteries of the Torstein before then as far as humanly possible, so I would not have a nagging distraction gnawing at the back of my mind when I ought to be focusing on college studies.

So I slipped outside in the dark of the night, not bothering to clothe myself in shadow, for my father was in Berlin for business. When I reached Hans' cottage, I saw that he waited for me with the front door open, clad in the typical casual dress of summer: socks, sandals, khaki shorts, a plain gray T-shirt. He nodded at me in greeting and commented that he had made tea. I smiled my acknowledgement and handed him his book, then headed for the brown couch.

Both electric lights in the room were switched on, and I noticed when I sat down that a single jarred candle also burned upon the windowsill, its flame a flat black. I snickered to myself, wondering whether Hans had lit that candle for effect, and when he returned to the room carrying two mugs of herbal tea, I remarked, "It's a good thing you were born in this era and not in the time of candlelight. Your fire doesn't really give off any light."

He set my cup down upon the coffee table and then rested himself upon his chair, regarding me with an appraising look. "It creates all the light I require," he stated at length, raising his mug to his lips, his expression chiding.

I considered that for a moment, and then a thought occurred to me. "Since your fire is black, does that mean you can see in the dark whenever you're using your element?" His eyes always turned a shining obsidian whenever we danced as Teutons, and if my own element cloaked my vision in a veil of blue, I figured that was a valid question.

Hans' thin lips curled upward rather imperiously. "It is useful, yes, to bend the darkness as I bend my flames."

An enigmatic answer, but I could expect nothing less from a Teuton priest. That caste tended to keep a lot to themselves. I was lucky that Hans had deigned to teach me anything about my background, to be honest. I relaxed upon the couch, taking a sip of tea and glancing once more toward the flickering candle. I tasted hints of mint and lavender, likely pulled fresh from the small herb garden he kept behind his cottage. "So according to that book of yours, Prince Otto von Bayern went insane before his suicide, before creating the Torstein. And it seemed to imply that the reason he went mad was because he'd failed to lead the Teuton people to victory over the Saxon invaders."

Hans nodded once and drank from his mug before adding, "Yes, that and the fact that he was unable to protect Muniche from the ravaging horde. He failed in his most sacred duty as keyholder. He lost his home and his Lady to his enemies."

I frowned, thinking of my elderly friend, hoping that Marga had gotten in touch with her to schedule one final gathering. I suddenly reflected on the fact that she had represented München during World War II, when my hometown had been annihilated by bombs and artillery. I shivered all over at the idea of that, then lifted my eyes to Hans and whispered, "Do you think . . . do you think I should tell *her* . . . that I found the Torstein . . . ?"

Hans looked disturbed at my suggestion; his hands tensed around his mug. He did not answer for some time, his eyes turning to the side to concentrate on the black flame upon his candle. "If you were to tell any of your acquaintances, I would agree that she would be the most trustworthy," he admitted in a respectful tone. "She has kept many secrets over the years, though few as significant as this. Before taking that step, however, we must be sure about its true nature."

I pulled the stone from the pocket of my shorts for a moment to study its multifaceted hues. "You're right. And I'm still planning to test it before I leave for college. I just have to figure out *where* and *when* to go." And I would have to get it done very soon, if I wanted to share the secret with Lady Muniche.

"There's something else I wanted to discuss with you tonight, Swanie, aside from ruminations on the Torstein itself." Hans' face had grown rather serious, and his dark blue eyes seemed to burn me, though they held no fire. "You said that you found this rock in the Leutasch Gorge, and at night. I happen to be aware that the Leutasch Gorge is a wild chasm, not a place for a young woman, Teuton or not, to be traversing at night." He paused, and I shrank back upon the couch, curling my legs underneath me. "Also, the worthy *Eihalbe* who resides not far from here met me while I walked home from work on the same day that you called. It passed along word that one of its own kind had directed you toward a mystery." Hans gazed at me heavily, his jaw clenched in what appeared to be disapproval.

I opened my mouth and shut it several times, wrapping my arms around my body, my tea forgotten on the table. "But . . . how . . . how did our *Eihalbe* find out about that? I thought they don't travel far from their trees."

Hans scowled at me and cleared his throat. "Unlike human beings, *Eihalbae* actually communicate with each other. I do not know their methods, for it's not my place to pry. And the resident of the Thaden silver oak is not 'our' *Eihalbe*. They belong to no one. They have no masters but God."

I looked away from Hans, his words cutting me to the core. "I . . . I didn't . . . mean it like that . . . ."

"Well I certainly hope that you were respectful in your discourse with the one who showed you the path." Hans' eyes burned black now, and the flame on his candle had begun to lick in a frantic manner.

"I was as respectful as I know how to be. I thanked the *Eihalbe* for everything it told me. I didn't ask questions. I never would!" I cried out, my cheeks burning in embarrassment, my ice gradually pricking the hairs on my arms.

"You'd best tell me all that you held back the last time we talked," Hans said, setting his mug of tea onto the floor and folding his hands. "I should have guessed that you found the stone after some mindless indiscretion."

I choked back a sob, blinking fiercely against the tears threatening to coat my corneas with ice. *He'll think far worse of you once he knows the whole story,* I knew, and I worked to take several deep breaths, my right hand shakily extracting itself from beneath my left arm to reach up and remove my glasses. I began to tell Hans the story, staring down at my knees while I did so, my ice-heightened vision picking out every tiny flaw in my skin. To my surprise, a sense of relief washed over me as I spoke of my elemental adventure. It was good to get it out in the open, even if Hans did not approve. When I revealed the hiding place of the stone—a crevice some thirty meters above the stream itself—a strangled cry broke from the direction of his chair, prompting me to pause and look toward him at last.

Hans' hands gripped the armrests of his chair with an intensity so strong that it surprised me to not see smoke rising from beneath his fingers. "You . . . climbed . . . a *cliff* . . . using your ice . . . ." He looked horrified.

"Well . . . sort-of . . . ."

"And you stirred up the Leutascher Ache to a violence that you could not counter . . . ." Hans shook his head slowly, closing his eyes, disgust for me dripping from each word he spoke. "Swanie . . . the Leutascher Ache belongs to Teuton lands . . . it runs into the Isar itself . . . and you could not . . . control . . . it . . . ." The flame on his candle calmed while he spoke. Apparently he felt the need to flaunt his own expertise in the face of my failure.

I buried my face in my hands, totally ashamed. "I'm sorry . . . ."

"Ach, Swanie! Have I not taught you discretion? Have I not taught you the importance of never overextending yourself? It is glorious to dance, yes, but to do it upon a river that proved itself far stronger than you . . . ." He broke off and opened his eyes to stare into mine, his disappoint-ment shredding my soul. "How *could* you do such a thing?" His eyes had returned to their natural dark blue.

I was trembling, goose bumps covering every portion of my skin. My ice had begun to shed traces upon the couch. "I was . . . an idiot . . . I should have . . . danced upstream . . . ."

"You should not have danced at all," he corrected me in a clipped tone. "Not alone, and not in such a place. You could have been *seen*. The Leutascher Ache is very close to the road. If you couldn't bridle your elemental urges, you should have worked your magic in the spiritual realm."

I could not deny this, and that dark presence that had raked my soul with such terrible precision from the edge of the ravine surfaced in my memory. "Someone *did* see me," I admitted, and when I saw shock cross Hans' face, I added, "but it was a Teuton. My ice sensed him right when I snatched the stone. He stood at the top of the gorge, clad in the darkness of the night, watching me, mocking my helplessness, it seemed. And just when I had given up all hopes for lost, thinking I would fall to my death . . . he conjured up an elemental storm the likes of which I've *never* seen . . . it was like energy and darkness and water and wind all combined . . . and it swept me back to the place where I'd started the dance . . . my sandals were still lying there . . . ." My voice trailed off, and I shivered a little at the memory of the relief and uncertainty I had felt at the close of my experience.

Hans gawked at me with eyes as black as night. This final confession of mine had disturbed him enough to allow his fire to take hold again. He had clasped his hands together to avoid burning anything, but I could sense the heat radiating from him. The flame of his candle grew to twice its original size. His mouth opened, then closed, and he exhaled one breath of smoke. "That's not possible," he said.

"I know it's not," I agreed, "but that's what happened. And if it hadn't, I'd be dead. Unless the *Eihalbae* lugged me to the ground." I did not think that they were capable of such a thing, even as a group. Though I had no concept of the extent of their magic, the one that had spoken to me had looked small and wispy.

But what if the Eihalbe *who spoke to you found that dark Teuton after vanishing over the rim of the gorge? What if that's why he rescued you?*

Hans gawked at me without speaking for a full minute, while I sat pondering that unexpected rescuer, trying to decide whether there was a connection between him and the *Eihalbe* who had showed me the path. "He had to be a priest, because I think he was wearing black robes," I commented at length. "Do you think maybe he was like a guardian of the Torstein, to make sure no one disturbed it?"

"Couldn't be. If that were the case, he would have let you die." Hans looked thoughtful, and I watched the flame on his candle shrink back to its usual size as he pulled his fire back.

"Then who was he, do you think?" Curiosity ate at me, and I leaned forward to put my glasses back on and take hold of my mug of tea, which had grown cold. "I'm thinking maybe it was the *Eihalbe* who told him I needed help."

Hans shook his head once and reached down to lift his mug of tea from the floor. "There is one thing that you would do well to keep in mind, Swanie, and that is that not all Teutons walk the path of virtue. You ought not to take chances alone at night. Some of our people still practice the forbidden arts, and Wuotan's paths are not to be taken lightly." He eyed me darkly and took a sip from his mug, likely having heated the tea through the power of his fire.

"Do you think maybe we should go over defensive principles again before I leave on some sort of adventure?" I inquired, thinking of the few times in the past few years when Hans and I had fought with our elements for sport.

A snicker escaped Hans' lips, and he responded, "Unless you're planning on traveling several millennia backward to heathen times, I doubt that will be necessary. You know the basics, how to shield yourself with ice, how to use your fingers as claws, how to use your element to enhance your speed and stamina. And you also know that discretion is the key point." He narrowed his eyes at me.

I lowered my gaze, chastened, and we exchanged a few further thoughts on the circumstances that led to the creation of the Torstein before I departed for the night. I considered many things as I walked leisurely back to the house through the trees, gazing at the sky and thinking of the many unique traits of my people. There were the elemental gifts, the blood rituals, the realm of the spirit, the possibility of travel through time . . . and many, if not all of these powers, harkened back to the Teuton people's oft-forgotten affiliation with the heathen deity Wuotan. *But he has nothing to do with any of it now,* I reassured myself, pushing my doubts aside. *Just because Teutonic powers may have originated from a demon doesn't make them inherently bad.*

On Sunday morning, when I sat in the dining room eating breakfast before heading for church, Hans strode into the room dressed in a tan suit, prepared for church himself. He carried a section of the morning paper, which he laid onto the table beside my plate, tapping one finger at a small article off to the side. "And that, Swanie, is why you must always use discretion . . . and caution."

He was gone before I could comment, but when I looked down at the article I saw that it covered the disappearance of an Asian tourist from the resort town of Mittenwald, where my friends and I had passed quite a few hours during our trip. The female tourist was part of a large group and had vanished without a trace.

I frowned pensively in the direction Hans had taken, wondering whether he attributed this mystery to human trafficking . . . or perhaps to that shadowy rescuer of mine whose power seemed unequaled in the realm of mortals.

Chapter Twelve:
A Disquieting Portal

I spent the greater part of that week debating with myself about where and when to travel using the Torstein, as well as how to keep it safe while I was at college. Regarding the latter issue, I ultimately decided to keep it closed up in a ring box during my stay in the university's dorms. Beth and I planned to room together, and hopefully none of our soon-to-be-peers would show interest in something so plain and small. If anyone disturbed it there, I could always continue to stuff it in my pants pocket like I had been doing since my return home.

I had to shelve my original hopes of visiting my brother or my mother using the stone, because *Niofirgeban* had been quite clear on that. Time travelers, it had asserted, should not travel to their own past because the temptation to alter history would be too great. The book had pinpointed that as the direct reason why Prince Otto had been unable to recall the end of his Song of Time in his final days, because he wished to fix his past mistakes. So I could not leap back ten years for a play date with Dane, or fifteen to share a heart-to-heart with my mother. Though the truth of the matter saddened me a bit, I reminded myself that the rest of history was open to me instead, countless eras holding infinite possibilities.

On Friday afternoon, I made my decision. I had considered many options, but I realized that I wanted to go somewhere familiar and close by the first time. That way I would not be faced with problematic language and culture differences like those in the Middle Ages. When it came to the recent past, I knew of one event that I would really appreciate. So I hunted for Hans shortly after lunch that day, ultimately finding him in one of the second-floor offices, busy with Thaden finances. He was dressed for work, wearing gray suit pants, black shoes, a spotless button-up shirt, and a gray tie. He looked awesome.

His serious mien mellowed a bit when he saw me come through the door, and I made my announcement immediately, without bothering with preliminaries. "I've *decided*," I stated with a grin, closing the office door behind me.

Hans smiled knowingly and made a few notations on the document in front of him before rising from the padded chair and coming around to stand in front of the oaken desk. "And what is your decision?" he questioned, also wasting no time with pleasantries.

"Well, I figured I'd better go somewhere easy first," I began, scuffing my sandals a little on the floor. "Somewhere recent so I won't have to worry too much about culture differences. And I won't have to make new clothes before I go." While I had garnered some experience with sewing thanks to Lady Muniche's talents with her loom, I had no time to waste hunting for appropriate fabrics and patterns.

Hans' face sharpened with suspicion. "You're not planning on going to your own past, are you?"

"No!" I replied, shocked. "I read what it said in *Niofirgeban*. As much as I'd love to talk to Mutti or Dane again, the Torstein isn't the way."

"Good," Hans said, quirking a slight smile and sitting down onto the desk. "So what, then, did you decide?"

I hesitated, looking down at the floor again, suddenly embarrassed about my choice. It was an emotional choice after all, and perhaps Hans would find it silly. "Well . . . I was trying to think of something . . . interesting . . . ." I stumbled over the words. "And I realized that what I really, *really* want . . . is to just *see* my Mutti again. Before I was born." I broke off sharply, awaiting his reaction.

Hans held his peace for a moment, then breathed out a sigh. "I suppose that would be a reasonable desire." His tone did not sound disapproving.

I looked up at him and saw that his expression was soft now. Encouraged, I explained, "I . . . I'd like to go back and see her church wedding with Pappi. That would be before I was born but not too long ago. June 17th, 1978."

Hans nodded, his gaze towards the far wall. "You'd have to be careful not to let anyone know who you are," he commented. "Particularly your mother."

I shrugged. "No one would believe me, anyway, but I won't say anything. I'll have to be there for just two hours or so. I just want to see the wedding."

Hans still looked contemplative, his forehead creased. "It was at the Frauenkirche downtown. You would have to be dressed quite nicely to get inside."

I nodded. "I'm going to go through some of Mutti's old dresses and see if I can fit into one. And I was actually thinking of using one of the turrets of the church as my destination. Nobody should be up there since Opa Hobart rented it out for the wedding." Both Hans and I played the Frauenkirche organ each month, so we knew every part of the old cathedral's interior, even the areas inaccessible to the general public.

"So when are you going to do this?" Hans eyed me speculatively.

I thought quickly through my options. Tomorrow night I was to have dinner at the Hofbräuhaus with my father, and Sunday was church followed by a gathering at Lady Muniche's apartment. Since I needed to appear presentable for all of those events, I would have to eliminate the distraction of anticipation. So I looked Hans straight in the eye and stated, "Now."

I spent a little over an hour preparing myself in my bedroom. Hans, at my request, had dragged one of my mother's old trunks of clothes down from the attic and promised to meet me up there once I deemed myself presentable. It did not take me long to find a decent dress amongst my mother's clothes. I chose a lovely lavender summer dress, long, with a frilly collar and short sleeves. Apparently I had become quite similar to my mother in build, for I had no trouble fitting into the dress aside from its length. I fixed that by slipping on a pair of silvery sandals with six-centimeter heels.

I spent about thirty minutes preparing my face and hair in front of my bathroom mirror—foundation, blush, lavender eye shadow, silver mascara, clear lip gloss. I even curled my mid-length black hair and put half of it up in a silvery clip, leaving a few crinkly strands hanging in front of my ears. Lastly, I put on a pair of silver earrings and squirted on a touch of perfume, choosing to use contacts for this venture since my glasses would not match the style of the late 1970s. I spent an extra minute checking every angle of my appearance in the mirror, giggling because I looked so old fashioned. Then I skipped back into my bedroom, snatched the stone off of my queen-sized bed, and headed for the attic as swiftly and sneakily as I could in such attire.

The attic was on the fourth floor of our house and had little use aside from storage. Crossbeams hung from wall to wall, and the wooden floor creaked with every step. Several small hexagonal windows let in a token bit of sunshine, and thankfully Hans had switched on one of the bare bulbs hung on a beam, or I likely would have tripped over something with my tottery sandals. I stood before him soon after ascending the crooked staircase and did a quick pirouette on my heels. "Well? How do I look?"

Hans' expression suggested that perhaps I had risen up from the underworld. He muttered something foul under his breath and said, "You look exactly like Camilla." His dark blue eyes glittered with shock.

I blushed a bit and looked down at the floor, flattered and embarrassed all at once. "But Camilla's going to look a lot better than me, where I'm going."

Hans chuckled and his expression softened. "That is true. Before you go—" he turned away momentarily and lifted something from one of the nearby trunks "—I figured you may have need of this, since that dress has no pockets." He held a small silvery purse out to me, obviously one of my mother's. "You wouldn't want to drop the Torstein by mistake."

I shivered once at the mere concept of doing that. "Good point. And that's perfect, since I'm wearing silver sandals." I took the purse from his outstretched hand, taken aback by its weight. "I probably ought to bring tissues in case I cry or something." Upon unclasping the purse, I saw that *some*one had already stocked it with tissues, a few mints, a pen, and, "A camera?" I pulled it out of the purse and stared at it, then at Hans. "You can't honestly think this would work with time travel. I mean, these things didn't even *exist* in the 70s." It was one of my father's digital cameras, small but decent.

Hans shrugged. "It may not, but I'd say it's worth a try. Perhaps you could snap some covert shots of the wedding, with the flash off of course."

I snorted a bit and put the camera back in the bag. "Whether it works or not, I certainly hope it comes back with me, or I'll have to buy Pappi another one. Are the batteries charged?"

"Yes, and the memory card is empty."

Hans was thorough, if nothing else. Then I noticed that a single brass key lay at the bottom of the purse. I pulled it out. "What's this for?"

"That's the master key for the locks in the Frauenkirche. In case you need to sneak around some of the back rooms."

I squinted at it. "They had to have changed the locks since the 70s."

Hans' wry smile turned wicked as he confirmed, "They did. I do not own the current master key."

I shook my head in disbelief and placed the key back into the purse. "Hans, sometimes you really freak me out," I informed him, stepping back.

Hans gave me a dark look. "It's not my fault you have this unnecessary fear of fire, Ice Princess." His expression was calculating.

I had the feeling that if we continued this discussion it would end in one of two ways. Either I would flee from him down the stairs, or I would kiss him. Neither of those outcomes would end well—as much as the greater part of me desperately wanted to kiss him—so it was time to get on with this. Hans certainly had more business to finish before the end of the day, and I ought not to delay his work due to my own foolishness. I swung the purse over my right shoulder and gripped the stone more tightly in my left hand. "All right," I said, trying to steady myself as the enormity of what I was about to do washed over me in a flood. "It's time." I glanced over at Hans, who nodded at me seriously. I took a deep breath, trying to concentrate. Then a sudden inspiration hit me, and I whipped my head toward him again. "You should come with me."

Hans frowned and shook his head. "Now you're stalling. I can't come. I was there, and I'd rather not run into myself."

"Hmm. Good point." The mere thought of such a meeting made me snicker in spite of the gravity of the situation. But I did not wish Hans to misuse the stone if it turned out to be the real thing. "I didn't realize you were at my parents' wedding," I commented, tilting my head at Hans.

"I was the organist."

I snickered again. It figured. Then I held up my left hand and gazed at the rock. "Okay, I have to concentrate," I murmured, working to clear all thoughts and images from my mind—everything but the mental image of Saturday, June 17th, 1978, downtown München, three-fifteen p.m., a landing halfway up the south tower of the Frauenkirche. The wedding was at four, so that should give me enough time to get inside the nave. Slowly, I began to recite the correct phrases in Teutonica: "I go to observe, not to interfere. To become a part of the past . . . ."

I clearly remember that at the exact second that the final word, "new," had left my lips, a brief but terrible ripping sound tore through the attic, and I could feel the rock trembling in my hand. The horrible noise practically knocked me off my feet. My heart leapt into my throat, and I thought of turning and running for the staircase. A half second later, the space in front of me split apart, gradually taking the hazy form of two ancient gates of crystalline black shot through with greens and blues like labradorite, impossible to fit inside the attic. I stood rooted to the ground in fright, staring as the gates opened inward with a creak that seemed to come from the abyss. I do not know what I expected to see on the other side of the gates of time, but it was not this whirling vortex of darkness splashed by fluxes of color and light pulling this way and that. My eyes bugged, and I could not move. How could I find the courage to go into *that?*

Hans' quiet voice reached me from somewhere behind, calming. "There is your portal, Swanie. The past awaits you."

I still could not move. "But how . . . how do I . . . close it . . . ?" I choked, barely speaking above a whisper. *So it's real. I really do have the Torstein.*

"By lifting your hand, the one that holds the Torstein."

Logical, of course. Tearing my eyes away from the frightening spectacle before me, I stared at my left hand, which still trembled from the force of the stone. I could not close the gate now; I had opened it. I *had* to do this. Moving just my eyes, I found Hans in my peripheral vision and whispered one final plea. "Please . . . won't you come with me?"

I saw him shake his head. "I will wait for you," he promised.

That was all I was going to get. I took a deep breath, steeled myself, and thought again of that day, and that time, in the center of my city. Then I stepped forward into the darkness, through the gates.

What I had expected upon passing through the gates I cannot say. What I found, however, has never left me, though for years I have tried to block it from my memory. It was not a simple step into the past, into the tower I had imagined. To this day, I do not know how long a time I spent in that darkness of oblivion, flying with inhuman speed through a current too strong to fight, twisted this way and that, having no control over my body. Perhaps it actually lasted no time at all and just seemed long and terrifying. But I do know for certain that during this entire frightening trip, I heard voices whispering to me from all directions in a language I could not understand. The voices did not sound particularly encouraging. I also heard eldritch moans, wordless cries of desolation, of hopelessness. And at the end, just before I burst through the other side of the portal, I heard an intimidating, horrifying laughter coming from all around me.

I landed sharply on a floor of stone, the gates of time still open behind me. Hyperventilating though I was from the journey itself, I remembered Hans' words and lifted my left hand swiftly while still gripping the Torstein. The portal vanished more quickly than it had come. I looked around, still catching my breath. No other people were on the snug landing with me, and I could tell that I certainly had landed in one of the turrets of the Frauenkirche. I unclasped the silver purse and stashed the Torstein inside, then closed it firmly, knowing that I must protect the gateway stone no matter what. My heart hammered in reaction to the mad journey I had just completed, but my ice remained confined within.

I hugged the purse close to my body and whispered to myself, "Okay, Swanie. Okay. This is definitely the Frauenkirche. Now. What time is it?" I glanced around at the landing one last time before heading for the spiral staircase, descending until I came to a small window that provided a halfway decent view of the city. The main roof of the cathedral was directly below me, much of it coated with tarp. "Because of the restoration. Of course," I told myself, recalling how damaged the cathedral had been from the bombings during World War II. I squinted toward Alter Peter's tower in the distance, trying to make out the time on its clock. Though I could not quite read it clearly from such a distance, it did appear that both of its hands were pointed just below the three. Just after three-fifteen.

That was when the triumphant smile finally broke across my face.

Chapter Thirteen:
My Parents' Wedding

Before heading further down the staircase, I pulled the digital camera from my mother's purse—after assuring myself that the Torstein was still safely inside—and took several snapshots of the cathedral's roof covered with tarp. It had not looked like that for quite a few years now, so I figured that if the pictures actually latched onto the SD card for the journey home, that was pretty solid proof that I had truly traveled time. I took one picture of myself beside the staircase making the rock-on sign with my fingers, then put the camera back inside the purse and mounted the stairs once more.

When I reached the first accessible side doorway into the main body of the cathedral, I decided that I might as well try out Hans' master key. Though I could follow the staircase down to ground level, the fact that I had not yet encountered any tourists made me think twice about that plan. *I know Opa Hobart rented out the cathedral, but I doubt that would have included the towers, too ... unless Mutti wanted to get some professional photos made inside them. And I don't need to run into her or any of my other relatives on this venture, even though they wouldn't recognize me. I need to remain as incognito as possible.*

The aged key did indeed turn the lock, and I slipped quickly into a dank and dusty passage that led toward the upper galleries of the Frauenkirche. I recognized where I was thanks to the after-hours explorations I had done over the past year on the nights when I had practiced on the organs here. *Maybe I should visit the main organ loft before heading down to the nave,* I thought to myself, *so I can find out what songs Mutti chose for her wedding.* My father owned a recording of the event that I could have watched anytime, but I had rarely done so and could not recall the music.

It took me less than a minute to reach the loft. No one was there yet, so I slipped inside the gate and cocked my head at the keyboards, stops, and pedals. This particular organ was the predecessor to the one that I knew well, so its setup was slightly different. I knew that it would still sound majestic when played, due to the excellent acoustics of the cathedral. I had to resist a strong urge to sit down on the bench, unlace my heels, and attempt to play something awesome without organ shoes. That would have been a bad idea, since someone likely would have come to see *who* had begun to play so early. I could hear countless conversations drifting upward from the guests trickling into the nave below.

Instead, I leaned over the bench to read the list of songs for the wedding. Three songs rounded out the prelude, starting with Louis Couperin's Chaconne in G Minor. Next was Widor's Toccata, Symphony V. I hoped to master that song while at college. My mother's favorite organ piece completed the prelude, Vierne's Final, Symphony 5. I adored that piece and could play it quite well, mainly because I knew that she had loved it.

My mother had chosen a quieter song by Pachelbel for the processional, and she would enter to the traditional Wagner wedding march from *Lohengrin*. There would be one special number, Bach's "Jesu, Joy of Man's Desiring." My mother's best friend Linda Reynolds—known to me as

Aunt Linda Fischer—would be singing that song as a solo. The recessional was set to be Mendelssohn-Bartholdy's "Wedding March" from *A Midsummer Night's Dream*, and two preludes and fugues by Bach were listed as the postludes.

I continued leaning over the organ bench, my hands resting atop it, thinking about the songs on the list for at least a minute. I felt slightly dissatisfied with the songs even though I knew that Hans would play all of them splendidly, because my favorite organ piece of all time had been left out. "Oh well, it's not like she knew that would be your favorite song. You don't even exist, now," I murmured to myself. I sighed and stood up, glancing down at the clock on the organ. It read three thirty-four. I needed to get going, and soon, for the prelude would take fourteen minutes not counting the processional. But then I noticed a daily calendar sitting atop the organ beside the clock, and I yanked out the camera. I clambered up onto the organ bench, leaned toward the calendar, and snapped a picture, grinning and pointing at it with my free hand.

As I stuffed the camera back into the purse, I noticed the pen lying there at the bottom and had a sudden inspiration. I pulled it out, leapt onto the bench, and grabbed the daily calendar, tearing off today's date. I turned it over and wrote, *Play this one: Praeludium in C, Buxtehude.* I dropped the note onto the organ bench, gave a cackle of laughter, and slipped out of the loft.

I headed swiftly down the hallway toward a side staircase, knowing that I had little time if I wanted to get a decent seat. Just as I reached the stairwell I heard someone coming up. In a rather foolish panic, I jumped back and darted behind a triptych bearing scenes of Christ's triumph over Satan. I waited while I heard the footsteps approaching, sounding sure and steady, and I peered cautiously out from my hiding place to see who it was. My gray eyes bulged, and I clapped my hand over my mouth to hold back a scream. It was Hans.

I stared at him in awe as he passed by on the way to the organ loft. He wore a jet black tuxedo with tails, snow white buttoned shirt, white vest, white bowtie, black shoes, and a black top hat. His face bore the typical serious expression; his left hand clasped a small stack of organ music. His dark blue eyes shone with the anticipatory fire of organ-playing, his face bore much fewer lines than I recalled, and his thick hair was as black as his hat, slicked neatly with gel. He was *thirty*-two. And he was indescribably more gorgeous than ever.

It took me a full minute to recover my wits enough to fly to the staircase and descend once Hans had passed. My heart hammered, my thoughts chaotic. *Oh my freaking word. I can't believe he used to look that good! The old pictures of him are nowhere near that good. I can't believe this. I'm going to die. Why did I leave that note for him? He'll never play my song, even though he has it memorized. I'm such an idiot. Why couldn't I have been born in the late 1940s?*

As I wove my way through the lower chapels to the front vestibule, I rolled my eyes at myself in frustration. When I returned to 1998, I would have to keep this part as my own secret upon telling Hans of my adventures. He would think I was crazy if I mentioned my momentary loss at seeing him in his youth. What a fool I was. Perhaps someday I could find a decent Teuton my own age.

At last I reached the vestibule and merged gracefully with the increasing flow of people entering the cathedral. I overheard quite a few speculations on the wedding, the reception, and the couple—my parents. One older lady clad in silvery Versace said to another, "They are such a charming pair, Camilla and Max, and of such strong Teutonic blood. I certainly hope their marriage lasts a long time."

"For fifty years at least, let's hope," her friend rejoined, and they tittered. I felt a stone hand clasp my heart when I heard those words, and the corners of my eyes welled with tears. *Fifty years, they hoped . . . but they had only six . . . .* Now I stood in front of an usher who handed me a program, and I struggled to force back the sadness of knowing the future as he offered me his arm to escort me inside. This unwanted knowledge proved to be a problem I had not foreseen. No matter where I chose to go on my next trip, I would know everything, as it were. Usually things never turned out well in the end. I sighed, ordered myself not to think of this now, and asked the usher politely to give me an aisle seat—the best one possible—on my mother's side of the church.

The usher directed me to an aisle seat on the twelfth row back to the left of the altar. I thanked him kindly and took my seat, noting that the rest of the row was already practically filled. I would likely have to move aside for two or three more guests, which did not bother me. I stuffed my mother's purse down between me and the arm of the pew, then began to peruse the program. It was intricately made and must have cost a small fortune to print off enough for all of the attendees. I glanced quickly around the auditorium and estimated that there were several hundred people already occupying the pews. The muted roar of conversing humanity filled the air, and just at that moment, the triumphant sound of the organ broke through with the beginning of Couperin's Chaconne. My mind flew again to the young Hans I had recently seen upstairs, and I valiantly fought back a blush and a snicker as I looked again at the program.

I scanned it in less than a minute, passing over the many familiar and unfamiliar names, paying more attention to the order of the ceremony. Following the processional, the preacher would welcome the guests. I smiled to myself when I saw that the preacher was, in fact, Harvey Martin, the missionary pastor of my church. I knew him well, but of course he would not know me now. I wondered briefly what he would look like twenty years younger, for my childhood memories of him were hazy. Then I continued scanning the program, noting that along with the usual preacher's message to the couple, exchange of vows, and special music, there would also be a unity candle and a brief communion. As I frowned, trying to reason out the purpose of a communion at someone's wedding, there was a pause in the music. Then I heard a blast of swift and complicated pedalwork. I dropped the program into my lap and twisted my neck to stare up at the organ console. Hans was playing Buxtehude's Praeludium!

I sat rooted to the pew while Hans ran through the five-and-a-half minute piece, dazzled afresh by its beauty and magnificence. It was so perfect for a wedding; how had my mother not thought of it herself? I did not even notice the lady waiting to enter my row until an usher tapped me lightly on the shoulder. I slipped into the aisle with a muttered apology, still staggered by the music flowing grandly through the cathedral. I retook my seat in an instant, shaking my head in wonder as the piece came to its rousing conclusion. *I can't believe he actually played it. Wow . . . I wonder if he remembers this . . . .* I resolved to buttonhole him the moment I returned to 1998, and a wicked grin spread across my face.

Hans skipped the Widor piece altogether and went straight to Vierne's Final once the Praeludium had finished. I hoped that my mother would not give him too much grief about changing that one song. She may not have even noticed. My gaze bounced from the program to the organ loft to the auditorium at large, and I tapped my foot as I waited for the Pachelbel piece to begin. At last the opening notes began, and I turned slightly in the pew to get a good view of the processional, pulling the digital camera from my mother's purse. My grandmothers came first, ushered in by two attendants, and I snapped a covert picture of each of them. Both looked much younger and dressed to kill, clouds of perfume following in their wake. Next came the seven bridesmaids and groomsmen. The women wore gorgeous light blue dresses with white lace while the men wore gray tuxes. I snapped pictures of each couple when they passed my seat. Lastly, the ring-bearer—my cousin Leon, looking incredibly young and silly—and three little flower girls advanced down the aisle, prompting murmurs from all sides.

The flower girls reached the front and took their places, the organ burst into a grandiose fanfare, and the crowd, now numbering over eight hundred, rose to its feet. I leaned as far out as I could without appearing horribly conspicuous, staring wordlessly at the tiny forms of my mother and grandfather just entering from the vestibule, seemingly a football field away. My eyes bugged and my mouth dropped open just a bit as I watched them progress gradually toward me. My mother's dress looked exquisite; it was of short-sleeved, sparkling white silk and lace, sprinkled with tiny diamonds, the train dragging at least a meter behind. Her long veil also shone with jewels, sweeping the floor behind her train. She held a gorgeous bouquet of light blue and yellow flowers with matching ribbons curling to the floor—her two favorite colors, I knew.

When she had come close enough for me to see her face, tears welled in my eyes. Her dancing blue eyes rimmed with thick black lashes gazed triumphantly ahead, and her tender smile looked so brilliant that my heart almost stopped beating. Her jet-black hair, exactly like mine, sprang around her face in bouncing curls, sparkling with glitter. My hands shook as I held up the camera and tried to take some pictures that would do her justice. Whether she saw any of us in the crowd while we gazed at her in awe, I do not know. The entire time I stared at her, tears trembling on my eyelashes, she was looking at my father.

I could not force myself to tear my eyes away from her until she reached the altar and the pastor motioned for the crowd to be seated. When I shakily retook my seat, the camera now in my lap, I finally looked to the right of the preacher to see my father. He looked almost as stunning as my mother, though that seemed nigh impossible. He was slim and young, his hair a very dark brown, his smile big enough to stretch from ear to ear at the sight of his bride-to-be. His posture was straight, his gray tux perfect, a light blue boutonnière in his suit pocket, his hands clasped before him in calm excitement. I held up the camera again and endeavored to get a halfway decent shot of him in spite of the distance between us. I could see, when I studied him, why my mother had decided to marry him. Aside from his handsome appearance, by his face you could tell that he was a good man.

The wedding itself flew by, and I hardly noticed any particulars of it, for my attention remained fixated upon my mother. I watched the grace and poise with which she moved, the beauty with which she spoke the vows, the adoration in her smile while she gazed at my father. During the special music, as her maid of honor Linda sang "Jesu, Joy of Man's Desiring" in its original German, I saw my mother mouthing the words silently to my father during the entire song. Her smile never faded; she was young and beautiful. I felt tears prick my eyes again at the knowledge that in six years she would be dead, bearing my father a son. Seven years later that son, Anton Gerhard, would die after years of suffering from cystic fibrosis. It was my mother's untimely death along with my brother's illness that caused my father to spurn everything Teutonic. He blamed her death on her Teuton blood, so I knew that he must have read *Der Weg* at some happier point in his life.

These dark thoughts finally brought the tears out of my eyes, and I pulled a wad of tissues from the purse to blot them before my mascara ran. Now I began to regret coming to the wedding in the first place. Why had I wanted to see this? Such promise, such future happiness, such possibilities—and I knew it would all end in agony. Despite having the wealth and success that most people craved, there were so many things that my family had lost.

At last, Pastor Martin pronounced the couple man and wife, and by then I had composed myself enough to take a picture as they kissed. I had a feeling that none of my pictures would come out very well, if they came out at all. I would check as soon as I got back, before dinner. Before I knew it, Mendelssohn's piece burst out from the organ and the crowd had risen to its feet. My parents descended from the altar, both laughing while they charged up the aisle in a shower of flower petals and rice. The woman behind me threw rice over my head when my parents passed; I was too busy snapping a couple quick photos of them together to pay too much attention. I watched them exit the nave just as the music transitioned to Widor's Toccata. Hans had not forgotten it after all.

I felt a strong urge to escape while the crowd stood waiting for the ushers to dismiss the rows one by one. I had seen what I had come to see. Now I needed to get out, to get back. It had been beautiful, but it would have been better if I could have kept those dark thoughts of the future out of my mind. Why could no one, not even such a perfect couple like my mother and father, have a happy ending?

I waited for at least twenty minutes, through the Widor song as well as both of the Bach preludes and fugues, shifting impatiently on my heels, before an usher reached my row and allowed me to depart. As soon as I had the chance, I slipped into one of the side chapels and through a small wooden door, forsaking the festive atmosphere. I would take one of the back ways to the south clock tower and climb to the same landing that I had used for my arrival. No tourists should be up there yet, so I should be able to open the gates of time in peace.

I halted my ascent on the level just above the main roof, then headed for one of the larger windows. When I peered out of the thick glass, the view took my breath away, as it always did. The sun sank toward the west, and I gazed toward it for a moment before turning my eyes to the city beneath me. The red and brown roofs of München stood out as sharp points of color in the late afternoon sun, and the tiny people and cars moving about the streets reminded me a little of an ant colony, with everyone at his or her own business or leisure. I looked again at Alter Peter's tower, the first one rebuilt after the war, smiling fondly at the sight of its many clocks. München, the descendent of that great Teuton city of Muniche, had always been something wonderful.

Reluctantly, I tore myself away from the view and retrieved the Torstein from the bottom of my mother's purse. I hesitated for a moment before picturing my attic and reciting the words necessary for a return. I had a feeling that I was in for yet another harrowing trip through darkness and helplessness, and I wondered if I would hear those troubling whispers, moans, and laughter again. I would have to do it one way or another, so I beat back my fear and concentrated on the Torstein and my own decade, then spoke the spell. "May I return to the time from which I have come, changed forever from what I have seen in the past. May I never forget the wisdom I have gained. May I continue my life and always consider that which has gone before me. Take me now to my home."

Again there was a hideous ripping sound, and again the air in front of me split open, forming into those ancient labradorite gates. The Torstein trembled afresh in my hand, and I watched in fear and fascination as the gates opened, again revealing darkness and tumult. I glanced back once more toward the window and the view of my city. Then I steeled myself and stepped through the gates, shutting my eyes in preparation. Again I felt myself tossed, pulled this way and that, hearing those mystifying whispers all around me, mingling with the moans that sounded as though they resonated from a very deep pit. And at the end, to my chagrin, that menacing laughter shook me, terrified me, made me beg silently for the journey to end, for my attic to reappear.

A moment later, I burst again from the gates, landing hard on that creaky, familiar wooden floor. I turned my right ankle a bit on my heels, but the pain meant nothing compared to the overwhelming relief and joy I felt at the sight of my surroundings. Yes, here was the dusty attic, the shadows, the trunks and boxes, the single light bulb with its dangling metal chain. And right there before me stood the man I loved, Hans, fifty-two again, still wearing his formal working attire, his expression suggesting insatiable curiosity and no little amazement.

I spun around to close the portal, just as I had in 1978, and it vanished with little fanfare. Then I turned to regard Hans, dropped my mother's purse onto the floor, and shook my head in wonder. "*That* was an adventure," I concluded.

Chapter Fourteen:
Is It Safe to Tell?

Hans received the complete rundown of my trip later that night, after I had made sure that my father had cloistered himself in his bedroom with the curtains drawn. We met at the gazebo this time, both of us dressed in black pants and shirts to help us blend in with the night. I laid almost the whole story of my trip to 1978 at Hans' feet while we sat opposite one another on the benches of the gazebo. He showed interest the entire time, particularly when I discussed the actual trip itself. He had not realized that the Torstein essentially pushed a person backward through the currents of time—his words—but he did not seem surprised about the whispers, moans, and fearsome laughter that had plagued me throughout the trip. "It's quite likely that those whispers, though you could not understand them, were meant as a warning," he inferred. "You said that they did not sound encouraging, so maybe they're meant to dissuade time travelers from taking another journey later."

His comments made me thoughtful, and I began to wonder whether having the Torstein was really a good thing at all. If some ethereal voices tried to deter time travelers from trying it again, perhaps I should not have opened the portal. "I'm not sure whether you should try this again, Swanie," Hans warned me when I mentioned the moans and the dismal laughter. "From what you've said, it appears that traveling time awakens forces that should not be given sway. The Torstein is an indescribable power, that is true, but great power often bears unwanted consequences."

"Maybe the Torstein shouldn't exist in the first place," I blurted, a feeling of dread washing over me at the thought. What had I unleashed here?

"Maybe," Hans agreed, "but the fact is that it does exist, and unless you plan to break the cardinal rule of time travel and change history to halt the creation of the stone, it will continue till the earth perishes in fire." Hans' face betrayed a bit of amusement, for he knew as well as I did that I would not dare to break such an integral rule. He concluded his philosophizing with the admonition, "You are now the owner of the Torstein, and it will likely be yours until your death. Therefore it is you, and you alone, who must decide whether it should be used or not."

Our late night conversation gave me much to think about, and I returned to my bedroom just after midnight, trembling with worry over the Torstein. *What if this rock isn't supposed to exist or be used in the first place? What if Prince Otto von Bayern was playing a devil's game when he created it, and what if it was a demon—maybe Wuotan—who moaned and laughed when I used it? What sort of repercussions might this have on me? Should I dare to use it again, and alone? Should I tell anyone else about it?* And the most frightening thought of all: *What if someone tries to steal it from me? Will it really be safe in a ring box?*

One humorous aside from our chat at the gazebo involved Hans' playing of my favorite organ piece at the wedding. He was disconcerted, to say the least, that I had suggested the piece. He informed me darkly that he had thought my mother had left him that note, or that she had sent a friend of hers to do so. He said that it had seemed odd to him at the time, for he had not realized that my mother knew that song. "Maybe she didn't," I told him with a shrug, "but I know it, and we both know it's my favorite. It made my day to hear you play it for the wedding." I had blushed and looked down, grateful for the dimness of night to hide the emotion that swelled within me at the memory of a young Hans. He seemed to find little comedy in that incident, but neither did he reprimand me. He merely assented that I certainly had become a part of history by concocting such a scheme.

I spent the greater part of Saturday evening with my father at the Hofbräuhaus, relishing the tasty Bavarian cuisine and traditional folk music. My father ordered the roasted knuckle of pork, while I got the Sauerbraten platter. Once we had finished our meals, I sat back against the wall to observe my father candidly as I sipped my Apfelschorle. His posture was very much at ease, for the Hofbräuhaus was one of his favorite places. He had already greeted quite a few other guests as well as waitresses throughout the evening, his businessman's smile ever perfect, introducing his daughter to this client, to that coworker, his personal stein never running short of dark München beer. He flourished in the company of others, I observed, and I felt a rush of pity at the idea of him living alone in our huge house while I was away in the U.S.

His gray eyes ranged throughout the room at large, resting for some time on the musicians, then at last returning to meet my gaze. "It's going to be lonely around here without you, Swanie," he remarked, guessing my thoughts, his left arm draped across the back of the wooden bench upon which he sat, his right hand curled around the handle of his stein.

I quirked a doleful smile at the truth of that and nodded toward the people crowding the room. "Maybe you should finally find yourself a serious girlfriend," I suggested. "I've seen enough of the women in here shooting you curious looks." My father had been a widower for nearly fourteen years now, and despite his charm and wealth, in all that time he had never dated anyone, to my knowledge.

My father's lips twisted a little. "Most of the available women I meet these days want me for my money, nothing else. I'm not desperate enough to lock myself into that type of relationship." He took a sip from his stein, then murmured, "Your Mutti was one of a kind. No one else can compare."

The sorrow in his tone struck my soul, and I remembered the obvious adoration with which she had gazed at my father during their wedding. It troubled me that I could not mention my new possession to him since he distrusted all things Teutonic. My thoughts drifted from there to another possibility, and I said in a soft voice, "Maybe . . . maybe one of *our* people . . . would take you for more than just the money." I dared not speak the word out loud. My body tensed automatically as I awaited his response.

A darkness crept over my father's face, and he looked away, stiffening his posture. "True as that may be, I can't do that again. That mystical madness took everything from me last time." He heaved a sigh and frowned, his eyes roving over the crowd once more. "By the way, you do realize that you'll have to see a doctor before you leave." He looked back at me with a grave expression.

He had conveniently changed the subject, like he did whenever I hinted at the Teuton people. But the topic he had decided to bring up instead prompted me to freeze and look at my hands, images that I had long fought against threatening to pollute my brain afresh. "I know," I said in a dead voice. I chewed on my bottom lip and continued to stare at my hands, wishing for the thousandth time that I could find some magical formula to counteract my irrational fear of doctors. My brain knew that there was no need to fear them, but the idea of actually entering a medical office and walking down that hallway, assaulted with those sweet chemical smells and too-calm clinical voices, nearly negated all of the progress I had made over the past six years. I had weaned myself off of the pills years ago, and my last really bad panic attack had happened long before that. Since Hans had first taught me how to reach the spiritual realm, I had taken to going there whenever I felt an attack coming on, for that transcendent domain held little room for negativity.

"The only thing you'll really need to have done is the TB test," my father said at length, breaking the sustained silence between us. "And I'm sure I could convince my physician to come to our house to test you."

I pried my eyes off of my hands and looked toward him where he sat across the table from me, his gray eyes sympathetic. "Really, Pappi? You'd do that for me?"

"Of course I would," he answered, reaching his free hand across the table. I managed to lift my right hand from my lap to lay it in his, the firmness of his touch comforting me. "I don't want you to have to go through unnecessary trauma. But on that note, you might want to talk to the doctor about birth control too. Colleges tend to be dens of drunkenness and sexuality, as I'm sure you've heard." He winked and let go of my hand.

I made a face at my father and reached for my glass of sparkling juice. "I'm not really planning on doing that stuff. American boys aren't my type."

My father certainly caught my hint, but he took a swig from his stein, which a waitress had recently refilled, and pointed out, "You know you'll have to actually go to a hospital whenever you get pregnant. Our family doesn't have the best track record there, and I wouldn't want you taking the risk of trying it at home."

I wondered whether he was discussing the subject of Teuton blood with me without naming it outright. "I'm not planning on having kids anytime soon, either," I noted, my thoughts running in a different direction at the memory of my mother and Dane. "But . . . do you think . . . when you have the doctor come . . . could you ask him to take some of my blood to test for the CFTR protein?" My father looked stricken when I spoke the words, but I plowed swiftly ahead. "Because if I have that mutation, I might just not have kids at all." There was no way I would want any of my own children to suffer like Dane had. I had resolved that years ago.

My father looked at me in silence for a long time, long enough for me to start tapping my foot along with the folk song that the musicians played. I finished the rest of my juice and looked around the room again, wondering if I had crossed a line I should not have crossed by asking that question. Finally, though, my father cleared his throat and said, "I can ask him to check you for that, yes. But you should know that people get cystic fibrosis only if both of their parents have the mutation."

I nodded absently, for I knew that quite well, and a moment later I invited my father to come visit Beth and me while we were at the university. "Maybe you could find a decent American wife since all the Germans are only after money," I suggested, and he laughed and pledged that he would do his best to visit. Not long after, we left the bustling beer hall to meet my father's chauffeur, Thomas, and we headed home seated beside each other in the back of his blue Rolls Royce. I rested my head upon his shoulder during the ride, silently hoping that one day he would be able to look past my mother's tragic death and accept his Teutonic heritage.

On Sunday afternoon I drove to Lady Muniche's apartment after church, squeezing my Ghibli into a spot at the curb several apartments down. This would be the final gathering of my Teuton friends before we all went our separate ways; I knew that Erika would be heading back to Vienna first thing Monday morning. As I strode briskly toward the Lady's purple door, clad in a pale orange summer dress dotted with artistic roses, my hair pulled back in a white clip that matched my heels, I thought again of the Torstein, which I had left at home. Hans had agreed that it would be both safe and wise to tell my mentor about it, but I had not yet decided whether I should spill its secrets to my five friends. *It would be a lot more exciting to travel time as a group, especially if I go somewhere far in the past next time,* I thought.

Sonnig met me nearly as soon as I had opened the door, yapping and wagging her tail in obvious recognition. "Down, you silly thing!" I scolded her, shutting the door and kneeling down to rumple her fur. She had been recently groomed; a lock of hair sprang up between her ears, held in place with a pink bow.

"Winter's mistress just showed up," Marga announced from where she sat on a knit cushion between the TV and loom. She wore cloth shorts and an FC Bayern T-shirt, a Coke already in hand, her brown curls frizzing wildly upon her shoulders.

I stuck my tongue out at her and breathed out one breath of frost in response. "I banish all who scorn me to the Arctic." I gave Sonnig one final pat and headed for the couch, where Erika had saved a spot for me. The Yorkie scampered toward the kitchen, probably wishing to check on lunch's progress.

"What took you so long?" Trudi leaned back on her hands on the other side of the TV, the yellow beanbag in a lump on her lap. "We're about to die of starvation sitting here smelling Lady Muniche's feast in there."

I sat down beside Erika, who had claimed the center couch cushion. Ina and my other cousin were nowhere to be seen, so I guessed that they were helping in the kitchen. "Got held up coming through town." I set my purse down on the floor and took a whiff of the air. I recognized the scent of bacon grease. Perhaps the Lady had chosen to prepare us a Bauernfrühstück.

"Why didn't you just take A99 around? Pretty sure there's something going on in the Englischer Garten this weekend." Trudi's narrowed eyes implied that she doubted my discernment.

I rolled my eyes at her and gestured at my attire. "Church?"

Trudi made a scoffing noise, though she wore a skirt herself, likely having attended mass that morning. Erika elbowed me and said, "I'll go get you something to drink. I think your options are Coke and Fanta."

"I'll take the one with caffeine," I said with a yawn, watching her colorful skirt sway as she departed the parlor. I wondered absently whether she would ever put her artistic prowess to use in designing clothing.

"So," Marga blared in a tone that prompted me to turn to face her. She had crossed her legs and set her Coke down on the floor beside her, her blue eyes glittering toward me in an accusatory manner. "Erika hinted that you two did some things while you were in the lake country."

I felt my cheeks burn as my cousin turned to stare at me, her mouth agape. "We didn't *do* any things. That was Ava and Morgen, my two rich friends."

Trudi burst out laughing. "See, I *knew* that would make her blush!"

I threw a pillow at my cousin and hit her square in the neck. "You jerk."

"Ow!" she complained, chucking the pillow back at me, but I was ready and caught it, stuffing it back in its place between me and the armrest. Erika reentered the room with my bottle of Coke in one hand and a loaded plate in the other. Traudl and Ina followed close behind, bearing plates and silverware, effectively ending the conversation. Within two minutes' time, everyone had sat down and bowed their heads while Lady Muniche blessed our lunch, having seated herself in her recliner across from the rest of us.

No one talked much while we ate, for the Lady had cooked a savory breakfast stew heaped with scrambled eggs, bacon, potatoes, onions, green peppers, and cheese. I pondered the dilemma of the Torstein while I ate, my gaze shifting from Erika at my left side to my cousins on my right, both of whom now sat on beanbags devouring the stew as though it was their first meal of the day. *Would this group of five Teuton girls really be the best cohorts for another trip through time? Would all of them be able to keep the secret? Of course they have experience keeping secrets, but the Torstein is something they can't tell their parents about, or their siblings. What about the darkness and evil that Hans thinks is involved? I bet Ina would have misgivings about that, and probably my cousins, too.*

"So, Swanie," Erika began in a conversational tone after finishing her final bite of stew. I looked toward her, and she smirked, her red eyebrows arching over her mischievous eyes. "You think we should tell them?"

"Tell us what?" Ina inquired, sounding only slightly interested. Since Erika and I very rarely talked about Teuton young men, our discussions hardly interested her. She had fed at least a fifth of the bacon on her plate to Sonnig.

I blinked at Erika, unsure to what she referred. "You mean . . . ?" I invoked my ice into my eyes for a second, blurring my vision behind my glasses.

Her forehead creased. "Yeah, what else is there to tell them?"

I had actually been thinking about the *Eihalbae*. Erika and I had danced in spirit form upstream upon the Leutascher Ache two nights after I had found the Torstein, and both of us were certain that we had not been alone in our dance. "So what do you have to tell us?" Lady Muniche prompted. When I looked toward her, I saw curiosity in her gaze, her smile broadening.

"We danced as Teuton spirits on the lakes," Erika blurted proudly.

"You *what?*" Marga sounded taken off guard.

"Wait, are you saying—"

"You can both *do* that?"

"Every time I try it I turn into a gargoyle—"

"—and I practically burn alive!"

My cousins were talking over each other, with Traudl spewing what she likely believed to be gargoyle noises from her throat. Trudi wiggled the fingers of her right hand in a vague approximation of igniting flames. "It's really not that hard when you're in a lake," Erika said with a laugh.

"Well, you two are both water elements, so of course it'd be easy." Marga had wrinkled her nose at us. "I guess if I wanted to enter the realm of the spirit, I'd have to bury myself first." My cousins roared with laughter at that.

Ina, meanwhile, shook her head at the three of them and rose to her feet. "I've always found entering the spiritual realm to be a freeing experience," she said in a breezy tone, drifting around the room to collect all of the plates.

"You can just put everything in the sink, Ina dear," Lady Muniche told her when she had reached the old woman's chair. "Rudi will take care of our mess after he's done weeding out back." After Ina had left the room, our mentor leveled her gaze upon Erika and me, her mien more solemn than usual. "While I'm glad that the two of you have uncovered the mysteries of the spirit, I urge you to be cautious whenever you explore the unseen realm," she stated, her blue eyes locking with mine. A chill crept up my spine when she went on. "The spiritual realm hides dangers for women who go there alone, especially for unbonded women like the two of you. I speak not only of devilish forces, but of the Teuton priests who stalk the shadows. There are some who would punish a woman wandering there alone."

Erika had grown stiff beside me, her mouth pressed into a thin line. After a pause, I gathered that it was up to me to answer Lady Muniche's warning. "Nobody saw us, Lady Muniche," I said, my voice shaking more than I liked. "I was actually keeping my senses on guard for other Teutons the entire time. Anytime I sensed one, Erika and I returned to our bodies right away."

"Good," the Lady commended me before shifting her gaze toward Marga and my cousins. "The rest of you need not fret about being caged in your mortality. Your future partners may lead you into the spiritual realm one day, and even if they don't, all of you have a keen grasp on your personal elements already."

I followed Lady Muniche into her kitchen later that afternoon when she went to warm up some of the stew for Rudi, who had finished outside. He occupied one of the chairs at her dining nook, the smells of fresh earth and mulch clinging to him as he nodded at me in greeting. I nodded back and sidled to the Lady's side, where she stood turning a dial on the stove. "Lady Muniche, could I come visit you one last time before I have to leave?" I asked her, leaning my right hip against the dishwasher, which was churning. When she turned her wrinkled face toward me,

I explained in an undertone, "There's something I need to tell you."

She smiled at me and answered, "I'll have to check my calendar. I know that I've got at least three groups of young Teuton girls coming to meet me in the next three weeks, along with some of the priests from the council. But I'll carve out some time for you and call your house once I know when." She patted my left hand in a reassuring fashion, and I exhaled in relief.

Chapter Fifteen:
Lady Muniche's Advice

I spent the greater part of the following weeks packing and repacking for my trip to the U.S., choosing one minute to take some trinket and promptly reevaluating the next morning. Life would be more complicated this time around thanks to technology; in past years I had brought zero electrical devices with me. Now I would need to bring my laptop and printer and their respective converters and adapters. I e-mailed Beth several times, trying to decide which dorm necessities I would need to buy once I arrived. She emphasized the importance of a hot pot—something that apparently could mimic a portion of a stovetop—as well as a mini fridge and microwave. I pledged to use my own funds for any of the more expensive equipment. Since my father planned to deposit four thousand dollars into my Bank of America account each month along with paying my bill in full, I would be far from broke.

I heaved a sigh and closed my e-mail client on my final Monday at home, rolling my leather office chair back from my desk and swiveling to face Lise, who was in the process of vacuuming my floor. She had transitioned into the position of head housekeeper after I had outgrown the need for a nanny, but I still looked to her for motherly support. When she caught my gaze, she switched the vacuum off. "Just e-mailed Beth again asking her to look at car ads. Have to buy one before we head for Virginia, and we've got only five days to get it done." I lolled my head back as though I could not handle such pressure.

"How much money is your Pappi giving you for your car?" Lise asked.

"Twenty-five thousand, I think. Not enough for another Maserati." I grinned.

Lise moved toward my couch and beckoned me to sit down with her. "Well, if you want me to, I can ask Siggi what he'd recommend. I'd think you should go for a reliable car since it needs to last four years."

I plopped down at the opposite end of the couch, running the fingers of my left hand along its bright cerulean fabric. "Sure, I'd appreciate his advice," I said. Siggi was Lise's husband, our groundskeeper, and he studied cars as a hobby.

I knew that Lise was looking at me, but I stared in a daze toward the glass doors to my balcony, shut against the heat of summer. The Thaden house was one of the few in Germany fully equipped with central air conditioning, a godsend for Lise and all of our other servants. Sebastian had said more than once that our house had spoiled him. *Hopefully the dorms will have good AC and heat,* I thought. *It's bound to get cold in the mountains.*

"Swanie, I don't mean to pry, but lately you've looked like you've swallowed an elephant." I gave Lise an arch look and patted my stomach, though I knew quite well that was not what she meant. She wrinkled her nose at me and reproved, "Oh, don't be like that. You know what I mean. And it's not just the stress of going to college. It started weeks before you bothered to pack."

My lips curled into a wry smile. My former nanny knew me too well, and my thoughts slipped into my right hand pocket, where the Torstein rested as always. "You're right, but it's not something I can tell you," I said.

She raised one graying eyebrow at me. "It's a Teuton thing, isn't it?"

"Yeah, but it's kind of a personal Teuton thing."

"Very well." Lise nodded at me and rose to return to her duties. "But if you ever need to talk to somebody other than Hans about it, I'm always available. No judgment. But you already know that." She waved her hand toward me and turned the vacuum cleaner back on. I smiled in acknowledgement and stretched out on the couch, closing my eyes to muse for a while. As much as I longed to tell Lise about the Torstein, as an outsider she would have no sound advice to offer on that front. Tomorrow afternoon I would confide in my elderly mentor, and I looked forward to sharing my secret with a fellow Teuton woman.

Thomas drove me to Lady Muniche's apartment shortly after lunchtime the next day and promised to retrieve me in two hours. I thanked him and vowed to be ready to meet him at the appointed time. Then I pointed my feet toward my elderly friend's purple door, where she stood awaiting me. The Lady wore a comfortable lavender summer dress, her silver hair curling around her ears, her blue eyes sparkling with fun, their color matching her crystal earrings almost exactly. "Dear Swanie, I've been looking forward to your visit!" Her honeyed voice was welcoming as she wrapped me in a warm embrace.

I eagerly returned her embrace, inhaling the minty scent that suffused the air around her; she had likely cared for her herb garden today. "Lady Muniche, it's so good to see you again!" I said, and when she pulled back to smile at me, I added, "And I have *so* much to tell you!"

The Lady's smile widened, and she turned toward her parlor with the words, "Well, let's get to it then!" She opened her door and shooed Sonnig away, then said, "Take any seat, and I'll be back in a few moments with some chocolate."

She bustled into the kitchen, and I set my purse down onto her blue-and-white-checkered three-cushioned sofa, knowing that I would seat myself there once she returned. A floral scent saturated the room from the rods of incense burning upon the windowsill, and I saw that the front window was open, inviting the warm breeze of summer to make its way inside. My eyes traveled over the other furnishings of Lady Muniche's small parlor: the TV, the upright piano, and the intricate sewing loom upon which she had fashioned countless beautiful costumes and hangings for Teutonic festivals. A large swath of light yellow fabric spilled from the loom now, and I stepped forward to look at it more closely.

"That will be hung at a tent at the Wiesn when it's finished." The Lady had reentered the room carrying a tray laden with various types of chocolate and two cups of sparkling cider. She set it down upon a side table, then glanced back toward the loom and noted, "You should remember from Teuton history that though the Oktoberfest today is mainly focused on beer, it was once the harvest festival of our people, many centuries ago. And some of the breweries still remember that truth."

Lady Muniche settled herself upon her recliner across from the sofa, her left hand wrapped around a cup of cider, her right hand clutching several chocolates. But her gaze remained upon the fabric spread across her loom, a numinous smile gracing her lined face. I walked to the couch and sat down, taking hold of the other cup of cider, vexation at my own destiny coming to the forefront of my mind. "And I'll be missing four Oktoberfests," I sighed before taking a sip of cider.

"By your own choice, Swanie," the Lady reminded me, her smile forever brilliant. "You're off to conquer the world, to experience its grandeur, and as there is nothing tethering you to this city, I say go for it!"

She had a point, and we spent some time discussing my upcoming college studies, Lady Muniche's delight at my opportunities constantly radiating from her bearing. We talked about business and organ music, and I sought her opinions on some of the electives that I would need to finish my degree. "I have to take four semesters of a foreign language, and I haven't decided which one yet."

"And what languages do they offer at your school?" she inquired.

I considered what I had seen in the catalogue, then said, "Spanish, French, German—like I need any help with *that*—Mandarin Chinese, Russian, and Latin."

"Take Latin," she advised without hesitation.

I blinked at her, taken aback by her certainty. I had studied Latin briefly in school, just for two years, and had forgotten most of it. "Why Latin? A lot of people say there's no point in studying a dead language."

"Well, you're already fluent in German and English, and you had four years of French in high school, yes?" I nodded, for I had studied it in the U.S. as well as in my last three years at home. "Then the obvious choice is Latin. Those who would say not to learn a dead language tend not to learn from history, and they repeat the same problems again and again." The Lady nodded sagaciously, her eyes twinkling.

That made a lot of sense, and it brought my thoughts back to the Torstein. I shifted a little on the couch and picked up a couple more pieces of chocolate—all of them had some sort of cream filling. My mentor had fallen silent, gazing at me from around the rim of her glass, so I figured that it was time to open the real subject at hand. I honestly suspected that Lady Muniche would have far more insight on such things than Hans, in spite of his priestly status. "So I had a crazy adventure recently that I've been wanting to tell you about," I began, and when the Lady's blue eyes lit up with anticipation, I narrated the entire story for her. I told her that I had found the Torstein hidden in the rocks after awakening my ice during a dance at the direction of an *Eihalbe*, and I told her what I had learned about it from Teuton writings, and finally I discussed my trip to my parents' wedding in 1978.

When I had finished, I reached for the final piece of chocolate, heart-shaped and white on the outside. When I bit into it I discovered that it had a strawberry filling. I chewed slowly, savoring the taste, and lifted my gaze to my elderly friend, who looked back at me in silence, her eyes betraying extreme concern for me. Perhaps she was waiting for me to ask a question, or perhaps the details of my tale had rendered her speechless. "So apparently, I really and truly *do* have the Torstein," I appended, pulling it from the pocket of my shorts to let the light catch it. "And it really does have the power to take me back in time. I'm trying to decide where I should go next, and whether I should bother going anywhere. It would be pointless to just keep it hidden, but I'm really not sure . . . ." My voice trailed off, and I looked from the mystical stone in my hand to my friend.

A long moment passed in silence, and at last the Lady spoke. "So right now there are only three who know of the Torstein's entity. You, Johannes, and me."

"Yes," I confirmed. "Hans said I shouldn't tell too many people, since it has the potential to be used for evil."

The Lady nodded. "I would agree with him on that point. Teutonic powers in general cannot be tapped by outsiders, but the Torstein may be outside of that sphere."

I trembled all over at that possibility. "But would any outsiders actually *know* about the Torstein?" I asked, thinking it was unlikely. I tucked the stone back into my pocket since my mentor did not seem inclined to study it herself.

The Lady frowned a little, the creases in her face deepening. "The existence of the Torstein is mentioned in *Der Weg*. While I doubt that too many outsiders would read our Teutonic lexicon and believe it to be factual, it is available to any and all. Though we carefully guard the secrets of the uniqueness of our blood, you know as well as I that even outsiders could interpret our written records as truth. Where do you think the fantasies about humans controlling the elements come from? And the folklore of vampires and fairies? These are *our* tales, Swanie, lingering upon the earth even today."

That was food for thought. "Do you think maybe I ought to let the council of München know that I found the Torstein?" I inquired. "Or that maybe next time there's a conference of a larger group of Teuton priests, Hans should go and inform them that the Torstein has been found?"

My elderly friend chuckled, and to my surprise, she shook her head. "If you do that, Swanie, then you ensure that the Torstein will be taken from you. Teuton priests, as wise and skilled as they are, would never deign to trust a woman with a power of that magnitude." She eyed me pointedly.

"So we should keep it to ourselves."

"That we should."

A worrisome notion suddenly came over me. "What if Hans decides to tell?"

The Lady chuckled again and waved her left hand dismissively. "Don't you worry about that. Next time I see him, I'll share a few of my thoughts on the subject, and he won't dare to reveal your secret."

I felt a wash of relief and took a moment to finish my glass of sparkling cider. "What about my Teuton friends?" I asked, getting up to set the empty glass on the tray beside Lady Muniche's chair. "I mean, the first time I went to the past, I went somewhere for just a couple hours, somewhere that wasn't too different from the here and now. But if I use the Torstein again, I might want to go somewhere more noteworthy, you know? And if I do that, I'm not sure I'd want to do it by myself."

Sonnig trotted back into the room while my mentor thought about it, and I reached out to rub her fur while she sniffed at my sandals. She looked up at me with a hopeful expression, as though she wanted to sit on the couch with me but could not quite make the jump herself. Traces of gray had begun to stand out among the black hairs on her back and on her muzzle, so I smiled wryly and set her beside me. She was so much lighter than my cat Thunar. If I tried too hard, I would throw her by accident.

"Actually, I'm impressed that you've decided not to tell any of your Teuton girlfriends yet," Lady Muniche said at length. "But you've always struck me as the most rational of your particular group of friends, so maybe I shouldn't be surprised. I would caution you, though, when it comes to revealing your secret to anyone else. Most people your age wouldn't grasp the seriousness of the situation."

I bowed my head, recognizing the truth of that. "So I guess it's my burden for now," I murmured, uncertain whether that would turn out to be a good thing or not. We spoke of a few more things regarding the Torstein before I rose to leave, knowing that Thomas would be returning for me shortly. As I stood at her doorway moments later, the summer Föhn stirring my hair, I voiced my final question, looking into the eyes of my most trusted mentor. "Lady Muniche, where do you think I should go, the next time I use the Torstein?"

"That is for you alone to decide, Swanie," she replied, her blue eyes shining with delight. "All of history is open to you now. You need only to choose which era you want to claim as your own." She patted my cheek, then gestured for me to go, for my ride had arrived. In parting, she pledged, "I'll see you at the Maypole."

On Saturday, August 22nd, I flew out of München bound for Philadelphia, Pennsylvania. My summer had been quite eventful aside from the few hours of time travel, but I looked forward to beginning my studies again. I could hardly wait to see Beth and her parents, since I had not seen them in three years.

I said good-bye to my father at the airport that morning, and he wished me well and admonished me to do my best, even if things got hard. Several hours earlier I had given my farewells to my father's entire staff, elbowing Sebastian in disgust at his insistence upon my "finding a boyfriend in Virginia." I doubted I would find any Teutons there, so if I got a boyfriend he would be just that—a boyfriend, never a husband.

I remember standing at the front door of my house about eight-thirty that morning, staring into Hans' face in sorrow, knowing that I would not see him again until May, since I intended to spend the Christmas holidays in New Jersey. "Enjoy yourself, Swanie, and learn as much as you can," were his words of wisdom.

I nodded, bridling my emotions. "I will," I whispered, then worked to make my voice stronger. "Keep everything in kilter here, Hans. I don't want to come back to chaos in May." I quirked a smile, grasping at the tiny strands of humor.

Hans smiled back knowingly and promised, "Don't you worry about that." Then he leaned forward to place his hands on my shoulders and murmured in my ear, "Keep the Torstein safe." He backed away just enough to look at me seriously, and I nodded and patted my purse, where the ring box lay at the bottom. His hands slid down my arms, the right one pausing just long enough to stuff something into my left hand. "I'll see you on the forum," he said with a nod.

Some time later, in the backseat of the car, I unfolded the paper in my hand. It was a worn page torn out of an old daily calendar, reading June 17th, 1978. On the back was the scrawled message, *Play this one: Praeludium in C, Buxtehude.*

Chapter Sixteen:
American Life

Beth and her parents met me at the Philadelphia airport on Saturday afternoon, the heat and humidity striking me the instant we stepped into the parking garage. "Ach, why is it always so hot over here?" I groaned. I had noticed it only vaguely on the jetway since I had flown commercial this time.

Onkel Jens gave a mirthless laugh, lugging my two bags that had no wheels toward his car, a Volkswagen Jetta. "It doesn't start getting better until October," he reminded me, and I groaned again.

Beth nudged the rolling suitcase that she pulled into mine. "Come on, you know you can just turn yourself into the Snow Queen whenever you want."

I eyed her in muted annoyance and righted my suitcase. "This isn't the time to play bumper cars. Some of us have been up since one a.m. your time."

"You didn't sleep on the plane?" Beth sounded surprised as she hefted one of my suitcases into the Jetta's trunk.

I snorted quietly and shifted my bags so that all four would fit in the trunk. "Kind of hard to sleep when you're traveling back in time," I muttered, prompting my cousin to shriek with laughter. Actually, I had spent much of the flight watching two different movies and fervently hoping that my father could convince one of his cronies to fly me across the ocean next time. I missed having the option of exploring the lavish compartments of private jets. The bathroom had gotten more repulsive as the trip had progressed.

Once we had all piled into the car, Beth began rattling off information about the various cars she had seen in recent newspapers. Aunt Linda reminded us both to buckle our seatbelts since we were about to get on I-95 outside of Philadelphia, "Where they always drive like hooligans," she clarified.

Meanwhile, I leaned my head against the side window. "I've already decided what car I'm getting, so the running commentary isn't necessary," I told my cousin, who sounded quite enthusiastic about the prospect of compact hatchbacks. "And I need a nap so I can stay up until tonight."

"Okay. But what car are you going to get?" Beth did not seem to get my hint. She leaned toward me from where she sat behind my uncle, her brown eyes bright and excited, matching her short hair almost exactly. "You can't just leave me hanging like this."

I sighed and met her gaze. "I'm getting a Toyota Celica. Goodnight." Onkel Jens turned the radio on, and Beth soon began singing along with a recent pop-country song, leaving me to peacefully snooze.

I purchased my dark blue Celica on Monday, paying with a batch of hundred dollar bills that my father had given me before I left home. The salesman eyed Beth and me with a look of surprise when I produced the cash, for we had driven to the dealership in her car, a very used Pontiac LeMans. It took a while to get the paperwork squared away since I usually lived in Germany, but thankfully my Aunt Linda had already arranged insurance on my behalf under the policy that covered Beth's car. Naturally I promised her to pay the difference, since the rate would certainly skyrocket with the addition of a brand new Celica. "Have to use my four thousand a month for something," I told her, and she agreed without complaint, remarking that Max von Thaden always insisted upon spoiling his child from afar.

Beth and I resolved to go to Ocean City on Tuesday for one final celebration before things got scholarly in the Appalachians. Ocean City was my favorite place in New Jersey, a shore town that I had visited often during my years with Beth's family. She told me that I would have to drive since I was better at parallel parking, which made me roll my eyes, but she had a point. I had gotten good at squeezing my Ghibli into impossible places in downtown München, and I knew that finding parking in Ocean City during the summer months often proved tricky. "You're going to have to remind me how to get there," I told her that night as we settled into our respective bunks. Beth had had a bunk bed since I had first stayed with her family at the age of five. Back then there were railings around her top bunk.

"No problem, just don't complain about miles the entire trip." I heard Beth shifting around under her blankets above me.

"You just have no idea how long miles are," I said, remembering how I had shaken my head at the 25 MPH sign at the entrance to her street. "And how slow they are. Really, you need to come visit me in München. You haven't been since I was what, eight?"

"I don't know. My dad says it's really expensive to fly three people over there. And my mom doesn't like planes."

"I said *you*, not your parents. We've got six guest rooms. You've never even seen my house, and I think you'd love it. It was built in the seventeen hundreds by people with ties to the Bavarian kings." I raised my right hand to the panel of wood above me, tracing its grains, finding the letters I had carved there on my last visit.

"Yeah, you and your giant house with all those manservants and maidservants," Beth said with a snicker.

"Has there been any *development* between you and your aging Teuton crush?"

I felt myself blushing as my fingers traced the letter *H*. "Pretty sure my Pappi would kill me if I told him I want to date his accountant."

"And what makes you think you'd have to tell him?" Beth's head appeared over the side of the bunk, the streetlight outside casting her face in an orange hue. "I mean, you're already keeping the Teuton stuff secret from him, right? How hard would it be to go on occasional 'dates' in your backyard?"

"We talk about Teuton stuff in the backyard." I brought my hand back down.

Beth glanced toward the carving I had traced. "You know I covered for you on that, right?" she declared, sounding triumphant. "My mom asked me about it after you left, and I said the *H* stood for some soccer player." She giggled.

I chuckled in response, looking up at the poorly carved *S+H*. "It's nothing but a dream," I murmured, trying hard to will myself to believe it. "He doesn't care about me that way, and he never will. I'm starting to think maybe he's asexual."

"One of the girls in my high school class was asexual," Beth commented, her face vanishing from my line of vision as she lay upon her mattress again. "She said she just wasn't interested in getting intimate like that."

"Hmm," I responded, not really grasping how someone could be completely uninterested in sex. Though I was still a virgin, I certainly wanted to experience true elemental copulation once I found myself a decent Teuton partner. *Maybe I should give that silly boy from Regensburg a chance. Maybe he's not as offspring-obsessed as the boys in München.*

"I have a surprise to tell you about tomorrow," Beth informed me through a yawn. "Since I'm sure you've been keeping new Teuton secrets from me, I've kept a few from you, too. But you'll find out in the morning."

I smiled a little, my weariness pulling my interest beneath a heavy shroud. "Did you get a new boogie board or something?"

Beth snickered. "You'll see."

I woke just after nine a.m. the next day, having slept a dreamless sleep. Beth stood brushing her hair before the full-length mirror on the back of her bedroom door, already having clad herself in a hot pink and orange one-piece bathing suit. I yawned and slid my way to the floor, knowing that I would have to root around in one of my smaller bags for one of my own bathing suits. "About time you got up. I was starting to think you'd died." Beth shot me a grin and laid her brush onto her dresser.

"Have to sleep in while I still can. You know we're both going to end up with eight o'clock classes." I opened my bag in the corner in search of proper attire.

"Yeah, you're probably right. You want breakfast, or do you want to wait until we get to Sugar Hill?"

"We can split a pack of Pop-Tarts if you haven't eaten yet," I suggested, and she exited the room while I stripped off my tank top and cloth shorts, tugging on my silvery bathing suit instead. I spent a few minutes taming my hair and putting it up in a tie before heading down the hallway to the bathroom.

We shared a pack of Pop-Tarts and drank orange juice from plastic cups while sitting beside each other on a floral-printed couch. Beth stared blankly at a silly cartoon on TV while she ate, and I busied myself with petting her family dog, a tan-and-white Sheltie named Jenna. "You might want to check the tides online before you go, so you know where to plant your towels," Aunt Linda reminded us from the doorway to the dining room when we had finished our breakfast.

"Oh yeah, good point!" Beth jumped to her feet and darted back down the hallway to the spare room that housed her family desktop. It was an old IBM with a dial-up internet connection.

I brought the cups to the kitchen to wash them at the sink, trailed by Jenna, who had apparently missed me.

Either that or maybe I still smelled like Thunar. "Do you want us here for dinner, Aunt Linda?" I asked while drying my hands.

"It's up to you two whether you're here or not, but if not, you'll miss Jens' burgers. He's going to grill when he gets off work." She winked at me, her eyes and hair brown like her daughter's. Beth really did not look much like my uncle, aside from the nose, which she was not pleased to have inherited. I wondered privately whether her American looks meant that her Teutonic blood was less than forty percent. I did not know whether her blood had ever been tested.

"That settles it. We'll be here for dinner," I resolved, bending down to ruffle the fur around Jenna's face.

Just as we started loading our beach stuff into the trunk of my Celica—two boogie boards, three towels, and a small sack containing things like sunscreen and tissues—a silver Sunfire with tinted windows pulled up to the curb in front of Beth's house. I glanced toward it briefly, wondering what its purpose was, and a second later I noticed Beth's brilliant grin. "You're taking two of us to the beach today," she informed me, waving toward the young man getting out of the Sunfire. "Unlike you, I've actually managed to find a guy my own age."

My mouth dropped open, and I rounded on my cousin. "You mean you have a *boyfriend?* And you didn't tell me? How long has this been going on?"

"We just started dating a couple months ago, so it's not like it's been *that* long." The young man approached while she spoke, and I scowled at Beth before turning to face her newfound partner, instantly smoothing my face into an expression of cool interest—a trait I had learned from my father. He looked about six feet tall with natural blond hair arranged in neat spikes atop his head, a pair of reflective sunglasses concealing his eyes, a chain with a Christian cross hanging around his neck, his right arm stretched out to greet me. He carried a boogie board over his left shoulder, his beach towel draped over his right.

"I'm guessing you're Beth's cousin Swanie. I'm Joel," he greeted, and I took his hand for a firm shake.

"You're right on that count, but apparently my secretive cousin failed to tell me that she's dating a surfer dude." I shot Beth another nasty look.

"Hey, I don't surf," Joel said with a laugh, moving to place his boogie board and towel among those already in my trunk. "Wow, this is a nice car!"

"She just paid cash for it yesterday," Beth interjected, apparently feeling the need to brag about my wealth.

I shut my trunk and rolled my eyes at the two of them, the notion of being the third wheel tingling at the back of my neck. This was something I had not yet experienced, for none of my Teuton friends were seriously dating aside from Marga. "No need to portray me like I'm some cash cow," I told my cousin, moving to the driver's side door to pull the seat forward. "I'm guessing you're both going to sit in the back?"

"Now your name is Thomas!" Beth squeezed my shoulder and slipped into the backseat, quickly followed by Joel, whose long legs would certainly be awkward crammed into the back. At least the driver's seat was pretty far up thanks to my short stature. I caught a whiff of what smelled like Axe deodorant.

Joel proved to be a welcome addition to our entourage, as it turned out. He had a playful sense of humor and seemed to enjoy discussing our shared interests and speculating on various landmarks that we passed on the drive. Joel's family lived in Medford, where his father ran a real estate business, and usually on beach trips they went to Long Beach Island rather than Ocean City. He good-naturedly griped that he had yet to convince Beth of LBI's superiority, and she declared that she would always prefer Ocean City since it was a dry town. "Not as many drunks bumbling around there, and the beaches don't stink of alcohol. The one time I went to the beach in Atlantic City, it was awful."

"Full of people in speedos, too, like Germany," I put in, for Beth and I had discussed the Atlantic City clientele on many occasions. While I was fully used to seeing naked sunbathers in the Englischer Garten in München and dodging bar-hopping groups when out with my Teuton girlfriends, I enjoyed Ocean City's family atmosphere. It was a refreshing break from the norm.

We ate lunch at Sugar Hill Subs on the way to the beach, a small business in Mays Landing that Aunt Linda had discovered years ago when she still had to work. I ordered a half of an Italian sub, my permanent favorite, stuffed to the brim with Italian meats and provolone cheese, topped with olive oil, lettuce, tomatoes, onions, and hot peppers. That along with the pizzas was one of the signature meals of New Jersey that I actually missed when I lived at home. Although all of the ingredients could be found in Germany, I had yet to find a suitable roll to complete the sandwich.

We spent several hours on the beach at Twenty-Fifth Street after scouring the area for a parking spot. Generally speaking, in the peak of summer, your best bet for parking in Ocean City fell toward the streets and avenues farthest from the public bathrooms. Joel declared that he could just go in the ocean if need be, which inspired Beth to rehash a story about one of the boys in her high school class who had allegedly pooped in the ocean. "There's no way he could have done that without being noticed," Joel proclaimed, while I shook with laughter at the mental image of such nonsense. "I mean, what if it floated? Did he just say, 'Oh, what's that?'"

The weather was perfect for relaxing on the beach that day. A pleasant breeze drifted from the southeast, the ocean rough enough to provide a decent ride on a boogie board. While the three of us stretched out lazily on Beth's giant blanket after a wondrous dip in the ocean, I glanced toward Joel through my prescription sunglasses. He lay on the opposite side of Beth with his hands behind his head, vibrant American flag patterns garnishing his soaked bathing suit. "So what are you going to study in college?" I asked. He would be accompanying us to the mountains of Virginia on Friday, mainly because he was 'very interested' in Beth and did not want to embark on a long-distance relationship.

"Marketing," he answered, his mirrored sunglasses turning in my direction. "My dad hopes I'll be able to run his business someday. Have to start somewhere."

"I know the feeling," I responded, remembering how much I would rather just immerse myself in music and art. At least I would have electives to round out my education.

"See, you two have more things in common than you know," Beth remarked, sounding pleased. I looked toward my cousin, where she lay between us with her face buried in her towel, letting the sun tan her back. Did she think that she needed my approval to date someone? I wondered whether my initial reaction had unsettled her. *Well, it's a lot easier for someone with blood like hers,* I knew, turning my face toward the sun again and shutting my eyes. *She can pretty much choose any guy in the world.* I sighed and endeavored to nip my envy in the bud.

Chapter Seventeen:
Clinging to My Identity

The three of us drove down to Virginia on Friday and spent the weekend settling into what was to be our home for the school year. Our dormitory was tucked away beside a fountained lake toward the back of the campus, situated on a street lined with dormitories and frat houses. It seemed that freshmen were the main occupant of our building, which meant that raucous parties would soon be unavoidable. Beth and I shared a room on the third floor with a small hallway that connected to Joel's room and our shared bathroom. There were several common areas on each floor, consisting of an outdated kitchen, a game room with pool tables, dart boards, and pinball machines, and a spacious chamber that consisted of nothing but tables and couches. "I certainly hope they pay people to clean these rooms," I muttered to Beth as we peered into the kitchen. I doubted that the resident assistant at the desk in the hallway would bother to monitor any parties.

"Probably student workers," my cousin figured, "but now you know why I said we need a fridge and a microwave. No way would I stick my stuff in that kitchen where anyone could get it." She curled her lip.

I agreed wholeheartedly, the spoiled part of me recoiling from the concept of living in such conditions for nine whole months. *Oh well, it's part of becoming an adult, I guess,* I told myself, trailing Beth's course back to our room.

On Sunday night, after we had both fully plotted out our class schedules—we would register tomorrow along with the rest of the freshman horde—Beth and I sat on the beanbag chairs Aunt Linda had given us, leaning back against our beds while sipping cans of soda and splitting a bag of popcorn. We had closed the door to Joel's portion of our apartment, because neither of us had decided how we felt about his roommate yet. He was a short guy with round glasses, a comb over, and a thick southern drawl. I had trouble understanding his dialect, since New Jersey's version of English was the type that I knew best. I still mocked my father whenever I heard him speak his British English, which usually incited him to swat playfully at me. I wondered how he was doing all by himself in the Thaden house.

"So you still haven't told me whether you've learned any wacky new Teuton secrets over the past three years," Beth commented at length, leaning her head back against the mattress of the bed she had chosen, the one closest to the window. Her brown eyes shifted toward me with a conspiratorial look. "I still think back to that night you first told me when I was working on my book about invisible cats."

I grinned. "I remember that book." It had been quite an imaginative tale, as most of Beth's were. She already had a talent for creative writing. Her plan of study encouraged her dream, unlike mine.

"Yeah, you came creeping up on me and spouted off this story about blood and elements and Germans and some ancient tome of devilish magic. I thought you were trying to prove you could think of stories as good as mine."

"And then I snatched your pencil and coated it with ice." I took my glasses off and laid them atop my blankets, then wiggled my eyebrows at Beth while a veil of blue overtook my vision.

Beth shook her head at me and looked away, chewing on some popcorn. "It took me a long time to forgive my dad, you know," she admitted, sounding rather disenchanted. "And sometimes I'm not sure whether I've really forgiven him. When I think about all your cousins on the Thaden side having these cool abilities I don't, it doesn't really sit well with me. I don't know. I love my mom, though."

I looked down at my small bowl of popcorn, pulling my ice back into my soul. "Technically if you want to blame someone, you need to blame my Mutti," I noted, reaching back to put my glasses on again. "If she hadn't stayed with your mom's family as an exchange student, your parents would never have met."

Beth looked pensive, her eyes moving from mine to the window to her right with its view of the lake. "Sometimes I think I need to do the blood-transfer." The yearning in her expression was clear, but I saw her shudder anyway.

"That's something you definitely *don't* need to do," I informed her, wishing that I had never mentioned that topic three years ago. "What person in their right mind would want to have their arteries cut out by a priest while they're conscious?"

"Yeah, I know," Beth said, her eyes on the ceiling. "And it's not like I know anybody to ask aside from you or my dad."

"And you wouldn't be okay with your Teuton blood costing one of our lives. That's exactly right," I finished for her, injecting a finality into my tone. "Being a Teuton isn't all fun and games, anyway. My list of potential husbands is practically nonexistent."

"Are you jealous about me and Joel?" Beth rose to her feet to stretch before turning for the sink to rinse out her bowl.

"Kind of," I admitted, though the truth was more like, *A load.* "I don't think he's really my type, though. I prefer black-haired guys."

"Like Hans," Beth translated over the sound of running water.

I gave a derisive noise. "His hair is more gray than black nowadays."

"All right, it's confession time," Beth announced when she had finished with her bowl. She marched over to where I sat and plopped down right beside me. I met her gaze with a bit of uncertainty, never fully prepared to lay myself bare before anyone, outsider or not. "Are you planning on staying pure until marriage?" she asked, her wide eyes searching my own.

I felt my forehead wrinkle at her question. "If I wasn't, pretty sure I would have taken up with one of my Pappi's business cronies by now. Did I tell you that at his winter party last year, one of them stuck his tongue between my lips?"

"No! Oh, gross!" Beth gagged.

I smirked at her. "I bit it."

She clapped a hand over her mouth. "You're kidding me!"

I shrugged my left shoulder. "It was just the tip. But that guy didn't come to our summer party, so apparently his only interest in my Pappi was to get a chance at me." I curled my lip in repugnance at the licentious habits of the wealthy. "I may not be a perfect Christian, but I still have my standards."

Beth grinned and wrapped her right arm around my shoulders, pulling me into a supportive hug. "Me too," she confessed, "and Joel agrees. We want to find a good church to attend while we're here so we don't get sucked into the party culture. I'm here to learn, not to lose my dignity."

I hugged her back, grateful for a roommate who shared my values. "Actually you might want to ask Kevin about that." I pulled away from her and got up to wash my own bowl out. "I think he said he's studying theology."

"Oh gosh, really? No wonder he looks like a nerd. Well, at least he shouldn't be too much of a problem for Joel, if that's the case. He'll probably spend most of his time studying."

When I finished at the sink and sat back down beside my cousin, she looked toward me lazily and repeated her earlier query. "So what wacky Teutonic magic did you learn in München over the past three years?"

I pursed my lips and considered, thinking first of the Torstein, which rested in its ring box on the shelf above my pillow between my alarm clock and box of tissues. As much as I wanted to share that secret with my cousin, something held me back for now, so instead I said, "I've learned a lot, probably more than I should know. Hans showed me some tricks about defending myself if someone ever tries to rob me or kidnap me. Check this out." I stretched my right arm out in front of me and allowed my ice to creep over my hand entirely, my fingers growing transparent, the nails extending into sharp points.

Beth gaped and shied away from me. "Good grief, Swanie, you could give Wolverine a run for his money with those!"

I laughed outright, thinking of the varied elemental abilities of the X-Men. "Not really, because his claws are metal, like my cousin Traudl. She's broken my frozen claws off before." I flexed my icy fingers, relishing the clinking sound they made.

"Does it hurt when she breaks them off?" Beth cringed as she gawked at the clear spikes extending from my fingernails.

"It did the first time because she ripped the nail off of its bed, too. Since then she's fought with a bit more decorum." I chuckled.

Beth slid closer to me and lifted a finger to touch my frozen hand cautiously. "Wow, it's *cold!*" she exclaimed, shivering.

"Of course it's cold, but it doesn't bother me." I pulled my element back, and my hand unfroze within seconds, returning to its natural tanned color, the heat of my blood driving away the chill.

From there, I told Beth some of the other things I had read in *Der Weg*, and I mentioned my love for my elderly mentor, the Lady of Muniche. I talked about my Teutonic friend Vreni, whose blood status was high enough to sense her element but not to control or create it. "I feel so bad for her, but at least she managed to find a decent Teuton boyfriend. If they stay together long enough, one day he may be able to awaken her fire."

"I can't get over the fact that Teutons use their elements while having sex," Beth remarked, her expression tinged with disapproval. "I mean, it would be *cold* getting in bed with you. You're going to need someone with a hot element to counter you." She paused for a beat and then spoke what I was thinking. "Is *that* why you're in love with Hans? Is it because he's fire?"

"I don't know, and I think I'm going to get in the shower. I don't hear the water running in there right now." I got to my feet and headed for my dresser to retrieve a fresh pair of underwear and a towel.

"I'll tell Joel goodnight while you're in there. Want me to say goodnight to Kevin on your behalf?" Beth shot me a sneaky grin on her way to the side door.

"Don't tempt him; I'd freeze him to death," I answered, and she chortled as she struck out for the guys' room.

In the coming months, I acclimated to both my new surroundings and my class and practice schedule. My private organ lessons quickly became my favorite class, right behind ceramics, which Beth and I had decided to take as a break from the humdrum of book learning. I had two business classes with Joel, and we sat next to each other during the lectures, commenting and making jokes about whatever happened to strike us. I was not particularly a fan of accounting, even though my math skills were decent enough. If Joel had not poked me every now and then, I would have fallen asleep during every single lecture. I had wanted to take it at noon, but by the time freshmen were allowed to register, eight o'clock was the only option left for Accounting 101. Beth got stuck taking World History 101 at that hour, which may have been worse in some ways. Luckily several of my high school classes had counted toward my history and English requirements.

By the end of October, I found myself barely able to wait for Christmas break and the chance to visit New Jersey once more. College life was not hard overall, but I looked forward to the holidays when I could enjoy more free time. The six hour time difference between Virginia and München made it difficult to coordinate a proper time to chat with Hans or any of my Teuton girlfriends, since they would generally be asleep once I had finished eating dinner. I tended to catch Hans on ICQ on Friday afternoons, and on weekends I chatted regularly with Erika, who was thrilled to be delving deeper into her studies of watercolors. Most of the time, though, I ended up too busy to sign onto ICQ or the Teuton forum, or I logged on and waited for Hans in vain. I wondered sometimes whether he purposely stayed offline when I could actually be there. He probably wanted to reinforce Sebastian's suggestion that I find a boyfriend at college.

His lack of response often frustrated me. On the last Friday in October, I signed onto the Teuton forum for the first time since Tuesday and discovered a half dozen new messages from that nineteen-year-old in Regensburg, each one more flirtatious than the last. In the final one, sent at eight-thirty a.m. German time, he wrote, "I just found out that I can get a couple of free tickets to the Christmas rock festival in Nürnberg from one of my buddies. It would be great if you could come. Then we could finally meet in person while doing something we both like."

I shook my head in disgust and muttered a curse in Bayerisch, glad that I was alone in the room at the time. I really had no interest in meeting the boy, even if he did have decent Teuton blood. I doubted my father would be too happy if I started dating an aspiring artist—and a broke one at that. I thanked my lucky stars that I could give the boy a good excuse this time, and typed that I would still be in the U.S. during the holidays. After sending the reply, I glanced down at the list of users signed on at the bottom of my computer screen and breathed a sigh of relief at the presence of *Das Dunkle Feuer*. I pulled up the personal messenger again and wrote a new one: "That idiot from

Regensburg, *Idealismus,* won't leave me alone. He just asked me out to the rock festival in Nürnberg this Christmas. I think you should ban him." I clicked the send button and returned to checking the new posts.

Three minutes later a reply popped up. "His behavior has been better than some on the public portion of the forum, and according to Regensburg records he is ninety-one percent Teutonic. If his only fault seems to be his attraction to you, it's your business to deal with it, not mine."

I groaned in irritation and replied, "I've tried to discourage him since he started this up last February. It's not my fault he got a crush on me because we both enjoy metal music. Some of the others think he's gay, since he likes designing comics. I wish he was." I snickered to myself and hit *send.*

Hans' reply popped up less than a minute later this time. "Tell him you're married."

He was not taking this seriously. "That won't work. He knows I'm single. Maybe I should claim I've gotten a boyfriend here at school." A wicked grin spread across my face as I considered that plan.

I had finished reading the new posts on the German history forum before a new message popped up. My gray eyes flew open and I slammed my fist down on the desk when I read this one. "Maybe you *should* get a boyfriend there at school."

I seethed and typed a scathing reply. "I can't do that, you idiot. I'm the only Teuton here. And absolutely *none* of the boys I've met so far, here or in Germany, Teuton or not, have been my type. You know that."

I began to regret what I had said the instant after I hit *send.* I should not have called Hans an idiot. He was far from that. But he certainly could be obtuse at times. I sighed and finished looking through all of the new posts, waiting fifteen minutes before Hans finally responded. "Maybe if you'd deign to give some of them a chance, you'll discover that they *are* your type. You need to pull the blinders from your eyes, Swanie, or you'll be single your entire life."

That was the last straw. I clicked the browser closed and shut my laptop, pushing the chair back so swiftly from the desk that it almost toppled over. I crossed the floor to the sink and splashed my face with cold water, then stared at myself for a long moment. The strain of schoolwork, organ practice, and guy troubles, on top of worry about the Torstein and whether or not I should use it again, had put dark lines under my eyes and set my mouth in a permanent frown.

All of the boys I had ever met ended up trying to woo me, usually because of my father's money, and like him, I refused to date someone that shallow. Here in Virginia, I had already been asked out by five different guys in my classes. Some of them knew about my wealth, while others just thought it would be fascinating to go out with a foreigner. None of the five had really hit it off with me. "And why can't *you* just give *me* a chance?!" I cried at the mirror, speaking Teutonica and thinking of Hans. He never would. I knew that. If only he would.

Chapter Eighteen:
The Teutonic May Dances

The rest of my freshman year at college passed in an unremarkable fashion. I made some new friendships, most of which were as shallow as the ones I had built with Beth's peers years ago. Most of my fellow business majors had chosen their field of study. I was the outlier who had signed up for business management only to please my father. When groups of us met for meals or study sessions, oftentimes chatter would arise along the vein of climbing the corporate ladder and solidifying a legacy, topics that inspired little excitement for me. I enjoyed losing myself in resounding tones of organ music whenever I practiced, the power of commanding such a great instrument speaking more deeply to my soul than the concept of being Swanhilde von Thaden, CEO of Süddeutsche Getriebe.

By the time graduation rolled around on the first Saturday of May 1999, I could hardly wait to leave the university behind in a trajectory for Dulles Airport. My father had arranged for me to fly back to München on a jet owned by one of the most prominent business owners in the city, and thus I looked forward to actually sleeping on the plane, since it would doubtless have beds. Beth and

Joel planned to follow me to the airport in his Sunfire, and once I had gone, Beth would drive my Celica back to New Jersey for the summer. I warned her that if she chose to use my car all summer instead of hers and I came back to any sort of scratch, she would never hear the end of it. She pledged to treat it respectfully and not let Joel take it anywhere; he promised to egg her car in retaliation.

I pondered the Torstein again on the journey over the ocean, grateful that I would not have studies to distract me from its mysteries during the summer. My father wanted me to start trailing him part-time at work so I could get a taste of his responsibilities, but work should not occupy my mind in the evenings. I needed to think about where and when I should travel next and who I should bring with me. I needed to consult with both Hans and Lady Muniche about it. I still did not feel comfortable with bringing my Teuton girlfriends into this quandary. My two mentors had pretty much wiped that possibility from my options completely.

When I finally arrived at the doorstep of the Thaden house early Sunday morning, Sebastian and my father came flying out of the door, both of them looking overjoyed to see me. I hugged my father for a long moment, tears coming to my eyes as I told him how much I had missed him. He had missed me too, he said, and he was so glad to have me back for such a long summer break. "Things get boring around here without you," he claimed, giving me a fond smile.

"I can't see how that's possible with Basti here," I rejoined. Sebastian, who was pulling my suitcases up the ramp to the front door, abruptly let go of them and swung me into a late hug. He promised that he had been very well-behaved during my absence, which made my father laugh. Once inside, I greeted Lise and Siggi at the foot of the front stairs, hugging them both.

Some time later I found Hans standing alone in the kitchen sipping a cup of black coffee, dressed in a gray suit and blue shirt for morning church at ten. He set his mug down and looked up when I entered the room, and the fire in his dark blue eyes, combined with his welcoming expression, took my breath away. In a single second I forgot about all of the foolish boys at college; I was back where I belonged. Hans' thin lips opened into a glorious smile while I stood frozen in the doorway, and he walked slowly towards me and stated, "It is good to have you home."

I desperately wanted to throw my arms around him, but I held myself back, as always, and replied simply, "I'm so glad to be back."

Though I had not returned home in time to witness any of the traditional German festivities involving Maypoles, which took place on the same day that I departed Virginia that year, the Teutons held their own smaller May festival on the third Saturday of the month. I had attended the May dances for the past three years, and I could hardly wait for the next one. The celebration would be held, as always, at the Teuton meeting place of München, a glade cleared out of the forest beside the Isar some distance outside the city itself. Everyone who gathered there would be of higher Teutonic blood, and along with the typical folk and Maypole dances there would be food and beer, stories and games, and possibly elemental stunts. I especially looked forward to catching up with my girlfriends and Lady Muniche.

The third Saturday of May dawned beautiful and breezy, the sky dotted with puffs of cumulus, the temperature pleasant enough that I did not need a jacket. I asked Lise to ensure that the stays and ribbons of my pale blue Dirndl were properly fastened. She did so with enthusiasm, taking the time afterward to braid my hair and tie two light blue ribbons to the top and bottom of the braid. "The whole of München will be lining up to dance with you, Swanie," she praised, examining her handiwork with my attire and hair.

I smiled at Lise and snatched my purse off of my bed, then turned for the hallway, prepared to slink my way down the back stairs *en route* to the side gate, where I would meet Hans on the street to drive to the festival. "Let's hope I have the stamina to withstand them all! Do you happen to know where Pappi is?" We had both exited my room, and I raised an eyebrow at my former nanny.

"I think he's still out and about with his business friends. He mentioned that he'd be having dinner at the Löwenbräu tonight."

"Good, good!" That solved the issue of escaping without notice. I pointed my feet toward the back staircase and warned in parting, "Don't you say anything to him about where I've gone!"

"I would never! Enjoy yourself!" Lise waved at me as I departed, and I flashed a grin in her direction before turning all of my attention to what lay ahead. Before leaving the house, I paused in the kitchen to grab a container of cookies frosted with black and yellow, the colors of München. I had gotten them specially made from a local bakery.

Hans had parked his black BMW by the curb outside the side gate. He stood waiting for me when I emerged from the ivy-coated wall, opening the passenger door for me like a proper gentleman. "I see you took the traditional route this time," he observed, appraising my Dirndl with a satisfied expression.

"My summer dresses have too much lace and veils to withstand the vehemence of ice," I explained with a sly smirk. I seated myself, and he shut the door behind me after making sure that all of my clothing had made it into the car.

"We'll have to hope that the lowered gate and the banner that says 'private event' will be enough to deter any unwanted visitors, if you truly wish to set your ice free," Hans remarked once he had gotten into the car himself. He wore a black T-shirt, black shorts, and black shoes, his priestly robes lumped in the back seat for the moment. "I often fear that one day, someone will go too far at one of these May dances. It's the largest yearly gathering of Teutons at the meeting place in the forest, and the *only* one that we have apart from the crowd that calls München its home. One day some drunken fool will shoot a glaring lightning bolt across the Isar in the dark, and it'll be seen and reported." Hans pulled away from the curb with a skeptical expression, guiding the car in a southwesterly direction.

"But that's why you and all your cronies come to these festivals dressed like the Grim Reaper, to keep all of us peasants in check," I pointed out, referencing the other five priests on the Teuton Council of München.

Hans looked sideways at me and said with just a hint of humor in his tone, "Well, this peasant beside me had better be ready to dance. Quite a few younger people are coming, if we can believe the chatter on our forum."

"Yeah, I know. Even Vreni says she and her family are coming."

After driving for about twenty minutes, we reached the parking area for the trail that led to the Teuton meeting place of München. A dirt lot off of a woodsy road, it was already practically filled with cars, and I suspected that more people would be arriving as dinnertime drew closer. Hans got out of the car first and then came around to open my door for me. Afterward he retrieved his cloak from the backseat and put it on, keeping the hood down. Lastly, he grabbed a rolled blanket from the hatch along with a container of Bavarian potato salad that he had likely made himself. Thus accoutered, he nodded at me with the words, "Shall we?"

So we struck out for the trail and squeezed around the gate with its notice about the 'private event.' I saw that the warning was written in German, Bayerisch, and English. "They should have put it in Teutonica, too," I joked.

"That might have made it too obvious." Hans winked at me and grinned a toothy grin, his feet seeming to glide along the trail beneath his robes, their shadow blending with the shades of the forest.

When we reached the end of the kilometer-long path, we paused at the opening for a moment, observing the goings-on in the clearing. Over a hundred people were already present by my count, and a group of about fifteen men were in the process of raising the Maypole—which looked to be about ten meters high—in the center of the glade. To the left of the trail stood several folding tables, around which a cluster of ladies gathered arranging the food and beer. Near the riverbank some distance from the trees a fire had already been lit, tended by a knot of young adults. Various people had set up lawn chairs and blankets, their lively conversations filling the air. A coterie of children darted along the outskirts of the clearing, chasing a blond boy who had stolen the ribboned crown of the Maypole.

I looked up at Hans, shaking my head a bit at the collective celebrations of our people, and he handed me his container of salad. "Go deposit this with the rest of the food, would you? I think I'd better put an end to this before the streamers get tangled." Several of the women had begun to chase after the children, but none of them had managed to catch the leader of the pack.

I started toward the folding tables but kept my eyes on Hans, who abruptly stepped into the trees to throw his blanket over top of the blond boy. I heard him squeal, and he dropped his prize as Hans scooped him into the blanket and threw it over his shoulder, child included. The other children ground to a halt and stared up at Hans in horror, and I heard him say in an eerie voice, "You had all better start behaving, for Krampus has come early, and he will catch every single one of you!"

The children shrieked and scattered, and I started laughing outright. One of the women snatched the May-pole's crown from the forest floor as Hans deposited the blond youngster onto the ground, setting him free with an inaudible rebuke. The kid took off, looking scared to death, and I continued to chuckle when I handed the platter of salad and the container of cookies to a grizzled older woman at the tables. "Maybe they'll *all* start behaving now, including those bunglers trying to raise the Maypole," she commented. I struggled to calm my laughter, and an instant later I heard several familiar voices calling my name.

I met my girlfriends at the riverbank, exchanging enthusiastic hugs with Erika, Trudi, and Traudl, and greeting Marga with a grin. Vreni waved at me from where she sat a short distance away with her boyfriend Stefan; they were using sticks to push leaves around the light green surface of the Isar. Someone had laid a striped blanket out beneath a linden tree at the water's edge. I saw that it held a growing collection of purses, so I added mine to the pile before turning my full attention to my friends. "So where's Ina?" I inquired, moving to situate myself on the riverbank not far from Vreni. I wanted her to feel more included in the group despite the low state of her blood.

"Oh shit, she doesn't know." I twisted my neck around to face Traudl, who stood beneath the linden tree at the water's edge. Trudi whispered something to her, both of my cousins eyeing me in a rather despondent fashion.

"I don't know what?" I pressed, a touch of worry scratching at my chest.

Marga plunked herself down at my left side, the only one of us clad in casual clothes. She ran a hand through her brown curls before favoring me with a tragic look. "Ina's engaged," she said in a low voice. "She accepted the offer of a wealthy broker named Walfrid who lives in Berlin. He's a Teuton, but he's lived up there for two decades now. His first wife died last year after giving him a child."

My eyes bugged, and I had to consciously order my ice not to explode in my veins at this news. "You . . . you've got to be kidding!" I cried out. "She wanted either Fonsi or Mane. I know it!"

Marga shook her head once and chewed on her bottom lip, its sparkling gloss reflecting the sunlight. "What she really wanted was to never have to worry about money for the rest of her life. She wanted to join a family like yours."

"So she just . . . met some rich dude who lives in Berlin and agreed to leave her family behind? How much older is he?" I drew my arms around my body, imagining a stern, suited businessman claiming my airy friend.

"I think he's in his late thirties. He and his first wife were together a decade before they decided to try having kids. Didn't work out so well."

"But Ina's ninety-five percent!" I exclaimed—she was the only Teuton friend I had whose blood matched mine. "I mean, it's not like she's going to have better luck! Hopefully he only wanted one kid." I shuddered and plunged my fingers into the grass beneath me, trying to steady myself.

"Hopefully," Erika said, sounding disgusted, coming over to sit at Marga's side. "But we all know how Teuton men are. They want all women to breed."

"Hey, *I'm* not like that!" Stefan cut in, apparently having snooped on our conversation. I glanced toward him, running my gaze over his Lederhosen and light green traditional tunic. "I actually want to build a life with my partner, thank you very much." He pulled Vreni close and gave her a peck on the cheek. Erika made a vomiting noise, and I snickered, watching my cousins have a splashing contest at the water's edge.

"What about you, Marga?" I probed, my eyes on the runnels of liquid coating Traudl's ponytail. Part of me really wanted to freeze it, but I needed to catch up on my friends' lives first. "So how's it going with you and the Teutonic dude? He didn't come today?" If he had, I figured he would have attached himself to our group.

"We broke up," Marga said, turning her gaze to the opposite bank, tapping her fingers on the sides of her thighs. "One of Stefan's cronies invited me to dance at the New Year's festival, and I haven't looked back since."

Maybe Marga's the Teuton version of Morgen and Ava, I thought to myself. I heard one of the council members announce the outset of the dances and got to my feet, holding out a hand to Marga. "Is he someone I know?" I asked.

"Not sure if you've met him. He's from the Allgäu and came here for college. His name's Ivo, and he couldn't come today because he's bartending."

"Huh," I said in response, not really having much to add to the topic. Erika snagged two streamers of the Maypole and held one out to me, officially inviting me to my first traditional dance of the day.

I took the time to study the Teutonic Maypole after accepting a streamer from Erika. Like its Bavarian counterparts, it was painted from top to bottom in the state colors of light blue and white; the streamers were of yellow and black, the colors of München. Instead of the usual representations of local industries, painted placards of the most common Teutonic elemental categories decorated either side of the Maypole. The four primaries were at the bottom: earth, air, fire, and water. Further up I saw increasingly smaller images including whirlwind, stone, snow, and lightning.

"I see that they went with snow instead of ice *again,*" I remarked to Erika, whose yellow streamer already showed traces of dampness as the dance began. "I don't get why our people seem to think snow is the catch-all for frozen water."

"Maybe we should make our own Maypole and set it up in Lady Muniche's back garden," Erika mused, weaving her damp streamer with mine, which I had dutifully sprinkled with ice. "Water, ice, yellow fire, metal, air, and earth. That pretty much covers the basic categories right there."

"If we included Lady Muniche too, we'd have wind, so all we'd be missing is energy," I noted, thinking through the Teutons I knew who claimed energy-related elements. None of them would really fit in with our group.

"If we're going to include Lady Muniche, then we'd be obliged to include her boyfriend. Rudi's lightning." Erika gave me a sly look, and we both giggled, the dance soon becoming too spirited to continue our discussion.

I danced around the Maypole three times but spent most of the event watching the other dancers. Our conclave of Teutons and Teutonic Germans had grown to nearly two hundred people, and the Maypole had only twenty-four streamers. I danced once with Trudi and once with Vreni, who looked thrilled to be involved when I offered her a streamer. She had cropped her hair short and dyed it purple, its color matching her Dirndl perfectly. I felt Stefan's eyes upon us the entire time we danced, and when we had finished he playfully complained that I should not claim his girlfriend for myself. "I've known her a lot longer than you have, so suck it up," I retorted with a sneer, prompting both of them to laugh.

I saw that Hans danced only once at this particular gathering, partnered with Lady Muniche herself, her wind seeming to both agitate and complement his black fire with an artistry that I had not yet achieved. Lady Muniche also danced with a couple of children, with Rudi, and with the oldest priest on the council; I knew him only as Herr Dantzler, an authoritative figure that I preferred to avoid. I wanted to try to speak with my elderly mentor alone for a minute or two, to ask her further advice on my plans for the Torstein. I had left it in its ring box in my room. Since nobody had disturbed it there during my months in the dorm, I had grown more complacent about its safety. Though both Hans and Lady Muniche had implied that others may seek it out and try to use it for evil, I had yet to face any potential rivals on that count. As long as I could keep its existence under wraps, I had begun to doubt that I would ever have to deal with villains trying to steal it from me.

After the Maypole dances, the majority of the gathered Teutons gravitated toward the tables in search of food and drink. I managed to edge my way closer to Lady Muniche as I heard her ask Rudi to fill a plate for her. It was odd to see him clad in the priestly robes, since I usually encountered him in his handyman role. He caught my eye and raised a hand in greeting before heading for the tables, and the Lady turned to face me, doubtless having wondered who Rudi had thought to acknowledge. "Ah, Swanie! So good to see you back home," she greeted, her blue eyes shining with welcome as she reached out to embrace me.

I hugged her tightly and said, "It's really great to be back. As much as I love America, there's nothing like being among my own people." She pulled back from me and offered a sympathetic smile, and then I quickly plunged into the subject that had gnawed deeply at my brain during the past few months. "What do you think if I . . . brought my cousin Beth . . . on my next adventure?" I asked her, lowering my voice considerably. I glanced around at the others standing nearby. None seemed to be paying close attention to us. "She's been my best friend and confidant since childhood . . . and I know she's trustworthy."

Lady Muniche looked into my eyes, her own appearing both thoughtful and enthusiastic on my behalf. After a moment's pause, she bent her head close to mine and murmured, "Well it sounds like you've found the perfect companion for your next adventure. I say go for it." She smiled, and a sense of vindication clasped my heart.

Chapter Nineteen:
Personal Preference

Following the Teutonic May dances, the remainder of my summer in München fell quickly into a routine. I began to work for my father as his personal assistant on Mondays, Tuesdays, and Thursdays, storing the extra money I earned in my savings account. I spent most of my free time at the house, lying outside working on my tan on the expansive back deck, swimming in the pool, or enjoying peaceful walks in the shade of our gardens and woods. I practiced the organ at home and at the Frauenkirche and Alter Peter. I also went roller blading around München with my Teuton girlfriends, and sometimes we would stop at one of the many cafés as a group to chat about events in our lives. At one of these gatherings, Erika pulled me aside to ask whether she could visit my house by herself at some point. She wanted to use me as the subject matter for one of her paintings for her senior art show in Vienna. I readily agreed.

She came on the last Friday in June, and we spent the entire afternoon outside in the forest while she worked on her art. I dressed in one of my more Gothic dresses for the occasion since I knew Erika liked that style; it consisted of a black corset with dark pink swirls and a skirt of layered magenta veils. I put on a flowered choker that matched the corset and made up my face in appropriate fashion, using contacts instead of my usual glasses. Erika posed me in the gazebo and beneath a fir tree beside the stream, sketching me in both positions and taking pictures of me in many more. "I may have to create an entire series of paintings with you as the model," she remarked at one point. "It can be the 'Gothic Teuton Maiden' series."

I guffawed and trailed the fingers of my right hand in the water of the stream. "You'd better take a few shots of me with my ice awakened if you want to go that direction." She responded that she did not intend to insert any fantasy into this particular series of paintings, so I shook the dampness off of my fingertips and kept my ice confined in my soul. "So why did you pick me for this exercise out of all your Teuton friends?" I asked while she continued with her sketches. "Do you like to draw short women or something?"

"No one will know you're only a hundred fifty-six centimeters when I paint you."

That was probably true. "Well, Marga's the best looking of us now that Ina's gone. But maybe you have trouble painting curls." I grinned toward my friend.

Erika shook her head and muttered, "All the women in your family are oblivious to their charm. Now quit talking. I'm trying to sketch your face."

I did not particularly agree with her assessment. If I really had 'charm,' one of the young Teuton men in the city would have asked me out by now. My cousins had started having luck on that front at long last, for Mane had shared two dances with Trudi at the May festival. And according to Traudl, they had gone out to dinner twice since then. Traudl did not expect to land a guy at all, for she considered her element to be 'unsexy.' I think she had long ago resigned herself to experiencing traditional family life by proxy through her fiery sister.

Four hours and six cigarettes later, Erika deemed her efforts complete for the moment, and we returned to the house for dinner. My father was out with his business friends, so I invited both Sebastian and Gregor to eat with us at the dining room table. Erika got along well with both of them, chatting with Sebastian about metal music and praising Gregor's Dampfnudeln. We watched *Titanic* on the big screen in the game room afterward, my friend commenting on the artwork and cinematography, pointing out details that I had not noticed before. Though I admired visual art, music was my first love, and thus I preferred to simply enjoy the soundtrack, musing on the emotions it evoked.

We made our way upstairs to my bedroom just after ten p.m., Erika having imbibed more Riesling than proper. Luckily her stomach seemed to tolerate it, but I did have to guide her up the stairs. "I didn't behave like a proper guest," she lamented as I led her into my bedroom and closed the door behind us. "We should be having a girls' night in, and all I did was drink."

"Hey, you worked hard all afternoon. It's fine as long as you don't throw up." I smirked at her, and she staggered toward the bathroom.

Later on, we sat on the lounge chairs outside on my balcony, the deepening twilight pulling night's cool shroud over our conversations. I had changed into my summer pajamas and put my glasses back on, gazing at the ever-increasing stars, many of them dulled thanks to the city lights of München. "You know the thing I worry about the most?" Erika said at length, clicking her lighter to ignite another cigarette. I rolled my head toward where she lay several steps away from me, clad in a breezy nightgown that left little up to the imagination. She had her right knee pulled up with her left calf balancing upon it, her hazel eyes blinking at the dark treetops. "I worry about becoming München's Lady after our old friend dies."

I wrinkled my forehead, the topic taking me completely by surprise. "What?"

"Let's be real, Swanie." Erika shifted her eyes toward me and took a drag on her cigarette. "Lady Muniche is ninety-three. How many people do *you* know who've lived much longer than that? And once she's gone, someone will have to take her place at the keyholder's side." She grimaced and tapped her cigarette over the ashtray on the table between our chairs.

She had a point. "I don't even know who the keyholder is," I said, thinking back to all that I had read in *Der Weg* about the two honorary leaders of Teuton cities. The Lady housed a city's soul, some sort of supernatural entity that bound her and amplified her wisdom. The keyholder kept the literal and figurative "keys" of the city. Centuries ago when walls surrounded the larger cities, the keyholders would unlock the gates each morning and secure them each night. In modern times, the keyholder was expected to govern the Teutons that called his city home, to punish those who misused their powers, to foster the success of the Teuton community. But though I had learned a lot about my people since my first elemental dance in 1992, I did not know the identity of München's keyholder.

"Nobody knows who he is," Erika corrected with a bleak snicker. "Our Lady friend says that he prefers to—"

"—work behind the scenes," I finished for her, having heard Lady Muniche repeat that mantra many times. Though every Teuton in our city knew and loved our elderly mentor, her male counterpart preferred to skulk in the shadows. Years ago she had actually been married to the previous keyholder—the man who had fathered her two daughters—but that one had died long before I was born.

"I think Rudi's the keyholder. And I don't know about you, but no *way* would I want to marry that old dude, no matter how good he may be at keeping my house from falling apart." Erika's tone sounded quite acerbic, and she gestured with her free hand while she spoke, as though she wished to fight fate itself should the bonds of the city fall upon her.

"He's not *that* old," I reminded her, though the idea of marrying the stocky man of lightning did not appeal to me, either. "I think he's not even fifty yet."

"Do you actually *like* him that way?" Erika eyeballed me in disbelief.

"No! But you know as well as I do that no one can fight the bonds of the city. They're stronger than the spiritual bonds that priests weave around their wives."

"Teutonic rituals are all a bunch of misogynistic crap," Erika spat, puffing on her cigarette and glaring at the moon. "Don't want women knowing the spells, so let's take them out. Don't want women misusing their gifts, so teach the priests how to bind them. Women need to breed and preserve Teuton blood for the future. It makes me so *angry!*" Erika cursed and ground the tip of her cigarette into the ashtray, extinguishing its garish glow. "It pisses me off that I have to worry about men, men, men. I don't even *like* men."

My eyes widened, and I looked toward my friend again. "Are you saying . . . that you're . . . ." I did not know if I should speak the word. Maybe I was misreading her meaning.

Erika met my gaze and plunked her legs back down on her chair. I could not make out her expression in the gloaming, but I sensed that she was trying to gather her courage. "I like girls," she clarified, her posture extremely tense. "And I know that Teutons think that lesbians are worthless. But there's no way, *no way* I'd want this city to bind me to a man. And I don't know how to escape it."

I stared back at her, at a loss for words. I abruptly wondered how long she had known, and how long it had eaten away inside her like a worm. *And here I've been thinking the Torstein is a burden* . . . . "Well . . . maybe you can find a Teuton girlfriend," I suggested.

"Don't make me laugh." Erika rolled her eyes and leaned back against her chair. "You know we're all taught that we're supposed to marry and have kids. I'm probably the only Teuton lesbian in existence."

"You can't be the only one," I said immediately, trying to come up with some way to ease my friend's fears. "I'm sure you can find one somewhere. Maybe try hinting about it on the forum where you have a bit of anonymity."

"Yeah, and just shout the truth for Hans to hear. Besides, having a Teuton girlfriend wouldn't disqualify me from becoming München's next Lady."

"You'd have to be married in a Teutonic wedding or bound in the spirit," I recited.

"No Teuton priest would marry me to a woman. Everybody knows that."

I could not disagree; all of the priests that I knew were traditionalists, Hans included. I looked from the sky to Erika, the moonlight illuminating her red hair with a ghostly sheen. "Have you told your parents yet?"

She winced. "The only people who know are my friends in Vienna. There's actually a girl I'm starting to like there. She looks similar to you, but she's Greek. An outsider." Erika sighed and slipped her hands behind her head. "I don't know if I'll ever tell my parents, to be honest. I might just move away permanently after I graduate." I could tell that Erika was trying hard to sound casual, but her entire body looked taut.

"But your parents seem open-minded, though," I pointed out. "After all, your dad did the blood-transfer on your Mutti's behalf. I don't think they'd disown you."

"I don't know. I don't think I'm brave enough yet." Erika got to her feet and stretched, then shuffled to the edge of my balcony, leaning upon the railing as she stared down toward the deck and pool. I remained in my seat for a few moments, unsure how to comfort my friend, for it had become clear that her struggles were far different from mine. But eventually I got up and walked to her side, laying my bare arms upon the railing and gazing out across the gardens to the trees.

"What about you, Swanie?" Erika asked, the freshness of her element reaching cautiously toward my ice. "You're the only one in our group who never really contributes to girlie chats about guys. Aside from me, that is."

I knew what she was really asking. I could detect the hopefulness in the mist that swirled around me, settling upon my skin. I looked again at the forest below, my eyes easily catching the warm glow of the lights at Hans' cottage. At this hour on a Friday, he was likely reading something, maybe Kafka, maybe Goethe. *She just opened herself up to you. It's only fair for you to do the same.* "That's because there's only one guy I like," I admitted in a whisper, shivering a little as my element cooled my veins.

"Ah." I caught the disappointment in Erika's tone, but when I looked toward her, she just nodded. "Hans?"

I felt taken aback. "Is it that obvious?"

"Maybe not to everyone, but I've seen your eyes following him at the festivals. I was starting to wonder whether you'd actually admitted it to yourself."

"It's just a dream," I repeated, slumping a bit on the railing and looking away from my friend. She had pulled her element back, so I worked on doing the same, though I suspected that it would cool me until we put this subject to rest.

"Am I the only person you've ever told?"

"You and my cousin Beth. I don't feel like it would go over well in our group, knowing that the rich girl's in love with her Pappi's accountant."

"Yeah." Erika sounded sympathetic now, and after a pause she asked, "Have you ever told him how you feel?" I recoiled at the mere idea, but Erika pressed on. "Maybe you should. How can you be sure he doesn't feel the same?"

"He doesn't. I'm just a student to him, a silly, naïve teenager."

I turned away from the railing, intending to go back inside. I had had enough of this discussion already. I never felt comfortable confessing the foolishness of my heart to anyone, friend or stranger. Before I could get far, Erika took hold of my left shoulder, prompting me to halt. When I looked up at her face, she spoke a question that chilled me to the core. "But if Hans offered to bind your Teuton spirit and make you his wife, would you agree?"

I could not meet her gaze, and I felt myself blushing despite the ice churning in my veins. My silence apparently spoke more clearly than my voice. Her fingers squeezed my shoulder in a supportive manner before letting go. "There's nothing wrong with wanting that," Erika said quietly, "but since he works for your Pappi, you'll probably have to make the first move. And I know you're strong enough."

We ate breakfast with my father the following morning around nine-thirty. He looked like he had not slept well, but he showed polite interest while Erika told him about her senior art show and the various subjects she intended to portray. I held my peace during most of the meal, preferring to concentrate on my farina while my brain replayed Erika's advice on repeat: *You'll probably have to make the first move . . . bind your Teuton spirit . . . make the first move . . . I know you're strong enough . . . you're strong enough . . . .*

I was not strong enough, and by the time I had finished my meal, a sense of annoyance had crept into the pit of my stomach. I looked from my father, who sat listening to Erika with a tired smile, sipping casually from his company coffee mug, to my closest Teuton girlfriend, bubbling over with zeal about her craft.

How can both of them just act so nonchalant about everything? Erika just told me that she likes girls, but now she's brushed it off to talk about painting like her prefer- ences are no big deal. And there's my Pappi, the Teuton who pretends that the magic of his blood doesn't exist. And then there's me, trying to live a normal life while longing for the love of an old man . . . and keeping all the secrets of time travel, let's not forget about that. Why am I the only one who can't find peace with normal life no matter how hard I try . . . ?

"Erika's favorite subject to paint is women," I cut into their conversation, my irritation with myself having over- come my discretion. I picked up my glass of orange juice and shifted my eyes toward my friend's face. Pallor had overtaken her countenance. "You should tell him why that is."

Silence fell around the table, and Erika glared at me with an affronted look. My father averted the impending eruption with a businessman's practiced finesse. "I would guess that's because women's bodies are more aesthetically pleasing than men's, generally speaking." I caught his reproachful glance.

"That's certainly true," Erika allowed, "but I'll admit that sometimes women are just as aggravating as men." She ate a spoonful of farina and glowered at me.

"But men are the ones that bind us. And that's what Erika wants to avoid." I looked pointedly toward my father, who had pushed his chair back from the table. I thought I detected an abrupt glow of comprehension in his gray eyes.

"True. And the old priests are the worst." Erika laid her spoon down with a resounding clang, her hazel eyes leveling a warning at me. I had gone far enough. If I explored this subject any further, she would certainly tell my father what I had told her last night: that I was in love with his servant, a man nearly eight years his senior.

Gregor passed through at that moment to collect our dishes and silverware, and when he had gone, my father rose from his chair and nodded once at Erika. "If that's what you want to avoid, I'd suggest talking with your dad about it," he advised. Then he headed toward the back staircase with coffee mug in tow, leaving my friend and me staring at each other in confusion. Was that supposed to be some sort of hint?

"Your Pappi's weird," Erika declared at length, and I had to agree.

Chapter Twenty:
How Could I Stop Loving Him?

After Erika had gone home, I spent the remainder of the afternoon and evening thinking about both the Torstein and my unrequited love for Hans, listening to a variety of metal music while I pondered. I played two albums by the Finnish band Nightwish twice; thus far, the singer of that band impressed me the most out of all of the metal singers I enjoyed. I had my father to thank for my discovery of that band. He had happened upon their show at a conference in Helsinki over a year ago. Their lyrics spoke deeply to me that day, while I ruminated on my impossible desires.

What if I've been looking at this wrong the whole time? Maybe I should take Hans on my next trip through time. Maybe if we share some crazy adventure, he'd finally reciprocate my feelings. And if we got together in the past, it's not like my Pappi would have any say about it. But who am I kidding? He'd just come up with some stupid excuse like he did last time. "I'd rather not run into myself." My best bet would be to convince Beth to come, and then stay in the past long enough to get over my ridiculous yearnings for my father's servant. If we travel to somewhere in Teuton history, maybe I could find some other fiery Teuton who could break Hans' hold on me. Maybe . . . .

If I decided to take a trip several centuries into the past, I would have to prepare extensively first. I supposed that with the language barrier, I had about a thousand-year window in which I could safely travel. I spoke Teutonica decently enough, and my Latin was improving thanks to my college studies. I also needed to consider dress and customs. I would have to sew several outfits that matched the time period as closely as possible. As a woman I knew that wherever I went, I would likely have little sway in the past because of widespread chauvinism. Two women would not be much improvement, but Beth had a boyfriend. Maybe it would be wise to ask both her and Joel to come.

Around sunset that day, I suddenly had an inspiration while lying on my bedspread stroking Thunar's gray fur. *Maybe I should get some outside opinions on this. And there is a way . . . .* I jumped to my feet and darted for my desktop, signing onto the internet and logging into my account on the Teuton forum. I did not waste time checking messages or new posts. Instead, I moved the mouse to the "start new topic" button and clicked, then paused with my fingers hovering over the keyboard, trying to decide exactly what to write.

About five minutes later, a new topic appeared on the German history section of the Teuton forum. Titled "If You Could Visit Any Time in German History, Where and When Would You Go?" my topic asked the readers just that question. I also requested that those who posted should explain their choices, as well as any pitfalls that might occur if they actually visited such a time. I ended my opening post with the warning to not turn the topic into an RPG—there was a separate forum for those. Pleased with my ingenuity, I pushed my chair back and returned to the main page of the forum, noting the five users currently logged on. My screen name, *Eistänzerin*, showed up first, followed by *Das Dunkle Feuer*. I took a quick look at the unread posts before clicking the browser closed and shutting my computer down for the night.

I patted Thunar's head on my way to the bathroom, intending to prepare for bed. I had not gotten a decent amount of sleep the previous night thanks to Erika's presence; her snores had kept me awake. I used the toilet first, then washed my face and let my hair down from its bun, peering closely at my visage in the mirror, scowling at the presence of a few new blackheads on my nose. Hopefully I would outgrow such things soon; I would turn twenty in August. I dumped my outfit into the hamper and put on the pajamas I had worn the previous night—white halter top and very short gray shorts. Then I retrieved my toothbrush to clean my mouth of the day's food, my final task before calling it a night.

While brushing my teeth I thought I heard something outside, and close by. It sounded almost like something sizzling, crackling, but I knew that nothing ought to catch fire out on my balcony. Ignoring it for the moment, I finished rinsing my mouth and wiped it on a blue hand towel, then reentered my bedroom. The first thing I noticed when I swept my eyes over my room was Thunar. He stood poised at the center of my bed, his fur sticking out, his round eyes ogling the curtains that concealed my balcony. I frowned and glanced that way as well. The noises I had thought I heard while in the bathroom had ceased, but I felt a chill travel down my spine, telling me that *some*thing was out there.

I crossed the carpet quickly and lifted one edge of the curtains away, just enough for me to hit the power button for the light on my balcony. It came on and lit up the table, chairs, and plants outside with a yellow-orange glow. I could see nothing unusual, but Thunar was still staring, so I had to investigate. I gathered my courage, prayed a quick petition for protection, and unlocked the glass doors to the balcony. I took a deep breath, then yanked them open and stepped outside.

At first my eyes detected nothing out of place as they slowly adjusted to the darkness. I glanced over the gardens

188

and the trees further out; all seemed peaceful. I paced forward to the balcony railing and peered over the side, down towards the deck and pool. Everything was dark aside from the light next to our back door. The light in my father's bedroom had already gone out. I shook my head in disgust at my own imagination. "There's nothing here," I murmured to myself, turning to go back inside.

A dark form stepped out abruptly from underneath one of my trellises hung with lilacs, and I froze in horror, an icy gasp escaping my lips. The figure moved forward into the light, cutting off my path to my bedroom. I cursed and half spun toward the railing, preparing to leap off and trust my ice to bring me safely to the ground. An instant later I recognized Hans wearing blackest black, the robes of the Teuton priest. I sighed in relief, trembling with belated shock. "Hans, what are you trying to do to me, cut my life short by a decade or two?" I demanded in a whisper.

In response, he stepped further into the light so that I could see his face. His black eyes blazed, his expression set into a rigid mask of fury. "You posted a very dangerous topic on our forum." His voice sounded as dark as his clothing.

His accusation did not entirely surprise me. I walked forward, reopened the door to my room, and beckoned him. "Come inside."

He refused, but I paused just inside the doorway, the cool night air chilling me in spite of my element. Hans stood just a few steps away from me, his eyes still burning with black flames. "I almost deleted the topic then and there," he informed me. "But I figured it would be better to confer with you first."

His ire frightened me, but I was determined not to show it. "Well, that was nice of you," I remarked, then ran through my apology. "How else am I supposed to decide where and when to go next? I didn't even hint at the Torstein in my topic. It's supposed to be just for fun. Maybe somebody on our forum would have some good ideas . . . ." My voice trailed off, for I knew that my excuses would not sway him.

After a moment of silence, Hans spoke again, sounding a bit less angry this time. "You need to remember, Swanie, that the Torstein is a very serious matter. It isn't something to be treated lightly or to be lightly talked about." He narrowed his eyes at me and said, "It holds a power otherwise unknown to man. Such power can corrupt even the most honorable man's good intentions. If it had not been for that power, our people would not have fallen."

I froze again at his words, my mind racing over everything I had read about the fall of the Teutons in the eleventh century. Nowhere had I found anything that implied that the power to go back in time had had anything to do with it. *Der Weg* attributed the invasions to the prosperous Bavarian trade routes. I stared up at Hans in shock. "I . . . I didn't know . . . it was because of that . . . ."

Hans glowered at me darkly, then pulled a small sheaf of old, dusty papers from somewhere beneath his robe. "Over the past year, I've conducted some more research on the Torstein, though there's little else to be found." He thrust the papers at me and ordered, "You need to read this."

My eyes focused on the papers. They looked almost like animal skin of some kind, the edges torn with faded ink scrawled across one side of each page. I took them gingerly from Hans' hand and asked, "What *is* this?"

"Some information I found on the Torstein written just a few years after its creation. It's written in Teutonica, so you may have some difficulty understanding it, but if you truly plan to use the rock again, you certainly need to read all of this."

I gawked at the crumbling papers. "These are originals?" I was amazed. "But who wrote them . . . ?" I squinted more carefully at the faded writing. It looked like some form of Carolingian miniscule.

Hans made an ominous sound in the back of his throat. "Sometimes to fully comprehend mystical things, one must step into the darkness. That was written by a Black Priest who went by the name of Wolfgang."

My eyes almost popped out of their sockets, and I clutched the papers more tightly, fearing that I might drop them. "A *Black* Priest?" I squeaked, my voice far too shaky. "One of the followers of Wuotan, the devil?" I stared up at Hans, who regarded me distrustfully. "But we're not supposed to *read* their writings . . . ."

"Sometimes the Cursed Ones write the truth."

Though I had no idea what he was talking about, I also found myself unable to doubt him. Black Priests were anathema to the Teutons, but perhaps this Torstein also had some dark roots. Then another thought struck me. "Where did you *get* this?" I inquired of Hans. He frowned at me severely and did not reply. "Do we have to return it?" I persisted.

Hans shook his head and turned away, his cape flaring behind him as he strode toward the railing of the balcony. "No, I received it freely." He paused at the edge of the balcony and looked back at me, his eyes filled with mystery and foreboding. "If you have any questions about what you read, do not hesitate to consult me." In the next instant, he flew off the balcony in a wave of black, heat rippling out behind him. I gaped in shock and ran to the railing, but he had already vanished into the night.

My plans for sleep were now completely shattered; I was wide awake. Hans had given me three pages of Carolingian miniscule, obviously torn out of some very old book. It took me over an hour to piece everything together from the faded ink. I used a magnifying glass and my bright desk lamp to be sure that I read everything correctly. When I finally finished, I laid the ancient sheets carefully aside into one of the wire bins on my desk, pushed back my leather chair, and pondered.

The writings of Wolfgang had shed much more light on the Torstein and the art of time travel than I had expected. Many boundaries were laid out plainly on the pages, including some things I had not considered. For one thing, a keeper of the Torstein was advised not to go back further than the year in which the stone was created, due to an escalated probability of losing the rock. The second page of the writings stated exactly what Hans had suggested—the power to travel time was not supposed to be held by man at all. It had originated from man's bargaining with Wuotan himself. It was a devil's power, not to be tapped by Christians.

For the remainder of the night, I sat in the chair or lay on my bed, glancing now and then at the box which held the Torstein, thinking about all that I had read. *It's a devil's power . . . . That means I shouldn't use it at all if I really want to call myself a Christian. But since I've put my faith in God, couldn't I use the Torstein anyway? It shouldn't make a difference regarding my eternal destiny. The power of Wuotan . . . . It shouldn't have worked for me in the first place if I wasn't supposed to use it. I have to use it again, no matter how great the risk may be. But it's dangerous . . . . Now that I know the truth about the Torstein, will God punish me if I use it again? Will I mess everything up somehow?*

I thought also about my topic on the forum, realizing that Hans had never said whether he planned to delete it or not. He would probably leave it up to me. Now I worried, though, if maybe it would generate some suspicion. If another user like *Teuton Brother* joined our forum, maybe for the sole purpose of seeking out classified information, would they guess the true purpose of my topic? The sun had begun to rise over the trees of my backyard when I finally fell asleep. Right before I slept I thought of Hans again, and how magnificent he had looked standing on my balcony, clad entirely in black, sweeping like a fire over the railing when he had left. And I wished for the thousandth time that I could have him somehow.

My father held his summer party that year on the first Friday in July, the 2nd. I had begun to dread these parties with all the drunken adults and flirtatious college-age boys. So I decided to give everyone a scare and dress in the vein of the Gothic subculture, something that the wealthy generally despised. It took me close to an hour to properly prepare myself in front of my bathroom mirror. I chose a sleeveless all-black dress with a full, grandly layered skirt and corseted blouse with tiny buttons up the front and ruffles across the top and bottom. I strapped on an armband bearing black ribbons, black angel wings, and a silver cross. I included a black choker with silver cross and beads for my neck. I curled some of my hair and wound it with black ribbons, leaving the rest hanging straight down my back like a dark curtain. I put in my contacts and applied black eyeliner and mascara heavily, using deep red lipstick and shiny metallic nail polish. After adding the finishing touch—black dancing slippers, invisible beneath the massive skirt—I left my room to present myself downstairs.

My cousins waited for me at the base of the front stairs, both clad in typical summer dress. Traudl wore a light pink flared dress with flowers, while Trudi's was of pale blue in the same style. Both of them shrieked when they saw me and gushed that they should have thought to wear their Gothic dresses. "Maybe we can load up one of your stereos with some Bauhaus or Lacrimosa," Trudi suggested with a giggle, taking hold of my left arm and guiding me into the parlors.

"That would freak all these brats out, I bet," Traudl predicted, turning her nose up at an elderly man in a tux that I recognized as a top official from the local utility company. "They just want to hear violin music all night." My father had hired his usual string group to provide music. They were set up in the front parlor, currently playing Vivaldi.

"I prefer Nightwish, actually," I commented, pointing my steps toward the dining room to investigate the available food.

"What's that?" Traudl sounded distracted, having attached herself to my right arm above the armband.

I was about to reply when I found myself facing Erika, who stood in the side hallway clad in a cap-sleeved maroon blouse and layered black skirt, her short hair patted down so precisely that not a strand waved free. She wore maroon lipstick and black eyeliner, black crystals hanging from her ears and a frilled choker trapping her neck. She looked me up and down with a pinched expression. "Swanie, you really need to stop dressing like that in front of me," she chided, her hands on her hips.

"I'm trying to scare off any freaky men who want to stick their tongues in my mouth," I explained, looking down at the base of my skirts.

"Hmm. Valid point. If you're wanting food, come on. I just sampled some of the chocolates myself. Exquisite." She snared my right hand and tugged me away from Traudl, who was talking with our Opa Hobart. Trudi's grip also slipped away, and I shrugged it off, knowing I could catch up with both of them later.

My choice of attire succeeded at keeping the worst of the sex fiends at bay. I saw Sebastian once in passing, and he laughed outright at my costume and asked whether I planned on attending a Halloween party later on that night. The ladies that I knew superficially greeted me with smiles and drifted away to gossip among their friends, some of these groups shooting me the occasional look of censure. My father shook his head when he saw me but kept his mouth shut, for as the host he had more important things to attend to aside from his daughter's choice of dress. My cousins caught up with Erika and me out on the deck, where we had staked out territory for our meal. "Opa Hobart said you look like you're going to a funeral," Trudi mentioned with a snort as she started on her filet mignon.

"Fair words from the guy who's almost ninety," I muttered, not particularly caring about my grandfather's opinion of my clothes.

Trudi snickered, and Traudl put in, "He might decide to complain to your Pappi about it, so prepare yourself."

"My Pappi won't care. He knows I got this dress specially made, and that's the point at these parties. Make sure you look rich even if you're not." I rolled my eyes and began to saw my cordon bleu.

I drifted here and there with Erika and my cousins throughout the evening, keeping my eyes peeled for Hans, who seemed to have blended in with the crowds a bit too successfully. I finally met him coming down one of the hallways carrying a plate of hors d'oeuvres around nightfall. He spluttered a curse when he saw my outfit and demanded harshly if I was trying to lose my virginity that night. I snickered, pleased that I had caught him off guard, and said, "Maybe I am."

He frowned at me and, when he stepped around me to continue down the hall with his plate, he murmured in my ear, "I'll want to dance with you later, after midnight." He was gone around the corner before I could answer, but I grinned in anticipation. That was the reaction I had been hoping for.

The party dragged impossibly long after I had finally seen Hans. I danced with Erika and my cousins and took part in a Rook tournament with three of my father's male business contacts, all of whom seemed dreadfully amused by my expertise at that game. Hans had taught me how to play, so of course I would know all the ins and outs. Afterward I said farewell to my three girlfriends. They had all ridden in Traudl's car, and Erika had to get home to prepare for her younger brother's birthday party the following day. Once they had gone, I decided that I could wait no longer. I sauntered away from the chattering guests, removed my contacts to toss them deftly into a trash can, and headed outside.

I spent the next half hour or so resting on the bench of the gazebo, relishing the stillness of the cool summer night. The chattering of the stream soothed me, and presently I laid my head back against one of the gazebo's posts, concentrating on the ice within me, preparing for my dance with fire. At last he arrived at the edge of the glade, having cast off his serving attire for the night, dressed once again in robes of black. "You're early," he said by way of greeting, standing at the doorway to the gazebo, watching me.

"I couldn't wait any longer," I whispered softly in Teutonica, rising from my seat and turning to face him. A cool blue glaze perfected my vision, and frigid breath escaped my lips as I departed the gazebo and took his hand.

We danced for a long time that night under the stars, with no music but that which rang in our hearts. I had not danced with him since my return home, and it was a liberating experience. I felt as though we were flying high above the city, above the world, that his black fire could lift me to heaven. My love for Hans would never die, even in eternity, I believed. How could I not love this man, so strong yet so gentle, who danced like no one else in this world? Ah, these foolish, youthful desires that could never come to be! I had to enjoy them while they lasted.

When our dance finally ended, I stood still for a moment while Hans held my hands, silently recalling that autumn of 1992. "What are you thinking about?" Hans asked softly, his voice still sounding other-worldly.

"Our first dance," I answered, my thoughts years away.

"Ah yes, I like to remember that, as well." Hans paused, not having let go of my hands, and a beautiful smile lit up his face. "You have gained much experience, since then. That first time, you did not even touch the water."

His black eyes were on the stream, and I tilted my head to look at it too. We had danced upon it quite a bit, and a sizeable wave of frozen water stood poised on its banks, an array of dripping icicles decorating its peak. "I made that sculpture for you," I whispered shyly. "It's waiting for you to finish it."

Hans chuckled and let go of my hands. "So it is." He took a single step away from me toward the stream, touching just the tip of my wave with his hand. The ice cracked with his heat and changed abruptly to water, steam rising as the wave fell back into the stream with a splash. Hans laughed quietly again, and I could not help laughing in amazement at his feat. Then he turned back to face me again, and I saw that his eyes burned now with something more than fire. He stared at me in intense concentration, taking in my whole appearance, my outfit, my hair, my face. He stepped toward me, and I began to tremble as I sensed the heat of his blood. His eyes never left mine now, and slowly, carefully, he lifted one hand to brush it gently across my hair and down the side of my face. My heart began pounding; I could not move. I stared back at him, shock, passion, love, and a little bit of fear racing through my veins while I watched his lips form the Teutonic words, "Such beauty . . . is wasted . . . ." Then he leaned toward me, his hand soft under my chin. I took a shuddering breath and closed my eyes.

When our lips met an instant later, I trembled in earnest, relishing every movement of his lips, cataloguing every feeling, every emotion, in my mind. *This* was heaven. For years, I had dreamed of him kissing me, and now it had finally come true. I could have held onto that moment forever, never letting go, but soon he pulled away from me slowly, his eyes still shining for an instant with passion. My eyes certainly reflected his wonder. But then, just as quickly, horror overtook his expression, and he turned from me as though to flee into the woods. I ordered my feet forward, stretching one arm toward him. "Hans . . . ." I gasped.

He stopped his retreat at the edge of the trees and spun swiftly around, his robes enveloping him like a cyclone. To my surprise, he looked furious. "Child, it is a dream, a dream," he snapped at me, "and if it is not that it will become something wrong. I have to leave now, or I will do something wicked."

There were so many things I wanted to say, needed to say, but now the moment was lost. We were dancing Teutons no more. The servant and the master's daughter had returned to reality. I sagged, euphoria crashing into melancholy. But there was one thing I had to say before he ran from me. "Hans, that . . . ." I choked, then forced myself to go on. "That was . . . my first real kiss."

Hans' harsh expression softened for an instant, but then he shook his head and said, unsmiling, "Assuming I can keep my head, that will be our last." A second later, he was gone.

Chapter Twenty-one:
Sorting Things Out

For several minutes after Hans had fled, I remained frozen at the banks of the stream, unable to think. That one golden instant of my life had come and gone so fast, I had barely had the time to fully appreciate it. The memory of that kiss swirled around in my head while I stood staring blankly at the trees, encompassing me with its perfection. Fire and ice, melding together into one just for a moment, and I knew that I would never forget. Years from now, when I had finally found a man decent enough to marry, I would still remember this night. I would forever compare every kiss, every touch, to how Hans had made me feel. My heart pounded out a jagged rhythm, and I closed my eyes as I sank into a reverie. *One perfect kiss . . . . Oh, my darling, can you not love me the way I love you? You must, oh you must, or you would not have kissed me that way . . . .* I thought of the words he had said just before his lips met mine: "Such beauty is wasted." *Yes, it is wasted, wasted on others and not on you. It should be yours, should be ours. How could I imagine that I could ever love another?*

"Do I even want to know what happened here?" The unexpected voice cut into my dreams, drawing me back to reality again, the reality that I wanted to leave behind: we had kissed, and he had left. He had been angry, at himself, at me? Would he ever agree to dance with me again? Would he ever speak to me again? Would he even *look* at me again? Had I ruined everything? Tears of icy shame began to well in my eyes when I finally unfroze, turning to regard the person who had entered the clearing. Sebastian. Who else would it have been? He stood at almost the exact spot where Hans had paused in his flight. He still wore his serving attire, but the casual disarray of his crinkly hair and unbuttoned vest told me that he was off for the night. He regarded me with a disturbed expression, concern darkening his usually cheerful features.

I breathed a sigh of relief that it had been Sebastian who found me and not one of the other servants or guests. I knew he had said something when he saw me standing there by the stream, but I could not remember what he had said. It had broken my concentration, but the memory of the kiss still revolved in my head. I regarded Sebastian blankly, and he looked me up and down, likely trying to discern my mood, and what exactly had brought me into such a mood. At last he shrugged and jerked one thumb back toward the trees. "Your Pappi finally let me go for the night since the party's almost over. I was heading back to my place when Hans ran past me with the speed of a demon, streaking for the side gate." I froze again at his pronouncement. Hans had not gone back to his cottage. I had really frightened him off. "It scared the shit out of me," Sebastian continued, oblivious to my reaction. "Hans doesn't usually run like that. So I figured I'd better take a look around, find out if something had happened out here." He paused and quirked a smile at me. "But all I see is you, and you're not that scary."

Sebastian laughed, and I tried desperately to form some sort of intelligent reply. I had nothing. In my mind, all I could see were Hans' black eyes glowing with passion, then that horrible instant when they became furious. All I could feel were his soft lips on mine, his tongue in my mouth. Sebastian waited for me to say something, anything to satisfy his curiosity. At last I whispered the only thing I could think at that moment. "We kissed." My eyes were half-closed. In spite of Hans' terrible reaction, a contented smile graced my face.

Sebastian's eyes widened in what looked like astonishment, and he stepped further into the glade. "*Seriously?*" He glanced around quickly as if to ensure that we were alone, then stared at me again.

"I think . . . ." I stumbled over the words. "I think . . . he got really mad . . . he ran away from me . . . ." My voice broke, and the tears welled up again. I spun away from Sebastian and brushed angrily at my eyes. *Why?*

Sebastian came beside me and drew me against him, putting his sturdy arms around my frigid shoulders, comforting me like any good friend should. He pulled me gently toward the gazebo while I struggled to regain my composure. "Come on. Let's sit down." He led me inside, keeping me steady as I stumbled on the wooden floor, helping me sit down onto one of the benches. He retrieved a handkerchief from one of his suit pockets, using it to wipe away the tears that had escaped my eyes in liquid form. "Tell me what you can," he urged kindly.

Though Sebastian had not known the gravity of my feelings for Hans, that night I laid everything at his feet, finally. I knew, as well as he knew, that he would keep silent. It took me some time to explain what had taken place just a few minutes earlier, holding back sobs as I worked to put everything into words. It would have been much easier had I not seen that wretched fury in Hans' face when he had spat the words, "Child, it is a dream, a dream!" at me. When I finished the tale, having left nothing out, I leaned into Sebastian's white vest, staining it with my tears while he rubbed my back in sympathy. By then my ice had begun to confine itself within my soul, so my entire world was a blur behind my tears.

I do not know how long I sat there in that gazebo, sobbing on Sebastian's chest. I do know that once my tears had finally begun to run dry, depression had descended upon me in a stormy cloud. I realized suddenly that all this time, for almost seven years now, I had been clinging to a ridiculous hope that maybe, just maybe, there could be some mutual future for Hans and me. Although I knew that my father would never allow it, that my friends would never understand it, that our age and class differences would account for far too many complications, I had still believed. "It is a dream," he had said, and he was right. But how could I let go of such a glorious dream, even if it could never be? How *could* I? I must . . . Sebastian would say that now, of course. I must find a way. There *had* to be a way. But my heart sank deep into rebellion at the mere idea . . . I *loved* him!

"I never realized that things were so serious between you two," Sebastian said at last. I still lay with my head upon his shoulder, but I looked up at his face when he went on. "I mean, I figured you had a crush on him, but I didn't know it was like this." He sighed, his mouth twisting into a frustrated frown.

I managed to give a quiet snort of laughter at his words, in spite of the enormous weight bearing down on my heart. "He doesn't even know," I informed my friend. "Beth and Erika were the only ones who knew, and now you. I've never said anything about it to him."

Sebastian looked thoughtful. "Maybe you should tell him."

I arched away from him in horror, shuddering at the thought. "I couldn't do *that*, not after what he did tonight! He'd be furious with me. He'd say I was just a child. That's all he sees me as, a child." I shook my head and wiped my face again with Sebastian's handkerchief.

"Yeah, you're what, over thirty years apart in age?" Sebastian glanced at me briefly, then looked toward the stream. "I guess that really couldn't work out."

"My father would kill me, or he would kill Hans," I predicted, for I had imagined the dismal consequences of my feelings many times before. "He'd think Hans had seduced me. But I love him, and I don't know how to stop . . . ." My voice trailed off, the pain of unrequited desire growing within me.

Sebastian shook his head again, his expression suggesting that he desperately wanted to help me but could not think of anything sufficient. "Haven't you felt this way about anyone else?" he asked. "Someone at college or someone here? Maybe one of the younger Teutons you know? *Any*one?"

"How could I?" I demanded of him, a touch of anger creeping into my tone along with my sadness. "Teutons just want children, and the Germans my age want sex, money, and beer. Most of the guys at college aren't much better." I scowled.

A short guffaw escaped Sebastian's lips, and he agreed, "Yeah, unfortunately it's the older men who have more realistic expectations. But you're going to have to let Hans go eventually, Swanie. It's not healthy to cling to something you can't have."

"I know, I know," I sniffed, wiping away a few angry tears. "But I just know that whenever I do decide to marry somebody, I'll be thinking of Hans the whole time. I'll be remembering what it's like to dance with a priest, to kiss a priest, to watch him manipulate fire. And I'll be wondering . . . and wishing . . . ach, I'm such an idiot." I sighed in frustration at the pain in my heart. It would never go away. Everything Sebastian had said was good advice, I knew. But I needed to get away now, just like Hans had run. I needed to get back to my room, lock myself in, and collapse onto my bed, alone with my remorse. I wiped the last tears from my cheeks and handed the handkerchief back to Sebastian, rising from the bench.

He took it from me and also got up, still looking sympathetic. "It'll all work out someday, Swanie." I cracked a sarcastic smile and turned for the gazebo's arched doorway, not particularly agreeing with his prediction. Before I could make my exit, Sebastian added. "They say it's better to have loved and lost."

I rolled my eyes and left the gazebo, my skirts swishing as I headed for the path to the house. "I've heard that one before, and I don't know if I agree," I said.

Then Sebastian asked something that prompted me to stop dead in my tracks. "Would you rather Hans had *not* kissed you like that?"

I froze, pondering for a moment, but I already knew that I would never willingly give up those fleeting seconds of heaven. "Nope," I declared.

Sebastian stood at the doorway to the gazebo, a wry smile curling across his face, and he nodded knowingly. "I rest my case."

I reentered the house through the side door, taking the same route I had taken seven years ago with the man who had just deserted me. This time the back staircase was empty of people, though I heard suggestive sounds drifting into the halls from various rooms. I quickened my pace and shut myself into my bedroom, locking the door behind me just in case any of the drunks had a secret Goth fetish. Thunar greeted me with a cheerful chirp, and when I switched the lights on I saw him stretching luxuriously atop his cat tree. Serene and spoiled, he wanted for nothing, not even the love of a human.

I shed all of my fancy clothing and washed off all of my make-up, feeling as though my efforts had been for nothing. Though Hans had seemed to approve of my attire, he would doubtless run the other way if I ever wore this dress in front of him again. The only one I had actually impressed was Erika, and while I liked her as a friend, I had no interest in her as a lover. I stared at my reflection in the bathroom mirror for a while after I had dried my face, my gray eyes demanding answers that I did not have. "Traveling time may be the only way to let him go," I whispered to myself, "since you can't seem to manage it here." I needed to focus on that, not on blissful memories of his fiery lips meeting mine.

I threw on my summer pajamas and attempted unsuccessfully to sleep. Giving up around three a.m., I retrieved the three pages written by Wolfgang, taking them and a water bottle from my fridge out onto my balcony. I settled myself onto my favorite lounge chair and studied the Black Priest's writings again, trying to allow the mysteries of time travel to supplant my thoughts of Hans. *Time's currents cannot be turned backward without cost. They were created to progress, and those who force them to regress must respect that to do so is contrary to nature.*

Respect the price. The advice of the *Eihalbe* resurfaced in my brain, and I felt my forehead wrinkle at the similarity there. *Have the* Eihalbae *read the works of Wolfgang?* I wondered vaguely, lethargy creeping along the edges of my thoughts at last. *They don't live by the rules of the Teutons. Teutons say that the writings of Black Priests are profane . . . but maybe the fairies aren't of that opinion . . . .* I closed my eyes for a moment with my hands resting upon the three pages that lay on my breast. *The* Eihalbae *should know. They possess the knowledge of centuries, of ages, and they share all of their knowledge and observations among their own kind . . . only rarely deigning to share it with humans . . . .*

I had begun to drift off on my lounge chair when a wispy voice crept into my mind, one I had not expected to encounter again anytime soon. At first I imagined it to be a dream, for it addressed me the same way its counterpart had at the walls of the Leutasch Gorge. *"Zoubaraera Teutona . . . ."*

My eyelids sprang open, and I invoked my ice into my eyes to enhance my vision. Then I caught sight of the *Eihalbe* balancing upon my balcony's railing, its back to the gardens. It sat with its silvery hands clasped in its lap seeming to conceal something, its sleek legs crossed at the ankles, its waiflike wings beating invisibly at its back. Perhaps it trusted its wings for stability; even for so small an entity, the railing would be a precarious seat, like a human perched upon a tree branch. The fairy's multicolored eyes observed me in silence, its hair gently swishing in the soft breeze of night.

I ogled my unexpected companion without speaking for at least a minute, feeling myself at a loss, like I had felt when the *Eihalbe* had spoken to me while I wept upon the elm's trunk. *They always have to show up when I'm least expecting it. I'll bet if I spent the entire day and night camping beneath the silver oak out back, not one fairy would stoop to acknowledge me.* I cleared my throat and shifted into a more upright position in the lounge chair, setting the aged papers down onto my lap. "Noble *Eihalbe* . . . good morning," I greeted in Teutonica, not knowing what else to say. I did not think myself in need of guidance upon my own balcony around three-thirty in the morning.

The fairy's eyes shifted from my face to the pages in my lap, and I reached for the bottle of water sitting upon the table to my left. "The Teuton witch consults the dead for advice."

I detected no judgment in the fairy's words, but its choice of terminology prompted me to look down at the faded handwriting again. "Well . . . information on the Torstein's potential seems hard to come by," I pointed out, taking a swig of water and returning the bottle to its place. The fingers of my right hand tightened a little on the pages in my lap. "I . . . I guess I shouldn't . . . believe everything written on these pages, though."

"Not everything dead is destructive. Decay consumes the dross and revives the treasures within."

This *Eihalbe* seemed to enjoy inserting new puzzles into my brain. I did not know how to take its advice, for it flew in the face of what my Christian faith had taught me. Or did it? "Thank you," I murmured automatically, peering down at the yellowed pages in my hands. "Death has haunted my family for a long time, actually." My arms trembled a little, and I took several deep breaths, ordering myself not to dwell on those things now. I had more pressing issues at hand. "These days my heaviest burdens come from love," I confessed, lifting my head to meet my companion's mesmerizing gaze again. *Love. Or something like it.*

The *Eihalbe* looked back at me in silence, not having altered its posture in the slightest since I had first noticed its presence on the railing. I started wondering what it held in its hands; its counterpart in the gorge had not hid them from me. Its kaleidoscope eyes gazed steadily into mine, as though it waited for me to translate its proverbs. *Consults the dead for advice . . . decay revives the treasures within.* "Maybe . . . maybe . . . since I can't figure out . . . how to quench my love here and now . . . the dead people in the past . . . might be able to help me?" My eyebrows came together as I spoke. I felt like I was grasping at straws.

The fairy rose abruptly into the air and fluttered toward me, holding both hands out in my direction. My eyes widened at the sight of a small silvery acorn, and my heart pounded in a mixture of excitement and confusion. How could this *Eihalbe* possibly find me worthy to plant a new silver oak tree—*me* of all people? I could not fathom it, but I knew better than to spurn its gift. I opened my right palm beneath where the fairy hovered, and it dropped the acorn into my hand with one final admonition: "Opportunity springs from the seeds of decay."

Chapter Twenty-two:
Planting New Seeds

I awoke late the next day, Saturday, rising from a strange tangle of dreams involving silver oak trees, the labradorite gates of time, and dances with a hooded man whose fire clashed powerfully against my ice. When I sat up in bed, my eyes drifted first to the ring box on my nightstand and then to the silver acorn beside it. Memories of the previous night returned in a flash. *The Eihalbe who embodies the silver oak in my own backyard saw fit to offer me one of its fruit, an honor attained by very few Teutons. And that means that I have to plant and nurture it so a new tree will grow, one to ultimately take the place of the hulking oak in the copse beside our stream. Hans said that oak is nearly seventy years old . . . .*

I shook my head and looked away at the remembrance of Hans. I knew that I would have no luck finding him that day even if I sought him at his cottage. Part of me longed to share what the *Eihalbe* had told me last night, to get his interpretation of its counsel. Another haughty part of me wanted to brag about the fact that apparently I was worthy of a silver acorn if not of his love. I doubted that he had ever been offered a silver acorn before.

I ended up sharing my good fortune with Lise instead. Though she was not a Teuton herself, she had noticed that the aged tree on Thaden grounds that appeared to be a white oak tended not to shed acorns like its kin. Outsiders mistook silver oaks for white oaks because they looked nearly the same to people who had no element to show them the spiritual veil. Unlike your typical white oak, though, a silver oak did not drop its acorns; they served as nourishment for the *Eihalbae*. Thus the mystical oak trees remained few and far between even in Teuton lands.

I explained all of this to Lise again—she had certainly heard it before, back in the days when I had excitedly babbled to her about Teutonic folklore—and she suggested that we both go shopping for the perfect planter for my future tree. By midafternoon, the *Eihalbe's* offering lay nestled in a bed of topsoil mixed with the natural earth from my personal forest, encased in a sizeable pot glazed in silvery green. "It's too bad I can't bring any of my pottery home from college," I remarked when we had finished with the planting. I stood back looking at where the planter sat at the right corner of my balcony, paces away from my lounge chair. "It would have been amazing to make a special container just for this tree."

Lise favored me with a fond smile and brushed the dirt off of her hands. "I can see what you mean, but I think the one we chose works perfectly. You said that its color is exactly how the tree's leaves should look in a few years." She winked at me, her expression that of one who has long heard tales of Teutonic legends while uncertain of the truth of them all. She knew all about my ice and Hans' fire, but she still considered *Eihalbae* to be fictional.

I grinned a little and thanked her for her help. I spent the remainder of the afternoon on my computer, catching up on posts on the Teuton forum and talking with a few of my friends through ICQ. Ina was actually online for once, gushing in the chat about her upcoming wedding, scheduled for the last Friday night in July. She and her fiancé would be returning to München for the festivities before taking off on a month-long honeymoon to various parts of

Asia. Ina mentioned that her step-daughter Lea would stay with her paternal grandparents while they were away. *She's such a cute baby, chubby and full of energy! She's just learning how to walk. Watching her pull herself upright makes my heart want to burst,* Ina wrote. It seemed that she was thrilled to be a mother, without question.

Does Walfrid expect you to give him more kids? I typed back after a pause, truly curious. I did not type out the rest of my thoughts: *Or did he learn his lesson after the first wife died?* As happy as I was for my oldest Teuton friend, I had felt a twinge of doubt since Marga had told me of her intentions. Marga had said that Walfrid's first wife had died just last year, and apparently the child had only just begun to walk. That meant that Lea was less than a year old.

What sort of man grabs onto a new woman less than a year after losing his wife?

We've talked about it a little, Ina responded at length, *but right now he wants me to concentrate on mothering Lea. I never knew how much I love babies until I met her.*

I'm glad you've gotten used to changing diapers, I typed back with a smirk, glancing briefly toward where Thunar lay sleeping on my blue couch. Though I did not carry the gene mutation responsible for cystic fibrosis, sometimes I imagined that I would be better off raising cats. At least they cleaned themselves.

OMG wait till you hear about the blow-out she had a couple nights ago. It was so hilarious! Ina went on for nearly a paragraph about jellybean-sized poop that Lea had attempted to eat, and I gagged a little and turned my attention to the forum. How could anyone consider an event like that hilarious?

Thus far, my topic on time travel had garnered just a pair of responses, and none of the users had raised any questions. *Idealismus* had commented first and declared that he would love to be there for the fall of the Berlin wall, "to see the moment when the German people triumphed over Communism." While I understood his intent, that period was off limits for me since I had been alive at the time. Fonsi, under the username *Drachenreiter*, replied that it would be awesome to witness the bomb plot against Hitler during World War II. I agreed with him on that, but I did not really want to insert myself into the madness of the Nazi era.

I ended up typing out a new comment, asking other users what they thought about journeying to the Middle Ages, which years would be the most enlightening, what preparations would have to be made first. Despite the rampant chauvinism and overarching control of the Catholic Church, I had begun to daydream about visiting the days of Teutonic prosperity from centuries ago. If I was expected to learn and apply lessons from traveling time, I figured that I may uncover mysteries long forgotten if I went to such a time, an age when Teutons used their gifts more freely. Maybe I could learn more about why it was dangerous for Teuton women to bear children, and maybe I could find a way to solve that problem.

I watched the topic carefully in subsequent weeks as users suggested various events from the Middle Ages. Marga, under the username *Sirene78,* offered a few hints on how to prepare, asserting that a journey through time would be similar to visiting a third world country. "You'd want to get your vaccines updated first and pack things like soap and tampons," she wrote. Her comment prompted *Idealismus* to chime in about the dangers of smallpox. I rolled my eyes at that, for no matter where I chose to go, I had no plans to stay there indefinitely. I should not have to fear ancient diseases during a few months' venture into the past. And if I contracted something awful like smallpox, I could just use the Torstein to return. The writings were quite clear that a time traveler's body remained unaffected by any ailments incurred in the past, once they returned to their own time.

On a Thursday night halfway through the month of July, Marga caught me on ICQ while I chatted with Beth about the upcoming semester. *Hey Swanie,* she greeted. I glanced briefly at her message and returned my focus to my conversation with Beth. She was bemoaning the fact that she had to take a class on writing poetry for her degree, and I typed out a sympathetic reply, since I enjoyed neither reading nor writing poetry. Then another line of text appeared beneath Marga's greeting that brought me up short. *What's going on with your topic about time travel, not wanting it to be an RPG? You put a fantasy topic in the history forum.*

I lifted my fingers off the keyboard and took several shallow breaths, chills creeping gradually up my spine. Had she discerned the real purpose of my topic? I looked toward my nightstand, where the Torstein rested inside its ring box. *Maybe I should have put it in the RPG forum. Admin fail,* I typed back. My fingers had begun to grow frosty with ice, and I felt my heart hammering beneath my tank top.

I was starting to think you'd dug up the Torstein or something, Marga answered, adding a wink after the words. I scooted my chair back from my desk and clasped my hands together, working to stem my encroaching panic. Marga had figured it out. All of my secrecy had crumbled before me. I squeezed my eyes shut and placed my palms against my temples, silently ordering myself to breathe deeply, not to surrender to the sensation of constriction scratching at my lungs. *No, Marga doesn't* know *that you found the Torstein,* I told myself. *She's probably just waiting to see how you react to her claim.*

After a good ten minutes of shaky breaths and icy flakes dampening the atmosphere around me, I tugged my chair forward again and responded to my friend's message with finesse. *Pretty sure if I'd found it, all of you would know. We'd be planning a grand escapade of München's finest maidens.*

Marga replied with several LOLs. *Nah, if I had the Torstein I'd want to go out west in the U.S. and get me a cowboy.*

I snorted and shook my head, my tension dissipating. *He'd better be brave enough to do the blood-transfer,* I typed to her before turning my attention back to my cousin, who had declared that the only poets she liked were

Edgar Allan Poe and Emily Dickinson. I took up the new subject with gratitude, feeling as though I had dodged a bullet. Marga went on for a while about her dream cowboy before signing off.

By Friday the 30th, I had not spoken with Hans once since the incident at the party. It seemed that he had chosen to skillfully ignore me any time we crossed each other's paths in the house. I really needed to talk to him again, to beg his forgiveness about that night at the party, to ask his opinions on what the *Eihalbe* had told me, to find out what he thought about my evolving plans for the Torstein. But every time our eyes met, his face looked like it had been carved from stone, and a very, very dark stone. He would avert his gaze quickly and not look my way again. He never seemed to sign onto ICQ anymore, and he had not sent me a message or replied to any of my comments on our forum, either.

If he prefers to pretend I don't exist, then I guess I'll have to bring all of my questions before Lady Muniche instead of him, I thought to myself that afternoon while I did my makeup for Ina's wedding. I had decided to wear a striped blue dress with a skirt that nearly swept the ground aside from the slits up its sides. It was one that I often wore when I played the organ at church because it did not trap my legs. I had already put in contacts, and I stared minutely at my eyelashes while I put on my mascara, metallic blue eyeliner and eye shadow completing my look. *She might even be there at the wedding tonight. There'll probably be a good amount of guests since they're not having a church wedding.*

Traditionally, German couples marry first at the registry office, similar to the justice of the peace in the U.S. Then a day or two later, they may choose to have a church wedding like my parents'. Ina's family was not religious, so she and Walfrid had simply invited their closest friends to celebrate at their Teutonic wedding, an ancient ritual common to our people. I had read all about this type of ceremony in *Der Weg* but had not yet attended one. My anticipation for this night glowed in my eyes when I looked at my reflection. I would have to keep a careful guard upon my ice if I wanted my contact lenses to survive.

I picked up Erika at her family's house before turning my Ghibli southeast toward the forest clearing where we had celebrated the May dances. We exchanged speculation on the wedding, Erika having clad herself in a short-sleeved dark blue dress that complimented her element nicely. "I really don't know what I think about what happens tonight," Erika remarked, a cigarette balanced between two fingers, its tip hovering outside the half-lowered window. "I just feel like Ina jumped into this too fast. She's only known the guy since March."

That was news to me. "I've been trying to figure out what kind of guy chooses a new wife less than a year after the first one dies," I noted.

"Right? It's like he's picked out a new horse or something." She puffed on her cigarette and cursed when several ashes dusted her dress.

"Well, Marga did say that he and his first wife waited a decade before having Lea," I reminded her as she swept the ashes to the floor.

"Give me a break. 'Waited a decade.' More like he was making her take fertility drugs the whole time." Erika curled her lip and took another drag.

"So who's coming tonight?" I inquired. I had not snooped the guest list.

"Ina's mom and brother, some of Wally's family and friends, our group, Lady Muniche, and the priest, I think."

"Wally?" I repeated, the epithet prompting me to cackle.

"What? Should I call him 'Friddy' instead?"

It took me a while to regain my composure, and by the time I did, we had made it to the parking area. I counted eight cars already present and backed in next to Traudl's Honda. "Who's the priest, do you know?" I asked Erika as we climbed out of my car and struck out for the trail.

"Some friend of Wally's. But I think he's from Passau."

I snorted. "You'd better not accidentally call him that to his face."

Erika shook her head and sneered, "Ah, these rich Berlin bastards who don't believe in nicknames."

When we reached the clearing, I made my way over to where Lady Muniche sat in a lawn chair beneath a towering willow. Most of the guests congregated in that same area, and I recognized Rudi positioned behind where the Lady sat, his robes hiding his identity from most. But I caught the flash of lightning behind his glasses when he acknowledged me, and I waved back before crouching beside my mentor. "Welcome, Swanie dear," she greeted with an easy smile, her pale yellow dress seeming to brighten the clearing more than the burning fire beside the stream. She clasped my hands in hers and said, "This is your first Teutonic wedding, isn't it?" Her eyes sparkled with what appeared to be delight.

"That it is, *Leitalra*," I answered, addressing her more formally than usual since there were quite a few people gathered around.

Her smile turned devious, and she released my hands. "Watch closely then, dear child, for one day you'll find yourself in Ina's position."

"I'm not looking forward to the blood, actually," I admitted in a low voice, trying not to let it carry over the sounds of others' chatter.

Lady Muniche chuckled and leaned close to me. "When you're in love, you never notice the pain," she promised me.

I brought my lips to her left ear and whispered so softly that I could hardly hear myself. "I'm thinking of using the Torstein to see how our people lived in the Middle Ages. What do you think about that?"

When I pulled back to meet her gaze, I saw that the creases on her face had seemed to deepen, her blue eyes appearing lost in thought. I saw the cloaked form of another Teuton priest approaching to speak with Rudi, so I rose to my feet, ready to return to where Erika stood with my cousins. I did not particularly want to be overheard by a priest from Passau that I did not know from Adam. "Swanie." Lady Muniche's voice caught me before I could make my escape, and when I turned back toward her, she murmured, "It would be instructive in more ways than you know."

I pondered the Lady's words throughout the entire wedding, hardly noticing the ceremony's progression. I saw that Ina wore a gorgeous gown of white patterned with swirls of silver, likely a representation of her element, the air. She walked to the table set up before the stream—the Teutonic altar—with the grace that always characterized her movements, her left hand clasped firmly in the right hand of her betrothed—who also wore the priestly robes. I had not realized that Walfrid was a priest. When I saw how his presence seemed to overshadow her before the table—a shrouded specter much taller than my tallest girlfriend—I felt a chill deep inside.

It would be instructive in more ways than you know. For some reason I imagined that what Lady Muniche had meant was that in the Middle Ages, Teuton women were even more oppressed than they were in the modern era. Something about the aura of Ina's fiancé bothered me, from the tightness with which he held her hand to what sounded like a studied coolness in his voice when he repeated the vows. I heard Ina give a soft yelp when the priest cut her wrist to collect her blood in the goblet of sorrows and create the pink scar of marriage, but Walfrid did not flinch at all. I saw her wince when she drank the required sip from the cup, and I watched her betrothed chuck the goblet over his shoulder with a bit too much force after taking a sip himself.

What am I really watching here? I asked myself when the pair had finished speaking the vows, Ina's voice stumbling over the words with what could have been an overflow of emotion. *I didn't realize this guy's a Teuton priest. Do priests have secret meetings to discuss the fates of the single women in their cities? Is that how he met Ina so soon after his first wife died? Has he already bound her heart—and if he has, does she really love him? Or does she just want to be rich?*

I glanced at Trudi and Traudl standing to my left while the couple pointed their feet toward the post on the banks of the Isar, where their right hands would be permanently joined in blood marriage. My cousins appeared to be caught up in the event, their blue-gray eyes shining with joy for our friend. Trudi's hands were clasped together in front of her, and I wondered whether she pictured this very thing happening to her in a few years' time. At least if she married Mane, I would not have to second guess her fate. I had known him for years now, and he was a decent man, just not my type.

The couple had placed their right hands atop the post, Walfrid's covering Ina's entirely, signifying his position as head of their family. I did not have a clear view of Ina's expression from where I stood, but I could see Walfrid's clearly. The firelight illuminated his serious mien; he looked like he was contemplating ways to break her. *Ina, what have you done?* I thought to myself, longing to rush forward and shove them apart, though I had no authority to do so. But it was too late now, for the officiating priest had voiced the binding proclamation: "May the couple seal their marriage with a kiss, and may the union be complete!"

I turned away when they kissed, a strange nausea churning in my stomach. I found myself face-to-face with Erika, whose pursed lips and anguished eyes told me all that I needed to know. Ina had made the wrong choice, and we both knew it.

When I congratulated the couple after the ceremony, my voice sounded dead, so I worked hard to inject some hopefulness into my tone. Walfrid greeted me with the words, "Ah yes, the icy maiden with the fiery patriarch." His grip nearly crushed my hand as he shook it once.

"What?" I said belatedly, his choice of words plunging me into bewilderment. *Fiery patriarch? Does he mean Hans? Patriarch?* But he had already moved on to greet my cousins, and then I found myself in Ina's embrace, her soft voice thanking me for coming to her wedding. I could not find any words to say in response, but I held her tightly for a moment, all of my positive notions about Teutonic marriages shattering into pieces at my feet. *They can't all be like this. My parents loved each other. I know it. And Erika's parents love each other.*

I had not expected one of my good friends to pick wealth over happiness.

Chapter Twenty-three:
On Speaking Terms

As August progressed, I did my best to shift my attention to the upcoming school year, sifting through the catalogue of sophomore classes. I would finish my studies of Latin in the spring, and I would need to practice speaking it to get prepared for my next journey through time. Beth and I exchanged a few messages discussing what art class we should take this time around; she wanted to continue with ceramics. I ultimately encouraged her to do so while I would sign up for fiber arts and costume design, both of which should improve my sewing. Maybe I could actually create a dress or two that I could wear in the Middle Ages.

Despite my anticipation for new classes and the chance to reconnect with my cousin, a gloomy mood settled upon me as the day of my departure drew closer. Hans and I were still not on speaking terms, and I had far too many topics I needed to discuss with him. Erika and I bemoaned Ina's fate in grand detail when we got together at a beer garden right before she left for Vienna, and I very nearly spilled the secrets of the Torstein to her. My multiplying Teutonic burdens seemed to have coalesced into a slab of stone in my heart, wearing me down and eroding my opti-mism. When Hans finally confronted me on my balcony the Friday before I was set to leave for the U.S., I had no time to reveal all of my worries to him.

On that Friday afternoon, I rested upon my favorite lounge chair, clad in my silver-splattered one-piece bathing suit and a pair of dark prescription sunglasses, alternating between napping and listening to a CD by Within Tempta-tion, a Dutch band that I had recently discovered. Their music style reminded me of Tristania, harder music with female vocals interspersed with death grunts. One of the first songs on their album mentioned traveling time, which spoke too clearly to my uncertainties. I was in the process of singing along to the female part in the song "Grace" when I began getting the impression that I was no longer alone on the balcony. I opened my eyes and saw Hans standing just a meter away from my chair, wearing black cloth shorts, sandals, and a Coca-Cola T-shirt. I sat up, removed my sunglasses and hit the *stop* button on my portable CD player, sliding my headphones into my lap. I blinked at him while my eyes adjusted to the late afternoon sunlight, unsure what to say. Fear began to creep up my spine while I waited for him to speak.

"Forgive me for my intrusion, Swanhilde," he began finally, as I shaded my eyes with my left hand, "but I came up here to apologize for what I did on the night of your Pappi's summer party." He paused, looking down at me with an expression suggesting that he might be expecting a slap.

Relief flooded through my veins at his words. *If he's apologizing, maybe we're still friends after all* . . . . Irrita-tion also seeped into my heart, and I did not give him the kindest reply. "Well," I began, laying my hand back down onto the chair since my eyes had finally adjusted, "it took you long enough." I invoked my ice into my eyes out of habit, and his body came into clearer focus.

Hans did not look particularly surprised, but I saw his own eyes narrow at the sight of mine changing color. "I suppose you're upset with me for ignoring you all these weeks."

"A bit," I agreed, though that was an understatement. "I thought you were never going to talk to me again. And I was starting to worry that I'd be on my own now with the Torstein and everything. I mean, I guess I could have said something to you, apologized, but I don't know. You acted so . . . ." I broke off, realizing that I was rambling and also rather frightened to go on.

He looked down at me darkly and supplied the correct word. "Distant?" I nodded after a moment's consideration. "I suppose I should also apologize for my behavior toward you. I could have said something earlier, but I needed time, time to consider the repercussions of . . . everything." He grimaced, his eyes darkening.

I was not sure if I really wanted to have this conversation, but I waved him to the other chair. "Sit down," I suggested.

He remained standing. "You realize that what happened was a terrible mistake on my part. You are my employer's daughter. I should never have touched you like that." I opened my mouth to comment, but he lifted a hand for silence. "What happened will likely stay with you for some time, clouding your ability to truly see anyone else. It is for that that I apologize most, and with the greatest remorse. You should be spending your free time seeking decent college-age men, not fantasizing about men old enough to be your father."

My mouth had gone dry at the truth of his words. My mind raced, trying to come up with something proper to say. At last I choked out an abject lie. "I . . . I'll . . . get over it." I smiled a horribly fake smile up at Hans.

He frowned and looked out across the gardens. "It was a dangerous thing from the start, tutoring you myself on the ways of the Teutons. I wouldn't have done it at all had it not been your Mutti's wish."

He had told me that before. I likely would never have known anything about my Teuton blood—due to my father's grand abhorrence—had it not been for my mother.

Apparently at some time before her death she had come to Hans and requested that once I had reached a proper age, he should train me in Teuton history and traditions. In spite of where this training had led, I certainly did not regret it. "Well, I'm glad that you . . . taught me everything anyway," I told him. "If it hadn't been for you, I would never have found the Torstein."

Hans' lips formed a wry half-smile as he acknowledged this. "True. But we must both be cautious, or our friend-ship could lead into more dangerous grounds."

I nodded, recognizing the truth of that. Already, with him standing on my balcony with no one else around, I sensed my desire for him springing to life again. I shoved it aside and asked him, "What then is left for us?"

Hans cocked his head at me and replied simply, "I offer to be your friend, as it has been, that and nothing more. I shall not kiss you again." He smiled a bit and held his right hand out, an offer.

More than anything else, I noticed that he had *not* said, "I shall not touch you again," or "I shall not dance with you again," and that alone sent rays of hope shooting through my despair, lightening my mood considerably. I set my CD player and headphones onto the table to my left and rose from my chair to stand before him, formally accepting his proposal. "In that case, I'll be your friend as well, and I'll try to keep my youthful lusts in check." I grinned as I took his hand, glad that I felt confident enough to joke about such a serious matter.

His expression turned fierce, but I could tell it was feigned, and he ordered, "See that you do," shaking my hand once, firmly.

My ice vividly sensed the heat of fire in his blood, so I stepped away before I did something stupid like throw myself into his arms. There were so many things I needed to tell him, but I had no clue where to begin. The devilish forces inherent to the Torstein and time travel? The *Eihalbe* and its counsel? The silvery acorn in the planter behind him? My fears that Ina had married an abusive priest?

When I finally opened my mouth to speak, I heard myself saying, "I think I'm coming home at Christmas."

Hans looked taken aback, and his black eyebrows came together. "I thought you enjoyed spending last Christmas with the Fischers."

"I did. It's just that . . . there's a lot I need to talk to you about . . . and I have to finish packing tonight." I broke off, realizing how desperate that had probably sounded to him. Thinking fast, I appended, "And I have to start preparing for my next journey with the Torstein."

Hans had leaned back against the railing, and he folded his arms across his chest when I broached that subject. "I saw the comment you made on your thread, and I read all the responses it generated." He frowned, his dark blue eyes reproachful. "You may be taking it too far at this point, Swanie. I'm sure you saw that two users have already brought up the fall of Muniche." I nodded once and rubbed my hands against my bare thighs, trying to dry their nervous sweat. "It won't be long before someone mentions Prince Otto's discoveries and connects them with the topic itself."

"You're probably right," I said, thinking back to the conversation I had with Marga several weeks ago. My topic had inspired her to think of the Torstein while other users had brought up familiar events like the Black Plague and Gutenberg's invention of the printing press. "Do you think I should delete the topic?" I asked, suddenly feeling as though spies eavesdropped on us.

Hans sighed and let his arms fall back to his sides. "I'll leave it up for another week and then delete it myself. I've been blocking a rash of bots lately, so it's best to refrain from discussing sensitive topics, I think." I agreed with him and looked toward the silvery green planter again, wondering if I should bring that up before he vanished into oblivion like the Teuton priest he was. But then he thrust his right hand into the pocket of his shorts. "You're leaving for the U.S. tomorrow, I know, and your twentieth birthday was Wednesday, so I should have given this to you earlier."

He pulled a tiny wrapped box from his pocket and handed it to me.

I accepted it and tilted my head at him playfully. "A birthday present? I'm pretty sure there aren't any new Nightwish albums out right now." He had gotten me their second album as a welcome home gift back in May.

The package was far too small to hold another Gothic metal album, and Hans chuckled tolerantly. "Just open it," he advised.

I did, casting the wrapping paper onto the floor of the balcony, then carefully lifting the lid of the white box inside. I stared, and my hands began to tremble when I saw what he had given me. It was a necklace, a gold chain, and upon it hung a small golden locket shaped like an oval, scintillating in the sunlight. I could not find any words to say, as I took it from its box and held it up to see it better. It was beautiful, held closed by a tiny hinge on the left side, its borders decorated with tiny rose petals. "I figured you could put some picture in it to remind you of home while you're away at college," Hans explained. "Something Teutonic perhaps . . . or simply something you love."

I already knew *exactly* what I would put into the locket, and I fought back a blush at the thought. I would wear it every day. And I would have to search through all of my pictures of Hans before leaving tonight, print one out on photo paper, cut it down, place it inside . . . . "Thank you, Hans," I said as calmly as I could, placing the chain back into its box and closing the lid. "That's really great, actually."

Hans looked satisfied, and he acknowledged, "I knew you'd appreciate it." I placed the box onto the table beside my lounge chair, and Hans turned toward the railing. That was when I realized that I had no idea how he had gotten onto my balcony in the first place. There was no way he had come through my bedroom. He never went in there.

He stood at the railing and traced the fingers of his right hand along the top of it, seemingly judging the distance to the ground. "Are you going to jump off like fire again?" I queried, moving forward to look over the side myself. Directly below us stood the back deck and the pool.

Hans raised an eyebrow and gave me a rather suggestive smile. "Want to come with me?"

I gasped in alarm, stepping back from the railing. The idea that Hans could sweep to the ground safely from the second floor balcony did not seem shocking to me; he was fire, after all. But me, the *ice* princess? And in the daylight? "I don't know . . . . Someone might see," I pointed out with a frown.

"Your Pappi won't be home until five." Hans' tone sounded calculating.

That made me think of something else. "Why aren't you still working?" I eyed his casual outfit in speculation.

"I finished early." He glowered at me impatiently and held out his hand. "Are you coming?"

My lust for him had returned again, and I considered what might happen if I agreed. I would probably land in the pool, freezing some of it perhaps, but the exhilaration would likely end with my desire for Hans growing stronger than ever. So I shook my head slowly and declined. "Maybe some other time, after dark."

Hans shrugged once and pulled his hand back. "Suit yourself." He vanished over the side, and I looked over the railing to see him land somewhat gracefully upon a potted plant right beside the pool. The plant abruptly began to sizzle with a dark fire. I heard Hans grumble in annoyance, and he patted it a few times until the fire went out. I gave a cackle of laughter, and he smirked up at me. Not long afterward I went inside, thankful that my friendship with Hans was no longer in danger.

I put both Nightwish albums into my stereo while I zoomed around my room packing and sorting. Last year I had spent weeks getting everything situated. Now I no longer felt the freshman panic, so I had procrastinated on my packing. I had to chase Thunar out of my suitcases three times, his furry gray face appearing more wounded each time. "Ach, Thu, you'll still have Lise to play with you," I reminded him as I set him upon his cat tree. "And she and Basti will make sure you've got food and a clean litter box. Don't forget, you'll have my entire bed to yourself." I kissed him on the nose, and he rumbled quietly in response.

About a half hour before dinner, a short knock at my door startled me out of my closet, where I stood thumbing through all of my fancy dresses. Last year I had brought only three, two of which I had worn to an orchestra concert and a Shakespeare play that the college had staged. This semester there was to be an opera, and in the spring a Ukrainian choir would perform a collection of folk songs. I had not yet decided which dresses to bring with me, but I vacated the closet and answered the knock at my bedroom door.

Sebastian stood there still dressed for work, holding a thin package out to me. "Happy birthday again, Swanie. This came for you today," he said.

I tilted my head at the package, bemused. I had already celebrated my birthday with the people that mattered—my close family and friends—so it took me off guard to receive two more presents today. "Kind of late, isn't it?" I inquired, taking the box from his hand. It felt light and unobtrusive, and when I looked at the return address, I saw that it was from Erika.

"The mail service from Vienna must be slow. You coming to dinner? Gregor's setting up a sandwich platter, I think."

"Yeah, I'll be down there in a few, but not for long. I'm packing like a Tasmanian devil right now." Sebastian laughed and said that he would see me downstairs, and I carried the box to my bed after shutting the door behind him.

I slit the tape on the unremarkable box using an icy fingernail and retrieved the card inside. It was a print of one of Erika's sketches of me in my Gothic fuchsia skirt, and I saw that she had clearly exaggerated the beauty of my face, hair, and bust. I snorted quietly and opened the card, which read, *Dear Swanie, Don't ever forget that women don't need men's approval. We are the conquerors who can please ourselves without making a mess. Happy Birthday. –Erika*

I laid the card onto my bed and gave a slight shake of my head, unsure what my friend meant by such a message. But then I shook the box, and her gift slid its way out onto my bed, encased in a smaller package decorated with flowery ribbons.

She had gotten me a vibrator.

Chapter Twenty-four:
An Outsider's Perspective

I left for Philadelphia on Saturday morning and spent the rest of the day trying to compensate for the additional six hours. I gave up and crashed around nine p.m., curled beneath the blankets of my bottom bunk in Beth's room. Like the previous year, my cousin and I would have several days to relax before striking out for Virginia. Since Hans had closed himself off to me for two months, I looked forward to unburdening myself to my closest friend. As an outsider, she may offer advice that a Teuton would not.

We went to church together as a family on Sunday morning, and quite a few older people greeted me warmly and mentioned that they prayed regularly for my ministry in Germany. I shied away from those comments and talked vaguely about playing the organ at my church back home. "These people don't seem to realize that I *live* in Germany. I'm not a missionary there," I muttered to Beth after a sweet lady with gray curls praised my willingness to live morally in a foreign country.

Beth snickered. "It's my mom's fault more than anything else. She always adds you to the prayer list when you go back to München. I think sometimes she wishes you were her daughter, too."

I glanced toward Aunt Linda, who had staked out territory for our family at a pew five rows from the back of the church. Onkel Jens had disappeared to put on his choir robes; he sang tenor. "Well, you're a better daughter than I could ever be. Stellar student with a summer job at the library and a simmering relationship with a good Christian guy."

"I'm not a stellar student. I got a B+ in World History," Beth reminded me, and an instant later Joel crept up behind her to give her a hug. She squealed.

"Hey Swanie, glad you're back," Joel said as Beth wormed her way out of his loose embrace. She turned around to smack at him, but he caught her right hand in his. "Shot another squirrel yesterday right through the brain. Wow, you smell nice." He leaned forward to sniff Beth's hair.

"Sensual Amber," she clarified, squeezing his hand and letting go. "Don't you have to tune your guitar?" She nodded toward the stage.

"Yeah, probably." He ran a hand through his gelled hair and turned for the front of the sanctuary, where the worship team unpacked their instruments.

"Did you shoot the squirrel with a gun?" I asked as he moved away from us, trying to recall whether Joel had ever mentioned anything about hunting before.

He twisted his upper body back toward us, both hands raised in a parody of nocking an arrow. "Archery," he responded, sending his imaginary arrow in a straight trajectory for Beth's chest.

"He just shot you through the heart," I said with a grin.

"He's done that well enough already," she complained, smirking back at me before lifting a hand to greet one of her friends.

I did my best to pay attention to the sermon, though jet lag still tugged at the edges of my consciousness. Though I generally appreciated the messages that Beth's pastor delivered, I found myself thinking about the modern style of worship music that her church had now fully embraced. The songs seemed repetitive and shallow to me, some of the lyrics sounding lovesick enough to get in bed with God. *Give me the organ any day,* I thought to myself while I fought to keep my eyes open. *Can't open the gates of time with an electric guitar. And metal musicians don't fudge the notes. I heard Joel mess up at least eight times.*

We ate lunch with Joel's family at an Italian restaurant in Marlton called Franco's, one of my favorite eateries in New Jersey. I talked with his younger sister Gloria before the food came, having just met her that day. She was a high school senior who played violin in a local youth orchestra, and she planned to study violin performance in college. She bubbled over with information on the trials inherent to learning violin, mentioning that her cat constantly swatted at her strings whenever she had to replace them. I laughed at that mental image, glad that Thunar was not the type to skulk around the organ pedals. He disappeared whenever I practiced at home, likely because he disliked my preferred instrument's volume.

Joel's father and Onkel Jens talked business, and the mothers discussed a wider variety of topics from gardening to home décor to baseball. Shortly after our entrees came and I dug into my pepperoni stromboli, Gloria asked me a question that was honestly stupid. "So I guess you're really good at speaking German?"

I looked across the table at her, feeling my forehead wrinkle at how she had worded her query. She seemed educated enough about music, but maybe that was as far as her cleverness went. "I would hope so," I responded in Bayerisch, knowing that no one at the table would understand that except Onkel Jens.

Gloria's expression appeared dumbfounded. "What was that?" Beth asked through a mouthful of lasagna. Her grasp of German was far from perfect, but she always worked to follow along whenever I spoke it.

"Dialekt," I answered with a snarky grin, cutting another bite of my meal.

"Hey, no closing all of us out like that. It's not fair," my cousin chided.

"She didn't close *me* out," my uncle remarked in Bayerisch from the far end of the table. I caught his eye and exchanged a knowing grin. My aunt rolled her eyes at him.

"I just finished studying French last year," Gloria put in, sounding as though she longed to reel the conversation back toward her. "It wasn't easy," she noted in horribly accented French, brushing a blond curl back from her face.

"You'd better not try that in Paris," I said in the same language.

I had spoken too swiftly; she blinked at me and asked me to repeat myself. Instead, I carefully explained, "French people expect everyone to know their language from birth, along with all the letters they don't pronounce."

My French exposition was met with silence. Then Onkel Jens harrumphed at me. "Cut it out, Swanie," he said in Bayerisch.

I looked around the front of Beth and Aunt Linda and commented, "Didn't realize your French was as good as mine," in dialect.

"Yours sounds like you're dragging it across grooved asphalt."

"Really?" I muttered in English, shifting my attention back to my stromboli.

"You watching the Phillies game this afternoon?" Aunt Linda interpolated, likely an attempt to bring peaceful discourse back to our table. I concentrated on my food, uninterested in chatter about America's pastime. After I had taken several bites, I noticed Joel staring at me with an unreadable expression.

"How do you put up with this all the time?" He posited his question to Beth, gesturing between Onkel Jens and me with his fork. "Can you understand them when they go off like that?"

"Only when it's German. But usually my dad doesn't indulge her jabbering since she's here to perfect her English." She kicked me lightly in the shin.

"My English is already perfect," I shot back with a glare.

On Sunday night my cousin and I chatted about our respective summers for over an hour before bed, having shut ourselves into her bedroom with glasses of iced tea and a bag of pretzels. Beth's summer had been mostly unremarkable. She and her parents had spent two weeks in Ocean City, and Joel had joined them for the final week. Afterward Beth had worked part-time at her local library in Blackwood until just last week, putting away as much money as she could while spending some here and there for trinkets and food. "I think Wawa saw too much of me. I ended up getting a hoagie for lunch almost every day I worked," she rehashed, resting her head back against the mattress behind her. She sat to my left dressed in what had once been her high school gym uniform; now she used it as pajamas.

"Wish they had Wawa in Virginia," I said, thinking about how convenient that store tended to be for New Jersey natives.

"They do, but they're all near I-95. Sheetz is all we've got in the mountains."

"Yeah, Sheetz is pretty decent," I said, crunching a hard pretzel.

"So what sort of Teuton stuff did you do over the summer?" Beth inquired, tilting her face toward me. "I can tell you've got some crazy stories tucked away. I saw it in your eyes when we met at the airport."

I smiled at my cousin, gratitude welling within me. "It's been a wild summer on the Teuton front," I admitted, "and I've had to keep a lot of it to myself."

"Well, I'm all ears," Beth pledged, sitting up and folding her hands in her lap, looking aptly attentive.

I plunged into the Hans story straightaway, which prompted my cousin to gasp and cover her mouth as I laid out the details. When I had paused at the part where he had fled from me—taking a sip of tea to clear the resultant lump from my throat—she murmured, "So you finally kissed him."

"He kissed me," I corrected. "It wasn't like I pushed him into it."

"And you danced all romantically first," she added, sounding entranced.

I exhaled and shut my eyes, reminiscing on how complete I had felt with his fiery presence so close to my body, claiming the spirit of the night for ourselves. "It was the best elemental dance I've ever experienced," I related. "And he's an expert at kissing. It felt like we were molding into each other, like I could spend eternity in his arms."

"Guess he's not asexual after all," Beth remarked with a snicker, awakening me from my muses. I opened my eyes and looked up at the letters carved into the wood above my bunk.

"Guess not," I said, suddenly wondering how many other women Hans had kissed like that in his lifetime. There had certainly been others; the man was over fifty years old. Why had none of them agreed to marry him?

"But he ran off and left you there to blame yourself."

I shivered a little and rolled my shoulders, sitting up again and draining the rest of my iced tea. "I think he blamed himself, actually. When he finally apologized, he sounded frustrated with himself. He thinks now I won't be able to love anybody my own age." He was right about that. My chances had been lost long ago.

"Technically, the two of you have only been legal for what, two years? And he's known you since you were a kid, so the whole thing is probably really awkward for him." Beth gazed sympathetically toward me.

"Six years. The German age of consent is fourteen. And I've known him since he started working for my Pappi after my Mutti passed away. That was when my Pappi decided he didn't want to deal with his own finances anymore."

"Wait a minute. Are you saying that you and Hans could have had sex back in 1993 if you'd wanted to?" Beth had jerked into a sitting position, her expression appalled.

"I didn't know a lot about sex back then but yes. We can legally drink at age fourteen, too."

Beth blinked at me rapidly, her revulsion emanating from her posture like heat from a wood-burning stove. "And I always thought Germany was modern."

"We have a different outlook than you Americans. Here it's all about 'safety first.' In Germany if you do something stupid, it's your own fault."

Beth shuddered and pulled a handful of pretzels out of the bag between us. "I bet a lot of vulnerable people have been exploited with your laws treating fourteen-year-olds like adults," she said, crunching her pretzels one at a time.

I shrugged, never really having thought about it like that. "Maybe. But give Hans some credit. He didn't kiss me until I was almost twenty." I laughed through my nose, still not far enough removed from the event to properly scorn it.

From there we moved on to the subject of Ina and her husband Walfrid, a topic that I could not discuss without condensing myself into a ball. "It just seemed like it all happened too fast, too suddenly," I finished, my eyes riveted on the bag I had dumped beneath Beth's desk. "I didn't even know she had an actual boyfriend. It's like she vanished from ICQ altogether once she met him. And now they're married, and he gave off this creepy vibe at their wedding, like he wanted to control her every move. And they live in Berlin, so it's not like we'll be able to watch out for her."

I fell silent, and Beth sipped at her tea, appearing pensive. "Did she seem to be happy at her wedding?" she inquired.

"She did, but she may already be bound to him. I don't know."

"Can you remind me what that means again? Sometimes all this Teuton stuff gets jumbled up in my head."

"Sure. For some Teuton couples, once they decide that their relationship is serious, they meet in the realm of the spirit, and the man weaves a spell around the woman's heart to claim it for himself. Creating that type of bond enhances the trust and loyalty that the bound woman experiences, and technically it keeps her heart safe from devilish forces and villainous men." I rested my chin on my knees and wound my arms more tightly around my ankles, imagining what it would be like to offer my heart to Hans. *He would never take it. He still thinks you're a child.*

"And it's usually Teuton priests that bind their wives' hearts, right?"

"Yeah, usually. But anyone can learn the spell if they're curious enough. It's in the old version of *Der Weg* from the 1800s."

Beth held her peace for a time, and when I looked toward her, I saw that she had hunched in upon herself just like I had. She shook her head slowly, her upper lip curling in a revolted fashion. "I just don't know if it's a good idea to be with a Teuton priest," she said under her breath, avoiding my gaze. "I mean, I know you love Hans, but . . . if he ever decided to love you back . . . would you be happy if he forced you into some weird mystic bond? I guess it's all well and good if it's protective, but the way you describe it sounds like you're pretty much giving up your free will." She chewed on her bottom lip and sighed, then took up her glass to finish her iced tea.

She raised a valid point, but I had already justified it to myself many times over the years. "I think it comes down to whether or not you trust the priest. With Hans, I've known him almost my whole life, and if he ever offered to bind my heart I would agree, no questions asked." My lips curved into an empty smile, and I got to my feet to stretch. "What worries me with Ina's situation is how fast it happened. I don't think *I* could trust any guy to bind my heart after knowing him for only five months. Anyone could put up a front for five months."

Beth rose to her feet as well, picking up her empty glass and the bag of pretzels and turning for the door to the hallway. "You've got a point there. But at least she loves her daughter, and she'll never want for money. So I guess sometimes you have to make concessions depending on what makes you happy."

I followed my cousin down the darkened hallway toward the kitchen, where we would deposit our wares before going to bed. "It makes sense, I guess," I said, casting a quick glance into the parlor, where Jenna lay sprawled in her doggy bed. "And everybody's different, so I'll just have to try to find peace with it," I added as I rinsed out my glass. *But it's really hard to find peace with the possibility of one of my good friends signing her life away to some unknown priest.*

When I fell asleep that night, I entered a world of dreams in which a shaded entity repeatedly asked for my heart, his warmth seeping into my chest in a soothing manner. By the next morning I suspected that a small portion of my unhappiness may actually stem from a germ of envy. Ina had snared herself a Teuton priest, but the one I yearned for continued to hold me at a distance.

Chapter Twenty-five:
Drunken Assault

Upon returning to college, I discovered that being a sophomore afforded privileges about which freshman could only dream. Beth, Joel, and I were assigned to a newer dorm, and our connecting rooms sported a tiny kitchen in between, along with the usual bathroom. I was able to arrange my class schedule in a more pleasant fashion, avoiding the early classes altogether. On Mondays, Wednesdays, and Fridays my last class would end at two p.m., giving me ample time to chat on ICQ or the forum with my friends in Germany. I even managed to sign up for two hours of practice on the theater organ, the grandest one on campus.

Though I did not need to take any history classes for my business degree, I checked a few books out of the library on medieval fashion and culture, intending to peruse them on the side. Hans had deleted my topic on time travel as promised, but the varied responses to that topic stayed with me during my transition back into college life. By the end of September, I had resolved to use the Torstein to visit the darkest and most contested incident in Teuton history: the fall of Muniche.

The words of a user who went by the screenname *Waldzwerg* had really struck a chord within me. *Waldzwerg* had asserted that seeing the glory of the Bavarian empire in the years just before Muniche's fall and then watching its ruin would help quite a few people—Teuton or not—to better appreciate history. Teuton history would be far more intriguing to observe than simple German history, I reasoned, especially since few people cared about it in modern days. If I used the Torstein to go to the eleventh century, fitting in with society would be challenging, but at least I would know the language. The experience would improve both my Teutonica and my Latin.

I began to spend Saturday evenings backstage at the theater, piecing dresses together from unneeded fabric, working to improve my sewing skills. I figured that if Beth agreed to go with me, we would need at least three dresses each in styles that indicated wealth. One woman who was to be an understudy for the upcoming opera already had a degree in art history, and she gave me helpful pointers about what the noble ladies were wearing in eleventh century Europe. From her I learned that I would need to make head coverings to match each dress and that female attire should be made to accentuate a woman's form. I wondered how uncomfortably hot the summers would be when clad in multiple layers of dress. There would also be a lack of deodorant. I figured that I might have to bring a secret stash of twentieth century provisions along for the ride—definitely contact lenses since glasses were not yet in common use, and maybe tampons like Marga had said.

I returned to my dorm just before ten p.m. on the first Saturday in November, my thoughts a thousand years in the past, a sense of accomplishment putting a smile on my face. I had just finished stitching a dress of dyed blue linen, the first one that I felt certain could play the role that I needed. *I'll have to figure out what to do about shoes and bags,* I thought while I ascended the main staircase to the second-floor hallway, where I could hear raucous laughter going on. Beth and Joel had gone to the football game and likely would not have returned yet. I had heard a lot of cheering coming from the stadium on my walk back to the dorm, so our team had probably won.

Someone on our hall had invited half the campus over for a party, it seemed, for I soon found myself having to squeeze through groups of rowdy college students, most of them male. I could smell alcohol and marijuana, which meant that other drugs may be in play. *Should have come up from the side door,* I realized as I ducked beneath a bearded man's grasping fingers. He proceeded to puke right after I made it past him, and I moved quickly to my room, a respite from the fray. I still could not understand why so many people viewed college as a place to party rather than a place to learn.

I unlocked the door to my room and opened it, glad to leave the hall behind. The light was already on, and I paused just inside the room; had Beth come back early? Then I saw who occupied the room, and I froze with my left hand on the doorknob, my eyes widening in horror behind my glasses.

"Finally, she's here!"

"Sam's right. She's hot. Take a look at those tits!"

The first guy who had spoken lounged in the desk chair that I shared with Beth, wearing nothing but stained gray sweatpants, his chest scrawny and flecked with limp-looking fuzz, his black hair up in dreadlocks. He held a joint in the fingers of his right hand and looked only half awake. The one who felt the need to comment on my body sat on Beth's bed with a can of cheap beer cradled in one hand, his dark eyes sweeping over me from head to toe before remaining on my chest. I saw movement on my bed out of the corner of my eye but figured I had better address the two jerks first, since Beth and I did not generally open our space to carousing drunks. "Sam's room is the next one over," I stated pointedly, jerking my right thumb toward the doorway that joined our rooms. Unfortunately Joel had been assigned a derelict roommate this year. He had trouble studying in his room thanks to Sam's tendency to attract obnoxious friends.

"He's nearly done making Jell-O shots, and you'll be the first to try them," a low voice said from behind me. A thick hand fell upon the back of my neck before I had time to react, and I felt myself being pushed into the room, my purse detached from my arm and kicked into a corner.

I heard the door to the hallway close behind me, and a seed of panic began to grow in my stomach. *They want to rape me. No doubt that's their final goal.* I sensed my ice scraping at the edges of my veins, but I endeavored to rein it in. Yes, I could surely beat the crap out of these guys if I set my element free, but they may not all be wasted enough to forget such a spectacle. I would have to find another way out of this. *The game's already over. Beth and Joel will be back soon.*

I took a deep breath and tried to steady myself as the oaf behind me tugged my leather jacket free. "Let's get you more comfortable," he said in my ear, alcohol permeating his breath but not slurring his speech. Not drunk enough to forget. One of his hands worked its way across my face and pressed heavily against my mouth.

Suddenly an ape-like moan pealed forth from my bed. I had not yet had the chance to really focus on the activities in play there, but now I saw a muscular guy sprawled with his legs bare, chest heaving. I recognized him as a member of the university's basketball team—and he was rubbing his cock with my vibrator.

"Hey, Zack's about to get off with this ho's toy!" the jerk holding the beer can announced, sounding entertained.

"Just keep workin' it, man," the one with the joint murmured, obviously the least lucid of the four of them. If I invoked my ice before him, he would probably assume he was dreaming.

"Let's make her swallow it. Come help me." The bastard behind me let go of my mouth, pinned my arms in a steel grip, and shoved me toward my bed, forcing me to my knees. I took a deep breath in preparation to scream—not that anyone would hear with the rowdy party going on—but before I could make a sound, a fist struck my diaphragm, knocking the air out of me. I felt someone pull my ponytail back so that my chin was level with the athlete's cock while I struggled to breathe, darkness encroaching on my peripheral vision. I finally managed to suck in a breath through my nose as my eyes blinked at the throbbing penis. I could tell that he was seconds away from finishing, and it looked like his fingers had cracked my vibrator. I tried belatedly to struggle, but the two men who detained me had me beat on both strength and size. "Open up, bitch," the one pinning my arms ordered in a gravelly tone. "Open up and take it."

I pressed my lips closed and refused to respond. If they forced me to take that ridiculous athlete into my mouth, I would bite down as hard as I could. But he finished before the two could shame me further, a fair portion of his semen splattering my nose and mouth. I spit it right back at him and tried to twist my head away from my captors' grip, unsuccessfully. The athlete on my bed pushed himself onto his elbows as his penis shriveled, shifting glazed green eyes toward my vibrator, which no longer buzzed. "I think I broke it. I worked it so hard I broke it."

"Let's break *her* next." Something struck my abdomen again, and I gagged, clinging to consciousness, my jaw falling open as I gasped for breath. *I can't let them do this. I have to use my ice . . . no one will believe them . . . .*

Before I could focus clearly enough to freeze my blood, the half-naked man on my bed had jammed the lip of a glass bottle into my mouth, dumping its clear contents down my throat. "That's right, drink. It'll help you relax. Drink like a good girl." The low voice crooned in my ear, and I felt someone's hands pulling my pants to the floor. I could still hardly breathe, and the tasteless liquor burned my throat. Vodka. At this rate they may succeed in making me black out, and if my friends did not return in time, I would have no memory of how I had lost my virginity. *Come on, Swanie, you've had a lot to drink before. Concentrate on what's deep in your spirit . . . in your blood . . . freeze yourself . . . freeze this room . . . .*

"Isn't she supposed to be rich? Maybe she's got some jewels hidden around here somewhere," the athlete said, prompting me to choke on the liquor. "Come over here and hold this while I go through her stuff."

I coughed and tried to struggle again, and the bottle fell away from me while my lungs gasped for air. Some of the vodka had gone down my windpipe. My vision blurred behind my glasses, and I coughed and choked, rough fingers probing the flesh between my legs. "Aw, shit, the front door's closed." Apparently he had found my tampon. "Have to go in the back." The fingers slid to my anus.

I tried to scream but managed only a frail croak. At least I could breathe again. My bleary eyes focused on the guy with the dreadlocks, who had crouched down before me, what could have been pity shining in his drowsy eyes. "You really have a beautiful face," he told me quietly, "in spite of the glasses." His fingers, softer than those of the oaf who was in the process of spreading my butt cheeks apart, stroked the side of my face and then slipped the end of his joint between my lips. "Take an easy breath, love. I'm taking care of you."

I had never smoked once in my life, and the sweet fumes of the joint caused my lungs to rebel again. I coughed violently and fell completely to the floor, catching a short glimpse of the athlete peering at a small object in his right hand. He was still sitting on my bed, and he was holding the Torstein. "No—" I choked out, the word scraping my throat on its way out. "Don't—"

"This doesn't look too valuable. But you seem to think it is." He snickered, but now all I could see was the gray carpet beneath me, and I felt something thrust its way up my rectum. I screamed, loud enough this time to garner some attention at long last.

I had trouble following the exact sequence of events, but Sam and one of his other friends—who had been finishing up their Jell-O shots in the kitchen—came at last to investigate my cries. I heard several voices arguing followed by a jolt of anguish in my rear. My arms free at last, I brought them to the floor to drag myself toward the bathroom. My intestines were churning. I needed the toilet.

And I needed to force myself to throw up. The alcohol had begun to impair my judgment.

I collapsed onto the rim of the toilet just as my intestines erupted. It felt as though the muscles back there had forgotten how to control themselves, doubtless thanks to that big jerk's brutality. I knew he had not used a condom. *He better not have herpes or something,* I thought while I crouched and whimpered, thin arms wrapped around my torso. Somehow my shirt had survived, which was honestly surprising, especially since the idiot with the beer can had crowed about the size of my breasts. Eventually I noticed my pants and underwear bunched around my ankles. My underwear was dotted with blood.

I dropped my head into my hands, shivering and waiting to be sure that the cascade from my rectum had ceased. I worked to think clearly, trying to push aside the vodka's soft shroud. *I have to get back at that fool who raped me. Make sure none of them ever try it again. And I have to find out whether that pale freak took the Torstein with him. I should never have brought it here with me. Damn.*

After using about half of a roll of toilet paper to wipe the stains from my butt, I knelt before the toilet and stuck two fingers to the back of my throat. The vodka burned my throat again on its way back up, but I had no time to waste. I needed to be able to grasp my element properly and clean up this mess.

Chapter Twenty-six:
Taking Control

After I had finished vomiting the majority of the vodka, I flushed the toilet and crouched down before it, resting my forehead upon the now-closed lid. Although I knew what I needed to do, my body would not obey my brain's commands. It had curled itself into a ball of quivering flesh, salty tears leaking from my eyes. That had been my first experience with abject violence in my short life, and all of the death-related trauma from my childhood resurfaced in my mind, rendering me useless. *What good am I if I can't stand up for myself in a group of outsiders? Why didn't I scream the second I saw them lounging in my room? Why didn't I bite that one jerk's fingers? I couldn't think . . . I couldn't fight . . . and now my incompetence may have cost me the Torstein . . . .*

"Swanie?" A male voice from the bathroom doorway attempt to break into my murky swamp of despair, its tenor soft and vaguely familiar. "Swanie? Hey . . . can I get you anything? Some water or tea? A blanket?"

I sniffed and worked to stem the flood of tears. I took two shaky breaths and managed to raise my forehead from the toilet lid, turning slowly toward the doorway, my fingers clutching the toilet as though it could safeguard me. The chill of its porcelain soothed my icy spirit in an outlandish way. I allowed my right hand to fall to the floor, and I squinted toward the man who stood beside the sink. He was very, *very* tall with buzzed dark hair and slanted eyes, his expression looking deeply concerned. I thought I knew him. But what was he doing here? "Min-ho?"

"In the flesh. Jeez, Swanie, if I'd known what they were doing to you in there, I would've stopped it sooner." He looked extremely upset.

I blinked at him and shifted around so that I sat beside the toilet rather than facing it. I flexed my fingers and wrapped my arms around my knees. "Why are you here?" He had never seemed to be the wild type to me. I knew him thanks to organ performance class; he was a sophomore piano major studying organ as his second instrument. And he played as a reserve for the university basketball team.

"I was helping Sam with the Jell-O shots," he answered, sounding apologetic. "Decided to try 'hanging out' for once. Bad idea, apparently."

A tiny laugh contracted my chest. "I don't recommend it."

"They're acting like animals out there. It's disgusting." Min-ho glanced to his right, toward Sam and Joel's room. "But really, do you need a blanket or something to drink? I can see what I can find in the kitchen here." He looked at my face again, worry evident in his bearing.

I looked down at myself, realizing that my pants and underwear were still bunched up between me and the floor. "A new . . . set of underwear . . . would be good, actually," I admitted, my reason slowly returning in the presence of a friend. He nodded, and I shakily gave him directions on where to find a pair.

In his absence, I pulled myself to my feet and shuffled my way out of a set of clothing that I would probably throw away. I laid both of my hands down on the sink to steady myself as I looked at my reflection in the mirror. Face flushed and sopping with tears, locks of black hair tugged free from my scrunchie, shock shining in my gray eyes.

Never in my life had I expected to have some drunken brute force himself on me from behind. I had to ensure that it would never happen again. My ice began to cool my blood, and I took my glasses off and set them down beside the faucet, allowing my irises to turn a frigid blue. *I'll make them regret this.*

Eventually Min-ho reappeared, holding a pair of underpants and shorts in one hand and a bottle of Deer Park water in the other. "Got you this whether you want it or not," he said, setting it down onto the sink. Then he stepped back into the hallway and turned away, giving me privacy to clothe myself. That man deserved an award for not having gawked at my pelvis once.

I came to his side in the hallway a moment later, unscrewing the cap of the water bottle as I did so. "Thanks," I told him. "Really. It's a relief to know there's some decent guys in the world."

He made a scoffing sound, his hands on his hips, his face turned toward the guys' room once more. "More of them would be decent if they didn't drink themselves silly. Think I'm just going to go back upstairs to my room once you're sure you're okay. Was going to spend some time dancing, but it's not worth it."

I smiled and took a drink, the cool water cleansing my throat, restoring my icy spirit. "Beth and Joel will be back soon. I think they went to the game."

Min-ho heaved a sigh and looked toward me again. I had leaned against the wall just beside the bathroom doorway, my weak eyes focused on the dark kitchen. "Do you want me to call security or the police?" he inquired, prompting me to look up at his face. "I mean, that mammoth definitely raped you. You could probably get him expelled or arrested."

"Mammoth." I giggled, sensing my ice lurking impatiently in my blood. It was time to take matters into my own hands. "No, don't worry about it. That would just drag things out, and he'd probably get off with the way the laws are."

He tilted his head at me. "Then you want him to get away with it?"

I gave him a small smile. "I'll take care of it. But hey, did you happen to see whether Zack took anything with him when he left? I think he stole something that belongs to me." I bit my lip and glanced toward the room I shared with Beth. Our entire apartment seemed to be empty aside from Min-ho and me. I wondered if he had beat up any of those jerks, and whether Sam had helped.

My friend shook his head. "No, I didn't notice. I was too busy punching the mammoth. What did he take? Your wallet?"

"It's . . . more like a . . . crystal. A red crystal."

"I can get it back. I'll threaten to get Zack kicked off the team if he doesn't give it back." Min-ho's expression hardened in resolution, and he rubbed his hands on his light blue jeans, looking as though he was fully prepared to beat up his own teammate. I had never imagined him to be a tough guy, even though he played on the basketball team. His fingers commanded the piano keys with a fluidity that few could claim.

"Thanks," I said with a smile. If he could get the Torstein back, that would cross one task off of my to-do list. "Can you go get it now? I can just sit here while you're gone and keep trying to pull myself together." I slid down to the floor and took a deep breath, resting the back of my head against the wall.

"Sure. But you might want to lock the doors behind me, especially if that big brute's going around bragging about what he did." Min-ho grimaced.

He had a point, so I returned to my room and turned the lock. The mess that the jerks had left behind twisted my stomach. I saw semen and some other liquid staining the floor beside my bed, and there were small patches of blood here and there. Those could have belonged to me or to whichever guys Sam and Min-ho had attacked. The lazy guy's joint lay not far from my bed, having singed the gray carpet. A crumpled can of discarded beer lay steps from our desk, and the chair was on its side just beneath the window. I suddenly began to see why Erika disliked men; they behaved like sloppy beasts when in groups.

I locked the door to Sam and Joel's room behind Min-ho, and he pledged to do a secret knock upon his return. The guys' room was disorderly and smelled like week-old pizza. Its floor was littered with junk, all of which looked like it belonged to Sam. *We've got to get out of this place. All of us,* I decided, planting myself on the floor against the door to the hall and nursing my water bottle. *This must be why Joel spends more time in our room than his. We have to get our own apartment somewhere off campus so we don't have to deal with this crap.*

When Min-ho returned, he looked aggravated. "My opinion of Zack just got a whole lot worse," he stated as I shut the door behind him. My heart sank, for I figured that he had been unable to retrieve the Torstein. But when I turned to face him, I saw that he held it between his index finger and thumb.

I pressed my right hand to my heart, breathing a heavy sigh of relief. "Ach, Min-ho, thank you *so* much. I owe you big." I held out my left hand, and he dropped the stone into it. I curled my fingers around it possessively, feeling the prickling in my blood as it sensed the stone's magic.

"Ah, it was no problem. It's just that Zack took things a little too far." His eyebrows came together, and he wrinkled his nose and leaned against the door. "I told him it meant a lot to you because it's a family heirloom. I know I made that part up. But then he said, 'Oh, did she get it from Hitler?'" He looked disgusted.

I rolled my eyes, that jibe not wounding me as much as it could have if I had not already spent several school years in the U.S. Brainless peers had thrown the Nazi rhetoric in my face many times before. "That just proves his IQ is under fifty. Wonder how he got that sports scholarship?" Min-ho guffawed, and we shared a moment of mockery at Zack's expense. "Did you happen to see the mammoth out there?" I asked after our laughter had quieted.

My friend rolled his own eyes. "Yeah, he's in the game room dancing like a weasel and trying to hit on a short blond. Looks like he's got a black eye now."

I thanked Min-ho and told him that he could go back to his apartment if he wanted, that I was fine now. The water had refreshed me, and my element stoked my urge for vengeance. But to do what I had to do, I would need to eliminate witnesses. He looked me up and down for the first time since he had found me in the bathroom, likely trying to discern whether I had truly recovered. I reminded him that my friends would be back soon and that I could just keep the doors locked until they got here. At last he nodded and prepared to return to his apartment. "If you have any trouble with any of the guys here after this, let me know," he said on his way out. I smiled and promised that I would.

Once he had gone, I locked the guys' bedroom door and took a deep breath, shutting my eyes to summon my ice to the fore. When I reopened my eyes, all of the natural fuzziness had gone from my vision, and the remaining water in the bottle that I held had frozen. I deposited the bottle on the kitchen counter, then darted back to my room to put the Torstein in its rightful place. It seemed to sparkle more than usual in response to my ice, and I smirked at it before closing its ring box. It seemed as though the entire Teuton universe yearned for my revenge.

I shut myself in the bathroom and locked the door, then stood before the mirror and coated my body with ice, setting my spirit free. Watching its clear solidity overtake my face was a thrilling experience, and my spirit burst into the night sky directly, anticipation coloring my robes a numinous dark blue that matched the waters of the lake. I spent a moment reveling in the cold of the night air, and then I ordered myself to focus. *Okay, Swanie. The two you need to punish are partying in your dorm right now. Don't need to worry about Beer Can and Joint. Just get the brute that stuck his cock in your butt and the fool who stole the Torstein.*

I pictured myself in the game room amid the partygoers, and reality blurred around me as my spirit appeared in the room. The pool table and foosball table had been shoved against the walls, and a thick group of students swayed in the center of the room. Someone had brought in a stereo that blared a popular rap song, and a disco ball had been duct taped to the ceiling, casting squares of color upon the floor and the dancers. The room smelled of beer, cigarettes, and sweat, and one guy had a naked girl backed up against the wall, thrusting himself between her legs while she moaned in a pitiful fashion. I heard a gravelly voice calling out from the far side of the room, declaring to the world at large that he had screwed Hitler's child.

That's Max's child, you Beidl, I corrected, keeping my thoughts to myself. Then I flung my spirit toward where he stood holding a plastic cup of cheap beer, breezing through the people between us, likely prompting the lot of them to shiver. The brute actually looked similar to a wooly mammoth, his face and head covered in brown fuzz, his thick chest and stomach spilling over his baggy sweatpants. He stood right before a window that was wide open, inviting fresh air into the tangle of partygoers. I centered all of my elemental power into my fists and slammed them into his diaphragm, having learned years ago how to manipulate the physical world as a spirit—one of very few priestly secrets Hans had shared with me.

The jerk made an *oof* sound, a look of shock crossing his face. He staggered backward, his legs wobbling under him, and I shoved against him once more at just the right moment. He tumbled through the window with a strangled cry.

I encountered Zack on my way out of the room and punched him square in the jaw before returning to my body. I caught a whiff of blood just as I departed.

Chapter Twenty-seven:
Consulting with Beth

By the time Beth reappeared, I had scrubbed the stains from our bedroom floor, cleaned up the trash, and changed the sheets on my bed. I brought my extra blanket down from a cabinet to use until I got a chance to wash everything. Completing basic tasks pacified me even more than my acts of revenge, though I replayed the scenes again and again in my brain while lying on my bed fingering the Torstein. Whether those two idiots would connect their misfortunes with their vile acts in my room, I could only guess. But it gave me a distinct feeling of accomplishment to recall the crunch of Zack's teeth against the knuckles of my spirit. I had likely knocked at least one of them out.

I heard the lock turn and looked toward the door to the hall, a furtive smile playing on my lips as my cousin slipped inside and fairly slammed the door behind her. "It's a madhouse out there," she remarked, locking the door and setting her purse down onto her dresser. "Not sure what they're celebrating, but they've gone all out this time. They were loading somebody into an ambulance a few minutes ago. People said the dude had fallen from a second floor window."

"Really? That's insane." I could not wipe the smirk from my face. I stuffed my right hand between my pillow and my head in a show of indifference.

"Seriously, the crowd at the game was a lot more civilized, probably due to the mixed company. I saw some kids there." Beth snickered once, having divested herself of her coat and gloves, her brown eyes drifting toward the door that led to the guys' room. "I'm going to make some hot chocolate. Do you want some?"

"That sounds wonderful," I said, closing my eyes to relax in the meantime. I turned the Torstein over and over in my left hand, fully intending to bare my heart to my cousin that very night. Sleep would have to wait, because I wanted to call my father to ask him for money for an apartment. Right now it was close to five a.m. at home, and he did not wake until seven-thirty on Sundays. Hopefully Beth had no plans for a lengthy snooze tonight.

"Why does it smell like cleaner in here?" my cousin queried upon reentering the room. I heard her set one mug onto the desk. "It's really potent," she went on, sounding as though she drew closer to where I lay.

"Careful where you step," I warned her, opening my eyes again.

Beth had halted several paces from the head of my bed, and when I met her gaze, I saw that realization had begun to dawn in her eyes. "What happened?" she asked in a muted tone, placing her free hand around the mug that she had prepared for me, as though to protect it from the truth.

I gave her a hard look and pushed myself up onto my elbows. "I was raped."

She gasped and took the Lord's name in vain, dampness welling in her eyes. "Was it some guy from the party?"

"Yep. It happened right in here, thanks to our friend next door who thought it would be smart to open up our apartment to his pals."

"Oh Swanie!" Beth looked horrified, and she sank down to the floor at my bedside, her round eyes staring up at my face. "Are you okay?"

"Not really. But neither are they." I smiled a wicked smile and clutched the Torstein tight against my left thigh.

She shied back a little. "Wait. Are you saying that it was the guy that fell?"

"He fell for a reason."

Beth blinked rapidly, my mug of hot chocolate sitting forgotten on the floor beside her. "But . . . how? He was huge!"

"The power of a Teuton's element is also huge." I slipped the Torstein under my leg and rose into a sitting position myself. "Can you hand me that mug? Something warm would probably be really good for me right now, even though my ice thinks otherwise."

Beth passed me the mug and then rolled the desk chair to my bedside, her expression wavering between sympathy and respect as I related the entire story to her. When I had finished with my return to my mortal body, she shook her head slowly in what appeared to be amazement. "Wow, Swanie. Just . . . wow. They had the brute strapped down with his neck in a brace when they loaded him into the ambulance. He may very well have permanent damage."

"Should make him think twice about raping anyone, let alone a Teuton." I sneered, feeling no remorse whatsoever. Hans had taught me how to defend myself for a reason, though I had never expected to use my spiritual form in such a way.

"So you pushed one out a window and punched another in the mouth. But you gave the other two a pass even though one of them helped pin you down while Zack was jerking off. I didn't even know you had a vibrator." Beth's cheeks flushed, and she gave me a side eye, bending her head down to take a sip from her mug.

"Erika gave it to me for my birthday. But I'm going to throw it out. How am I supposed to know if Zack's got any diseases or not?" I gagged, the mere thought of pressing it to my genitals nearly making me sick.

"Good point." Beth's shoulders shuddered a bit, and then she leaned back in the desk chair, her expression inquisitive. "I thought you were a virgin like me."

I eyed my cousin in disbelief, then remembered that she had attended a private Christian school throughout her childhood years. She had likely been led to believe that a woman's pleasure comes from penetration. "You can be a virgin and still masturbate. Men do it, and so can we."

"Do you do it after I fall asleep every night?" Beth still looked doubtful.

"Not *every* night. I'm not a sex addict. And I've never done it with you in the room. Honestly!" I rolled my eyes at my cousin and sipped some hot chocolate.

"Maybe I should get a vibrator. But I don't really want to visit a sex shop. Do you think about Hans every time you use it?" Beth looked playful now.

I felt myself blushing, and I looked away from her. "Sometimes. Why are we talking about this?"

"Because my cousin's been using a vibrator without telling me. You're such a terrible friend." When I looked back at Beth, she wagged her tongue at me. "What about the guy with the beer? Aren't you going to get back at him, too?"

I shrugged. "I probably should, but he wasn't the one who shoved his penis up my butt."

"And why did you punch Zack again? Because he ruined your vibrator?"

It was time. I set my nearly empty mug upon the shelf above my pillow and dug the Torstein out from beneath my left thigh. "No. Because he tried to steal this from me." I held the stone up to the light, its dark ruby glimmer calling silently to my Teuton spirit.

Beth cocked her head and looked at the stone, her forehead wrinkling as she reached her right hand toward my most prized possession. "Is . . . is that . . . ?" I could tell that she was trying to remember all of the stories I had told her since I had first learned about my ancestry. Comprehension dawned in her brown eyes, and her index finger froze several centimeters from the stone in my hand. "Is that the *Tarstein?*" she whispered, hesitant.

A loud laugh burst from my lips. "*Torstein,*" I corrected. "Gateway stone. And yes, it is. It's the secret I've been keeping from you and almost everyone else for the past year and a half."

I handed the stone to Beth to let her study it while I related the tale of where and how I had found it. A grand relief pervaded my chest as I laid out the details. I had not realized how different—how refreshing—it was to speak of my experience with someone my own age. As much as I loved both of my mentors, I found it more freeing to unburden myself before my cousin, rehashing some of the minor details that I had thus far kept to myself. I told her how scared and hopeless I had felt when I had collapsed on the trunk of that tree, how mortified I had been that an *Eihalbe* had chosen that moment to acknowledge me, how I had cried out in terror toward the shrouded entity that had seemed to scoff at my predicament.

"Who was it that saved you?" Beth asked, speaking for the first time after I had described the elemental storm that had carried me back to the riverbank where I had begun my dance. "Do you think it was a human or something else?"

"I . . . I'm not really sure . . . but I think Hans thinks it was a Black Priest," I admitted, looking down at the Torstein in my left hand. Beth had handed it back to me not long after I had begun to tell my story.

"Those are the evil Teuton priests, right?"

"Something like that. They're Teuton priests who've committed some sort of unpardonable sin and are exiled from our people. *Der Weg* doesn't really offer a lot of information about them, and trying to find out more from Hans has been like pulling teeth. I just know that they serve Wuotan directly, and I guess he gives them supernatural powers in return." I tossed the Torstein from one of my hands to the other, thinking back to what little the Teuton history tome revealed about Black Priests. *Those who work the forbidden arts of Wuotan should be left to their dark devices, shunned by the righteous.*

"Serving Wuotan directly," Beth repeated, sounding pensive. "How do you even . . . *do* that? Wuotan's a demon, right, so what kind of worship does he expect?"

"Some people think there's human sacrifice involved." My cousin recoiled in her chair and I waved one hand in a nonchalant manner. "That's probably just a legend. But Hans knows." My eyebrows came together as that realization hit me. "He probably knows all of it, because he gave me three pages on the Torstein that were written by a Black Priest."

Beth favored me with an arch look, her torso still pressed against the back of the desk chair as though she dared not come close to me. "So a Black Priest wrote his own set of lore about the Torstein while sacrificing people on the side, and you still think having the Torstein is a *good* thing?"

My forehead wrinkled, and I looked down at the stone again. "Well . . . ."

"Really, Swanie, I thought you were a Christian. Do you really think it's smart to dabble with stuff like this? I mean, traveling back in time is like resurrecting the dead, in a sense." My cousin's face had paled, her dark eyes focused warily on the amulet in my hand.

I had never really thought about it that way, but a germ of uncertainty settled in my stomach. Had I not done that very thing on my first journey into the past? I closed my fingers around the stone, suddenly questioning all of my motivations. "I . . . I already used it once . . . to see my Mutti," I said in a choked whisper, squeezing my eyes shut as images of her in her fabulous wedding dress surfaced in my mind.

"You . . . you *what?*" Beth's voice sounded stricken.

I took a shuddering breath and slowly recounted the story of my trip to 1978, glossing over the details to focus on my feelings. How lost I had felt in the currents of time. How triumphant I had felt when I realized that it had worked, when I saw that the hands of Alter Peter's clock read three-fifteen. How amazed I had been to see my mother in all of her splendor, to see her kissing my father in devoted love. How the lighthearted chatter of the two elderly ladies in the foyer had crushed me, speculating on a future that my parents would never have.

Joel knocked on the door that connected our rooms before I had finished, so I shut my mouth and put the Torstein back in its ring box while he and my cousin shared a goodnight kiss. I overheard her telling Joel the short version of my rape in a low voice, so I turned my back to the room and concentrated on the memories of my parents' wedding. A hopeful event with a joyful audience concealing the one who knew what was to come—one child who would never know his mother, another who would grow up watching her father's descent into alcoholism, his rejection of his Teuton blood.

"Swanie?" Joel's voice pulled me from my glum reverie, and I rolled onto my back to acknowledge him. He stood beside my bed dressed in black sweatpants and a Daffy Duck sweatshirt—his pajamas. I caught the scent of mouthwash, and he had recently slicked his blond locks back from his face. His hazel eyes shone with pity as he murmured, "When Sam gets back, I'll make it clear that he's not allowed to let his pals into your room again. I'll even beat him up if you want."

"Thanks, but I took care of it already," I said with a chuckle, grateful for Joel's support either way. Hopefully he would not mind relocating off campus.

After he had gone, I finished describing my parents' wedding to Beth, who had sat back down in the desk chair, appearing engrossed in my story despite her misgivings. "I can see how having the Torstein would be a blessing for someone like you," she conceded, "but it really sounds like there's something dangerous at play with Teutonic time travel. The way you describe what's beyond the gateway . . . ." Her voice trailed off, and she pursed her lips at me, looking unhappy.

"You're probably right, but what's the point of having the Torstein if I'm not going to use it?" I asked. "It's been lost for over five hundred years, and I doubt the *Eihalbe* would have directed me to it if I wasn't supposed to use it. And it's not like I'm the only Teuton who has ever traveled time. Prince Otto and his brother Paulus did it back in the eleventh century using his forgotten song."

"And then the Bavarian empire fell to the Saxons. Definitely no connection there." Beth raised an eyebrow at me, and I frowned, rolling onto my left side. "Is *that* why you decided to minor in organ? Is it because you're hoping to figure out how to play Prince Otto's song?" Beth demanded in an accusatory tone.

"You're making a lot of assumptions right now," I retorted, looking down at the blanket beneath me. My Aunt Linda had gotten it for me from Ocean City, and quite a few of the shore town's landmarks were stitched into its fabric. I traced the depiction of the giant Ferris wheel at Wonderland Pier.

"Some of it just seems a little too convenient, you know?"

"Well, that's why I need to use the Torstein again to go to eleventh century Muniche. I want to see the fall of my city, to understand what really happened. Why couldn't the Teuton people defeat a clan of outsiders with no elemental aid?"

Beth held her peace for a moment, and I continued to trace the Ferris wheel, not looking at her. I understood her hesitation about time travel. No doubt she was worried about what would become of me if I kept jumping here and there in history. But I had been preparing for months now, and I had one dress complete. Besides, if all of the writings about time travel were correct, I would not have to fear my fate in the past. I would return in the same moment that I had left, no matter how many years I spent in another time. And if I lost access to the Torstein, death would send me back where I belonged. A frightening concept, but even Wolfgang's writings had confirmed what I had read in *Niofirgeban*.

"I agree," Beth finally said with a sigh. "I've questioned your histories on that subject myself, knowing what I know about your elemental gifts. There must have been something going on in the shadows that caused the Teutons' defeat."

I pushed myself up onto my elbows and tilted my head at my cousin. "Would you be willing to come with me when

I go? I'm kind of looking for a companion or two so I won't be completely on my own in the Middle Ages." Beth did not seem too sanguine about the idea at first, but I convinced her after careful explanation. By the time one o'clock rolled around, she had grown fascinated by the idea, bringing up necessary preparations that I had not considered.

I called my father's private line just after one-thirty. The phone rang three times before he answered, sounding more asleep than awake. Relief washed over me when I heard his voice. "Hey Pappi. I need some money," I told him.

A short pause. "How much?"

One good thing about my father was that he never asked why whenever I needed money, probably because he knew my spending habits. "Enough to get an apartment off campus for me, Beth, and Joel." I waited.

When my father responded, he sounded suspicious. "What happened?"

Chapter Twenty-eight:
A Father's Resolve

By the time I finished speaking with my father, my ice had nearly overtaken my blood, extending to the phone's receiver and sprinkling its lengthy cord. My father had reacted with appropriate ire, but I had hardly told him any of the details about what had happened. Instead, I had spent the majority of our conversation trying desperately to dissuade him from what he was about to do. And I had failed.

I sank down to the floor with the receiver in my right hand, my expectations caught in a wild tornado. Beth reentered the room just as I leaned my back against the door to the hall. Her tired eyes widened when she saw me sitting listless on the floor with the phone frozen to my hand. "Swanie? Did your Pappi freak out?" She crossed the floor and took my right hand in hers, prying the phone from my fingers.

"He's coming here," I squeaked, hardly remembering to speak English. My father had used a slew of Bayerisch curses that I had heard only rarely.

"Your Pappi's coming *here?*" Beth had succeeded in releasing the phone from my fingers. She climbed to her feet to hang it in its place beside the door, then bent down to meet my gaze.

"He's coming here, and I don't know what he's going to do. He's going to want to report what happened. He can't. He can't because of what I did. I can't give a police report. I don't want to be examined by a doctor." All of the shame and betrayal I had bottled up for the past four hours spilled over suddenly and I sobbed, icy tears seeping from my eyes.

Beth comforted me until exhaustion began to temper my cries, my element slowly retreating into my spirit. She assured me that we could convince him to keep his cool if we worked together, that we could talk him out of any reports he might want to make. Eventually her words became a low drone in my brain, and I think that she may have helped me crawl into my bed, where my body curled into a tight ball beneath my sheets and Ocean City blanket.

The next day, I did not wake until nearly noon. My body and mind seemed to desire hibernation after the assault, and I was all too ready to grant that wish. It was Sunday now, and I was in no state to attend church or any other event that required socialization. I might skip all of my classes this week, if only to keep a watchful eye on my father, to make sure he did not sneak off to alert security or the local police of the attack. I thought I smelled ramen noodles, and I shifted weary eyes toward the doorway to the guys' room. No one was in the bedroom with me, but I may have heard Beth singing a Sarah McLachlan song in the kitchen.

Okay Swanie, you have to pull yourself together and get up, I told myself, shutting my eyes and taking several deep breaths. *It's nearly noon, and Pappi will be here in a few hours. You and Beth need to figure out how to soothe him.*

My cousin and I shared a hearty batch of noodles complete with boiled eggs and mushrooms, a cheap meal that she had learned to fix with expertise. I did not speak except to greet her, preferring to concentrate on the food. Apparently I should have eaten something last night, for I felt ravenous. Joel was at church, and Beth had no clue where Sam had gone. "I kind of want to slug him myself," she said through a bite of egg. "He's a jerk for letting his so-called 'friends' into our room."

"Hmm," I said in response, thinking that maybe I should start packing my things before my father arrived. I remembered him saying that he would help the three of us find a suitable apartment off campus. Part of me longed to leave this entire country behind and return to my beloved München, where no broke bastards would dare to treat me like a sex kitten. But I wanted to finish my degree here, and I loved my organ professor. I did not want to have to start again elsewhere.

"I was thinking maybe you should tell your Pappi that you pushed your rapist out the window." Beth's declaration prompted me to raise my eyes from the ramen before me. I saw that her eyes burned with resolve. "I know he doesn't like hearing about Teuton stuff. But if you tell him that you did a Teuton thing to punish that freak, that might convince him not to file any type of report."

I grimaced at the concept, but I suspected that she was right. But my father knew next to nothing about my Teuton life; he did not even know my element. "You may be right," I sighed, looking down at my noodles again. "I'll probably just drop a few hints, though. I don't think he knows anything about the spiritual realm."

Joel returned from church around one p.m. with a bag of Taco Bell in tow. After assuaging his hunger, he retreated to his room to begin organizing his stuff in preparation to move. Beth had informed him of my plans that morning while I was still asleep, and according to my cousin, he had heaved a huge sigh of relief at the prospect of vacating the dorms for good. "He hardly gets any studying done with Sam in there," she told me. "And pretty sure that jerk has been swiping some of his cash. He's running out of places to hide it."

Beth and I spent most of the afternoon loading up our suitcases, though she took several breaks to work on a poetry assignment. I had two essays due that week, along with a test in statistics class, but I could not convince my brain to focus on studies in the aftermath of what had happened. Images of Zack masturbating on my bed kept invading my mind, and my anus was sore. Although I would not agree to be examined by a doctor, I prayed hard that afternoon that the mammoth had no diseases. I certainly did not want to deal with lesions lining my behind.

I made a habit of peeking out our window every few minutes to look down at the street below, waiting for the appearance of an exclusive rental car. I did not know how long it had taken my father to arrange a flight to Virginia, but I did know that once he got here, he would zoom in my direction without a care for speed limits. I hoped that he would not draw attention from any state troopers. I wondered vaguely whether he had instructed Hans to arrange for both a rental car and a hotel room. A selfish part of me wished that he would rent a suite at one of the nearby mountain resorts. I desperately needed a break from reality to keep my anxiety at bay—and I needed to figure out exactly *how* to tell my father what I had done without scaring him half to death.

My father arrived just after five p.m., having nudged a shiny blue Mercedes into a spot at the curb out front that few Americans could successfully negotiate. When I saw him step out of the car, I had to consciously refrain from yanking the window open and leaping to the ground from the second floor with my ice and the chilly air as my buffer. Instead, I darted down the side stairwell and through the door in a matter of seconds, barely remembering to stifle my element before throwing myself into my father's strong arms. I heard his voice consoling me in Bayerisch as my emotions broke free again, and I wept, burrowing myself into his jacket.

It took me a few moments before I began to realize that I certainly looked weak to anyone passing by on the sidewalk. I pulled slowly away from my father, who kept his arms around my waist when I lifted my head to meet his gaze, working to blink my tears away. "Swanie, my dear girl," he murmured, his expression soft and pained, though his gray eyes looked cold, yearning for vengeance. "That beast really hurt you, didn't he?"

"You . . . you can't . . . tell the police . . . ." I managed to say, my voice hitching. "Please, Pappi . . . promise me you won't." A fresh batch of tears welled around the periphery of my eyelids.

His forehead wrinkled in what looked like incomprehension, but he reached up to lay my head against his chest. "We'll talk about it," he said, and I shut my eyes again, weighing my explanations on the scales of my mind. He greeted my cousin in a louder voice and commented that she looked a lot like her mother.

"Hallo, Onkel Max," I heard Beth respond, her voice tentative. "Ich verstehe kein Bayerisch. Entschuldigung."

I slipped out of my father's arms and poked his chest, knowing that I needed to control myself until we were far away from here. "English, Pappi," I reminded him, turning around to see that Beth stood several steps away with our suitcases lying on the sidewalk behind her. Joel stood near the side door with his hands in his pockets, looking from my father to me with muted curiosity.

"Then Jens has done you a disservice," my father told Beth. "Bayerisch is a much lovelier language than German." His British accent inspired me to snicker, like it always did, and I skipped away from him before he could swat at me. I loaded the two suitcases into the trunk of his car while Beth introduced him to her boyfriend, who addressed my father in halting German. I smiled to myself, thinking again that Joel would be a useful addition to our imminent journey.

Beth and I rode with my father to a cozy cabin he had rented about a twenty-minute drive from campus halfway up a nearby mountain. My father said that he had reserved the cabin for the entire week but that it currently had no food in stock. "I can take a trip to the grocery store once we get settled, if you don't mind letting me borrow this car," my cousin offered.

My father's eyes met mine for a second in the rearview mirror. "Is she a decent driver, Swanie?" he asked me before steering sharply around a curve.

"She may be better than you," I answered, glancing out the side window at the steep drop beyond the guardrail. Beth cackled.

"Ach, you know automatic transmissions put me to sleep," he scoffed. "This stupid thing keeps trying to shift." Beth and I both started giggling and spent the rest of the drive up the mountain clinging to each other and moaning during every curve. By the time my father parked right in front of the cabin's porch, he seemed to have decided to brush off our antics, for he unloaded the trunk and tossed Beth the keys with the admonition, "Don't make me have to replace this car."

After I had brought the suitcases into a snug bedroom with matching twin beds, I wandered back toward the front parlor, where my father had likely taken up residence. It was an impressive cabin, complete with a hot tub on the back deck and a game room with air hockey, pool, and foosball just steps away from the small bedroom upstairs. The ground floor boasted a master bedroom and bath, a kitchen, a dining nook, and a parlor with a brown bearskin rug and a deer head mounted above the fireplace.

When I reached the bottom of the spiral staircase, I saw that my father had lit the gas fireplace and set two plastic bottles of Apfelschorle upon the coffee table. "Thought you said this place had nothing to eat," I said as I snatched up the bottle that had not yet been opened, plunking down upon the couch beside him.

"Bought you a couple six packs before I flew out," my father said, leaning against the back of the couch with a look of weariness. "I know how much you miss it when you're here." He shifted his eyes toward me.

I felt warm inside, and I twisted the cap off and took a grateful swig, relishing the zesty apple flavor. "Thanks, Pappi. What would I do without you?"

He hummed softly and took my left hand in both of his, gently warming my skin with his touch. I leaned against the back of the couch, following his example, feeling more relaxed than I had in a long time. "I'm always here for you," my father murmured, "and I always will be. You're my crown jewel, Swanie."

The corners of my lips wavered. "But you're not going to tell the police what happened to your crown jewel. Right?" I closed my eyes as tension marred my quietude once more.

He continued to massage my palm as though he longed to take my troubles away by his presence alone. And he would doubtless manage it as soon as he assured me that he had no intention of involving the authorities. But then he posed a question that made my eyelids spring open. "Did you kill them?"

I felt my jaw drop in slow motion. It took me a moment to gather myself and take another drink of Apfelschorle before I turned my head to face him. "No." The word came out more defensively than I intended.

My father looked pleased, though the dark anger had not left the depths of his eyes. "Good. But still, most people don't beg to leave the police out of a flagrant crime unless they contributed in some way." He raised an eyebrow at me.

I blinked at him, my excuses jumbling up in my brain. "It's not that," I said, dropping my eyes to my hand clasped in his. "It's just that . . . I know these things take forever . . . once they're reported . . . and rapists don't usually get convicted. Since that one guy's a basketball player, he *definitely* wouldn't get in trouble. I don't have the time to fling money at the courts around here, so I just . . . I kind of . . . pushed the main beast out the window." I tensed and chewed on my bottom lip.

My father did not respond, and his fingers seemed to have turned to stone upon my hand. I took a few shaky breaths, trying to gather my courage. *You don't have to be explicit about it. Just let him know that you used Teutonic magic to get it done.* "He didn't see that it was me," I finally managed to say. "Nobody saw. I did it in the unseen realm. I pushed him out the second floor window, and I think I heard something crack when he landed."

The silence dragged, the crackling flames in the fireplace the sole indication that life existed in our cabin. When I finally got brave enough to look at my father again, I saw that he wore an unreadable expression. He released my hand and leaned forward to retrieve his bottle of sparkling juice, his shoulders stiff. He took several drinks and cleared his throat, then said, "I think there's a word for that in English. De . . . defenestrate? You defenestrated your rapist."

My mouth fell open again; I had not heard that word since high school. "Well, I . . . I guess I did," I admitted, a sense of absurdity nearly provoking me to laugh. "I also punched the athlete in the mouth before I left the unseen realm. Knocked out at least one tooth." That part spilled from me in English, the term *defenestrate* swirling around in my mind, making it hard to rein in my smile.

"You're a lot more skilled than I thought," my father charged in a tone that sounded half dismayed and half dead.

I sidled away from him and gripped my Apfelschorle bottle more tightly. "I can't just hide my head in the sand forever, Pappi. It's not in my nature."

My father sighed, and when I looked at him, I saw that his countenance appeared defeated, the wrinkles in his forehead more pronounced than usual. "Just remember that your Mutti felt the same way you do now," he cautioned me with a solemn nod. "I don't want to lose you the way I lost her."

I set my juice bottle upon the coffee table and reached out to hug him, longing to wipe the pain from his face. "You won't," I promised. "I'm not having kids. And I'm not trying out any of the dark stuff," I added, though that was a lie.

Beth and I spent the entire week vacationing with my father, enjoying the comforts of the cabin as well as the offerings of the surrounding area. We included Joel on more than one occasion—Thursday afternoon at an indoor waterpark and Friday evening at an ice skating rink—and my father ultimately invited both Beth and Joel to visit us in München next summer. I urged them to take him up on that offer, for that would make it easier to coordinate our venture into the eleventh century.

My father spent some hours apart from Beth and me, each time claiming that he had business to accomplish. Once, he asked for my campus library card and my login in order to find out information about the school's finances—and about the two abusers that I had not punished. I told him that he did not need to worry about the guy with the dreads and the joint, for he had been too high to comprehend what was going on that night. But he told me on Friday morning after breakfast that the fool with the beer can was about to meet a reckoning, a vengeful glow in his eyes as he put on his coat and grabbed the car keys from the kitchen counter.

Beth and I exchanged one terrified glance while we sat across from each other tending our bowls of cereal. I could tell by my father's tone of voice that I had no chance of dissuading him now. So I cried out, "Please, Pappi, don't get caught! And make sure nobody blames me for what you're about to do!"

My father shot me a nefarious smirk and said, "Don't worry. They won't."

Chapter Twenty-nine:
The Cryptic Teuton Priest

My father left for München on Sunday, not having offered an explanation regarding his proclaimed reckoning. I heard tales floating around campus the next day about a male student who had gone to the hospital with "venereal complaints," which prompted everyone to speculate on whether he had chlamydia or something worse. Whether that story had any connection with my father's doings, I could only guess. I wondered whether he had cornered the beer dude in a dark alley and cut off his testicles.

Soon afterward, Beth, Joel, and I relocated to an apartment complex about fifteen minutes from campus by car. Most of the renters there were elderly, and the complex offered no student discount like the cheaper places nearby. Thus it became our reprieve from the insanity of college life, and the three of us made a new habit of staking out territory in the student center in between classes and practice. I enjoyed the freedom that being a town student afforded. I no longer had to fear someone combing through my possessions and swiping the Torstein.

Nightmares returned to me as a result of my trauma, and on some nights I would wake in a cold sweat, the smothering sensation I remembered from years ago tightening my chest. It angered me that the stout fool had covered my mouth at the outset of his abuse. That and the vodka down my windpipe doubtless reminded my subconscious of Dane's suffering, stirring up reactions that had not plagued me in ages. So I started spending half of the night in spiritual form whenever panic nipped at my heels, doggedly trying to train myself to function properly on a lack of sleep.

I flew to München on the Saturday before Christmas, excited for the chance to enjoy my homeland during the holiday season. Though I loved my cousin and her family, their traditions could not compete with wandering the Christmas markets and celebrating the New Year in mirthful German fashion. My father greeted me with appropriate fanfare when I stepped through my front door, enfolding me in a strong embrace and pledging once again to keep me safe from harm. I assured him that I could take care of myself at home, but his earnestness warmed my heart.

On Wednesday evening after dinner, I crunched through a dusting of fresh snow in my backyard to meet Hans at his cottage. He had decorated his front door and windows with twinkling white Christmas lights, and a ribboned wreath dotted with pine cones hung upon his door. He swung the door open before I had a chance to knock, and I kicked the snow off of my boots before stepping inside. A tree aglow with sparkling lights and tinsel stood in the far corner beside his chair, and I saw four Christmas pyramids set up in various places around the room, the flames atop their candles glimmering in natural yellow-orange. "Not wanting to give the impression of darkness during the holidays?" I asked as I removed my boots and set them by the floor mat.

Hans made a guttural sound in his throat in response, and I straightened up to shrug my way out of my winter coat. He stood waiting to take it from me, and I did a double-take when I saw that he wore the priestly robes, clad in darkness from chin to the ground. "Hey ho, I was wrong," I muttered in English as he hung my coat upon a hook beside his front door. I stepped away from him and glanced at the Christmas tree again. It looked about a head taller than me.

"Sit down, Swanie," Hans instructed. I sensed him sweeping past my back in a quest for his kitchen. "I've got Glühwein on the stove that's nearly finished, so make yourself comfortable."

I had thought I smelled a touch of cinnamon. I smiled a little and sat on his brown couch, feeling cozy in his parlor despite his arcane attire. "Are you planning on casting a spell on me tonight with your potions?" I called out to him, relaxing against the back of the couch and tugging the sleeves of my violet sweater down over my hands.

"Actually I have a meeting to attend tonight at midnight. We recently caught a Teuton criminal who had been robbing banks in his spiritual form."

"Oh gosh," I interjected, looking toward the clock that hung beside one of his paintings of München. It was only seven forty-five, so we should have enough time to discuss most of my recent experiences. "Is he going to be sent to that dungeon north of the city?"

"He will be punished, yes. But tonight we're going to find out what he did with the money." Hans reentered the room holding two steaming mugs. He handed one to me and turned for his chair, his face hidden in shadow.

I had no concept of what such an interrogation would entail. "Torture?" The word crept hesitantly from my mouth, and I drew the Glühwein close.

Hans chuckled and settled himself upon his chair. "You need not concern yourself with it," he said ambiguously, blowing on the contents of his mug.

I quirked my lips and rolled my eyes internally. Apparently tonight was to be an equivocal night on the Teuton priest front. "So did my Pappi tell you why he came to visit me?" I asked, figuring that it would be best to move on from the thief's approaching fate. I wondered whether he had studied for the priesthood or if he had just worked out the mysteries of the spirit himself.

"He said that you'd gotten tired of the vulgar culture in the dorms and needed advice on rental property." Hans' hooded head was pointed in my direction, his face still in shadow, his pale fingers cradling his mug against his chest.

I smiled a little, recognizing again that my father knew how to guard what few secrets I told him. None of his employees had any inkling of the assault I had experienced. So far I had told no one but Lise, who had emphatically reminded me that what had happened was no fault of my own. I considered how to word the truth for a few seconds, then decided to just drop it like a bomb. "Actually I was raped, and someone stole the Torstein." I blew on my Glühwein and took my first sip. I hoped that Hans would not ask for details. If he did, I may have to tell the story as a spirit to stave off any potential panic.

"What?" Hans stated after a beat of silence, his tone sounding flat.

I shrugged one shoulder and gazed at the wooden pyramid that stood on his windowsill, watching its blades slowly turn from the heat of the candles' flames. "I got lucky I was on my period at the time, so he went in my butt instead. And I got the Torstein back thanks to a friend of mine." I heard Hans give a scoffing sound, and I eyed him dangerously. "What's funny?"

He shook his head once and raised his mug to his lips. "I apologize, Swanie. It makes me laugh to this day that a rapist would run away screaming at the sight of menstrual blood."

I felt my own lips curving into an uncertain smile. "Apparently poop is less disgusting to men? I definitely shouldn't have wiped." Then we both started laughing in earnest, a small portion of my shame evaporating at the ridiculousness of it all.

"So did you have him arrested?" Hans inquired in a conversational tone, as though we discussed something as blasé as the weather. I saw his pale lips caress the rim of his mug, the only portion of his face that the candlelight seemed to touch.

"No, I attacked him in my spiritual form. I pushed him out a window, and he broke several vertebrae in his back. Now he's paralyzed from the waist down." I jeered through my nose at the brute's dismal fate. He would never rape again.

Hans remained silent for at least half a minute, and I watched the movement on the Christmas pyramid again while I waited for his response. Would he think I had gone too far? Would he reprimand me for using my ice in such a way? I took a deep breath, inhaling the mystical scent of the wine, silently praying for strength if my most trusted mentor decided to rebuke me. But to my surprise, when he spoke again he said, "God spare me from the justice of Swanhilde von Thaden."

I looked hesitantly toward him. "Do you think I went too far?" I brought the mug to my lips and moved a portion of wine around in my mouth.

"Whether you went too far is debatable. But I would advise you to keep your actions to yourself. When Teutons take the law into their own hands in a foreign land, they can't expect the legal system to back them up."

"Right. Of course. Beth and Pappi are the only people who know, so I should be fine. It's not like I'm going to make a habit of pushing rapists out of windows. It did give a sense of satisfaction, though," I disclosed with a smile.

"If you did, far be it from me to dissuade you." Hans sounded amused.

I grinned, grateful that he seemed to appreciate my act of revenge, though I had taken it in the heat of passion. I liked Hans for a reason. He did not seem to hold to the chauvinistic views of standard Teuton priests. I asked him whether he would be willing to keep the Torstein safe at his cottage during the upcoming semester. Although I lived in an off-campus apartment now, the potential for thievery had burgeoned like a cancer in the back of my mind. I did not fear thieves on the Thaden grounds, for if anyone ever thought to break in, they would go for the main house, not the detached cottages. Hans agreed with my assessment and promised to lock the Torstein into the safe in his bedroom closet.

From there, I updated him on my adventure plans. The addition of Beth had already proven to be a godsend, for she had dug up more information on clothing styles and culture norms from the library. She had also thought of things that I had not—we would need hairbrushes sans plastic, as well as edible provisions like dried fruits and meat. I planned on ordering handmade leather shoes and bags from a small shop downtown before I returned to the U.S., and I would also check the local Christmas markets for items appropriate to our upcoming venture.

Hans seemed disgruntled about my decision to take an American along on my next journey through time. I did my best to explain my reasoning, mentioning that my cousin had known about the Torstein for years already and that she had an interest in history as a library worker. I told him that I felt that it was safer to involve an outsider, since she would not be tempted to blab about her experiences to those with no knowledge of the potentials of time travel. As fun as it would be to bring Erika with me, her red hair would likely stand out in an era when widespread travel was uncommon. I did not trust any of my other Teuton girlfriends enough to share my secrets with them, so Beth was truly my best option.

"I suppose you make valid points," Hans conceded at length, rising from his chair and retrieving my empty mug from his coffee table. "If you wish to take the risk of meddling with evil, that's your choice, and it's not my place to dissuade you." He disappeared into the kitchen, leaving me wondering what exactly he had meant by that. Since Beth and I had gotten caught up in eleventh century plots over the past few weeks, I had only rarely thought about the dark roots of the Torstein.

"Are you pouring some more Glühwein?" I called out, hoping that he had made enough for seconds.

"I am," I heard him reply, and I got up to use the bathroom, looking forward to continuing our conversation. Discussing Teuton secrets with a priest was something that I always enjoyed, even when the priest in question chose to be enigmatic.

When I returned to the parlor, I saw that Hans had already situated himself in his chair once more, blowing softly on a new steaming mug. I sat down and took up my own mug, crossing my legs beneath me on the cushion. "So. The 'meddling with evil' factor. Can we figure out a way to get around that?"

Hans' figure appeared even darker now, as though he had set himself apart from both the candlelight and the twinkling bulbs garnishing his Christmas tree. "Prince Otto uncovered the mysteries of time travel thanks to Wuotan himself, according to the writings of history," he reminded me in a cautionary tone. "We both know that a demon's ways are not to be taken lightly. Consider the dangers of the blood-transfer, the one Teutonic ritual that invokes him directly. Also consider the counsel of God: demons are liars, their gifts soiled with death."

I stared at Hans, suddenly feeling cold even though I held a warm mug in my hands. "But . . . I mean . . . if we're going to use that argument, then we could say that Teutons shouldn't use their elements at all, since we got our blood from a pact made with Wuotan millennia ago."

"No one alive today knows the specifics of that pact, for it was made before written records became common. Enough good has sprung from Teutonic gifts over the years to raise doubts about their demonic origins. But the priestly records agree that the Torstein arose from Prince Otto's desperation to fix his mistakes, to destroy what we know of history. Wuotan was likely disappointed that the Prince chose to die instead."

"Well . . . I'm not planning on going back and stopping the fall of the Teutons. I'm not trying to tear our culture apart. I want to observe and learn, like the spell to open the gates says," I pointed out.

"And if your journey to the eleventh century results in your death? Would it be worth it?" Hans spoke the question in a grating tone, and I thought I could see his eyes glittering in the shadows covering his face.

I chewed on my bottom lip and took a sip of Glühwein before answering. "If I die in the past, I'll return to the present. That's what the writings say."

"I hope, for all of our sakes, that the writings are true."

He had certainly given me a lot to think about, but I did not wish to cancel my plans out of fear of death. Ritual suicide was the only way for a time traveler to actually die in the past. I clung to that claim like a lifeline.

As I prepared to leave Hans' cottage, I raised the subject of my girlfriend Ina who had seemed to vanish off the face of the earth after her marriage to Walfrid. "I'm honestly worried about her," I said while putting on my coat, feeling chilled again at the concept of what her priestly husband may be doing to her. "She married the guy after just five months, and he's a priest, and I know he bound her heart, and I'll bet he wants her to have kids when she's ninety-five percent. What if he's abusing her, keeping her far away from her family and friends?"

Hans sighed at me, standing at the doorjamb with his hand on the knob. "It seems to me that you're assigning blame where there is none. Ina wanted to marry a rich Teuton man, and that is what she found."

"I'm a rich Teuton, and I don't break contact with my friends when I'm in the U.S.," I pointed out, shoving my feet into my boots and lacing them. "And that freak she married called you my patriarch. What the heck did he mean by that?"

Hans snorted quietly. "A traditional sort," was all he said.

I straightened and scowled at Hans, placing my fists on my hips. "Well, I don't like it," I declared, "and I don't want my friend to lose her personality to some freak of a priest. You know she knew how to get to the realm of the spirit. I bet he put a stop to that."

"Enough, Swanie." Hans swung his front door open, and the frigid winter air swept into his parlor, tendrils of frost beckoning to my element. "Not everyone has the same tastes as you. You shouldn't imagine yourself worthy to judge your friends' choices of husbands when you've yet to find one yourself."

His barb cut deep, and I flounced out into the cold, pointing my feet toward the main house. Icy tears pricked the edges of my vision as I raised my face to the cloudy night sky with its intermittent flurries. *I don't care what Hans thinks. I've got to find out if Ina's okay,* I resolved. *And I'll have to go to the spiritual realm to do it.*

Chapter Thirty:
Preparations

I had too much to get done during the remainder of the Christmas holidays to check on Ina, so I resolved to do so as soon as I came home in May. Since I had no wish to make the long drive to Berlin, I figured that I could just drop in on her as a spirit sometime in the afternoon, when I should be able to catch her alone with her child. I knew her address, and my father had a map of Berlin somewhere in his archives, so it should not be too difficult to send my spirit there. I had never really tried to test the limits of the spiritual realm since Hans had taught me the basics; I had no clue exactly how far my spirit could travel from my physical body. Berlin was just over six hundred kilometers from München, so I hoped that the distance would not prove too far.

When I visited the leather shop to order shoes and bags, I ended up requesting a total of three bags rather than just two. I had not yet told Beth that I wanted to invite her boyfriend on our escapade, but even if we decided not to bring Joel, I had begun to suspect that we would need at least three bags for all of our supplies. We planned to travel to the year 1064, two years before the fall of Muniche, long enough to witness Teutonic peace and success before it all came crumbling down. Thus we would reside in the Middle Ages for two full years, hopefully finding some sort of employment in the city to keep us afloat with food and shelter. I suspected that I could find work as a seamstress, and Beth mused about attaching herself to a pottery shop.

Along with extra clothing, I intended to bring a digital camera so I could capture mementos of our trip like I had done during my parents' wedding. This time I planned to take one of my father's older digital cameras that ran on double A batteries; that way once the batteries ran out, I could replace them until none were left. I planned to bring a twelve-pack of batteries along with the two already inside the camera, which I figured would be sufficient. I bought three metal thermoses for water and a smaller bottle that I would use for vitamins. Beth had come up with that idea, for she asserted that it would take our bodies time to adjust to a medieval diet, and we may find ourselves short on things like Vitamin C. I hunted through my father's knife collection and set aside three that seemed practical.

The spring semester at college passed unremarkably overall. The mammoth never returned to campus, though I heard some people saying that he was confined to a wheelchair now. Apparently he had been trying to learn how to push himself around on leg braces, but his size had rendered his attempts futile. As for Zach, he continued to play on the university basketball team, only rarely cheering since he had lost one of his front incisors. Min-ho told me that his family was not particularly well off, so it may be a while before they could save up to get his mouth repaired. Beth asked me once whether I regretted what I had done. "Hard to regret anything when their assault revived my panic attacks," I told her. I usually managed to get a full night's sleep about four times per week. Too often, I would wake drenched in sweat with my lungs constricting in the darkness.

I finally brought up my plans for Joel on the Thursday before Easter. He had gone to practice guitar with the worship team in preparation for the Sunday service, so I took the opportunity to confer with Beth in private. Her forehead wrinkled as I outlined my reasoning—it would be best to bring a man along on a journey into the eleventh century as a bastion against chauvinism. Joel was fit and smart with the ambition to conquer new challenges. He had begun studying German last year and occasionally tried to use it in conversation with me. His archery abilities would also be useful in the Middle Ages, both for protection and in case our group ever needed to hunt for food.

"I see what you're saying," Beth sighed when I had finished. She lounged in the recliner in our parlor with a notebook on her lap, the fingers of her right hand tapping her pen distractedly. "But I'm not sure whether it would be smart to bring someone like him. He has no clue about Teutonic powers, for one thing."

"So much the better," I said from the couch, gazing up at the popcorn ceiling. "You're both coming to visit me in June—finally—so he can just come along on an unexpected side trip. If we didn't bring him, do you really think you could keep the secret from him once we return? After two *years* in the Middle Ages? With all kinds of mad adventures under your belt? It's been hard enough for me, and all I did was go back to 1978 for a couple hours."

"Yeah." Beth sounded noncommittal, and I tilted my head toward her, not really comprehending her hesitation. Our plan was to use the Torstein on her final night at the Thaden house, Friday, June 16th. The next morning she and Joel would fly commercial back to Philadelphia. Personally, I could not imagine keeping my mouth shut while trapped in a seat next to my boyfriend for over eight hours. "But we'd have to get him some clothing, too," she noted.

"That's no problem. Our dresses are finished, so that'll give me something new to work on before graduation. I just need his measurements. And I can put in a rush order for his shoes when I pick up our shoes and bags."

Beth was silent for a moment, and when she spoke again, the subject took me off guard. "Did people eat a lot of nuts back in the eleventh century?"

My eyebrows came together, and I looked toward my cousin again. "I'm . . . not sure. I know they ate a lot of grain and pretty much drank nothing but alcohol. No sugar, chocolate, or coffee available before Europeans started colonizing."

"Oh crap. That's true. I'll probably get headaches until my body gets used to going without caffeine." Beth winced, and I felt a touch of sympathy for her. Both she and Joel drank coffee every morning.

"I'm not sure about nuts, though, but it wouldn't surprise me if people ate things like chestnuts and walnuts," I mused, suddenly thinking that I ought to try to learn about herbal medicine while in the past. I might check to see if the campus library had any books on that subject.

"See, that would be a problem for Joel. He's allergic to tree nuts."

My jaw fell open just a little. That was something I had not known. "Oh. Is *that* why he never eats Almond Joy bars?" I felt like smacking myself. I should have worked that out before.

"Yeah, he doesn't like to talk about it. He keeps an EpiPen on him all the time just in case. But at least peanut butter doesn't bother him."

"Hmm. Well, I guess we'd just have to make sure he brings a pen or two with him. And I can find out whether there's nuts in our food before we eat any meals. But if we end up going our separate ways with employment, I'll have to teach him how to ask about nuts." I frowned, trying to piece the phrase together in Teutonica. I realized that I did not know the word for *nut*. Hopefully Hans knew what it was.

Beth ultimately agreed that Joel would be a useful addition to our conclave, though she was unsure how well he would take to the reality of time travel. I told her that we could break things to him gradually, starting with the magic of the Torstein. Once he had accepted that, I could broach the topic of Teutons, their history, their blood, their elemental gifts. I probably would not need to mention the spiritual side, but some of the odd blood magic may prove valuable for all of us.

The secrets of blood magic were held by the Teuton priests; your everyday Teutons knew little aside from their blood percentage. But Hans had mentioned a few other things to me in passing, things about which he had thus far refused to expound. For one thing, Teutons apparently had the ability to control blood flow, to stem the tide from a serious wound. I hoped to drill Hans about that power in particular, for I knew that such a talent could come in handy during the siege before Muniche fell. He had once hinted that Teutons could read someone's intentions using blood—I had no idea how that could be possible—and that burnt Teuton blood would invoke an indelible curse on a settlement.

My hopes for learning more before embarking on our medieval adventure mostly fell flat. When I returned to München the first weekend of May, I cornered Hans in his office the following Monday. I bluntly informed him that we needed to converse in either Teutonica or Latin until my departure because I needed practice with speaking both languages. He raised an eyebrow at me and stated in gravelly Latin that I was interrupting his work. I ignored his complaint and asked him about blood control in Teutonica, stating that I needed to know how to do it in case either Beth, Joel, or I got wounded during the siege. This prompted him to glare at me and reply that I might as well bring all of my American school friends while I was at it, effectively closing the subject. He did tell me that the Teutonic word for *nut* was *Nusi*, so the conversation was not entirely wasted.

I visited Ina on Thursday afternoon, having shut myself into my bathroom to cross into the spiritual realm undetected. I had stared at the location of her house on my father's map for nearly an hour that morning, trying to imprint it into my brain. Since I did not know anything about how the house looked inside, I would have to travel there through the air rather than by imagining myself there. If I had not spent so many nights exploring the spiritual realm in recent months, I may not have been able to pull it off. I had gotten used to traversing the Appalachians from high above, checking out all of the towns near to my apartment. I had even pushed myself to the Virginia coast one Friday night, a journey that had tired me until the waves of the ocean rose to restore my spirit. So I planned to fly straight to Ina's and then return to my body after I had finished chatting with her.

My plan worked marginally well. I sent my spirit as high into the atmosphere as I dared and zoomed to the north, keeping the sun on my left and A9 within eyeshot below. I pushed my spirit as swiftly as I could, snatching moisture from wisps of clouds now and then, watching Nuremburg pass by below and later Leipzig. *I bet Ina was really good at flying here and there in her spiritual form,* I thought to myself as my stamina gradually waned. *She could claim the entirety of the air to propel her along while I have to snag at clouds. I should have done this back in December, actually. Might have been able to find some snow then, too.*

By the time the Berlin metropolis appeared in the distance, I had truly begun to weaken, the robes of my spirit appearing more and more ethereal, their colors shifting from water's blue to the white of clouds. *I can do this. I have to do this,* I told myself. When I saw the River Havel below on the edges of the wealthy section of the city, I gave a wild cry and cast my spirit beneath its waters. I felt the rush of vitality they gave me, and I laughed in my mind as I gathered them into my spirit. The hue of my robes altered one final time to a murky bluish green; I felt like I had gulped down an alien tonic. Northern Germany did not belong to Teuton lands.

I erupted from the river with more verve than necessary, and I saw several passengers on a nearby tourist boat pointing in confusion at my brief water spout. No matter; I sensed no Teutons among them. I sent my spirit above the trees again and set my course for Ina's street, just a block from the Forst Grunewald.

When I reached her front door, I did not bother to waste time studying the house's design. I simply shut my ghostly lids and stretched my element forth, seeking the Teuton souls inside. I sensed only one and gave an internal shout of victory. That had to be Ina. Her husband was not home, probably at the stock exchange. What servants they likely had were not Teutons. And Lea was too young to manifest an element.

I breezed through the chambers of her house until I found her in the kitchen. She stood before the stove, stirring a pot of what smelled like Eintopf, a soiled apron protecting her sleek khakis and frilly blouse. She had the radio tuned to a classical music station, and little Lea sat perched in a swing, laughing as she smacked at a row of toys dangling from its frame. Ina sang along with the opera that currently played—the quality of her alto was not particularly great—glancing toward a second oven every now and then, checking on the progress of some sort of cake. And when she turned fully around to chatter for a moment with her daughter, I saw that her stomach was swollen with pregnancy. Just as I had predicted, the fool had decided to breed his wife, her high Teuton blood be damned.

I perched my spirit upon an empty countertop and spoke directly to Ina's mind. *So why exactly are you cooking? Shouldn't Walfrid have a hired servant to do that sort of thing?*

Ina's body jerked into an upright position, and she looked around the room, her eyes wide in what appeared to be shock. I noticed that her face was layered with make-up, prompting me to wonder if her husband was the type that expected his woman to look perfect all day every day. Ina had not bothered with makeup when we went to the metal festival two summers before. "Who . . . ?" She spoke at last in a quivering tone, her eyes having passed over me twice.

Swanie. I'm sitting on your counter.

Ina turned to face me, her eyes remaining their natural shade of dark blue. "Swanie? What . . . what are you doing here . . . ?" She sounded horrified.

Visiting my friend who's vanished off the face of the earth. It's a long way to Tipperary, though. I probably won't have the stamina to stay here long.

Ina swung away from me to retrieve Lea from her swing. "Since you're here, you definitely need to meet Princess Lea. Sometimes I call her that even though my master disapproves of Star Wars." My friend gave a nervous giggle.

She said the word *master* in Teutonica—*Truhtein*—which sounded odd stuck in the middle of a Bayerisch sentence. The fact that she had referred to her husband with that title prompted my heart to sink, although I knew that terminology was common for a bound Teuton wife. Now Ina balanced her daughter on her left hip, gesturing vaguely toward the counter where I sat, telling the child that they had a visitor. I smiled at Lea, though she could not see me. *I'm pleased to meet you at long last, Princess Lea. You could certainly take down any storm trooper.*

The little girl fell silent while I spoke, her pale eyes growing as round as an owl's. She had probably never had a spirit speak to her before. "That's Swanie," Ina said gaily, giving the child a kiss on the cheek. "She's a good friend of mine."

"Friend?" Lea repeated, her attention diverted by her mother's earrings.

"Swanie's a friend. Oh, don't touch that, Lea dear. You know Pappi likes my ears to sparkle when he comes home." Ina brushed the child's hand away from her ear and headed for the swing again. "I'd better put you back in your seat so I can finish dinner before Pappi gets here."

Lea did not appreciate this arrangement; she started wailing, interspersing her cries with the words *Pappi* and *nein*. I smiled to myself as Ina tried to quiet her. Children were nowhere near the top of my wish list. *How far along are you?* I asked my friend once she had returned to the pot on her stove. I sensed the exhaustion emanating from her spirit, and I wondered again why Walfrid had not hired a cook.

"I'm due in ten weeks, if I make it that far. My blood pressure is already too high. A doctor comes to check me over every Friday." Ina wiped a drop of sweat off of her forehead and dried her fingers on her apron.

I pursed my lips, my concern about my friend's fate growing ever stronger. *Why did Walfrid get you pregnant when he already has Lea?* Maybe that question was a bit too forward, but her husband's actions angered me.

Ina's shoulders rose and fell in a sigh, and she turned away from the stove to look toward where I sat, her eyes focusing on something to my right. "He wants a son, but this one's a girl, too. So I'll have to try again." She shook her head.

Ina, can you even see *me?* I asked, feeling as though there was a knot in the pit of my stomach. Her situation was worse than I had thought. The rich bastard had convinced her that it was her fault he had not yet produced a male heir.

My friend's face fell. "It's dangerous for the baby if my element runs free. So no. I can't see you." She cradled her swollen abdomen in maternal affection.

Chapter Thirty-one:
Dismal Fates

In subsequent weeks, I cast myself into my part-time work and my final preparations for Beth's and Joel's visit with gusto. What little I had seen of Ina's chosen fate disturbed me, but I had a feeling that Hans would downplay my fears. It seemed like Teuton priests always defended their own, even when a priest mistreated his wife. Or he would say that since Walfrid and Ina lived in Berlin, their affairs were not under his jurisdiction. There was no Teuton Council of Berlin since Northern Germany was historically Saxon territory; therefore, any priest with a narcissistic bent could relocate there and work his schemes without oversight.

Instead, I hoped to voice my concerns to Lady Muniche at the May dances, for perhaps she would have some sage advice on the matter. I could bring up the subject to my Teuton girlfriends as well, though Erika would be absent this time around. She had graduated with honors and joined an artist co-op in Vienna, hoping to gain some exposure that way over the next few years. She and her Greek friend Iliana were still an item, though Erika told me over ICQ that she had yet to decide if and when she should come out to her parents. She still fretted about her ultimate fate once our beloved mentor had passed away, commenting again and again that she desperately hoped that Muniche's spirit would sense the direction of her heart and not force her into a bond that she did not want. When I described my visit with Ina, Erika responded harshly: *That's exactly what Rudi would do with me. He'd force me to give him children since it's not like the current Lady Muniche was still fertile when her husband died.*

Sometimes I wished that I could unburden myself to my father, since he had always seemed sensible on the subject of relationships. But Erika had pretty much blurted to him that I had something going on with an old priest, and I did not want him digging further into that subject. I generally kept our private conversations focused on college life and my cousin's upcoming visit, about which he was vibrantly excited. He had already arranged for the four of us to tour Neuschwanstein castle, and he looked forward to discussing the U.S. real estate market with Joel. I smiled blandly at discussions like this, silently hoping that one day I could tell him more about my Teutonic life.

I drove myself to the May festival because I did not want to sit in a car next to Hans for a half-hour drive with my misgivings about romantic relationships with Teuton priests bottled up inside. I brought sugar cookies again, this time frosted in the Bavarian state colors of light blue and white, depositing them with the ladies manning the food tables before pointing my feet toward the banks of the Isar. I wore a light pink Dirndl with magenta bows and ribbons this time around, my now mid-length hair done up in French braids courtesy of Lise. I glanced at the group of young men raising the Maypole and caught Fonsi's eye. We exchanged casual waves before I turned to face my cousins at the water's edge. I wondered if Ina's marriage to Walfrid had upset him. They had been good friends.

"Is it just you two this time?" I asked my cousins, who were in the process of building a tower of small rocks from the shallows. They had dumped their purses beside the flat gray boulder that served as the base of their tower, so I dropped mine into the grass as well.

"Nah, Marga's over there with her priest," Trudi said, gesturing toward the far side of the clearing with her left hand. She delicately balanced another stone with her right hand as she spoke, and Traudl gave a squeak, likely expecting their tower to crumble.

I froze into a statue beside the boulder. "Ivo's a priest?" I gasped, pivoting around to look for my earthy Teuton friend. I could just make her out sitting on a blanket in a dell fringed with willows, her lips locked with those of a wiry young man with spiked dirty blond hair. Both wore traditional Bavarian attire.

"Not yet, but I think he's going to try to pass the initiation this summer," said Traudl, holding an off-white pebble between her left thumb and forefinger.

"Um, why is everybody lusting after priests?" I shuddered and tore my eyes away from Marga and Ivo. *Not again,* I thought.

"*I'm* not a priest," Mane interrupted, converging upon us from the direction of the Maypole. He swept my cousins' tower to the ground, prompting both of them to squeal and pummel him. He laughed and caught Trudi in his arms. "Come on, the dances are about to start. I think Fonsi wants to have one with you, Swanie." He fairly carried my cousin into the group gathering around the Maypole, his dark curls appearing obsidian in the sunlight.

"Sometimes I just want to rub his hair in the dirt," Traudl grumbled as we headed for the Maypole. Two of the priests on the council were already handing out streamers, their dark robes standing out amid a sea of Lederhosen and Dirndls.

"Why does Fonsi want to dance with me?" I muttered mostly to myself, keeping to the outskirts of the throng so that I would not be swept up in the first cycle. I did not usually dance with any young Teuton men at these festivals because thus far none of them had appealed to my blinded heart.

"Who knows? Maybe he's hot." Traudl sounded disinterested, and seconds later she had melted into the crowd, likely wanting to catch up with her sister.

Fonsi and I danced the second dance, my icy streamer weaving strangely with his, which glowed as bright as pure sunrays. The luster of my ice against his light nearly blinded me, and I laughingly told him that we had better call it quits after one dance. "Don't want to accidentally set something on fire."

My partner smirked, his brilliant irises dimming into their natural dark gray. "Good point. I need to talk with you about something, though."

We slipped through the crowd around the Maypole once our dance had ended and crept into the trees, bushwhacking a fair distance away from the gathered Teutons. I followed Fonsi's lead, not sure what had gotten him so tense. He looked over his shoulder as we progressed into the forest, as though he feared eavesdroppers. He halted at last behind a thick tangle of brush, planting himself among the roots of a towering elm tree, crossing his arms and meeting my gaze with a pinched expression. "Okay Swanie, we both need to keep our senses on guard. I don't want any priests to overhear us," he stated flatly.

I blinked in surprise, realizing that he must want to discuss Ina's marriage. *Hadn't really planned on mentioning what I saw to Fonsi, but . . . .* "Okay," I said, sitting against the neighboring fir tree so I could observe his body language. "My ice is on guard." I pocketed my glasses and turned my irises a frigid blue, allowing my spiritual senses to sweep softly over our surroundings.

"Thanks." He gave me a half smile and then dropped his hands into his lap, focusing on them rather than on me. "I know you went to Ina's wedding. Did she seem happy about her choice, do you think?"

Fonsi pulled no punches; his hands fidgeted in his lap. "She seemed happy," I answered, all of the negative vibes I had sensed at that event howling at me in my brain. "But shouldn't you be talking to Marga about this? She's Ina's best friend. I never really knew her all that well."

Fonsi raised his eyes to mine, his light lurking in the background, not potent enough to make me have to squint. "I wouldn't get anywhere talking to her. She's lost to the abyss of the Teuton priesthood. You're one of the few Teuton girls left with a solid head on her shoulders."

Heat rose in my cheeks, and I looked down at the needles coating the forest floor where I sat. "It seemed like everything happened too fast with Ina. She'd only known the guy for five months before she married him. I didn't really like how he hovered over her at their wedding," I confessed.

Fonsi sighed. "See, I'm like one hundred percent sure that the bastard bound her the day they met. And that's like drugging a girl's drink at the bar, only worse." I heard him ruffing his brown hair, and when I looked up again, I saw red blotches on his cheeks. "We'd been friends with benefits for over a year," he went on, anger polluting his tone. "And I've known her practically since birth. I know she wanted a successful man, and I've been trying really hard, you know? She seemed thrilled when I got the assistant management position at Lidl. It was like maybe things would work out between us after all. But then she sends me this message last March that she'd met some wealthy man in Passau that had a beautiful daughter. That's all she said, and I didn't know what to make of it. Two weeks later they're engaged."

"Scheiße," I murmured, my heart sinking into the depths of my intestines. *I bet Fonsi's right. I bet Walfrid bound her on the day they met, and he's been working at altering her desires ever since. Did she even realize what she was doing when they got married?*

"I've been trying to move on," Fonsi said after a short silence, lifting an elm leaf from the ground, gradually cindering it with his element's heat. "But she was my best friend, you know? I don't like that some priest stole her away from me."

"I went to see her right after I got back home," I disclosed, figuring that I might as well get the truth out in the open, even though it would not quell Fonsi's frustrations. "I found out he wants a son. That's why he took her. She's pregnant with another of his daughters. And he's suppressing her air to keep the child safe. Her *air*," I emphasized, hoping that Fonsi would grasp the absurdity of that.

Fonsi cursed in Bayerisch, a disgusted sneer curling his lip. "It's worse than that. I snooped on them in my spiritual form just before their wedding. I know that was wrong of me, but I wanted to put my mind at ease." He stared into my eyes, his own aglow with fury. "He had her bound in a room that I wish I'd never seen while he repeated black lies over and over to her, his energy jolting her heart every few seconds. She was crying, and her eyes could not see my spirit."

I felt sick. Though I had suspected that a wicked Teuton priest could use his enhanced powers to subdue a woman's heart, I had never heard the process described so vividly. Hans would likely deny that such atrocities ever happened. "But what . . . what can we do . . . ?" I whispered, a lump hitching the words in my throat. "Can priests order a Teuton couple to divorce? He's rich enough to just flee with her to some foreign country."

"I tried to convince her family to stop her wedding, but they didn't listen to me. I even talked to Herr Dantzler, and he pretty much forbade me from intruding upon others in my spiritual form. If I ever do it again, they'll lock me up."

I shuddered at the thought of the Old One on the council. Fonsi should have picked a different Teuton priest in whom to confide. "So basically we've lost her," I translated, feeling dejected. "But how many kids can she possibly have with blood at ninety-five percent?"

"Ninety-six. We screwed for over a year. She's at my level now." Desolation had darkened Fonsi's eyes, and he shook his head and brushed his hands off on his pants. "Thanks for listening, Swanie. I think I just needed somebody to believe me even if we can't help her. If the bastard kills her, though, I might invoke the rite of *Virstohran*."

My jaw dropped, and a cold hand grasped my heart. "But Fonsi . . . is . . . is that . . . even *legal* anymore?" He spoke of an ancient Teutonic ritual of vengeance against a perpetrator of blood crime.

Fonsi snorted. "Does it matter? I'll be able to make a strong case if she dies due to his cruelty. Besides, do you think his daughters will turn out okay growing up with an abusive father? That'll put them right into the hands of greedy priests."

I rose to my feet and brushed off the back of my Dirndl, not pleased with the direction of this conversation. I did not mind lamenting Ina's condition, but I was not sanguine about murdering Walfrid. Yet. "You should have gone into law," I told him over my shoulder as I struck out for the clearing, putting my glasses back on.

"Teutonic law I can do," he answered with a snicker, quickly catching up with me. "Want to dance again and burn half the trees down?"

"I need to catch up with my other friends, actually," I said, moving to put some distance between us. To his credit, he did not pursue me.

Back at the clearing, I headed for the table and filled a plate with food, ideas of primeval revenge swirling around in my mind. Vreni found me at the platter of Schnitzels and requested to speak with me alone while we ate. I agreed, frowning at everyone's secrecy. *Are all of my friends planning insurrections nowadays?*

We sat down on a pair of dark boulders a short distance downriver from the bustling clearing, my Teutonic friend uncharacteristically silent. She wore a green-ribboned Dirndl, her hair cropped short and bleached blond, her blue eyes gazing blankly at the opposite bank. "Swanie, I need your advice on some things," she said at length, her expression appearing rather downhearted.

I had a feeling that I knew what troubled her. Stefan had not followed when we had sought privacy. He had remained with the group of younger Teuton priests arrayed around the fire, roasting sausages. "Not sure if I'm any good at advice, but I'm listening if nothing else," I told her.

Vreni sighed heavily and took a bite of her sausage before unloading her troubles. "I *love* Stefan, and he loves me, and our families support our relationship. But now he's studying to become a Teuton priest, and here I am, unable to even *touch* my element." She glanced at the fiery glow filtering through the trees, her eyes alight with frustration. "He tested my blood the other day to see if he could do the ritual that reveals the percentage of Teutonic blood. And after sleeping with him for *two years*, I'm only seventy-seven percent. In two *years*, I've gained only two points of Teutonic blood!" She paused to hurl a curse, then used her teeth to yank the remainder of her sausage from its stick, chomping harshly.

I did not know what to say to comfort her, so I held my peace and chewed on a bite of Schnitzel. Though my trials had burgeoned in recent years, at least my Teuton blood would always be strong enough to avoid derision. Vreni brought up this very point a moment later. "They look down on me, you know. All of his cronies. I've heard them muttering together whenever they see us. How am I supposed to be the consort of a Teuton priest? I can't have his children, not yet at least, because there's a chance they wouldn't be fully Teuton. And apparently Teuton priests can do other things with their wives, things that we *can't* do since I can't control my fire. At the rate it's going, it'll be eight *years* before I reach eighty-five percent, and I don't want to wait *that* long before having kids!"

"You'd probably be safe getting pregnant once you're at eighty percent, since he is eighty-nine," I reassured her. "Teutonic blood is strong. Normally the blood of Teuton children follows after the blood of the parent with the higher percentage." I had read that in one of Hans' books years ago. Vreni looked doubtfully at me, and I gave her a reassuring smile. "That means three years. By then you two will have had time to get established, buy a house, start moving up in the world." Stefan was studying chemistry in college and intended to go into pharmaceuticals.

Vreni eyed me for a while, her fingers twirling her stick around in the water before us. "I don't know, Swanie," she said at last, "sometimes I think I just need to do the blood-transfer and get it over with."

"Don't start thinking that way," I admonished her, quaking at the mere idea. "You're going to be a Teuton eventually. There's no point in hurrying it along."

"Maybe I could get Hans to do it. He's been a priest long enough. He's probably good at stuff like that."

"Ach, Vreni, *no!*" I cried out, shoving her shoulder. "It's not worth it. Really. I don't want you to become a statistic in one of Hans' books. '90% of the time, one person dies during a blood-transfer, including Verena Scheele.'"

My friend shoved me back, then admitted, "You're right. I just hate waiting."

"As for those young priests who've been giving you grief, just ignore them," I advised. "Most of them aren't as well-off as you two will be, with your love. And once you can control your element, you can give them the fiery finger." I lifted mine and coated it with ice. Vreni favored me with a knowing grin and pulled me into a side hug, murmuring her thanks for my support.

Later in the evening I inquired after Lady Muniche, whose absence from the gathering troubled me. Several women informed me that she was not well and had been struggling with her health for several months now. Since I had been at college, I had not known. I would have to talk to Hans about this later, for I wanted to talk with her one final time before embarking on my journey to the eleventh century. I wanted to let her know that both Beth and Joel were coming with me, that we could hardly wait to learn what had really happened when Muniche fell. Maybe that sort of discussion could help take her mind off of her illness.

I spoke with Hans about it the following Sunday morning, while we sat together at the kitchen table eating breakfast before church. He wore a gray suit, light blue shirt, and checkered tie, while I wore a flowered indigo summer dress. A dark look came over his face when I mentioned that I would like to visit the Lady once more. "I'll have to consult with her doctor to see if she's well enough for visitors." Hans' expression looked pained, and he laid the morning paper aside.

When I studied Hans' face, I suddenly comprehended that she may not be grappling with a simple illness after all. Shock gripped my heart at the memory of her age. "Do you mean . . . do you mean that she might . . . ." I faltered.

"She does not have much longer to live," Hans replied gravely, his face ashen. "But she's ninety-four and has lived a long life. She has earned her reward."

I stared at him, fingering my glass of orange juice, numb with remorse for this aged Teuton woman who had been the symbol of our city for so long. I admired her greatly as a grandmother figure, and soon she would be gone. "I hope I'll be able to see her," I murmured, looking down at what cereal remained in my bowl, curling my toes at the thought of how empty the Teuton community of München would be without her. "I guess somebody else will get the job next," I noted, silently praying that Erika would be spared.

Hans grunted in annoyance. "It's not a job. It's a privileged position." He had switched from Teutonica to Latin for that statement, and I looked over my shoulder to see that my father had entered the kitchen, also dressed for church.

"The world will be much gloomier without her," I commented after a pause, piecing the Latin phrase together.

My father gave both of us a weird look and headed for the coffee pot. "Did you two decide to become scholars or something?" he queried in Bayerisch, pouring himself a cup. "So grim and serious!" he added in Latin with a leer, taking a sip.

I snorted and turned my attention back to my bowl of cereal. Hans lifted the paper from the table and took a sip from his own coffee mug before murmuring to me in Latin, "I'll let you know if she is able to see you." I nodded, then pushed my melancholy aside to chat with my father.

Chapter Thirty-two:
A Matriarch's Muse

I went to see Lady Muniche on the last day of May. I brought one of the medieval-style dresses that I had sewed for myself along with me because I wanted to ask her opinion of my design. Hans drove me to her apartment, and neither of us spoke much during the journey. I sat in the passenger seat with the dress of blue linen lying across my lap, watching the familiar streets go by, thinking that maybe I should not bother my mentor with sewing questions. Instead, I began to ponder her life and her role as Muniche. Though I had passed many afternoons in her home with my Teuton girlfriends, we had rarely discussed her experience as the female representative of our city.

If this is really her final illness, it might be time to find out more, I realized, my thoughts drifting again toward Erika, who planned to return home for a visit at the end of June. If the spirit of our city chose her at Lady Muniche's death, she may very well find herself compelled to forsake her art career in Vienna. I needed to lean just how much the spirit of a Teuton city influenced its Lady's destiny, whether the bond was truly something to fear, like Erika believed. I determined that I would leave the dress in the car and simply find out as much as I could about Teutonic mysticism from my most beloved teacher.

Hans parked across the street from her apartment and followed me to her door, turning the handle and holding it for me with a solemn nod. He had decided to wear his priestly robes to this rendezvous, which did little to quell my hesitancy. But I took a deep breath and nodded back, then stepped into her parlor, quickly seeing that Hans and I were not the Lady's only visitors today. Another priest from the council sat in her recliner, and I felt a sense of disapproval gnawing at me. *Do they figure they can just claim everything she owns for themselves now that she's possibly dying?* He showed little interest in me, but he rose to his feet when Hans closed the door behind us. "How is she, Oskar?" Hans queried softly.

"Not well. The doctor is attending her right now. Her pain grows ever greater, I'm afraid." The shorter priest heaved a desolate sigh.

I slipped away from the two priests standing in the Lady's parlor discussing her condition like a pair of Grim Reapers. I could not abide that sort of environment for long without remembering my brother's final days. I ended up in the cozy dining nook attached to her kitchen, standing before her fireplace mantel. Garnished with a collection of ornate-looking crosses, statues, and goblets, the mystic painting at its center snared my attention, as it had many times before.

The painting portrayed an artistic rendering of the spirit of Muniche and her keyholder reaching out to one another across an expanse of spiraling darkness. Both had been painted as gods, Muniche's gorgeous halo casting rays of light onto her pleading face. The keyholder was handsome, divine, but something held him back from fully touching the one he loved, his painted expression suggesting numerous possible explanations. Every time I studied the image, I always felt a rush of sympathy for Muniche's spirit, which yearned for a keyholder whom she could not touch. When I looked at him, I found that I could not hate him for his reticence, for whatever held them apart clearly could not be mended by man. At the bottom of the painting in Gothic letters stood an inscription in Teutonica: "Muniche and Her Keyholder—Unending Faithfulness at Indescribable Cost."

A hand touched my shoulder, pulling me out of my enchantment at the painting as I turned to regard the doctor. "She will see you now," he informed me quietly, "but you will have only fifteen minutes at most. She is not well." I nodded at him and glanced briefly at Hans. Then I turned for the hallway to her bedroom.

In the dim light of her room, I saw that a hospital bed had been wheeled inside where she now lay, hooked up to several monitors and IVs. The chamber smelled like medicine and death, not the soft scents of incense and candles that I recalled from prior visits. Several candles burned at the windowsill, flickering with the wind, and I wondered whether it was wise to have the window open at all with the Lady dying.

Behind me, the doctor urged me forward to her bedside. Only then did I realize that I had frozen just inside her door. I cautiously approached the hospital bed, trying not to cringe at the sight of my mentor's wasted body. She appeared so much thinner than I remembered, so much more wrinkled, her silver hair in disarray around her face. I stopped right beside her head as her clouded eyes met mine. I pulled up a stool from the nearby medical table and sat down. Her cracked lips slowly formed a welcoming smile. "Ah, dear Swanie," she murmured, her voice seeming to come from far away. "I'm so glad you're here."

The doctor had left the room, leaving the door open just a crack to give us privacy. I found myself wishing that he had stayed. I did not know how to properly address this woman, my friend, so obviously at the door of death. She still smiled at me, waiting patiently for me to speak, so I gathered my courage and decided to tell her the truth. "Actually, I was going to ask your opinion on some clothing I recently sewed, because I've decided where I'm going on my next trip into the past," I began carefully, watching interest break across her face at my words. "But Hans told me that you were . . . sick . . . so I . . . I figured I'd better just . . . forget about that, and just . . . just talk to you . . . ." I ran out of words.

She laughed, a weak, choking sound, and made a small dismissive gesture with her left hand, several tubes curling out of its veins. "You came to talk to me one last time, you can say it, child." The irony in her tone disarmed me a bit, and she chuckled again. "I know I'm dying, Swanie. You don't have to ignore it."

I stared at her, marveling that she could laugh about such a thing. "Doesn't it . . . bother you . . . at all?" I asked, truly curious. I knew death would bother me.

"Oh no, not really," she replied easily, her withered hands grasping at her covers absently. "When you reach this point, you are ready to go. It has been a long life . . . not without its regrets . . . and I'm ready for the next step."

I supposed I could not disagree with her, when she put it that way. "Ready to meet God," I commented, thinking that perhaps that would not be so bad.

"Yes, to see my Savior, and also my husband . . . ." She smiled again, closing her eyes in serenity.

"Your husband," I repeated thoughtfully, remembering some of the few stories she had told about him. At one point long ago, she had in fact been married to the keyholder of München. He had passed away shortly after her sixty-fifth birthday, and she had never forgotten him. I suspected that she kept that painting on her mantel as a reminder of him, knowing that someday they would reunite in eternity.

"Yes, he was a good man, my Hermann," she whispered, her gaze focused upon the flickering candles at the window. "It's been almost thirty years. How I have missed him . . . ." She sighed, suddenly looking weaker than ever.

I leaned over her bed, covering her left hand with both of mine, noting its chill. I tried to warm it, though I had no fire. "Should I close the window?" I asked her, concerned. "It's a bit drafty in here."

"No, I prefer the wind even if it kills me, for I am the wind." Her eyes turned back to mine, an almost impish smile gracing her wrinkled face. Of course she was right; she would not shut her element out of the room, even in death. I imagined dying myself, much later, with a bucket of ice lying next to my bed. I snickered a little and reached up a hand to brush some stray strands of hair away from her forehead. She gave me a knowing look and murmured, "You know how it is, Swanie. Your ice is strong even now. Your hands are cold against my skin."

She was probably right, and I folded my hands back into my lap. "Forgive me. I don't want you to be uncomfortable," I apologized.

She chuckled. "Don't worry my dear. Before you go, you can send Johannes in. His fire will do what your ice cannot, at least for a time."

I had a feeling that the doctor would return soon and ask me to leave, to let Lady Muniche rest. Now I did not want to go. I had so many questions for her, so many things I wanted to tell her, but any minute she might slip away like the wind, flying to heaven. My thoughts returned to her love for her husband Hermann, the previous keyholder of München, and I knew that I had to ask her one thing at least. "*Leitalra*, tell me," I whispered, leaning close, "when Hermann . . . died . . . what was it like for you with the new keyholder, a completely different man?"

She sighed again, a hint of sadness gracing her usually positive gaze. "When Hermann passed away, it was very hard for me for many years." Her eyes took on a faraway look while she related the story. "The new keyholder was young, just in his twenties, and there I was, an old woman thrown together with youthful lust. It never would have worked out between us from the start, where romance was concerned. For a while I was angry with Hermann for giving the keys to such a boy, when he knew that I likely had quite a few more years to live. But ultimately I realized that it does no good to stay angry with anyone, with Hermann or with the young keyholder. Bitterness is worse than the cancer that weakens me now. It eats away at your soul, at your heart, at all that is good inside you." Her hazy eyes bored into me as she warned, "Stay away from bitterness,

Swanie. Always be willing to forgive, even the unforgivable wrongs. You can forgive without leaving yourself open for harm, because it's how you find peace with things inside your heart. It releases you from experiencing the trauma over and over again."

Now a new angle of Muniche's painting grasped me when I heard her words. Yes, it could refer to her and the late Hermann separated by death. But it could also portray her relationship with the young keyholder, forever divided by age, immaturity, bitterness, her love for his predecessor. I nodded at her while I considered this, her words imprinting themselves onto my heart: *Always be willing to forgive, even the unforgivable wrongs.* "Were you ever bitter about...becoming Muniche in the first place?" I asked, her difficult life having disturbed me. "It wasn't your choice, after all. Maybe things would have been easier for you if... if the spirit of our city had chosen someone else."

The elderly lady snorted quietly, startling me. "Oh, child, what's the point of worrying about such things?" she threw at me. "We women never have the choices men have, and it doesn't matter. All that matters is what you *do* with the situations that are given to you. You can accept them and make them beautiful, or you can pine away your entire life about something you can't change."

I could not argue with that, though at my age accepting things tended to be hard at times. I still had not gotten past my childish love for Hans, nor had I ever tried to see my father's hatred for all things Teutonic from his perspective. Perhaps while I had spare time in the eleventh century, I should truly ponder these things. Maybe when I returned, I would be able to let everything go and live my life as I should.

"Do you think the city has ever chosen the wrong Lady?" I asked my mentor, thinking about all of the young Teuton women I knew who were not yet married. Erika. Trudi. Traudl. Marga. My younger cousin Leina. Mane's sister Binge. Stefan's sister Sophia. Manuela Dantzler, the daughter of the Old One on the council. All the others whose names I did not know. Which one would be bound by Muniche's spirit?

"That question has been debated over the centuries," Lady Muniche said, her eyelids sliding down a little as though she longed for rest. "There have been some Ladies who have misused their position. But such things are not in our hands, and how can one expect any human being to be perfect? The everyday Teuton, man or woman, should simply do their best to use their influence for good."

I heard a footstep outside Muniche's door, and I rose quickly from the stool, knowing that the doctor would come in and ask me to leave. Her wisdom on the subject of Teuton Ladies gave me much to consider, but there was one more thing I had to ask. Looking into the Lady's eyes one final time, I questioned, "What about the keyholder now? I don't know anything about him. What is he like?"

"Oh, he's certainly not without his faults," my elderly friend replied, smiling in spite of her words. "But he's not a bad man. He comes to see me often, though we are very different, and he has comforted me much over the years. His loyalty to our city will never waver, nor will his love for the Teuton people. What more can one ask for?" The Lady's left hand rose slightly from the bed, and she pointed one trembling finger in my direction as she stated rather covertly, "He loves me, though he does not comprehend it, for I embody the city he would die for. Maybe he'll have more luck with Muniche's next choice. I hope so, for he deserves better than me."

I could not see how that was possible, but I decided not to press the matter. Lowering my voice considerably, I told Lady Muniche of my upcoming adventure. "I'm going to use the Torstein again in just a few weeks, and I'll be taking my cousin Beth and her boyfriend Joel with me. We're going to the eleventh century to witness the fall of the Teutons."

An odd amalgamation of emotions creased her face, surprise mixed with both sorrow and pride. "You are a brave and strong woman to do such a thing. May you find inspiration and glory there and bring honor to your name."

I bent down to give the Lady a careful hug, my last farewell. "I'll miss you a lot. Tell Hermann I said hi, when you get to heaven," I whispered in her ear, trying not to cry. Icy tears pricked the corners of my eyes.

Lady Muniche laughed softly and patted my back with her left hand. "I will, Swanie, I will. I wish you a long and happy life."

I kissed her forehead, then turned for the door. Hans opened it a moment later, his expression rather fiery for some reason. He looked at me, then at the bed. "I'll be out in a minute," he said, shoving me into the hallway rather abruptly. I found myself regarding the Teuton doctor, the bedroom door shut firmly behind me. He smiled at me gravely and suggested that I wait in the parlor.

Upon reentering the parlor, I remembered Hans' claim that he would be out in a minute. It would probably be longer, I figured, since my mentor had wanted someone to warm her cold skin. I glanced briefly at her empty loom and at the short priest sitting in her recliner once more. He nodded gravely at me from beneath his black hood, his brown goatee standing out starkly against his robes.

It suddenly occurred to me that I had seen no trace of Lady Muniche's aging Yorkie since my arrival. "So what happened to Sonnig?" I asked the priest, thinking that the presence of a yappy dog would temper the grimness of the situation.

Oskar snorted in an offhand fashion. "Rudi's had her since Easter," he answered, sounding disinterested in the animal's fate.

"Ah." I turned my attention to Lady Muniche's piano, figuring that I might as well immerse myself in music while waiting for Hans. I pulled out the bench and retrieved a hymnal, flipping through its pages until I found her favorite hymn, "Fairest Lord Jesus." I situated myself on the bench and began to play, allowing the music to express the tangle of emotions churning within me. I hoped that Rudi was being nice to Sonnig. The poor little dog doubtless missed her beloved owner.

Before I had finished the second verse, I sensed Hans' presence behind me, listening to me play. I stopped after that verse and turned to him, ready to leave, but he held up his right hand. "Don't stop," he admonished, his face overcome with sadness for the dying Teuton woman. "Play it again, and we will sing every verse." I obeyed and breezed through an introduction. In a moment Muniche's small apartment rang with my voice, his, and Oskar's—soprano, bass, and tenor—singing one of the most beautiful German hymns in an impromptu elegy for her.

Chapter Thirty-three:
American Tourists

I had little time to reflect on Lady Muniche's frailty, for Beth and Joel were scheduled to arrive on Monday, June 5th. They both looked forward to seeing all of the wonders of München and the Bavarian countryside, so I hurried to finish preparing for our eleventh century journey before their arrival. I laid out an outfit for each of us: a red-violet dress for myself, a tawny yellow dress for Beth, and a long greenish tunic with tawny trousers for Joel. I had prepared all of our clothing in colors that generally belonged to the higher classes, for I suspected that it would prove easier to assimilate with society if we presented ourselves as wealthy travelers.

I folded the extra clothing and divided it between our three leather bags. The small downtown shop had come through in excellent fashion; the bags and shoes were durable with stitches that were obviously done by hand. I set the three metal thermoses temporarily in my bathroom closet, intending to fill them just before we would leave. I tucked the three sheathed knives in amongst our clothing, putting the digital camera and extra batteries in my bag while concealing the vitamin bottle in Beth's. I included wrapped bars of locally-made soap in each of our bags and folded the cloth packets for the food into squares for later use. I already had some victuals stashed in a cabinet: beef jerky, salted crackers, peanuts, raisins, and dried apple and pear slices. I put one roll of toilet paper into each bag for us to use until we grew accustomed to whatever the medieval Teutons used in the bathroom. Beth suspected that tattered rags would become the norm for both wiping and menstruation.

I breezed through the contents of my bedroom several times after deeming the majority of my packing complete. Although I had resigned myself to living in ancient filth for two full years, I still had a niggling urge to bring a few more modern conveniences along. I hesitated to bring a lot of plastic aside from the camera, since the disposal of such things would prove problematic. The batteries would be an issue, but I had already decided to bury those. I had stocked up on contact lenses and solution—transferred into a glass jar—since I could not wear my glasses in the eleventh century. But did I dare to bring along pads, tampons, or deodorant? And what about toothpaste? Without sugar my teeth should not necessarily rot, but I was still uncertain about how to keep them clean.

I ended up sticking my old Latin-German Bible into my bag, something that my Oma Betti had gifted me when I had first studied Latin in school. That would help me keep my Latin up to par in case Teutonica proved insufficient with some people. I included wooden hairbrushes in each of our bags along with tightly woven blankets in case we lacked shelter at the start. My locket with its picture of Hans would make the trip as well, but I planned to wear it as usual.

On Sunday evening, I visited the attic for the first time since my former trip into the past. I had abruptly realized that I had packed no valuables, and I doubted that I could find any eleventh century coins in the year 2000 unless I scouted out museums. How were we to rent a room or get food in Muniche if we had no money? Precious metals and gems likely had great value in the Middle Ages, so I hunted through the trunks of my mother's things until I unearthed the one that contained her jewelry. I claimed four twenty-four carat gold necklaces, three pairs of twenty-four carat gold earrings, four pairs of silver earrings, one amethyst ring, one diamond necklace, and one emerald bracelet, tucking them inside our woolen socks in each of our bags when I returned to my bedroom. As long as the Torstein worked this time like it had during my last trip, everything would come back with me, so I felt no guilt about swiping my mother's jewelry.

Thomas drove me to the München airport on Monday morning to retrieve Beth and Joel, both of whom looked incredibly exhausted as they advanced toward me beyond the arrivals gate, tugging their rolling suitcases behind them. "I am in desperate need of coffee," Joel said in greeting, a red Phillies hat slouched atop his head, proclaiming his American status to any and all observers.

"Didn't they have some on the plane?" I asked, reaching out to pull Beth's suitcase for her. Her short brown hair looked like she had slept on it wrong during the flight.

"It was really thin," Beth said in a dead voice, she and her boyfriend trailing behind me in my course for Thomas and my father's Rolls.

"It's so weird seeing German signs everywhere," Joel commented on our path to the parking garage. "I can only read some of these."

"It's not an easy language," I conceded in German with a grin, knowing that Joel had not particularly mastered the language yet. He would not have to study it during his final two years in college since he was a business major.

"Better than French," he responded in kind, and I laughed, thinking of his sister Gloria. I wondered whether she planned to keep studying French once she went to college herself.

Back at the Thaden house, I installed them into adjoining bedrooms on the third floor, promising to give them a full tour of the house and grounds once they had gotten some rest. In their absence I passed time on the internet, chewing on some Kinder chocolate bars to tide me over until lunch. I chatted with Erika on ICQ, mentioning my recent visit with our elderly mentor. *It doesn't look like she's going to be here too much longer,* I typed to my friend, a premature sense of loss churning in my blood. *I didn't even know she had cancer. Do you know what type it is?*

I heard it was ovarian. By the time they found it, though, it had spread to her lungs and spine, Erika responded.

I winced. *I wonder what our community will be like without her . . . .*

It definitely won't be the same. I'm probably going to stay here for a while. Iliana's got a fashion show coming up.

I smiled, pleased to learn of Erika's girlfriend's success. *That's awesome! When is it? Maybe I should go.*

It's July 22nd-31st, but she's got some models lined up to parade her outfits on opening night. You really should come. I think you'd like her a lot.

I raised one eyebrow and typed, *You trying to get my approval?*

Ha-ha. You're not the first person I'd turn to for relationship advice. Erika's blunt reply struck a nerve, and I rolled my eyes and pushed my chair back from my desk, glancing toward the three aged papers resting in their wired shelf. Of course she would not want relationship advice from someone hiding a mad love for an old Teuton priest and the dark secrets of time travel. Hopefully my upcoming adventure would squelch my heart's foolish longings once and for all.

I roused my cousin and her boyfriend in the early afternoon, bringing up a tray of sandwiches. "Gregor's going to cook a full-sized dinner tonight in honor of your visit," I informed them while we sat at the mahogany table in Beth's bedroom, consuming the platter that the cook had prepared for us.

"Excellent," Joel remarked through a mouthful of bread and cheese. "The plane food wasn't all that great to be honest."

We chattered about various summer events while the two of them nursed mugs of coffee. Joel had shadowed his father part-time, learning more of the finer points of the real estate business; I told him that we had that task in common. My father had focused my training on the financial aspects this time around, something that I found fascinating. Beth talked about a few weird encounters with customers at the Blackwood library, and both she and Joel bubbled over about days at the beach and nights prowling the boardwalk.

Once the two of them had deemed themselves presentable, I guided them through every room in the Thaden house apart from the attic. The third floor was smaller than the main two, consisting of our six guest bedrooms, two guest parlors, and four bathrooms. That floor of our house did not see as much use as the bottom floors, though my father always opened up those rooms to any business clients that visited from far away. Right now Beth and Joel were our only guests, so I jokingly told them that they could claim the entire floor for themselves.

On the second floor, I took them through my bedroom and bathroom. Both of them expressed amazement at the quality of my stereo, the décor on my balcony, and the inclusion of a hot tub in my bathroom. Beth seemed wholly entranced by the blooming roses climbing over my trellis, while my eyes drifted toward the silvery green planter in the far corner. A tiny sprig had appeared in its center, thanks more to Lise's care than to my own, for she had watered the soil faithfully during my absence. Part of me wished that the spirit of the new oak tree would one day thank the outsider who had nourished it in its infancy, but I did not know whether such interactions ever transpired.

After leaving my bedroom behind, I showed Beth and Joel the doors to my father's bedroom, bathroom, and office, places that I rarely entered since my father valued his privacy. Next I pointed out the door to Hans' office—I could sense his fiery spirit inside, doubtless at work on some important business matter—and then the cozy chamber that Lise and I had decorated as a memorial to my mother and Dane. Beth and Joel traversed the room with a quiet reverence, observing the photos, possessions, and articles of clothing that my once-nanny and I had thought best represented the two most beloved Thaden angels. Joel eventually asked me how they had died, and I related their stories in as few words as possible. "My Mutti passed away shortly after childbirth, and Dane died from cystic fibrosis."

Joel gave a quiet sigh and favored me with a sympathetic gaze. "I'm so sorry, Swanie," he murmured, the cross on his necklace catching the golden light from the sun shining through the window.

"Thank you. It's still hard." Beth came to my side and folded me in a hug, and I shut my eyes, fiercely ordering my tears not to break free. "Come on. There's a couple more rooms on this level that you've yet to see," I said, beckoning the two of them into the hallway.

I took them through the spare office, bathroom, the conference room, and the library, still one of my favorite places to lurk alone with a book. I pointed out the shelves that housed my collection of fiction, which prompted a conversation on *Lord of the Rings* and *The Hobbit* courtesy of Joel. He had heard that movies were being made of the first series, and he could hardly wait to see how modern cinematography would bring a classic fantasy tale to life.

I led them down the back staircase into the kitchen—both of them took too much time voicing their amazement at all of its features—the pantry, and garage. We spent a good half hour there while Joel admired my family's four cars: my red Ghibli and my father's blue Rolls Royce, black Ferrari, and silver Porsche. "There's another garage a short walk from here where our staff parks their cars," I noted, thinking that Joel would probably like Hans' BMW. "But you need to see the rest of the ground floor before we head outside."

We went back through the pantry, laundry room, and kitchen into the formal dining room, and from there to the music room, the game room, the exercise room, the family room, the front parlor, the interspersed bathrooms, and finally the sunroom which opened toward the side gardens. "This place really is a dream," Beth commended as she sat down beside the three-tiered marble fountain in the sunroom. "Really, Swanie, I can't understand why you give people like me the time of day. I could never afford a place like this."

Heat rose in my cheeks, and I took a seat beside my cousin and slipped an arm around her waist. "You're family," I reminded her, "and I'm not a snob like most of my high school classmates."

"Did your dad already pay off the mortgage for this place?" Joel inquired, his attention fixed on a small putto statue beneath a glade of peonies in the far corner.

"I'm not really sure," I admitted, "but I know that the family that owned this house before ours wanted to get rid of it. It was an unwanted inheritance, I think."

That evening after dinner, Joel got roped into a game of darts with my father and Sebastian, so Beth and I crept up to my bedroom in the meantime. I wanted to show her all that I had packed for our journey and find out whether she could think of anything I had missed. She went through all three bags, chuckling at the rolls of toilet paper and the glass jar of contact solution. "I guess you could just toss your lenses into a fire once they're worn out," she mused.

"Or I can invoke my ice into my eyes. I've ruined plenty of contacts that way. My element destroys the lenses."

Beth shook her head slowly, appearing disenchanted by my Teutonic abilities yet again. She pulled the knife from my bag and queried, "Do you honestly need something like this when you've got ice claws?"

"Better to be safe than sorry," I pointed out, "and I've actually been thinking that maybe we should get Joel an old-style bow and set of arrows to bring along. I mean, we're going to witness the fall of Muniche in two years, and I'll bet he'd want to take part in the battle."

Beth looked up at me from where she crouched before our bags; I sat on my bed absently stroking its comforter. "You do realize that the three of us might die in 1066, right? I doubt witnessing the fall of Muniche will be the safest thing to do."

That thought had crossed my mind more than once, but I repeated the same mantra that had quelled all of my fears on that front. "The only way for a time traveler to permanently die while in the past is by Teutonic ritual suicide. And you can't do that unless you're at the Rhine River. That's a long way from Muniche."

"Right. Still. You'd better be guarding the Torstein tightly when things start crashing and burning. We need to be able to get out at a second's notice."

"I know. I'll keep it ready." I looked toward my bedside table where the stone lay inside its ring box. Hans had returned it to me when I came home in May.

"Um, Swanie." Beth's tone sounded appalled, and when I looked at her again I saw that she held the twelve pack of AA batteries in her hand. She narrowed her brown eyes at me. "This is a really bad idea. You know batteries don't break down without messing up the environment."

"How else are we going to get a good stash of snap-shots? If they bother you that much, I can take a quick trip to Saxon lands and drop them in the Elbe." Beth glared at me, and I frowned. "Hey, they're going to rip Teuton lands apart. If any German tribe deserves to get their river poisoned, it's the Saxons."

Beth sighed, seeming to accept my rationale. She suggested that I add some gauze and rubbing alcohol to our bags to treat any wounds we may suffer. "Good idea. Wouldn't have to worry about that if the priest in the cottage would teach me blood control," I grumbled, setting a course for the pantry to find another suitable glass bottle. My cousin followed me, saying that she had yet to tell Joel about our time travel plans. She intended to swipe the four EpiPens she had convinced him to bring out of his suitcase before we assembled next Friday night to open the gateway. "Hopefully he'll graciously accept the existence of fantasy," I said.

"The two of you went on for a good fifteen minutes about Tolkien's works, so he should be all good there,"

Beth reminded me. "He also likes Narnia and all of the Star Trek shows, so he'll probably be elated." I snickered, and when we entered the kitchen, my cousin shifted the discussion to the various landmarks we planned to visit in the coming days. I grabbed onto the new topic with a sense of relief, my thoughts of a naïve American coming to grips with the concept of time travel transitioning to mental images of the great churches of München.

Chapter Thirty-four:
Glory and Tragedy

Friday, June 16th, 2000, dawned with clear blue skies and warm Föhn blowing from across the Isar. The two weeks I had spent with Beth and Joel had been truly refreshing, for it had been years since I had toured some of the elegant landmarks in my city. We had marveled at the Residenz, the Deutsches Museum, several of the larger art galleries, the BMW museum, and the full collection of churches: Alter Peter, the Frauenkirche, the Theatinerkirche, the Asamkirche, and St. Michael Kirche. We had lounged in the Englischer Garten and taken a sobering trip through the concentration camp at Dachau. And our castle tour had reawakened my pride for my people. Though King Ludwig had not been a full Teuton, records asserted that his blood had been at Teutonic levels.

Beth and I managed to keep our true plans for that final Friday under wraps, though we exchanged many loaded looks that afternoon while she and Joel picked up their last batch of souvenirs from the markets downtown. Joel declared that he planned to get to bed no later than ten p.m. since their flight to Philadelphia was scheduled to depart at nine on Saturday. "You may have to shake off my Pappi and Basti first," I said with a laugh. "They've really enjoyed goofing off with you in the game room." Those three had undertaken pool tournaments, chess tournaments, and dart tournaments during the past two weeks.

Gregor prepared Jägerschnitzel, Bavarian potato salad, white asparagus, and Germknödel for dinner at my request. I wanted my best American friends to sample some of my favorite foods during their final dinner in München. Joel expressed great astonishment at the colorless asparagus and asked me whether it would make his urine smell like ditchwater. I nearly choked on a forkful of potato salad at that metaphor; I had never thought about it that way before. "The taste is similar, so you can bet that the results will be similar," I told him with a wink.

I excused myself from the group in the game room around seven p.m., for I wanted to think alone for a while before we embarked on our journey to the eleventh century. Beth promised to join me once she had finished playing Rook with Joel, Sebastian, and my father. I told her not to hurry and struck out for the back staircase, separate seeds of worry having sprung up in my heart. I had not seen Hans all day, for one thing, and I needed to make sure he still intended to witness our departure and return. The plan was to meet him outside at the gazebo to open the portal in a place where it should not draw attention.

I reached my bedroom and flopped down onto my bed, petting Thunar absently when he approached to greet me. I retrieved the remote for my stereo and hit the *play* button, and seconds later the wonderfully Gothic sounds of the most recent Nightwish album, *Wishmaster*, erupted from my speakers. I had purchased the album online from Finland only two weeks prior. I had hardly gotten the chance to appreciate the songs or learn all of the lyrics, but I had already selected "Two For Tragedy" and "Wander-lust" as my favorite tracks. I played those and the rest of the album twice that evening while I lay on my bed staring up at the ceiling, thinking about my upcoming trip.

Tonight, once Beth and I lured Joel outside, I would have to explain to him a little about what we were going to do. He would not believe me—I was counting on that—but I needed him to at least think about the proper year, 1064. We needed to picture ourselves in the old city of Muniche on one of the medieval streets that I had seen in drawings, in June of 1064. That would be almost exactly two years from the time when Muniche fell to the Saxons, so it would give us a chance to fully appreciate how much had been ruined. I wanted to see Muniche in its prime, with trade flourishing and plenty of food coming in from the nearby estates, before the Saxons took it all away from us. For the Torstein to work, Beth, Joel, and I would have to picture the same time and place. Beth had already been properly instructed, but I would have to tell Joel something before opening the gates.

I also considered what it would be like when we first appeared in the city. Hopefully no one would notice the gates, just like when I went to 1978—no one had been inside the tower. I would have to close the gates quickly. Then we would have to find a place to stay temporarily, perhaps an inn, and I would have to teach Beth and Joel how to speak Teutonica. Then we would need to seek employment unless we could garner some aid from the local nobility. I had yet to decide whether we should try to present ourselves as tradespeople or as nobles fallen on hard times.

Eventually I took the Nightwish album out of my stereo and booted up my desktop, hopping onto the ISDN connection to sign onto ICQ. It was high time to seek out some trace of Hans, since it was after eight p.m. He was not on ICQ. I checked all three of my e-mail accounts. No message from him. I brought up our Teuton forum and checked the most recent login time for *Das Dunkle Feuer*. Ten-thirty the previous evening. Where the heck was he?

My digital clock read eight twenty-one, and I sighed in frustration, shutting my desktop down. I headed for the shower, probably for the last time in a long time. The three of us would doubtless stink like hogs in the eleventh century, which was not a pleasant thought. I pulled my hair up into a ponytail to let it air dry when I had finished, reentering my room wearing a halter top and shorts, my hands on my hips as I looked around and wondered how I was to get hold of Hans tonight. I looked toward my dark blue curtains stretched across the door to my balcony, and I had an inspiration. Perhaps he would appear there at some point like he had done in the past when he had news to share. I resolved to lie out there on my lounge chair and wait, bringing my headphones along with *Wishmaster* and *Awaking The Centuries*, the most recent Haggard album.

As I lay there watching the sky darken, quietly singing "Two For Tragedy" along with Tarja, Hans suddenly whirled onto my balcony in a fiery storm, stopping underneath my trellis, dressed in the all-black garb of the Teuton priest. I hit the pause button and rose from my chair to face him, my eyes widening when I saw his stricken expression. He panted as though the effort to bring him up to my balcony had been far too much for him, and he placed one hand, claw-like, upon my trellis, his entire body sagging. I rushed over to him, concern having taken my own voice away. "She is gone. Lady Muniche is dead," he whispered.

Grief hit me like a brick, and my hands came up to cover my mouth in shock. "No . . . ." I gasped. All thoughts of the Torstein and the eleventh century evaporated from my mind, replaced by a weighty sorrow for that honorable Teuton woman who had served our city so faithfully for over seventy years. Tears welled in my eyes, and Hans said nothing, but his face looked like he was on the verge of crying, too. I had never seen him cry before.

I realized that all of the other priests on the Teuton Council of München would be grieving now along with that keyholder, the one that Lady Muniche had claimed was a good man despite his faults. I wondered whether it was actually Rudi or some other priest I did not know. "Oh, Hans . . . I . . . I'm so sorry . . . ." I choked on the words. Tears trickled from my eyes, and a moment later I was holding him, surprised at how weak he felt in my arms, trying to comfort him though I could do no good.

For a long minute he did not resist me, and we stood together there under the roses. I cried softly, whispering meaningless phrases intending to soothe him, and he remained silent and still, sinking into my arms. At last he shuddered away from my embrace, taking a step out onto the balcony, his eyes on the sky. He sighed heavily, then murmured, "She is there now with her husband in eternal bliss. Although she has left so many of us behind, there's no point in weeping for her." He sounded like he was trying to convince himself.

I had never seen Hans so moved by anguish before. He had always come across as a hard man, showing as little emotion as possible aside from during our glorious dances with nature. I do not think he had wept when my mother had died fifteen years before, nor when my brother had succumbed to cystic fibrosis. But for my aged mentor I saw silent tears trickle down his face as he gazed at the night sky. I suddenly remembered the Torstein and my plans for that night. Hans looked like he was in no state to attend to that sort of thing now. "Do you think . . . do you think I should . . . postpone my trip?" I asked him cautiously, a bit worried. If I did, my cousin and her boyfriend would not be able to come.

For a moment he did not answer. Then he swiveled around to face me, and I saw that his expression had hardened once more into that impassiveness I knew so well. "Of course not, especially if you still plan to take your friends. What time?"

"Probably about ten-thirty or so, by the gazebo." His abrupt about-face had startled me all over again, and I recoiled from him under the trellis.

"I'll be there." A second later he flew off the balcony, the air hot behind him.

I went back inside shortly afterward, the twilight having grown oppressive to me for some reason. I lay back down on my bed and pondered the loss of that great woman, the Lady of Muniche, grief washing over me afresh. She had been my good friend in spite of our wide gap in age. If it had not been for her, I would never have learned anything about sewing, nor would I have come to appreciate my city so greatly. My thoughts drifted toward all of my single

Teuton girlfriends, and I wondered whether one of them was starting to feel the tug of Muniche's spirit. I felt no difference in myself, and I chewed on my bottom lip at the thought of Erika. Maybe I should log back onto ICQ to see whether she was online so I could let her know that our mentor had passed. Would she start wailing at me if I did so, crying that her heart had been bound by an absent keyholder?

I rose and moved toward my desk, but my bedroom door opened before I sat down. "Hey," my cousin greeted in a low voice. "Joel and I are going to go upstairs and take showers. Then I'm going to swipe his EpiPens and put on my medieval attire. I'm going to try to convince him to do the same before we meet you on the deck." Her tone conveyed a strange mixture of excitement and dread.

I shot her an empty grin, plunking myself into my office chair. "Sounds good to me. Think you'll be ready by ten-fifteen?"

"Should be. It's not even nine-thirty yet. I just hope he doesn't think I'm a complete idiot trying to dress him up for a Renaissance festival on our last night in Germany."

I laughed once and gestured for her to go. "Tell him I'll explain everything once he meets me outside." Beth mumbled something in response, and I heard the door close behind her. I turned my attention back to my computer; it had nearly finished the startup sequence. I tapped my foot impatiently, then signed onto the internet and ICQ. My eyes scanned the list of contacts, and I clicked on Erika's number. *Hey. You're not feeling like Muniche bound your spirit, are you?* I typed, wasting no time with pleasantries.

Her reply was slow in coming. *Has Lady Muniche passed away?*

Yes. Hans just told me a few minutes ago.

My heart hammered while I waited for her next response. I wished that she was chatting with just me. Anytime I chatted with multiple users, my conversations progressed much more slowly. I glanced toward the list of numbers again, thinking that maybe I should send Traudl and Vreni a similar message. Vreni should have nothing to worry about, though, with her low level of Teutonic blood. Marga and Trudi were not signed on.

I don't really feel any different, Erika admitted at length. *Is it supposed to happen right away when a Teuton Lady dies? Or does it take some time?*

I felt my forehead wrinkle as I thought about that. *I don't really know. But I don't feel any different either.*

Then maybe Rudi will inherit a good wife, Erika replied, and I snickered, telling her that I needed to get going since my cousin was still at my house. We said our goodbyes, and then I turned off my computer again. It was nine forty-five now. Time to get changed and check the bags one final time.

I put on my reddish-purple dress in the bathroom, studying myself in the mirror. I laid my glasses beside the faucet and put in a pair of contacts, taking my now-dry hair down and shaking it out around my shoulders. I tucked Hans' locket beneath the neckline of my dress, then wound my head covering around my hair, knotting it at the back of my neck. I was not entirely sure how medieval women wore such trappings, but I would learn soon enough.

I sifted through all three of our leather bags one last time, ticking off each item in my mind. Blankets, clothing, socks, jewelry, underwear, knives, vitamins, soap, food, water, hairbrushes, toilet paper, camera, batteries, contacts, solution, gauze, rubbing alcohol, Bible. Everything was where it should be. I put on my sturdy leather shoes and retrieved the Torstein from its ring box, gripping it protectively in my left hand. I wondered if it had any inkling of the portal it was about to open. *Silly. It's just a rock,* I reminded myself, lifting each bag onto my shoulders one by one. They were ponderous, and I put two over my right shoulder since that was my strong side.

Beth and Joel stood waiting at the steps to the back gardens, both of them clad similarly to me. My cousin darted forward to take one of the bags, and I handed her the one on my left, which contained her clothing. "What in the world is going on, Swanie?" Joel inquired, his hazel eyes following his girlfriend with an uncertain look. "Are we going to a costume party or something? You know we have to get up at six tomorrow." His blond brows slanted downward as he looked at me, but he did have the decency to step forward and take the bag I offered to him.

I chuckled quietly and shared a glance with my cousin. "Beth and I are about to embark on a grand escapade into eleventh century Europe, and we'd love to know whether or not you'd like to accompany us." I smiled and tilted my head at him, waiting for his reaction.

Joel looked startled at first, and then his face grew skeptical. "The eleventh century?" he repeated, looking from me to Beth as though he figured I was bluffing. He quirked a smile, still looking unsure. "So what, are we going to use a time machine?"

"Not exactly." I grinned, thinking that the Torstein was a rather *small* time machine. "But Beth and I *are* going to travel time tonight. You don't have to come if you don't want to," I added to goad him.

A short laugh escaped his lips, and he shook his head incredulously. "You just like, travel time every night? Just for something to do?"

"I haven't actually done it before," Beth put in, sounding entertained. "Swanie's the professional time traveler around here."

"I've only done it once," I said, rolling my eyes at my cousin, "and this trip will involve a lot more excitement and danger than my last trip. I'm all ready for it. I packed all this stuff—" I gestured toward the bag he held "—and Beth helped me do a lot of research. But there's no sense in wasting time, so to speak. Are you coming or not?" I eyed him in speculation.

He shook his head again, his hazel eyes wary while they looked from me to Beth. "You're crazy, Swanie," he stated, looking as though he wished to go back inside and crash in his bed.

This might be harder than I thought. I decided on the bluff. I stepped forward to take Beth's hand, guiding her down the steps into the garden. "Fine, we're going without you," I threw at him as we struck out for the trees.

"We'll miss you a lot! Hope we don't fall for any noble lords while we're gone!" Beth crowed in a teasing tone. I snorted.

Soon afterward Joel ran to catch up with us. "Hey you two, wait!" he hollered. I kept going, not looking back, entering the trail to the stream, Beth walking behind me since the path was narrow. Then I heard Joel panting not far away, and Beth halted with a squeak. He had grasped her left shoulder. "You really need to tell me what's going on, both of you," he said, sounding impatient.

I stopped short on the path, letting my bag drop, and spun to face him. He had apparently left his bag back at the deck. "I already told you, we're going to the eleventh century," I snapped. "If you don't want to go, then get back to the house and go to bed. If you do want to go, you'd better pick up your bag. You're going to want what's inside of it, trust me."

I could tell that I was wearing him down. He stared at me in frustration, then at his girlfriend, then back toward the house, then at me again. Finally, Joel harrumphed and spun around to walk swiftly back toward the deck. "Fine!"

Beth and I raised our eyebrows at each other, remaining where we stood on the trail while we waited for him to join us. "Maybe I should have told him about this earlier," she murmured, sounding like she regretted her secrecy. "I wonder what he's going to do when he finds out what Teuton blood means."

"Guess we'll see," I answered, shaking my head and shifting my bag a bit on my shoulder.

Joel stomped back toward us not long afterward, this time obediently toting his bag along. "So how exactly are we going back in time?" he asked as we advanced down the trail once more.

No point in denying it. "With a rock," I said.

"A *rock?*" Disbelief rang out in his voice.

"Yeah, a rock. It's a really long story, and when we get there I'll tell you."

Joel was silent for a moment. "How long have you known that your cousin's a time traveler?" he asked Beth in an accusatory tone.

I heard Beth give a short snicker. "She told me on the night she was raped. We both figured it'd be best to bring a guy along for protection."

"Hmm." Joel sounded thoughtful now, no longer wholly disbelieving.

I halted just before we reached the end of the trail at the glade by the gazebo and turned to face Joel again. "There's one more thing you *have* to remember," I told him, "and if you don't do this right, we could end up anywhere. We're going to the year 1064, in June, to the Teuton city of Muniche. Don't be thinking about anywhere else or any other time when I'm using the rock, do you hear me?" I did not consider the fact that Joel may never have heard the word *Teuton* before in his life.

"Muniche," he repeated, "is that the same thing as München?"

I rolled my eyes. "Pretty much."

"Is that why most of the world calls this city 'Munich' instead of München?"

Huh. I had never thought of that. "Maybe," I allowed, then motioned for him and my cousin to follow me into the clearing.

Hans stood close to the stream still clad in his priestly attire. He looked rigid but far past his emotional storm from earlier. He raised one hand in greeting when we approached him, his dark blue eyes sweeping over our clothing and the bags we carried. "Have you forgotten anything?" he asked me, speaking English for Joel's and Beth's benefit.

"I hope not. Do you think the clothes look okay?" I asked.

"They seem to." He looked us up and down again, then noted, "It appears that you guessed your friends' sizes quite accurately."

"She cheated, because she had Beth take my measurements," Joel said. Hans nodded sagely while Beth swatted at her boyfriend.

"All right, there's no point in dragging this out," I said, not wanting Joel and Hans to have some sort of chat to mock me. I held the Torstein up to the moonlight, then turned to Hans. "Do Joel and Beth have to speak the spell too, or just me?"

"Just you, since you are the one who holds the Torstein," Hans answered. "However, your companions should also picture the proper time and place in their minds, since they too will make the journey."

I nodded and looked back at Beth and Joel. My cousin gave me a thumbs up, and Joel offered an uncertain smile. "Eleventh century, I know," he said, still sounding rather incredulous. I grinned and turned to the stream, holding the Torstein up and reciting the now-familiar words.

Just like it had happened two summers before, when I finished the phrase "Restore me as I was, but new," a wretched crack rent the sky apart, and the air between me and the stream tore open vertically. The Torstein trembled in my hand yet again, and I gripped it more securely. I heard Joel curse somewhere behind me while the ancient gates gradually appeared, smooth labradorite, seeming to reach far into the heavens above. My cousin gave a soft cry of amazement, sounding like she had never fully believed in my tales until that moment. I regarded the gates in wonder and fear as they opened, creaking harshly, revealing those waves of darkness with the rivulets of light and color darting this way and that. My gateway had opened. It was time to go.

I tore my eyes away from the fearsome oblivion to look at Hans one last time. For some reason, a terrible feeling overtook me, convincing me that nothing would be the same when I returned. I was tampering with things that I should have left alone. I would not wind up unscathed again. I stared into Hans' dark blue eyes, wanting to say something profound, not knowing what would suffice. At last I whispered, "You'll wait for us?"

He nodded solemnly. "I'll be here when you return," he said in Bayerisch.

I took a shaky breath and turned to Beth and Joel. Beth had her hands over her mouth, her brown eyes staring at the portal in what looked like terror. Joel had the look of a scared rabbit, ready to flee into the woods as he gaped at the gates. I held out my right hand, an invitation. "Let's hold hands so we stay together."

"Through *there?*" Joel cringed, and I nodded. Beth locked her fingers with those of his right hand, clutching herself close to him. Joel drew in a shaky breath and then stepped forward bravely to grasp my hand, determination glowing in his hazel eyes. I turned swiftly for the blackness, and an instant later the three of us leapt into the obscurity, leaving all that I truly loved behind.

End of Book I

~*~

Turn the page to find out what happens when our three adventurers arrive in the past—and get just a taste of the quandaries they face in Book II!

His Name Was Augustin
Book II excerpt
© C.L. Carhart

Chapter One:
Arrival in the Past

The harrowing ride through the obscure currents seemed to last forever this time around. On my trip to 1978, I estimated that it may have taken about a minute or less according to my own internal clock. Truthfully, I believe that getting pushed backward through that awful darkness does not register at all, as far as time itself is concerned. But during our journey to the eleventh century, I felt sure that my body remained helpless to those jostling currents, pulled in all directions, pushed forcibly against a powerful undertow for an infinite eternity. I could hardly form a conscious thought during the traumatic passage, but I did think briefly of Beth and Joel, wondering how they were tolerating the experience. They had come with me—I knew that—but I could not sense them. I was alone.

Shortly after stepping into the currents, I began to hear those bothersome whispers all around me demanding my attention and my understanding. Since the journey seemed lengthier this time, I concentrated a bit more effort on trying to interpret those voices, wanting to discern of what exactly they sought to warn me. But they spoke a language I did not know. It was not German, English, Bayerisch, or

French, nor was it Latin or Teutonica. It sounded older, more rudimentary, yet also more profound. The whispers continued throughout my entire journey, insistent, warning, *warning* . . . .

Just as I began to believe that I could pick out a word or two, a dismal moan crept up from the depths, breaking my concentration. I may have discerned a shift in the whispers at that point, a hint of mockery mingling within their unknowable warnings. I struggled to focus entirely on the voices, trying to ignore how helpless my body felt with the moans seeming to work their way deep inside.

At last I caught just two words, both sounding similar to Latin: *obligure* and *damnere*. Obligate, perhaps, or obligation? Damnere—that was easy enough. To condemn, to consign to hell. Fear washed over me at the potential meanings of those two words. The realization struck me again that I should not have opened the gateway, not at all. I should not have used the Torstein twice, not after learning about its true nature from the forbidden writings. This time, I feared I would face serious repercussions.

The fact that I could see nothing but whirling darkness and intermittent bursts of light and color—nothing solid, nothing that would have a mouth or speak with a voice—disturbed me. While the persistent moans wove their way upward from somewhere below, it seemed that those niggling whispers came from every direction at once. Some spoke directly into my ears, close enough that I should have been able to reach out and touch *some*thing. But my hands remained immobile. I could not move any part of my body, for the currents were far stronger than me. A burgeoning terror overtook me, convincing me that this time there would be no end to these currents, to this darkness. I had chosen—*knowing* the writings—to go back to a time before the Torstein had been created. Would I never make it there alive? Would I remain entangled in the strands of time until the end of infinity? What about Beth and Joel? They were innocent outsiders. What had I done?

Suddenly that horrible, abysmal laughter rang out again from the darkness in a tone so deep it could not have been human. Panic raced through my veins at the thought of the alternatives. *If it's not human . . . then it must be a demon . . . Wuotan . . . ?* The laughter increased, piercing my soul, grasping at my heart with hands as black as the depths of the ocean. I tried to react, but I held no power against the forces that drove me backward, and even less power to smother the laughter. *Damnere . . . .* The word crept into my brain again.

Then finally, I found myself falling forward, bursting from the portal onto soft, brown leaves in the sheltering shade of a forest. I heard two *oofs* as my companions landed beside me, and I pivoted quickly to confront the gates, raising the Torstein in my left hand, silently ordering them to vanish before that wretched, laughing demon reached out to take me. They responded properly, fading much more swiftly than they had come.

I sighed in relief and collapsed on the ground, flopping down on top of my leather bag, the Torstein still clutched in my left hand. I closed my eyes and chuckled foolishly at nothing, the twittering sounds of birds and buzzing insects soothing my frightened soul. I did not think to question why I had landed in a forest rather than on the streets of medieval Muniche. My gratitude at my safe arrival impeded my judgment.

"Swanie?" My cousin's voice pulled me out of my reverie of relief. I opened my eyes and looked toward her, where she stood in the brush on the opposite side of Joel. She clutched the strap of her bag with both hands, the skin of her face as white as a sheet. "That . . . that was *way* worse than you described," she accused in a trembling voice, her wide eyes locking with mine.

I felt oddly jubilant at the fact that the three of us had survived the journey, and I heard my own voice chuckling again. "Guess our mental images of Muniche were a bit off," I commented, glancing around at the trees. I recognized white oak and birch interspersed with brambles, ferns, and moss. Maybe the medieval version of my city had a woodsy section like the modern Englischer Garten. I heard no sounds that indicated human activity, though. It was quiet in the glade where we stood, a soft summer breeze rustling the leaves overhead.

"So," Joel interjected more loudly than necessary, "I'm going to make an assumption here and say I'm dreaming."

I lifted myself off the ground and turned to regard Joel, who stood upon a massive birch root several paces behind me with his bag on the ground before him, his eyes dazed as he stared at our surroundings. I exchanged a quick look with Beth, knowing that we could no longer keep everything to ourselves. After all, we were *here*. "Well, Joel," I began, trying to discern how exactly I should explain what had happened. "Actually, we're not dreaming. We're in the eleventh century."

Joel focused on me, confusion in his hazel eyes, then looked around again. "No, I *have* to be dreaming this," he insisted, appearing thoughtful. "I must have fallen asleep while Beth was in the shower. She said we were supposed to meet you outside at ten-fifteen. I really need to wake up. I'm going to be late." He started smacking his arm, pinching his face. "Wake up, wake up," he muttered.

I gawked at him, shaking my head at the ridiculousness of it all. Beth took it upon herself to march up to him and take hold of his right arm. "No, Joel, I promise you, you're not dreaming. This is real. You wouldn't be wearing those clothes in a dream. You'd never seen them before." She gestured at his linen tunic and pants.

Joel continued slapping himself with his left hand, ignoring his girlfriend's words, still murmuring that he needed to wake up. Then his gaze traveled down to his shoes and the root where he stood, and he scooped up a small stick with a sharp point. Waving it at Beth and me in an ingenious manner, he announced, "*I* know how to wake myself up." Before either of us could yell at him to stop, he stabbed his own palm with the stick, drawing blood.

Beth screamed and grabbed for the stick, ripping it out of his hand before he could do any more damage to himself. I heaved an aggravated sigh and plunked my bag onto the leaves while she urged him to sit down. "For heaven's sake, Joel, listen to me!" I ordered as his girlfriend fairly shoved him down onto the root below. "You are *not* dreaming, and you need to stop trying to hurt yourself, because we are *in* the eleventh century! You could give yourself blood poisoning with a cut like that." Joel cringed and stared down at his bleeding palm as I turned to Beth. "He's got the gauze and alcohol in his bag. We'd better get that wrapped up before it gets dirty." His blood had started dotting the moss that coated the root where he sat.

"Right," Beth said, crouching down to unclasp his bag and dig for our small batch of medical supplies. Annoyance washed over me at the idea of wasting some of it now, two years before the siege. Maybe we should have left Joel at home.

"That really should have woken me up," Joel said while Beth dabbed his left palm with alcohol, softly chiding him as she worked. She began to wrap his wound, and he shook his head, disbelief still written all over his face. "But time travel is impossible. There is no way . . . ."

"Just think about it for a minute," I admonished him, watching my cousin work to repair what he had done. I wished yet again that Hans had agreed to teach me blood control. If I knew how to tap the full powers of my Teuton blood, I could have stopped Joel's bleeding already. Maybe here in the eleventh century, where ancient traditions still flourished among my people, I could finally learn the things that Hans was so loath to share. I smiled to myself at that idea, then focused on Joel, trying to discern the best way to convince him that we had traveled time. "If you're being honest with yourself, you'd have to admit that there is no possible way your unconscious imagination could have come up with what happened just before we got here," I pointed out. "Similar to what Beth said before about your clothes. You can't dream up something you've never seen before."

Joel's countenance paled, dull fear creeping into his eyes. "Those gigantic gates . . . those whispers . . . those awful moans . . . ."

I nodded at him in agreement. "My nightmares could never come up with something like that," I said, and it was true. Beth finished dressing his wound and tucked the remainder of the gauze back into his bag. Then she got to her feet again and retrieved her own bag, looking toward me with a determined nod. "That place in the darkness after we stepped through those gates? Those were the currents of time," I explained to Joel while pulling the strap for my bag back over my right shoulder. I moved to stand beside my cousin, feeling more at ease now that our crises seemed to be winding down.

"That was an incredible excursion we made," Beth remarked, bumping lightly against my left shoulder. "And I'm kind of hoping that the journey forward will be a lot less terrifying." I did not meet my cousin's gaze, preferring to concentrate on her boyfriend, who was in the process of regaining his feet. *No, Beth, the trip forward is just as terrifying as the trip back,* I thought.

"The currents of time," Joel murmured, realization dawning in his eyes at last. "Is that why it felt like I was being pushed against a tornado or something?" He rolled his shoulders a bit and situated his bag beneath his left arm, flexing his fingers around the gauze binding his hand.

"Yes, we were flying backward through the currents of time," I clarified, thinking back to those moments in the darkness. "It's kind of crazy, but it seemed like it took *forever* that time." I shared a look with my cousin and explained, "The first time I did this, I just went to 1978, and it wasn't quite so bad. *That* trip . . . ." My voice trailed off, and I shuddered.

"I guess an extra nine hundred years would make the trip a lot longer," Beth said, and Joel murmured in agreement. He seemed to have accepted the fact that we had traveled time.

I opened my left hand and looked down at the Torstein, glowing a muted ruby in the shade. Its powers overwhelmed me again at the idea of what we had just done. Then just as abruptly, my mind turned at last to the forest and to the medieval city of Muniche. *We were supposed to arrive . . . there . . . .* I stared at the Torstein, then around at the trees, then back at the rock. "Why did you bring us *here?*" I whispered to it in Teutonica, fear seeping into my veins again.

"Is that the rock you said would take us back in time?" Joel inquired, stepping forward to peer at it himself. He reached his unwounded hand down to touch it, but I closed my fingers around it quickly. "How does it work?"

I pulled away from him and looked around again, taking note of the ancient trees, the sunlight filtering through their branches, the dried leaves beneath our feet. "It's a long story, but I can't tell you yet. We have a problem. We were supposed to get here in the Teuton city of Muniche, but we're in the woods." I looked at Beth and saw that a touch of worry had creased her brow.

"Muniche. That's right," Joel repeated, apparently remembering what I had told him when we stood on the path to the gazebo. "What's a Teuton?" he asked, the word finally having made him take notice.

I gave him the shortest possible explanation. "The Teutons are one of the old German tribes from before the Christian era. This rock was created by one of them." I held up my left hand significantly and finished, "I am one of them."

Joel nodded, following along. "Barbarians," he said, and I frowned at him. Beth giggled in an impish manner.

"Maybe to the Romans," I allowed, "but that's not important right now. I'm trying to figure out why we're in the forest. Were you thinking about the city of Muniche when we leaped through the gates, like I told you?"

Joel's face clouded over, and he put one hand to his chin while he considered. "I was thinking of the eleventh century, like you said . . . . But I guess I was picturing some medieval battle in a field or in the woods, like on Middle Earth. Remember when we were talking about *Lord of the Rings?*" He grinned crookedly at me.

I groaned in despair, realizing that it was the fault of Joel's foolish imagination that we had arrived in a forest. "Sounds like we'd have been better off if you'd gone back to bed," Beth observed in a scathing tone. "*I* was thinking about the city of Muniche, Swanie."

"At least you listened to me, but your boyfriend had to be an idiot thinking about elves and hobbits, and who knows where we may have ended up?!" I snapped. "I don't have a map, and I don't have a compass. We may be on the wrong continent for all we know. We're going to have to do this again." Terror seized me at the idea of reopening those gates again and confronting those voices and that laughter. And Wuotan knew that I knew that it was he who laughed. He would try to take me . . . .

All at once, Beth clutched at my left arm. "Swanie!" she gasped in a low voice laden with horror, "I think there's someone out there!" Her eyes scanned the trees around us. Joel followed her example, moving to stand before us.

I froze, my element sweeping into my veins at the possibility of immediate danger. I endeavored to keep my ice out of my eyes so it would not ruin my contacts, but I allowed it to sharpen my other senses. My keen ears picked up the distinctive crunch of twigs snapping, and a moment later a man stepped out from behind one of the ancient oaks not five meters from where we stood. In the dimly lit clearing I could see that his clothing was brightly-colored, his complexion darker than expected, his hair jet black. And in his right hand he carried a spear.

The man stopped short when he saw us—two young, dark-haired girls standing behind a youthful blond-haired boy with three bags between them. He stared at us, confusion crossing his face. Apparently he had not expected to encounter the likes of us in this forest, but as I glanced again at his spear I felt a rush of sympathy for whatever—or *whom*ever—he sought. Three, then four more men, each looking about the same as the first, also emerged from the brush, all bearing spears. They halted as well, ogling us, and then began speaking excitedly amongst themselves in a language I did not understand.

I had a strong feeling that this would not end well unless I played the role of the peacemaker. I raised my right hand slowly, non-threateningly, disregarding the warning tug of Beth's grip. "Do you speak Teutonica?" I addressed the question toward the man who had first appeared, pronouncing every word distinctly.

There was a short pause, and then all of the brightly-dressed men began speaking at once, to each other, the word *Teutonica* on every pair of lips. That was when the first man leveled a furious gaze upon me. He slammed the base of his spear upon the leaves as he spat one word, an accusation. *"Teuton!!"*

I cursed, hesitating just one second longer. Then I grabbed Beth's hand to yank her into the forest and shouted, *"Run!!"*

To be continued . . . .

Book II comes out in June 2021
Order now from your preferred platform!

C.L. Carhart would be thrilled if you would leave a review for this book. Reviews help buoy an indie author's career, as well as her spirits. She appreciates your feedback!

Sign up for C.L. Carhart's newsletter for an inside look at her author undertakings, along with information on new releases and the occasional secret deal.
https://sendfox.com/clcarhart1066

Check out C.L. Carhart's website to see how Inessa Burnell brought her characters to life, and commission her for some fantasy art of your own.
https://www.clcarhart.com/characters

Arcane Gateway is available on library platforms! Ask your local library to order it in eBook and paperback so that C.L. can reach more readers.

Follow C.L. on social media:
https://www.facebook.com/CLCarhartAuthor
https://www.instagram.com/c.l.carhart.author

German Translations

ach – oh, ah

Almdudler – sparkling herbal lemonade

Apfelschorle – sparkling apple juice

Bauernfrühstück – farmer's breakfast: eggs, bacon, cheese, and vegetables fried in a skillet

Bayerisch – Bavarian dialect

Beidl – bastard in Bavarian dialect

Das Dunkle Feuer – the dark fire

Dirndl – traditional Bavarian dress often worn at festivals

Dampfnudeln – Bavarian yeast dumplings: served either as a main dish with mushrooms in white gravy, as a side dish, or as a dessert with vanilla sauce

Dialekt – dialect

Drachenreiter – dragon rider

Eintopf – one pot stew: typically made with meat, green vegetables, potatoes, and herbs

Eistänzerin – ice dancer

Englischer Garten – English Garden in downtown München

Föhn – warm mountain breeze

Germknödel – yeast dough dumpling w/plum jam, poppy seeds and sugar on top

Glühwein – warm spiced wine usually served around the Christmas holidays

Guten Morgen – good morning

Hallo – hello

Ich verstehe kein Bayerisch. Entschuldigung. – I don't understand Bayerisch. Sorry.

Idealismus – idealism

Jägerschnitzel – breaded veal with mushroom gravy

Leberkäse – corned beef, pork, and bacon finely ground and served warm in a loaf

Lederhosen – leather shorts with suspenders, traditional Bavarian attire for men

Mutti – mom

nein – no
Oma – grandma
Onkel – uncle
Opa – grandpa
Pappi – dad
Sauerbraten – beef marinated in wine & herbs, served with
    heavy gravy
Scheiße – shit
sonnig – sunny
Spätzle – egg noodle pasta, usually buttered and sprinkled
    with herbs
Süddeutsche Getriebe – South German Gearboxes
Tante – aunt
Waldzwerg – forest gnome
Wiesn – Oktoberfest

Teutonica Translations

Der Weg Teutonisch – The Teutonic Way
Eihalbe/Eihalbae – singular/plural, fairy of silver oak
Leitalra – Lady of a Teuton city
Niofirgeban – The Unforgiven
Nusi – nut
sconi – beautiful
Teutona – female Teuton
Teutonica – old Teuton dialect
Torstein – stone of the gate
Truhtein – master
Virstohran – ritual vengeance
Wuotan – demon lord of the Teuton people
Zoubaraera – witch

Pronunciation Guide
(for names and commonly used words)

Augustin – Au-GUS-tin
Bayerisch – BEYE-rish (eye is pronounced like eyeball)
Dane – DAH-nuh
Der Weg – Dare Veg
Eihalbe – EYE-hahl-buh (eye is pronounced like eyeball)
Fonsi – FON-zee
Ina – EE-nuh
Isar – EE-zahr
Ivo – EE-voh
Jens – Yenz
Leitalra – Leye-TAHL-rah (eye is pronounced like eyeball)
Leutasch – LOY-tahsh
Leutascher Ache – LOY-tah-sher AH-khuh
Lise – LEEZ-uh
Mane – MAH-nuh
Swanhilde – Swan-HIL-duh
Thaden – TODD-n
Torstein – TOR-stein (stein is pronounced like a beer stein)
Traudl – TROW-dool (trow is pronounced like cow)
Vreni – FRAY-nee

About the Author

C.L. Carhart has been writing since the age of 4, dabbling in everything from children's books, to fantasy, to historical fiction. Eventually, her lifelong interest in European history inspired her to create a paranormal fantasy realm based on the Teutonic people groups. *Arcane Gateway* provides a first glimpse at this other-world—a place rife with ancient mysteries and dark magic.

Born and raised in southern New Jersey, C.L. spends her free time hiking with her husband, enjoying metal music, snuggling her feline familiars, and dreaming of the wonders of Germany.

Made in the USA
Coppell, TX
28 February 2021

51019564R00203